04·12

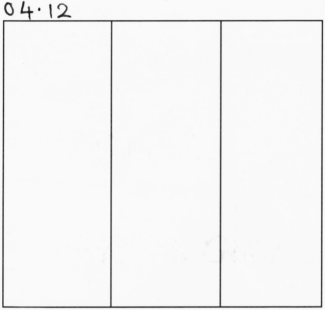

This book should be returned/renewed by
the latest date shown above. Overdue items
incur charges which prevent self-service
renewals. Please contact the library.

Wandsworth Libraries
24 hour Renewal Hotline
01159 293388
www.wandsworth.gov.uk Wandsworth

THE GAY MEN'S PRESS

by the same author :

Street Lavender
Mignon
Thornapple
N For Narcissus
Gaveston
The Bisley Boy

First published 1997 by GMP Publishers Ltd,
P O Box 247, Swaffham, Norfolk PE37 8PA, England

World Copyright © 1997 Chris Hunt

A CIP catalogue record for this book is available
from the British Library

ISBN 0 85449 243 7

Distributed in Europe by Central Books,
99 Wallis Rd, London E9 5LN

Distributed in North America by InBook/LPC Group,
1436 West Randolph , Chicago, IL 60607

Distributed in Australia by Bulldog Books,
P O Box 300, Beaconsfield, NSW 2014

Printed and bound in the EU by The Cromwell Press,
Melksham, Wilts, England

to Barbara Armitage

Author's Note

In researching the background to the story of *Duval's Gold* I read various works, from Daniel Defoe's *Jack Sheppard* to Peter Newark's *The Crimson Book of Highwaymen*. The three most valuable to me were *The Thief-Taker General* by Gerald Howson; *The Road to Tyburn* by Christopher Hibbert; and *Mother Clap's Molly House* by Rictor Norton (GMP, 1992), which was the particular inspiration for a good deal of this book.

Part I
I set out to become a Gentleman

Chapter One

SOMEWHERE along the Great North Road lies buried a hoard of golden guineas, the treasure of that best and bravest gentleman of the road, Claude Duval. Fifty years ago they hanged him, and the secret died alongside him. All we have is the rhyme:

> 'By stem and root as we are told
> Duval hid his crock of gold.
> Twixt Tollentone Lane and Alconbury Hill
> Duval's gold lies buried still.'

One thousand guineas, as is said. One thousand guineas. And therefore every ditch, copse and tree, every root, stem and stone of that sixty-four mile stretch of road is laced with meaning.

There is more than one way north. Some say the road begins at Shoreditch church — and this is the older road. That way you would quit London from Bishopsgate and so to Stamford Hill and Tottenham village and the long straight way, past the Ram and the Swan and the old woods, passing through Buntingford and Buckland, an ill-kept and deeply rutted road, often flooded — old Ermine Street — where the Caxton gibbet is your landmark. But the other road has the gold, and therefore you shall hear more of it.

This road leaves London by St John's Street, through Islington village and along the Hollow Way towards the heath; and where it joins Tollentone Lane you will see upon your right-hand side its gibbet; and so to Highgate Hill and Finchley Common, and so passing Whetstone, to Prickler's Hill. Then the Roebuck and the White Hart will be your landmarks, and when your horse takes you up Mardley Hill you will be well clear, and the way is open to the great long barrows and the Swan Inn, where the road branches; then up through the flat swampy fields and the Ouse floods, and so to Buckden.

Both these roads lead to Alconbury Hill and its swinging tree. Here, as at Caxton, there will always be some unlucky brother in his cage of chains, his carcase shifting in the wind, his crows upon his shoulder.

Who searches for a treasure on the road must follow the road's course, and its grim companions be damned.

I daresay that in this wicked world there will be few to disagree with me when I observe that a man with gold is more fortunate than one who lacks the same. Gold buys privilege and favour, a good horse, good wine, good lodging; gold buys a man from the gallows. A man with gold and friends in the right places need never bed with Mother Tyburn. I cannot think there will be any who consider the pursuit of gold to be an unworthy aim.

But I have only passed my life amongst a gang of rogues about the same pursuit, and therefore know no better, never needing reason for the tricks and schemes we dealt in, wherein greed and lust, betrayal, villainy and mischief were the way of it. Therefore if my sorry tale of thieves and swivers give offence I say I speak but as I find; and in defence I offer up the curious fact that our ministers of state may rob our nation of thousands of pounds with impunity, but the poor wretch who steals a shilling and some silver spoons is always hanged.

Mr Defoe, with his undoubted interest in low life and its denizens, would certainly have told the story with more excellence and learning if I had done as others have and sought his talents as a scribe; but Mr Defoe has made his name retelling the histories of those already dead or old, and I am neither. This eighteeenth century and I are of the same age, being twenty-eight years; and you shall hear the true and genuine account of my disreputable life and actions from my own mouth and in my own manner.

It was as a boy during the reign of Queen Anne that I acquired that liking for gold which was to influence my life's course. Jerry Dowlan was my mentor. A lean long-faced man, with little eyes and lank brown hair, a solitary man living outside the village, wearing a patchwork coat and moleskin breeches, he was a treasure seeker on the Great North Road. Our village Buckden straddled that road, and the coaches that went north and south stopped at the inns. Jerry Dowlan took me with him on his search for gold.

Long days we passed at this great work.

"This road has seen the tread of king and soldier, merchant and nobleman, since men wrote down their doings," Jerry said, "and every one of them bore money on him. There was the buying and selling, there was flight and ceremony. There was battles fought, there was murder done. Pieces of gold were tumbled down by chance or buried deep on purpose, never claimed. Castles and churches, inns and farmhouses, all along the way, and gold passing between them, travelling in purse and pocket, saddlebag and shoe, and fated not to reach its chosen destination. Waiting for the likes of me. And you, Davy, and you; since you are my chosen partner."

I was not his partner, I was a lad of eight years old; but I believe he took a certain pleasure in confiding to my eager ear his rambling thoughts, as we plodded on together in the misty silences of copse and spinney, and along the rough and rutted tracks.

Jerry Dowlan had a pendulum of glass upon a leather string; he kept it in a pouch inside his shirt.

"We have to look for humps and hillocks, Davy," he said, "and hollows never dug by paw and claw. Such as this."

And he would crouch upon the damp leaves with the dripping boughs about him, and his brows knit in a frown, his shoulders hunched, his breathing hard. In his brown hands the leather string would slowly circle and the holed glass take upon itself a life all of its own.

"Now she speaks," said Jerry. "What hev you to tell me, gal?"

In the leaves we'd scrabble with our digging fingers, rooting up the earth clods, fisting the mulch, sometimes to elbow and armpit; the holed glass never failed us.

"What is it, Jerry? Is it gold?"

"This here's a silver penny; I seen 'em before."

"It's like no penny I know. And is that Queen Anne whose head we see there?"

"Not a bit of it; that is an old king."

"What king?"

"How do I know? An old king, like I say."

Rings we found, tarnished and out of true; and sometimes a leathern boot, which we discarded, and a spear handle carved with heads and leaves, and a drinking horn tipped with silver. There were brooches also, made of coloured glass, bronze and amber; and broken swords. These it were that pleased me most.

"Take that one for yourself," said Jerry. "Keep it."

The hilt was too large for my hand, beautiful to the touch, engraved with shapes and marked with lettering. The blade was much worn, broken at the tip and heavy.

"Who would have borne this sword?" said I marvelling.

"Warriors," said Jerry; but he knew no more than that.

I was those warriors then, whirling that weapon in an unseen army, terrible and brave. At last, in combat with a tree, it split, the hilt from the shaft, and I kicked the two pieces from me, finding them now useless as the leathern boot.

Gold we rarely found.

And yet the lure of it, the rumour of it, the merest possibility, was enough to keep our noses to the earth like hounds upon a scent. Who was it first said that Duval had hid his treasure here —

'Twixt Tollentone Lane and Alconbury Hill
Duval's gold lies buried still?'

We did not know, but we believed him, and should we find that gold we would be rich for life. Duval's gold was the ultimate prize, but we were teased upon our way by small enticements, therefore hope burned always bright within us. A gold ring we found once, and a clasp that once had held a cloak, and a little crooked pin. But Duval's gold we wanted for the best of reasons — usefulness. Duval's gold was shaped in guineas of the realm, not in pins and combs and gewgaws — things which must be changed to cole, that is, money; and should we find it we could there and then go spend it.

Upon what, I wonder, neither of us having knowledge of the world of gentleman spenders? Upon a good horse — that I knew essential to a gentleman. A fine coat and a pair of long boots. A sword that did not break against a tree.

This unnatural son gave no thought to the easing of his mother's lot nor saw the acquisition of wealth as a means to bring her comfort and security. No pleasant cottage with beans and herbs growing in its garden figured in my visions of the future. Why waste my wealth, I thought in careless disregard, when I had Uncles a-plenty to enrich and comfort her, all wealthy, all with horses of their own?

One February day, beside a mere, I proved that I was not the henchman of a treasure seeker but a gold finder in my own right.

I was alone. Upon the branches of the bare trees hung strings of water drops. The moist leaves rustled as they fell. The surface of the mere was thick and murky, pitted with the falling drops. The new green of the spring barely disguised the hollows of the ground. I dug at a tree's root, where a mound showed clear enough. No birds sang. My fingers closed upon a sharp hard shape, an earth-encrusted thing. I scratched it raw and knew that it was gold. I thought to pocket it but pride made me eager for praise. I kept it to myself throughout one day and handled it. A strange thing, a mass of embossed curves like spotted snakes; I could trace the pattern of it and then lose it as another snake broke across the path of it; there seemed no reason in the pattern. At last vexation made me tire of it.

"It's gold, Jerry, I know it."

He fingered it. He eyed me craftily. "Where did you find it?"

I told him a lie. He knew it.

"Aye, that's gold. A buckle, I would say, and very fine. Not broken either, and the edge smooth. You done well, Davy. When I take it to the Collector I could say I found it. But I won't, since you and I are pals. Would you like to come with me and see him and tell him yourself?"

"I would."

All that Jerry found would never be of use to him if he had not his Collector waiting for his finds, as the Almighty and the Devil wait for souls. I was at last to meet him.

We travelled on foot along an ancient path, wide enough only for one. The path skirted fields and hedgerows, a way long used by pedlars, worn by their trudging. The grass to the sides of such paths is rough and hillocky, but if a traveller keeps entirely to the sunken dip of the path, it is easy going. We followed the edge of a wood, then we crossed open heathland, bypassing the villages on our way.

The Collector lived apart from the village, in an old house surrounded by tall ash trees, each bare-branched tree smudged with rooks' nests, the birds circling and tumbling above them with raucous cries. Briars and brambles grew up to the walls of the house. Its roof was gabled, dark with mosses, its windows small with leaded panes. A twist of smoke curled from a tall chimney.

Jerry thumped upon a small side door, which opened at the force of his fist, and laid bare a stone-flagged passage reeking of mould. Into this passage came a servant, elderly, wiping his mouth from quaffing beer.

"Ah — Jerry Dowlan..."

"The same. Is Lord Staughton at home?"

We followed the servitor up a winding stairway whose cumbersome banisters and dark wood panelling bespoke an earlier age. The boards beneath our feet were uneven and creaked as we trod. We were taken to an upper room, and in the doorway we were announced, as the important are.

"Master Jerry Dowlan and accompanying Boy."

The room into which we were ushered, being low, with heavy timbered beams and oaken wainscoting, possessing one small window merely, was dark. A fire burned in the hearth. Beside it, in a great carved chair, sat a man in repose, his hands and the white ruffles at his wrists gleaming pale amongst the shadows; and a black cat sat upon his knee, its eyes like green glass. The white fingers stroked the cat's black fur.

"Jerry, my friend... what have you brought me?"

The voice, coming out of the surrounding gloom, was, I thought, very beautiful. I knew why it seemed so — it was a gentleman's voice.

I owned at that time an inordinate respect for the gentry, knowing nothing of them except that, as with the possession of gold, it was better to be a gentleman than not, since gentlemen were wealthy, rode in coaches, threw coins when you held their horses for them, called 'Inkeeper!' and caused the same to run towards them, serving up the best of all the inn might offer. I had stood close to gentlemen before, but never in their parlour, and I gaped with awe at my good fortune, squinting to behold more plainly the one who was before me.

"Light candles," ordered he, as if in gratification of my wishes, and the servant moved about the room, and in his wake glowed flaming orbs that filled the room with quivering illumination. Then he withdrew.

Lord Staughton was very beautiful indeed. He would have been at that that time some twenty-five years of age. His face was lean and handsome with high cheekbones, a patrician nose and dark eyes beneath dark brows. His lips were finely formed, sensuous and firm. He wore a white shirt with ruffles at the neck and wrists, and close fitting velvet breeches to the knee, with white stockings and buckled square-toed shoes. About his person clung a dark red robe, open, of very rich cloth, satin as I supposed, the light playing upon it as he moved. His face was framed by the ringlets of a dark wig whose curls lay on his shoulders.

He put the cat to the floor most carefully and smiled at me and extended his hand. To my astonishment we shook hands.

"And who might you be, young man?" he asked me.

"Davy Gadd, sir. Master Jerry's partner."

"Davy Gadd...?" His lordship looked a query at Jerry, over my head.

"Yes sir." Jerry spoke as one man of the world to another, as if I was not present. "His Feckless Father ran away to London. Jonas Gadd, sir, you remember, five years ago, and left the mother. Selina Gadd, the..." He hesitated, and coughed behind his hand.

"Indeed," agreed his lordship smoothly, with a little smile. "The lovely seamstress living near the inn."

"That's right, sir, and Davy helps with the horses."

"Is that so, Davy?"

"I sleeps alongside 'em," I assured him. "There ain't nothing I don't know about a horse."

"That must be very useful," said Lord Staughton. "You must allow me to show you my own, when we have leisure. Have you any advice, perhaps, for one who also knows a little on the subject?"

"I don't like to see 'em at the plough," I told him earnestly. "Oxen are for ploughing, as has always been."

"But you concede their usefulness for pulling coaches?"

"Aye, if they must; but best of all they like to run, and so one master is the best for 'em, who takes good care."

"You speak from observation — or do you possess a mount of your own?"

"No; but I will do."

"I am sure that you are right. However, it is not in the capacity of horseman that you visit me today, I understand?"

Jerry stepped forward. "Davy have found a buckle."

It was a good buckle. I had done well. As my reward I was permitted to see the Collection. It was in the next room. This room contained tall cupboards, whose doors and drawers opened to reveal a wondrous display. Objects such as Jerry and I had drawn from the earth as mud-encrusted lumps were here to be seen as new. I was full of admiration for the cleansing process and the polishing. It was pretty to see silver pennies, brooches, clasps, tankards and weapons gleaming on their backcloth of blue velvet. But I could not see the point of such display. Gold and silver were for buying, selling, dealing. I perceived Lord Staughton as something of a gaoler, someone who took pleasure in the capture and the holding. *I have you now, my fine ones, you are mine...* And then what? Merely to look at them? I thought him strange.

"So," said he, "young Davy Gadd, you'll find me Duval's gold now, shall you?"

"If I can, sir." I could not help but ask it. "And will you put that away also or will you spend it?"

Lord Staughton stroked his chin reflectively, a little half smile playing about his mouth. "If I were fortunate enough to possess the treasure of that celebrated highwayman," he said, "I would — after first offering to your good self and Jerry here your fair share — divert it to a Cause dear to my heart. One to which that renowned Gentleman of the Road would give wholehearted approval. But first of all, I would sit, and run my fingers through the golden guineas, simply for the joy of it."

"Yes, I would do that," I agreed.

"And I," said Jerry, plainly considering himself too long absent from the conversation.

"And I would meditate upon a life of bravery and daring so merrily spent in flouting law and dull convention," said Lord Staughton. "I would consider nights beneath the stars, and the pounding of the heart that waits expectantly — the rattling of the coach, the drawing of the pistol, the confrontation, and the flight from danger." As he spoke he moved about the room, like a stage player, that moves knowing all eyes are upon him. He was a very dainty walker. "I would suppose myself that charming Frenchman, gallant, chivalrous and courtly, dancing a coranto on the heath with the partner of my choice, while yet holding the timorous coachman at pistol point. I would regret the passing of those same romancy days, when gentlemen of the road were gentlemen by nature, and not the louts of our own time." He paused and studied the gold buckle which he held between finger and thumb. "Each guinea would speak to me as eloquently as a rose. But," and he laughed, "I would not put them away. I would put them to work."

And yet you would not soil your hands to find them, I thought. And I wondered whether, if I found them, I would bring them docilely to Jerry or to Lord Staughton. I rather thought I would not. I rather thought that I would keep them for myself.

"Davy Gadd," Lord Staughton said, "you are a handsome boy. Has anyone told you that? Believe me, it is so. I hope that we will meet again. I think that if the years are good to us and we outlast the vagaries of time and chance we may prove useful to each other — say in ten years' time, when you are grown, and I... am not yet too well past my prime."

I did not understand him; but I thought he meant that he and I should search for treasure.

Selina Gadd my mother was considered to be comely. Certainly my Uncles so considered her. Whenever one or other of them visited us he brought her presents. I see her in those days, sitting in a chair by the window, wearing an overdress of yellow muslin sewn with little green and blue flowers and fastened at the front with bows of yellow ribbon. These bows often hung undone and showed a pale green dress beneath and much of neck and shoulder. Her nose was snub, her lips large, her teeth white and pretty, her cheeks rosy and her skin smooth. Her hair would have been chestnut, as mine was, but with lotions and potions she heightened it to a shade closer to buttercup. It was piled high with plenty of little curls about her ears, which seemed to drive the Uncles to extremes, and each must kiss these curls or twine them about his finger, at which point if I were there I would be sent away.

This was no hardship to me, as I had no interest in these visitors, all generally bloated in appearance, portly, red-faced, older than my mother, and by their dress and their demeanour pretty well-to-do, and predisposed to pat me on the head, while plainly wishing I were elsewhere. As a result of the presences of so many Uncles, I was often from our lodging, and my time was spent most pleasurably at the Lion or at the Sun, where I made myself as useful as I might.

All transport to and from the north came to Buckden. Carts and wagons, packhorses, chapmen with nags, postboys on fast horses, gentlemen riders and cumbersome coaches. I earned myself some small cole — that is, a few coins — holding horses, fetching hay and straw, sweeping up, shovelling dung, scraping mud from coach wheels, minding trunks, carrying tankards in the parlour, anything at all in that teeming bustle when the inns were busy. In all weathers they came to Buckden, some from Stilton, that is, hardly any distance at all, and others from Stamford and Grantham and Gonerby Moor and Newark and Bawtry and York itself.

They had notices upon a board in York which read: 'All that are desirous to pass from York to London or from London to York or any other place on that road, let them repair to the Black Swan in Coney Street in York and to the Saracen's Head on Snow Hill, south of Smithfield. At both which places they may be received in a stage coach, which performs the whole journey in four days (if God permits).'

When these coaches pulled up and the horses were changed and the travellers refreshed, I heard such tales — of flooded meadows where the coach might pass only by the help of a guide who went ahead and plumbed the water with a pole, and the heads of the leaders barely above the waves; and of haunted inns where a King once slept and now walked of nights, carrying his severed head; of Barnby Moor where the blizzards turned the coaches over; of the Bloody Oaks, which bled on the anniversary of a famous battle; and Gonerby Moor, where highwaymen lay in wait; and Gonerby Hill where a gibbet stood for all to see sticking up against the sky and where these selfsame highwaymen met their doom.

I never wanted to go home. I had a home, yes, of a sort, in lodgings down a side street, with my mother, and those Uncles who were sometimes there and sometimes not; but I was more at home at the Lion and the Sun, where they tolerated me good humouredly and paid me small attention.

I was a ragamuffin lad, wiry and strong, with a thatch of chestnut hair and a wide grin, a whiffling thrum-cap boy in ragged black cloth breeches, a homespun shirt and a coat of corduroy, the sort of stable riffraff that may be found in any inn yard, gawping at travellers. I was unlettered, I knew nothing but the inns, the horses, the road, the search for treasure. I had seen the travellers tumble from their coaches, stiff and grumbling, staggering to the inn parlour. I had seen the gentlemen riders with long leather boots and spurs, possessors of fine horses. I had heard about Captain Claude Duval, Gentleman of the Road. I would never be a gentleman by blood; but with a horse and pistol it seemed plain to me that I could be that other kind of gentleman.

Such was my intent. The road itself was my chosen home; I could foresee no other life than to be part of it. Night after night this was the substance of my thoughts as I drifted off to sleep in the warm hay of the stables at the inn and the dozing horses whickered in their stalls, and I dreamt about the road... that road which unbeknown to me I was so soon to travel.

Chapter Two

MY Feckless Father, Jonas Gadd, was a man for whom I spared never a thought. This comfortable state of affairs was soon to change. I became obliged to consider at close quarters this same betrayer of wife and child when my mother revealed to me her intention of bringing me south by coach to visit him at his lodgings in Bishopsgate in London.

"Will there be horses there?"

"Of course there will be horses."

Ma would have told me any lie to get me docilely to London, but I needed small persuasion — we were to travel in a coach.

Twenty years ago the travellers in the coach from York to London took five days to reach their destination. They slept at Doncaster, Newark, Stamford and Stevenage. If they came northward they slept at Biggleswade, Stamford, Barnby Moor and Ferrybridge. And now that great distance could be travelled in four days and nights only. I had seen the York coach, the four-stager, as it disgorged its passengers. Its wheels were black with mud and twice my height. Its doors hung open to disperse the stench within. Its weary horses steamed, with sweating flanks, horses which had come from Stamford and the Bloody Oaks, from Alconbury gibbet, and still reeking of the road.

Ours was a Buckden coach, Humphrey Harvey's coach. I knew it well, and grand enough it seemed to my small view, with its great wheels — fourteen spokes about the nub — and its big squat body wherein six folk might sit, or more if they be careless of their comfort. I studied it with awe and satisfaction as it stood there in the inn yard the night before we left. It was like a sleeping monster that would be wakened into life by daylight.

A hand now gripped my shoulder — Humphrey Harvey the coachy, on his way to bed, and drinking as he stood, a big man, his face brown and creased, frizzle-pated and loud.

"So, my nipperkin, you're coming south with us tomorrow," Humphrey said, and passed me the leathern jug. Ale, sweet and warm.

"Aye, to London, as it seems."

"To find your Dad."

"He ain't lost, Humphrey; he lives at Bishopsgate. We're going to live with him."

"And is that so?" he said and ruffled up my hair.

"Ma says so."

"Cod's teeth, then it must be so," said Humphrey comfortably. "But I'll tell you what — whatever you got waitin' for you in Bishopsgate, you got a merry journey coming up. We'll have ourselves a good time, and I'll show you all there is to see."

"Will we see highwaymen?"

"Wounds, I hope to God not! But if we do, I got my trusty old musket. Oliver Cromwell's musket that used to be. They found it at his house in Huntingdon and now it's mine, and good as new. No London prancer's like to get the better of a chap with Oliver Cromwell's musket. And you'll sit up beside me. You'll be fine with me; no need to be afraid."

"I ain't afraid," I said indignantly. "I ain't afraid of nothin'."

"Off you go home, boy, then," he answered. "Crack o'dawn's when we'll be leavin'. Crack o' dawn."

I was ready. I had run on ahead to be first at the coach, Ma tripping it behind me in her dainty shoes. It was early morning, so early that it seemed yet night, and dark, though it was springtime. The ostlers by lanthorn light were leading out the horses.

Ma caught me up, vexed and wild at my having eluded her, and quite abandoning her general simpering manner, displayed something of her truer nature as she shook and clouted me. Then mindful almost immediately of the presence of stablehands, which though inferior were nonetheless male, she calmed herself and firmly took my hand. She was got up in her new dress. It had a tight blue bodice and full gathered sleeves. Her skirt was of striped pink and lavender calico. A cloak half covered all this provender, but Ma had the skill of letting a cloak slip just a little to reveal her good looks. She had a black ribbon at her neck. She wore blue shoes with bows and heels. Her hair was piled high and hidden by a white cap which framed her face. She looked very pretty. All the ostlers thought so too.

Myself wore dun-coloured breeches and worsted stockings, flat leather shoes with tongue and buckles; and a shirt and cloth coat and cap. My coat had been provided by an Uncle, therefore was new and smart though dull in colour. I had a fine cravat which measured one foot wide and one yard long. We were a well looking pair, I thought.

For all that Humphrey had promised crack of dawn, it was midday before the coach was ready to depart and it was Humphrey himself who was the cause of our delay for he must sleep off his night's drinking. We all had time for a good breakfast and various beverages besides and I was bursting with impatience as the time dragged by. Then the chests and trunks and baskets were loaded on to the back of the coach and at last the passengers were called from the inn, six in all, now to be jostled together, thrown up and down over hillocks and ruts and obliged to know one another very well, and if one stank or drank or coughed himself to a consumption so much the worse. Ma went into the coach. All the men about the inn fell over themselves to help her up the steps and look at her white stockings. The only other female person was a farmer's wife who received small attention from the menfolk and who plainly disapproved of Ma.

Now came the moment of joy — the emergence of our coachy Humphrey Harvey from out of the inn parlour, a tankard in his hand, the which he handed to a potboy with a gracious gesture as he strode forth like the Hero he believed himself to be. As, to be fair, so did we all, for the coachman's is an arduous craft not to be taken lightly.

Majestically and slowly he approached the horses, wheelers and leaders, patting them, assessing them, seeing that the harness sat fair and the reins well buckled to the bits. Finding himself satisfied he mounted the box. He held the reins loose, he then tightened them in his right hand, and took up his whip; he fixed his old musket into position.

"Well, Davy Gadd, and shall you stay behind?" he roared; and up beside him I was thrown and took my place of glory.

The innkeeper bawled for all to hear that the coach was ready to depart.

"Safe journey!" cried the ostlers.

"Amen," said Humphrey Harvey, and with a great jolt we set off.

Out of Buckden, along a road of fine gravel, past flat fields where young wheat grew green and distant church spires showed against the sky. Unaccustomed then to the quickness of a single horse I thought us very speedy and immensely superior to the folk who travelled by wagon and on foot. For me it was a journey of pure pleasure. Perched high beside our coachy I was well content, and more so when he shared a flask with me whose contents I found very warming. It was black cherry brandy.

We came down through Little Paxton and St Neots and on to Tempsford, and so to Biggleswade where we drew to a halt at the Crown to dine. At Baldock we halted our regal progress for an overnight pause where to my great delight I slept within the coach itself, surprised that no one else was eager for the privilege. In the morning we were off again, going, as I thought, like the wind, but in actuality at the steady pace of the country coach, slow up the inclines, easy on the levels, and with no particular hindrance, the weather being fair and dry.

Six great hills now caught my attention, and Humphrey told the joke I guess he always told: "Which two are furthest apart? Look carefully as we go by and tell me right."

"Those two — no, the first two — no, which?"

"The first one and the last!" he cried in great good humour.

And so down to Knebworth, by Hangman's Lane and Mardley Hill, pausing at a roadside inn to eat, and thence to Hatfield and beyond. Then said Humphrey: "See that great stone in the grass."

"I see it."

"The very whetstone that gives its name to this place, and it's criss-crossed with the marks of the cutting edges of the swords they sharpened before a famous battle."

"Which famous battle?"

"A very bloody battle."

And at last to Finchley Common. "And here," said Humphrey, "is where we're most like to see highwaymen. But best not tell the ladies."

"What shall we do if one attacks us?"

"I shall shoot him with my trusty musket."

"Have you ever been stopped and robbed, Humphrey?"

"I have not. I daresay I've been lucky."

"Are you not afraid that today your luck might change?"

"I am not and I'll tell you why. It is after noon and broad daylight and we are not alone upon the road. There are those carts there, another coach back there, a drover behind, a wagon before. We are almost a crowd. And on Finchley Common we bunch up closer by general consent. Wounds, if I didn't think myself a match for any poxy villain on horseback I'd never have turned coachy! But we won't see no highwayman today. Keep your eyes peeled, Davy, nonetheless."

I scoured every oak tree, every copse. I longed for Humphrey to be proved wrong. I itched to hear the sound of the musket at close quarters. I longed to see a darkly handsome man, masked, on a proud black horse, a pistol in his hand, a wicked smile upon his lips, firm but not cruel, who maybe would bestow a kiss on Ma, who, for all that she was flighty was good looking and like to appeal to gentlemen of the road, I guessed.

"Ha!" cried Humphrey. "There's your highwayman!"

A gibbet by the roadside, and a tenanted one. I saw the rags flutter, and the bones within the chains. I saw the grimace of the teeth.

"Rot and perish all such rogues," said Humphrey vigorously.

"Humphrey, that was once a man like you or me," I protested.

"Not a bit of it," insisted Humphrey, "for we are honest God-fearing creatures and he was not. He stole men's silver and put them in fear. Death to them all, I say; brutes and scoundrels each one."

"And Captain Claude Duval?" said I.

"What of him?"

"He was a Gentleman of the Road and wore lace ruffles."

"And what good did it do him? He was hanged nonetheless."

"He was unlucky."

"Unlucky! As are they all. Captain James Hind — hanged. Swift Nicks Nevison — hanged. Jamie Whitney — hanged. And he came from that very town we passed through — Stevenage — and, so they say, took a full two hours repenting at the gallows. Maybe he was putting off the moment, eh? They all are hanged, Davy, sooner or later. They all become like him beside the road, grinning at the air and making a slow dance while birds sit on their shoulders."

Travellers a-plenty there were as we crossed that rough heath, and two more gibbets, tenanted, but Gentlemen of the Road saw we none.

Before we knew it we were passing through another village and

Humphrey was telling me that upon that very stone sat one Dick Whittington, who heard the bells of London calling him and telling him he would become Lord Mayor.

"He was only a poor young homespun lad up from the country," Humphrey said. "He thought the streets of London would be paved with gold. But when he got there he found they wasn't."

I twinged with sympathy for Whittington. A treasure seeker like myself.

"So he went home again?"

"Aye, but changed his mind, here on Highgate Hill. And back he went and rose to be a great man and gained great wealth."

"By honest means?" I wondered.

"Of course by honest means! Wounds, what do you take him for? A Worthy, he was. He built Newgate prison — the old Newgate prison, that is — and he did good works and was a great friend to the poor. And everywhere he went, a big grey cat went with him."

I must have paid good heed to that same story for I well remembered it in aftertimes, sometimes pondering the oddity that the long-dead Whittington and I were to be not a little bound together in the unravelling of our lives, though I a reprobate and he a Worthy.

It was the last I heard before I fell asleep; and this coinciding with the final halt upon our journey I was passed within the coach and slumbered like an infant against Ma; therefore saw nothing of the approach of London, awakening only to find that night had fallen and we had achieved our destination.

The first thing that I saw in London was a sight enough to fright a person of more anxious disposition than myself — a great black wooden head with painted eyeballs and a grimace full of teeth, upon his chin a beard, upon his head a turban, and this all superhuman in its bigness. This was the Saracen who gave his name to the inn into which our coach now trundled, and there were two more like him positioned within, each as fierce and large.

Now all was bustle as we entered the inn yard which, lit by many lanthorns, showed galleries and tiers stretching upward to a great height, and the glittering stars beyond. We went with the crowd into the inn parlour, where all was noise and confusion; but within a moment a familiar pattern had established itself, my mother being surrounded by a group of gentlemen who plied her with beverage and paid her compliments and caused her to laugh and smile and tease, as fresh as if she had never made a journey in her life. Satisfying her maternal leanings with a glance in my direction to ensure I had myself completed that same journey and was present, she then allowed herself the pleasure of the company of the gentlemen, assuming I would be at ease about the inn, the which, I must confess, I was.

The Saracen's Head, on Snow Hill, south of Smithfield, stood close by the church of Saint Sepulchre, where the condemned felons hear their last benediction, and within a stone's throw of Newgate Gaol where they lie penned. This I did not know upon that dark night when at eight years old I arrived in London Town, nor did I know that I had landed slap in the middle of a region that was to become familiar to me as my own hands; but let it be said that I felt instantly at home. An inn yard wheresoever was to me as the hearthside is to the dog, the lair to the fox — even an anthill like the Saracen's, four storys high, teetering with antiquity, thriving, unsavoury, rancid with unwholesome company.

With the joyous sounds of drinking all about me I prepared to explore the inn. Ad's blood, I knew the very song that they were singing —

'The man in the moon drinks claret
With powder beef, turnip and carrot.
If he doth so, why should not you
Drink wine until the sky looks blue?'

I had not stirred three yards from the parlour doorway when a gang of lads my own age set upon me for a fight; but I was as glad as they to scrap, and welcomed their attentions as relief from sitting stiffly in the coach. It was in this manner that I first encountered William Field, the first visible portion of him being the knuckles of his fist, and though there must have been in that unruly group some of the others who were to become friends or foes, he for the trouble he was to cause me is the one whom I most well remarked.

It would be pleasing to relate that he was ugly, vile, misshapen, outwardly revealing the extent of the malevolence within; but he was not so. Even as a boy, he bore some semblance of that fairness which fooled women and men alike into thinking him honest, till they knew him better. Yellow hair he had, and lizard-bright eyes, and a smiling mouth, and a face a delight to behold for the pleasing arrangement of its features.

This same face was now contorted to a leer of anticipation as he knelt upon my chest and squared himself up for the punch that would imprint itself upon my wincing visage; but at that very moment one of the others cried out: "Wait! He's one of Mr Hitchin's Boys!"

Will Field gave a howl and stayed his hand.

"Is that true?" he demanded, hanging over me in threatening pose. "One of Mr Hitchin's Boys? Are yer?"

"I am!" I yelled, no fool.

The hands that gripped me relaxed their hold, and all drew back in palpable disappointment, and, resigned to Fate's irony, conceded the defeat of their intent.

One laughed close to my face. "And if he is not, he soon will be!"

"And if he is not," Will Field promised, "he owes me one."

Within moments I was once again alone, my assailants vanishing as swiftly as they had appeared, and I unblemished was left to marvel at my unknown benefactor, Mr Hitchin, who all unwittingly had saved me from affray.

"There have I a mistress got," sang the gusty drinkers from within the bar room.

> 'There have I a mistress got
> Cloistered in a pottle pot
> Plump and bouncing, soft and fair,
> Buxom, sweet and debonair,
> And they call her sack, my dear.'

This echoed in my ears as I mounted the stair and found myself upon the first of the galleries that ran around the innyard.

"Where do you think you are going?" shouted a voice. I darted through a door in the twinkling of a bedstaff, and found myself in an unlit room with a pair of snoring sleepers in the bed nearby.

Here I crouched in darkness, and no hue and cry being raised, no pursuit ensued. I crept away, and venturing further along the gallery entered another room which proved to be empty. I fumbled about in the darkness for a while, but then hearing footsteps approaching and the sound of a heavy trunk placed down outside the door, I hid inside a cupboard and pulled the door tight shut.

Into the room now came its occupants, noisily preparing to bed down. Not wishing to expire from want of air in my small enclosed space and with no other form of escape offered me, I wrenched the panel from the back of the cupboard, wriggled through the gap and replaced the wood as best I might, and I found myself in a similar cupboard of similar stuffiness whose outer door I carefully opened and as carefully sneaked through.

Upon the instant I was seized by the ear from behind and pulled into the room, and I looked for the first time in my life but not the last upon the barrel of a pistol.

Chapter Three

"GOD's breeches, a rapscallion boy!" my captor groaned. "Curse my bad luck. And are there more of you?" He shoved the pistol into his belt. He grabbed a candlestick. He shone the flame into the cupboard, myself still held between finger and thumb, a yowling appendage.

"Shut your mouth," he snapped. "Or I shall shoot your tongue from out your gullet."

The illogicality of his threat eluded me at the time and I was silent though in pain. I braved his wrath then to remark: "I am alone. I am the only boy you shall find in your cupboard, sir."

He let me go, closed the cupboard door and locked it, and taking the candlestick, perused my face, as, of course, did I his. There lit by the leaping flame stood an extremely handsome fellow. His hair was thick, long, black and curly. His eyes were dark and glittering. His lips bespoke sardonic humour. His teeth, in an age of withered gums and black fangs, were white and gleaming. He was not, it is true, in the first flush of youth; indeed his face bore the lines of a life of some dissipation, and his figure ran a little to paunch. He wore a white silk shirt, with a lace cravat carelessly tied. His breeches were black, and tight about the hips; his boots were very fine indeed. The pistol at his buckled belt made him seem powerful and strong. All in all he was most plainly that for which my eager eyes had searched and failed to find upon our journey — a Gentleman of the Road, a highwayman.

As if in verification of my surmise I saw beyond him on the table nothing less than several piles of golden guineas, neatly placed in little towers of winking gold. My mouth opened so wide you could have placed an orange in it, had you one to hand.

Seeing in me nothing to provoke alarm, the highwayman relaxed his manner and surveyed me with perplexity.

"Now, what am I to do with you?"

"You might tell me the story of your life and your tales of the road," I said hopefully.

"Now why would you want to know about such wicked matters?" he said reprovingly.

"It is my intention to do likewise as soon as I am grown."

"More fool you," said he, but smiling. "Have you eaten?"

We sat down at his table each side of the guineas, to which I was man of the world enough not to refer, though they gleamed with preternatural brightness, quite outshining the humble bread and cheese beside them, of which we now partook.

Taking the stopper from a leathern bottle this gentleman now poured us each a mug of ale. He sighed.

"Ah," he said. "It's not like the old days."

"No sir."

"It was good in the old days."

"Yes sir."

"Truly," he maintained, "gentlemen we were indeed, though humbly born. On the road it matters nothing where you come from. You stand and fall through skill and bravery. You are a king. You follow in the footsteps of heroes. Take Jamie Hind..."

"Captain Hind! Did you know him?"

"Hold hard," he laughed. "He died fifty years ago. He was a kingsman, and took to the road against the Roundheads. Wounds, he robbed Cromwell himself! They called him the Grand Thief. A true gentleman he was, and gave his pickings to the poor."

We thought admiringly about him.

"Once," continued my new acquaintance, "he took forty shillings from a cull who swore that it was all he had. Well, Captain Hind must have the money there and then. But meet me here in one week's time, says he, and I will give you twice as much. And when the chap came to that same spot a week hence, Captain Hind through having had a lucky week, gave eighty shillings to the man and kept his word. They wouldn't do so now — they'd have his forty shillings and his head also!" Becoming morose he paused and drank, then brightened. "Mulled Sack," he said. "Do you know about him? Captain Cottington was his name, but they called him after the tipple he liked best."

"And did you know him?"

"Ah, he was before my time. Like Captain Hind he was a kingsman too and now has passed into legend. Only robbed the Roundheads. Hounslow Heath was his particular patch. Robbed the army pay wagon; took it right from under the soldiers' noses. And this is what he told 'em: All this cole belongs by rights to honest folk. It belongs to them and to me and not to the dogs of the Commonwealth. And here's a health unto his majesty, our young king Charles. And off he rode, and the money with him. Passed into Legend."

Passed into Legend! Once you have done that, you are unassailable. Calumny cannot touch you. Truth has no relevance. Captain Hind gave all his money to the poor — Mulled Sack spirited away the garrison's pay with all the soldiers looking on. Legend has it so. Dead fifty years, they lie safe enough from witnesses prepared to say it isn't so — no carping voice to blurt out: I was there and saw what really happened. But at that moment, there in the candlelight, beside the stacks of golden guineas, in the presence of the handsome stranger, all my faith was undiminished. I believed it all.

"And Jamie Whitney?" I enquired.

"Jamie? What of him?" His voice had altered. In recital of the brave accounts he spoke as one does with ale in the gullet, warmly, in heroic vein; now he sounded wary.

"Captain Whitney," I prompted, "who was so beautiful and vain that he ordered a suit of clothes to be made for him while he was yet in Newgate, so he should meet death as a gentleman?"

"Ah, so you know about that?" he laughed.

"It has Passed into Legend."

"Jamie was beautiful, yes," my highwayman agreed. "But there was more to him than beauty. Have you ever seen a likeness of him?"

"Never."

"I happen to have one here."

With studied carelessness he reached within the breast of his coat, which hung behind him on the chair, and brought forth a folded paper, which he opened. Then he parted the pillars of guineas and slid the paper across to me, tilting the candlestick the better for me to gaze.

The faded drawing, creased and much handled, showed a lovely face, fine featured, especially the eyes, which seemed to reveal a look of arrogance and amusement. He wore a long curled periwig, a hat with a plume, and a coat embroidered all over with little flowers.

"He was awaiting execution," said the highwayman. "That is the suit of clothes he had the tailor make for him. This portrait was drawn in Newgate, three days before his death. You hear such stories of attempted escapes from Newgate, secret plans, last minute rescues. Don't believe them. Have you ever felt the thickness of the bars on that great door? There were twenty of us in the gang. You'd think we'd have been able to arrange something. You'd have thought one at least would have had the wit to work his release. Idiots, all of us, all brawn and noise. Most of them dead now, gone the same way as Jamie."

"You were his friend!" I gawped, wide-eyed. "You knew him!"

"Oh it's a long time ago now," shrugged the highwayman. He took the picture back, folding it away. "Fifteen years since he died. He believed to the last, you know, that we would save him. He pretended to repent. They love a good repentance, do the crowds. There sits the ordinary — that's the preacher who comes with you to the gallows and waits to take your confession down — and then he makes a mint of money selling it, and to please the mob he tries to make you talk about your sins and let 'em know the lewd and luscious titbits they can read about in your confession. Jamie was an hour and a half repenting. And it was bitter weather — February — but the mob was easy; Jamie was so pretty they could bear to see him for as long as he chose to entertain them. But he thought he would be rescued, so he dragged it on and on, till even the ordinary had had enough."

"At Tyburn tree," I shuddered.

"At Smithfield," answered the highwayman. Jerking his thumb over his shoulder he added: "There — just back of this inn." He laughed brusquely and reached for a second bottle, filling our mugs. "Come now, young fellow; it was not my intention to make you sad. Jamie Whitney had a good life — why dwell on its end? And he was such a clumsy brute at first — a butcher's apprentice. Wounds, when I first saw him he was cleaving beef in Stevenage! You're too damned pretty to be chopping up dead beasts, says I. Piss off, says he, or you'll be next; but he knew damn well that he was pretty. Then his uncle in Cheshunt left him a small inn, and Jamie went to be its landlord. I went too. I'd got some pals I went about with and we used to drink at Jamie's inn. I first took him to bed there. Stripped he was the loveliest thing you've ever set eyes upon. You ever seen a young good-looking fellow naked, seventeen or so? Best sight in the world, believe me, boy. You don't want to be an innkeeper, we told him. Come out on the road. You'll never be a gentleman pouring ale at folks' beck and call. What's an innkeeper? But on the road you'll be a gentleman — silks and ruffles and a lacy coat — long leather boots and jewelled pistols. He was twenty-three. We had ten years..."

Thoughtfully we drank. Distantly the muffled sounds of singing rose up from below.

"But he was no gentleman at first," my companion chuckled. "What would you expect? You should have seen him, his first robbery! Clumsy! All he knew was innkeeping. You are part of a great Brotherhood when you set out upon the road, I told him. What is more gorgeous, said I, against the full moon and the branches of a winter tree, than a Gentleman of the Road upon a noble horse — his tricorne hat, the lace at his throat, the velvet ribbon of his hair. The coach approaches. He urges his horse forward. You do not, says I to

Jamie, at such a point cry 'Damn me you son of a whore, stand and deliver!' That is the language of common thieves and footpads. Why can't you rob a chap civilly instead of cursing and calling him names? Think of Claude Duval! Would he have spoken so? No, you must be soft spoken and polite, and doff your hat as you take their gold."

"And he took your words to heart!"

"Oh yes indeed. Jamie became the greatest gentleman of us all. So gallant and charming, and being so beautiful to look upon, much of his dealings were forgiven by the ladies, each one believing herself the object of his affection. They would hand over their rings and trinkets with a smile and tell him where he might come to them that night, and which their window!" He laughed throatily, as at some private joke that was between him and Jamie.

"There is no life like it, lad," continued he. "To take to horse and leave the town behind you, and then far away, with the man of your heart's desire. A ditch is a palace, a shack is a kingdom. Jamie and I, we slept under the stars, and none to hinder us. The road keeps many a secret."

There and then I knew that this was what I wanted for myself. I promised myself that one day I would have it.

"And the stories about him? Are they all true?"

"Of course they are, boy, every one and more! The rich bishop that he robbed, and gave the pickings to a poor clergyman... the coins he strew along the way to slow down the pursuit... the young lady whose wedding ring he would not take when he heard her husband was a Jacobite... all true, all true!"

"And so he has Passed into Legend! And you, sir, will you so? You speak but little of yourself."

"Pass into Legend?" guffawed he. "I will not! And do you know why? In order to Pass into Legend there is one small requirement made of you — you must be dead!"

"But the glory, sir, the cheering crowds — your story told in next day's broadsheets!"

"And yourself anatomized — that is, dissected by the surgeons, and your entrails flapping around your ankles. No, boy, if I gave advice to Jamie as to how to be a gentleman, I'd give you advice of a different nature."

"What?"

"Never tell your name. We Gentlemen of the Road, as you so rightly observe, are greedy for glory. We rob a coach — we cock our pistols to the sky and boast: tell them 'twas Captain Moonshine robbed you! Soon there's the warrant out for the arrest of Captain

Moonshine, his name and face are stuck on tree, on post, on house wall. When he's caught and hanged he makes a brave show and the mob follows, ladies weeping and throwing flowers. What is this thing, fame? How we love it, our name upon folks' lips, that name to last forever. I say a pox on it — a hundred aliases will stand you in better stead. Be Joseph here, there Will, there Jack; and let poor John be hanged, so long as you be not he."

"I had rather be like Jamie Whitney and Claude Duval, glorious and famous," I answered stoutly; "but," I added, "luckier."

"Aye, lucky," agreed my companion. "To have luck sitting on your shoulder is worth any of your talents."

Footsteps strode past our door. My friend, in an instant, had his pistol at the ready. The footsteps went past.

"Are you in danger, sir?" I whispered.

He gave me a wry smile. "I think it would be better were I not discovered in my counting house." He scooped up his gleaming guineas into a baggy leathern pouch. Then he paused. He winked at me. He took one guinea from the pouch and held it between finger and thumb. Nearer and nearer came that guinea to my vision, till the whole world expanded for me into a blur of gold.

"It's yours," he said.

"Oh sir!" I breathed, but I did not protest; and rapidly pocketed my wealth.

Now past our door came voices, so close indeed that a shoulder thumped the door as it went by; and my companion grew visibly uneasy. He stood up and put his coat on.

"Time to depart," he said. "And with, I think, some safeguard." He grabbed my arm, which motion lifted me bodily from my chair, and hustled me towards the door. "Now while it is almost certain that I shall not put a bullet in your ear," he said, "I may be challenged, and must seem most menacing."

"Where are we going?" I gasped, apprehensive and delighted.

"To the Devil," said the highwayman with a merry smile; but seeing that I started in some alarm he added: "Or rather to the Devil's lane. Devil's Lane's up Tollentone way. They say it's Duval's Lane. They say it's where he set out from, when he hid his gold."

"There's nowhere I would rather go," said I.

Cautiously my highwayman opened the door, and we emerged upon the upper gallery of the inn yard. Lights glowed below, but the vocal imbibers had gone to their beds. Held firmly in the highwayman's strong grip and pressed against his warm thigh I was hurried down the stairs, across the yard, and into the stable. A passer-by wished us good night. A stable lad began to saddle up a dark brown mare.

"Up you get, son," said my friend, for the boy to hear. We mounted. The stable boy watched us curiously, saying nothing. We rode out of the inn yard, past the mighty Saracens lit horribly by lanthorn glow, and we passed between the dark and silent houses. Through streets whose names meant nothing to me then we rode, in the direction of Islington village.

We were in open countryside now — no lights, merely the wind in the leaves, the mighty silences of the empty fields. Exhilaration seized me. I had never known such happiness.

A pistol shot rang out behind us.

"Damn me, we are pursued," my highwayman remarked. "And who the devil would have thought it! The parting of the ways, my boy."

He bundled me from the saddle and threw me well clear. I landed on a bank of grass and rolled over and over. A posse of pursuers on indifferent horses thudded past me. My friend had disappeared into the night. I lay there squinting at blackness, tangled in the undergrowth.

Had I at that moment a familiarity with the legend of Icarus, the boy who flew close to the sun and tumbled down to earth, I would have considered myself the equal of that hapless lad in misfortune. Yes, and had I known about Ganymede the lovely boy who was carried off by Jupiter in the form of an eagle for frolics upon Mount Olympus and if by some mischance the eagle had let fall the luscious lad upon the way, then truly such a fall could not have been more tragic than my own. To be transported by the Hero of my Dreams upon a fast horse to Duval's Lane at Tollentone for who knew what further excitement — then suddenly to find myself alone in the meadow in the wilds of Islington — this was too much for soul to bear! I bit my lip and needed all my fortitude to prevent an unworthy tear from coming to my eye.

But understanding that I myself might be in danger of pursuit for the information I might possess about my friend, should the posse return empty handed, I jumped up and darted away to lose myself amongst the trees.

Lose myself I certainly did, but not so far from the civilized world, for crossing the meadow I heard the sound of fiddles playing sweet and merry notes, and I saw a light that glimmered in the darkness; therefore without more ado, but silently, I made my way towards the music.

Chapter Four

THE open doorway of a farmhouse cast a beam of bright light upon the grass, and from that aperture came the cheery sound of fiddles and singing. I heard the song quite plainly. I made my way along the farmhouse wall warily, listening for the first baying of hounds that would make me scamper; but none barked.

"There was an old woman lived under a hill
And she good beer and ale did sell,
She had a daughter whose name was Cis
She kept her at home to welcome guests.
A handsome trooper he rode by
And called for drink most plentifully..."

Through a window I saw in the farmhouse kitchen a merry gathering of both men and women, those that worked about the farm, as I supposed, and all with the air of having well feasted. Not being much able to account for my presence here, and needing a place to sleep without the trouble of explanations, I did not enter but crept towards the nearby barn. The song pursued me as I went in.

"What is this so stiff and warm?
It is my nag, it will do you no harm,
What is this hanging under his chin?
It is the bag he puts his provender in...
Shove him in by the head, pull him out by the tail..."

I climbed a ladder to the hayloft and pulling the musty strands about me I made myself comfortable. I was just settling down to sleep when with great noise the joviality came to an end, and shouts and laughter travelled clearly across to where I lay.

"Goodnight then, Gabriel; goodnight, Peter. Once again, my apologies that my beds are full within, but I know the barn to be a comfortable place, and something tells me you will not mind being together. I'll call you in the morning. Sleep well!"

"Goodnight, Henry — sleep well yourself. And your good lady wife."

Into the barn with a lanthorn came Gabriel and Peter, two men in their twenties, with blankets over their arms and every intention of sharing my domain. They did not climb the ladder. Gabriel placed the lanthorn down upon a bench and sat down beside it. I could see that he was a stocky well-built fellow. His companion was slight, with dark hair, and bore himself with that air of assurance which men have that know they are considered pleasing to the eye.

29

"I think," said Gabriel, and I could hear the smile in his voice, "that Henry understood the favour he was doing us by offering us the barn, away from company. Away from his all-seeing wife."

"We dined well. Henry has a good table. Perhaps a little too much in the way of songs about women!"

"Peter," said Gabriel, of a sudden hesitant. "I'm not wrong? You wanted us to be together?"

"You're not wrong," Peter said, and he moved close to Gabriel and kissed him on the lips, a gesture of reassurance, no more.

I thought that of the two it was Gabriel who was the most in love, and Peter who accepted this as natural.

I lay looking down from the edge of the loft, gripping the ends of the ladder. I knew that I would have to flee the barn now and gave some thought as to how I might best achieve this aim unobserved. I had never been a particularly reflective boy, and in a world that I knew to contain many diversities, it did not strike me as odd that one man should kiss another. I merely wondered how I might move past them and make my escape. To this end I was obliged to watch them and listen to their discourse, a low-voiced exchange in a silence permeated by the rustling of mice amongst the straw.

"It's strange I never met you in the city," Gabriel said. "Strange that chance should bring us out into the fields for this encounter."

"You never go to Jermyn Street?" said Peter.

"I know the house you mean; but no, I never have. I was every night at the Exchange, and sometimes on London Bridge — until last October, when so many of our kind were discovered and apprehended. Since that time I am in such fear I stay at home of nights."

Peter muttered something to the effect that we lived in grim times. "Did you know any of the men that were taken?" I heard him ask.

"I knew John Grant, who cut his own throat rather than stand trial. The kindliest of creatures..."

"A shopkeeper, I believe?"

"Aye, knowing more of damasks and serges and muslins than the inside of a prison. Nor would he, I think, have been in any danger but that he trusted the wrong people."

"You mean he was betrayed?"

"In my understanding of it," Gabriel said, "we have to trust one another, especially in times of hardship. But lately we seem beset with deceivers, men who promise the earth and all manner of delight — which should in itself make us wary! Yet it does not, and — poor eager fools — we show our true leanings, and are trapped.

The perfection that stands upon London Bridge, with golden hair and tight breeches, turns out to be sent by the Society for the Reformation of Manners, and working for the Law." He laughed brittly. "One must admire them for their ability to find such fine examples of male beauty, unfortunately at some cost to ourselves."

Peter turned abruptly, moving a little further off into the shadows. His voice was low and brooding. "It's better in the end to trust nobody," he said. "I don't share your hopefulness, Gabriel, in thinking that we are loyal to one another in times of hardship. We are not. In times of hardship we are as hostile to each other as the vilest low informer, take my word. So we may save our own skin we will peach our lover with a merry unconcern, believe me." He turned back to Gabriel. "How do you know that I myself am trustworthy? I might have been sent by the Society."

"To Henry Yoxon's farm?" scoffed Gabriel. "A married man with children, and a sturdy churchman?"

"What if I had been sent on purpose to follow you, a man known for frequenting the Exchange last year? The Exchange, where lovely wicked lads sell their arses for a shilling!"

"Peter Bavidge! I had hoped for affection from you — and will you put me in fear?" Gabriel reproved him lightly, but I heard the alarm behind his pleasant manner.

Peter stepped back into the lanthorn light. He was smiling. "Be easy, I am no deceiver. We'll talk of kisses; we're wasting time making ourselves melancholy."

"Back there in Henry's kitchen," said Gabriel, "when we were feasting and singing and the fiddles playing, all I could think of was you and how I wished that I might see you naked."

"That's a wish easily granted," Peter laughed.

"And will you grant it, O powerful magician?"

"I will. I owe it to you for teasing you that I was sent by the Society of Reformation. Watch me now — I'll strip with foolery, like they do at the Rose."

Gabriel leaned forward and settled to be entertained. What had my highwayman so latterly remarked? — a young good-looking fellow naked is the best sight in the world? It seemed I was to be given a chance to judge the matter for myself.

It was plain enough that Peter Bavidge was a man that liked himself and thought himself a goodly sight to see. No silly modesty for such as he! Off came his coat and waistcoat, tossed into the hay, and he the while a-smirk and a-simper, bending his body this way and that for best effect. Now he took his shoes off and his white knee stockings and carefully unbuttoned his shirt and slid it off his shoulders. He had a lean and muscular chest, smudged with dark hair. As he unbuckled his belt I saw that this hair continued down his belly and beyond. Now he had bared his bum and off came breeches and all and there he stood with the shadows playing on his skin and his privy member jutting out enough to hang a towel on; and this I gawped at, spellbound.

Gabriel also. "Peter, you are very beautiful!" he said.

"Shall we go upstairs?" suggested Peter, stooping to gather up his clothes.

Upstairs? Into the loft? I rolled at speed behind a bale of hay, and when they clambered up the ladder I was well hid. They spread their blankets in a further corner, with murmured words and husky laughter; and I was able to climb down the ladder with no more of a rustle than a roosting owl. I crept out of the barn.

At that very moment out of the darkness came riders up to the farm house. I turned about and ran straight back into the barn.

If I had run the other way and hidden alone in a field my whole life might have taken a different course.

Gabriel's face showed white at the top of the ladder beside the lanthorn.

"Don't say you saw me, sir!" I said. "I'm in hiding."

He was down beside me in a moment, had bundled me into a manger and shoved hay about me. He was wearing only his breeches. Outside the barn there was noise and shouting. Henry Yoxon was brought grumpily from bed.

"Looking for a highwayman? From London? Recognized by the stable lad? We have none here. A boy abducted by the same? I have seen no boy. Search if you must."

They all came into the barn. I heard them moving about, poking at the hay bales with rakes and hoes.

"There is no boy here," Gabriel told them firmly. "I have been here for some while now and I would have seen or heard an intruder."

After a time the men gave up and left and rode away, and Gabriel eased me out of my confined enclosure.

"Why'd yer save me?" I said, rosy faced and spluttering with hay.

"Perhaps because I know something about having to hide," said Gabriel smiling. "And you looked pretty scared. What had you done?"

"Nothing, that's the joke of it. But they would want to question me about my friend, and I would not be telling."

"Where do you want to go?" said Gabriel.

"Well, back to the Saracen's Head, in London, I suppose. My mother might be wondering where I am. I am to be taken to my Feckless Father."

Gabriel asked no questions. "If you are still here in the morning I will take you into London in my cart. Go to sleep now; dawn is not far off."

Before I fell asleep I made sure that I had my golden guinea safe. I closed my palm protectively about it. Upstairs in the hayloft Gabriel had his heart's desire; but I had mine also.

Gabriel was a milk seller. He lived in Holborn and got his milk from cowkeepers in Islington — Henry Yoxon was one such — and sold it on the streets of London. He said it was worth going out of town for milk, as the country taste was still upon it, whereas town cows' milk tasted of the dark sheds they were kept in, and the sir-reverence in which they stood. Gabriel had a horse and cart, and it was in this conveyance amongst the milk that I returned to Smithfield early next morning. Peter Bavidge had left, gone away on horse-back; it was Gabriel and myself that made the little journey south.

Gabriel whistled as he drove. I saw by daylight that he was a pleasant-faced chap, not handsome but with an open frank counte-nance, large features and dark hair. He had a wide friendly mouth and a fringe of hair swept across his broad forehead, with thick eye-brows and a square jaw. The tune he whistled was the one they had sung last night, about the old woman who lived under the hill and had good beer and ale to sell. Gabriel had slept with Peter last night and now he whistled, merry as any lark. He did not know that I had seen him gaze with adoration upon Peter stripped. *What is this thing so stiff and warm, it is my nag and will do you no harm, what is this hangs under his chin, it is the bags he puts his provender in..*

But beautiful though Peter had seemed, naked, and his man-hood jutting like a rakehandle, myself I thought a golden guinea just as beautiful.

"Do you sing, Davy?" Gabriel enquired. And so blithe was he that morning on account of his night's work that he would have no other but that we should do so. I knew tap-room songs; but I knew a dozen more before we reached our destination.

Since the sentiments were my own, I liked:

"Honest shepherd, since you're poor
Think of loving me no more, for
Only wealth can influence

Woman's inclinations.
Gold alone doth scorn remove.
Gold alone incites to love
Gold can most persuasive prove..."

And we had 'Blowzabella my bouncing doxy', which we sang as a raucous duet, it being a song of wrangling. Then we sang 'It was a lass of Islington', about a maiden who came to London along the same road as ourselves, to sell her pears, and met with a vintner. Gabriel sang the vintner's part, and I the maid's —

"Quoth he, fair maid, I have a suit that you to me shall grant,
Which if I find you'll be so kind there's nothing you
                                                    shall want.
Prithee now consent to me and do not put me by,
It is one small courtesy, all night with you to lie..."

"It will cost you five pounds," says the maid, and they set about it; it had a jolly tune.

Our singing made us laugh, for both of us played the part with gusto, I squeaking as I thought proper for a maid, and Gabriel adjusting his agreeable features into a sinister leer, which in itself was droll to see, and Gabriel said I should sing for a living, but, as I said, he was in excessive good humour.

The sun was high, the sky was blue, the birds were chirping in the hedgerows.

And so in Gabriel's cheery company came I to London, singing.

Chapter Five

"YOUR father will whip you for your disobedience," Ma promised confidently, encouraging me thus to look forward to the encounter with the progenitor whom I had never known. She was pretty vexed; not, I think, at my absence, for she understood me to be self-reliant and with wit enough to make my way back from whatever escapade I had embarked upon; but that at my return a small crowd at the inn having interested themselves in my case, she was obliged to play the part of the distressed and tragic matron and had endured much noisy and unlooked-for sympathy when it had become surmised that I was abducted by a highwayman.

She no more than I had wasted time during our separation, and it was a smartly dressed and highly perfumed gentleman who procured a Hackney coach on our behalf, nay, must escort us all the way to Bishopsgate. A smooth and patronizing manner did not hide his irritation at my presence. As we sat pressed tight within the coach he put a hand upon the back of my neck and twisted my head this way and that to make me see the famous landmarks on our way which he must point out to us and prove himself immensely knowledgeable, we being from the country and knowing nothing.

"We are now passing beneath the arch of Newgate," he said. "It is adorned with the statues of Justice, Fortitude, Plenty, Liberty and Peace. Its tower is sixty feet high and considered very fine. Newgate gaol is where your highwayman would have passed the night had he been caught, and that way" (a three-quarter twist of my neck) "lies the way to Tyburn tree, where he would have been hanged. Newgate gaol," he added with a heavy-handed humour, "is where they put the naughty boys that cause sorrow to their mothers."

He chattered on about Cheapside and Poultry and pointed to the newly built St Paul's church, but I paid little heed, save when as we passed along Threadneedle Street he said: "The Royal Exchange. This is the second building of that name. The first was burned down in the Great Fire, forty years ago. You can buy anything there, anything at all."And he chuckled and winked at Ma, plainly having no inkling that I understood him well enough and knew that there were boys who sold their arses for a shilling. Not that I had a precise comprehension of what such transaction signified; but I believed it similar to the lass of Islington's pears.

"And what do you think of London?" he enquired in an arch inveigling tone. "Your mother finds it filthy, noisy, smelly and full of thieves. She has a fine discerning nature."

"I like London well enough," I answered with a shrug.

"And here he shall meet his father, and shall go to school and learn to read and write," Ma simpered, "and shall know London better."

The house where I would begin to do so was an old one, untouched by the famous fire, tall, several storeys high, pressed close against its neighbours, gabled, eaved, with crumbling plaster and small dark windows. Ma and I descended from the coach into the gabble of the street, the gentleman remaining and going on elsewhere, with fond words to Ma, and promises; and she and I entered the house and a low dark empty room within. No one was at home.

It was plain to me that Ma was disconcerted by this and also by the lack of furniture. She poked about, a frown upon her brow. A

35

scent of beeswax hung in the dank air, inexplicable in a room without a chair or table or the like. Hearing noises from above, Ma went purposefully up the stairs, which led out of this empty room, I following, and the scent of beeswax rapidly diminishing. The room above contained a bed and chest and wash bucket, and from the strewn clothes and the remains of food upon the table, seemed a place of habitation. A further stairway of rickety dimensions led up to the higher floor, and here to our surprise we found a heap of folk, all poor and tawdry, some asleep, some sitting in poses of disillusion, all of a mean and furtive appearance, who, it transpired, paid rent to Jonas Gadd in exchange for his revealing nothing of their presence to the landlord.

Ma and I returned to the middle chamber and set ourselves to wait. Ma pronouncing the food edible we consumed a leg of mutton and a loaf and drank warm beer. The noise from the street came up to us quite plain, the cries of the traders: "Pots to mend!" — "Lovely flahs!" — "New baked bread!" — "True Confessions — Sin and Vice Exposed!" — and we heard the jostlings of carts and carriages, the snatches of song, the fights, the bawling of abuse, the trills of laughter, and the whinneying of horses.

Ma dabbed herself about the neck with rosewater, and prinked a bit, and worked to convince herself in spite of growing doubt that what she did was right.

"A boy should be with his father."

"A father should know his son."

"I have nurtured you; he must take his share." Then, finally, in some exasperation: "Davy, I wish you'd speak! I never know what you think. Will you be good and do as your father says and go to school and learn?"

I did not see why I should assuage her guilt and misgivings. I was equable about my lot. I would stay or I would run away and look for Duval's treasure on the road; my intentions were straightforward, but I would not share them.

Eventually, with a great noise, there came something into the room below.

"Lord! Lord!" Ma said and fanned herself, and we went down.

A big door had opened at the back of the room, letting in much light and clamour and two men bearing a sedan chair. This they deposited upon the floor. One of the chairmen left. He that remained was my father Jonas Gadd.

He was a big red-faced man with wild dark hair and a huge neck, not tall, but having great muscular arms that hung in ungainly fashion from broad shoulders. His face was roughly hewn, all features big and coarse, his forehead knotted with a tangle of the veins beneath. His chin was heavily bearded and he stank of sweat. My strongest emotion on regarding him for the first time was surprise. He looked nothing like my Uncles, and did not resemble the kind of man in whom Ma presently interested herself, her tastes being now for clean well-washed persons with fine manners and access to guineas. That Jonas must have had some earthy charms when younger was apparent; but I did not think that time had on the whole been kind to him.

"Ah," he growled, recognition dawning. "So you are here!"

A violent argument then broke out betwixt Ma and himself, during which I climbed the stairs and sat down on the final step to wait for them to finish. The gist of the disputation was:

"I will not take him!"

"Jonas, you must. I have nurtured him till now. And now at last I have the chance of Betterment. My protector will give me all I need, but will not take the boy. This is a wealthy man, Joe, one I must not lose. He eats out of my hand. And older than myself and like to die the first, and no relations. There will be something in it for thee, Joe, if you prove a willing friend to me now. This is a chance that does not happen twice."

"What good is he to me? He will be a burden to me."

"He will go to school. You need not see him."

"He is too like yourself about the face. When I look on him I shall be reminded of past pains."

"I cannot help his appearance. He had to look like me or thee, and I think he made the wiser choice."

"He'll be a mother's brat, no doubt."

"No; I have had little to do with him. Innyards and horses are his best delight."

"Then leave him at the Saracen's'."

"Jonas! This is your son of whom we speak."

"Aye... so you say!"

"There is no doubt of that. How dare you say so to my face?"

"To your face and any other part of you I say it."

The disagreement now progressing to a screamed and bellowed quarrel I retired further, ate what food was left, and waited. At last after much wrangling my mother with a blackened eye came up to tell me she was leaving now and I would stay with Jonas Gadd who would do a father's duty by me.

Then she fell to hugging me and kissing me and making fond

farewells and promising that we should meet again, that all her thoughts were with me and that I was dearest to her in all the world.

"How can ye bear to leave him then?" said Jonas jeeringly, and spat upon the floor. The door then closed behind Selina and she disappeared from view.

"She'll have some poxy bum-firking partridge waiting for her with his carriage, I don't doubt," said Jonas. "Well!" he said and turned to me. "And do you want to go to school?"

"Not much," said I.

"What? Not learn to read and write and be a scholar and apprentice to a trade?" he sneered.

I shrugged. He grinned. He had a great wide mouth and big grey teeth like tombstones. "Well. Perhaps we'll make a man of you then and to hell with your mother. You can work with me. You can be my link boy. We'll go out tonight. Now come and meet her ladyship."

Whom did he mean by this but the sedan chair which he had brought into the room! I understood now why there was no furniture. The room was home to this same chair, indeed, as I was soon to find, a veritable shrine to it.

"Did you ever see such a handsome chair as this?"

This chair was as embossed and ornate as any throne. Carved and naked nymphs twined like serpents up and down the supports. Leaves and flowers made patterns in wood along the roof. More naked nymphs descended down the back. A tasselled fringe gambolled about the roof's edge, and above it gleamed a regiment of golden studs. The windows were of glass, their frames a riot of small beasts and birds, their curtains of crimson velvet. Below the windows were inlaid panels where more nymphs disported themselves. Each of the poles was polished smooth where it was held, the remaining shaft a further abundance of carving — ivy leaves and roses, picked out as neatly as the misericords in church.

Mere admiration for this work of art did not suffice; we must, it seemed, adore it, venerate it, treat it much as if the Queen herself was to be borne within. All afternoon it must be polished and repolished, every leaf and beak, every bosom, every tendril of hair.

Within, the crimson velvet of the seat must be brushed clean of mud, and that not being enough, it must then be picked clean of fluff, and the glass wiped and rubbed from inside and out, and, there being some slight distortion in the glaze, the face of Jonas, goblin-like, came at me closer and closer, till, most grotesque of all, his squashed lips showed pressed against it, as he breathed upon the pane, like some ogreish Jack Frost. No pleasant satisfaction did he seem to take in this work upon which we were engaged together, but strove as one demented and possessed. And if I did not polish as he said it should be done, he clouted me, which I considered unreasonable, since I had polished many a saddle to the approbation of their owners, and I said so, and received another buffet.

"She's livelihood," said Pa mistily, standing stock still like Balaam's donkey who saw an angel passing. "She's bread and butter, princess and queen. She must be handled like a lady. You wouldn't know how to do that; but I tell you, ladies like a firm and gentle touch, a man's touch, so you polishes this chair as if it was the white skin of a lady, with her smooth haunches like the ladies have under their silks and satins as they walk about and their smooth thighs touching and their petticoats rustling; so you keep that in your head when you polish this chair and you handle her most careful."

At night his fellow chairman Evan Bate came back, and we all went out together for trade, and I the link boy that ran on ahead with a flaming brand which we collected from a chandler's; and so out into the dusk of the city.

We trod the miry cobbled streets now lit by shafts of light from tavern, cookshop, bawdy house. We circumnavigated a brawl which I would have liked to stop and watch, but Jonas bellowed at me to be on my way. Time and again he promised he would belt me when we got back, for wasting time in gawping. But there was so much to see. Even obscured by dusk the city was a wonder.

Tall fine buildings five storeys high, and so many windows; and churches and towers and painted signs that hung and swung above your head — angels, beasts, kings' heads, ships, exploding suns — and coaches with good quality horses that all but ran you down, and gentlemen and ladies glittering with jewels. A line of posts along the cobbles showed where the road divided from the walkway, but hardened chairmen such as Jonas and Evan from sheer bravado took a pride in ignoring them and attempted with enthusiasm to mow down the unwary. At our knee roamed dogs and pigs rooting with relish for whatever savoury titbits might be sucked out from the ooze beneath our feet. From the main streets smaller streets and alleys led away, with women on the corners half undressed, and in dark doorways loiterers, giving the impression that just out of sight there was much going on.

We took a fellow from a draper's shop in Cheapside to a brandy shop in Fleet street, so near to the Fleet bridge that we all but puked from the stench of the ditch. Evening breezes carried the strong odours of decay and putrefaction far beyond the muddy banks of the infamous river. We took a chap from Poppins Court to Holborn. We came along Snow Hill and turned into Old Bailey especially so that Jonas and Evan could put down the chair to heave a stone at the window of a building on the corner.

"Here, boy, take a stone."

"What for?"

"Throw it, yer cod's head. It's a molly house."

By our concerted efforts we were able to break a window pane. Elated by success Jonas and Evan called into a gin shop for a drop of the blue ruin and we drank it in the street, standing beside the chair.

Our gin-drinking performance was repeated time and again, till we were all pretty fuddled. On the way back Jonas and Evan picked up a couple of drabs and brought them home in the chair and a very tight squeeze it was. On returning to the house the chair was carefully placed in the downstairs room, Evan and his doxy disappeared and Pa took his upstairs.

Noises of such violence ensued as might have made one believe it was an act of hearty mislike that followed rather than of passion. I had heard rutting pigs sound more cheery in their coupling. Never forgetful of my lurking presence Jonas called out time and again for me to climb the stair and witness him about his work and so discover how a man proved himself; but I declined. The female yelped like a barking dog and Pa was rasping in his breathing like a man in extremis. At last there came about a kind of silence, and I sneaked inside the chair and fell asleep curled on the velvet seat.

I was awoken when the female let herself out of the house and Pa came down in a rage because he had wanted more of her. Ascertaining with a howl of fury that I was within the chair he hauled me out and gave vent to his vexation upon myself. I had never in my life suffered a beating before and for so paltry a cause. In the process of the same, my being upended the better for him to deliver his blows, my precious guinea tumbled from my pocket and careened across the floor. Pa just as myself had some sixth sense where coinage was concerned, and pounced on it.

"Damn my breeches, a guinea! Where'd you steal this?"

"I never stole it; someone gave it to me."

"I'll give it to yer an' all for a lyin' brat. Well, you've lost it now. Young lads ain't got no use for guineas."

"It's mine! Give it back!"

He stuck it in his pocket. I noted which one. He aimed another swipe at me. He went back up the stairs and threw down a fusty blanket. He called down:

"You sleep there on the floor. If I catch you in that chair again I'll give yer a real thrashin', not a few slaps round the head. That chair ain't for the likes of you to sit yer arse on. You keep well clear of her. You sit on that seat again I'll have the hide off your rump, do you hear me? I said do you hear me?"

I told him that I did. I daresay they heard him at London Bridge.

I pulled the blanket round me. I would have run away that night if it had not been for my guinea.

Chapter Six

"TONIGHT," Pa said, "we're going up the Garden." Anyone who had supposed arbours of roses, statues, fountains and sylvan shades would have been disappointed. That night I was to see for the first time those dark alleys, those narrow streets and that brilliant and tawdry piazza which I later grew to know so well. Not that we — with our so precious chair and touting for custom as we were — took to those meaner ways, some of which we were too wide even to enter. No, we kept to the broader thoroughfares and saw merely the dark and gaping maws of the entrances to those vile warrens where no respectable cull might walk in safety. But their menacing presences accompanied us all the way.

Bravely bearing my bright brand I led the way at Pa's direction. The great bulk of St Paul's showed large against the darkening sky. Down the narrow slope of Ludgate hill we went, and under the arch of the gate, knowing ourselves near the Fleet ditch by the stench, and over Fleet bridge which I thought a pretty thing with its pineapples carved out of stone. Through Temple Bar we went, the dusk too murky for me closely to observe the rotting heads of miscreants and the dangling limbs, though I raised the brand the better to observe the same. Here we picked up a passenger; we carried him along the Strand, and I gawped up at the great tall houses of the rich and wondered what magnificence was hidden there behind those lighted windows.

The night-time streets were full of clamour — the music of fiddlers, the shouts, the beery singing, the neighing of horses, the rattling of wheels.

"Forward, forward!" urged Jonas all the time. "We give way to no one. Stick 'em with your fire if they don't move!" As for himself he was being very free with the clubbed ends of his poles, the which he handled as a rampaging knight his lances. Fearfully red in the torches' glow he followed me, always close enough to boot me onward; and thus we broke clear of the last houses and we entered Covent Garden.

I saw a whirl of tall eaved houses, the pillared portico of St Paul's church, the rows of colonnaded arches, all illumined in a welter of light that spilled in rank confusion from a variety of sources — the open doorways of the taverns and coffee houses and bagnios, the braziers of the street vendors, the brands of link boys, the swinging lanthorns and the flames of small fires alight beyond the posts that marked the centre of the square. Beneath our feet the mulch of sodden vegetable leaves from the market stalls; the smells of coffee, beer and perfume in our nostrils; in our ears the music of the ballad pedlars, the laughter of those on pleasure bent, the barking of questing dogs, the whine of beggars, the enticements of those selling food, drink and themselves.

A cully would have hired us, but Jonas told him we were taking no passengers and strode purposefully towards a tavern where they had heard that whores took off their clothes and walked naked between the tables. They laid down the chair near the doorway, taking it in turns to disappear within with slavering mouths and panting tongues, emerging belching and growling and half out of their heads with unsatisfied lust. Crowds streamed past me, rough louts pushed their way in, throwing the weaker from their path, and in the doorway constant scuffling went on, while some were bodily ejected by the giants employed to keep some order there. The entertainments within proving too strong to resist, the bibulous twain decided to remain, and fortifying me with gin, left me to watch the chair outside.

I waited by the chair, my brand burned out, munching a bun, swigging the gin, watching the pickpockets at work, and the fumblings of the lovers in the shadows. I saw the female whores about their work, and good-looking youths about the same concern, these less brash and loud. I saw a gentleman go off with one, and another slunk away as if to try another pitch.

And then I noticed lurking in the shadows who but my friend Gabriel that had brought me down from Islington and sang amongst his churning country milk, and now looking so shifty and uneasy that I made no sign of recognition; but I watched him nonetheless. After a while a youth, the one I had seen earlier, joined him, their heads close as they spoke; then they moved off together and were gone.

No sooner this, than a strident shriek showed me that I too had been recognized, and by that wretch Will Field, whose gang had tried to flatten me in the Saracen's Head. His yellow hair gleamed like a halo, his whole face happily contorted into that grimace of anticipation of one who hoped to finish what had been denied him previously.

"You! You never was what you said. You was never one of Mr Hitchin'sBoys. Was yer? Was he, Mr Hitchin?"

I saw now to my alarm that Will Field was in a veritable flotilla of small personnages of like kind, scabby bedraggled urchins of the street, and all, I had no doubt, willing enough at his command to hurl themselves upon me for the joy of it, and I with my one weapon the once burning brand now cold and useless, much at a disadvantage. And now to make matters worse it seemed that Mr Hitchin, he whose name I had made so bold as to take in vain, was with them, much to my detriment I could be sure. But who was Mr Hitchin, and who were his Boys? I stared, wary, curious.

A big broad cumbersome man was Mr Hitchin, about thirty years of age, with an uneven stance and a shambling gait and a belly overhanging his breeches. I saw that he was pretty ugly. His head was too small for his body, planted on his shoulders without courtesy of neck. His eyes were small. His lips were loose and over large, his chin receding into his cravat. He towered above me like a wall.

Will Field was darting up and down in ill-concealed delight, slamming one fist into the other palm in earnest of intention.

"He's a liar, Mr Hitchin! He said he was one of us. He ain't though. He came here on a coach down from the north."

"Thee name, boy," Mr Hitchin said, bending close to my face.

"William Page," said I. It was the first name that came into my head, but I remembered well the advice of my highwayman friend to deal in aliases.

"William Page." Mr Hitchin licked his tongue around the name and found it palatable. "And are thee from the north indeed?"

"Yes sir; that is, from the north road."

"And thee told Will Field that thee belonged to me?"

That was how he spoke, Mr Hitchin, in that odd manner.

"Yes sir," I replied.

"Fortuitous half truth. For thee are just the kind of Boy we like to have about us, William Page. Where do thee live?"

"Cheapside, sir," I lied.

"Ask for me at the Blue Boar in Barbican. Anyone will tell thee where to find me. For thee and me, Page, shall be friends. I may have work for thee, with money in thee fist."

His breath smelt rank and gummy. He turned to Will Field. "Why did thee say he lied? Bad lad! William Page is one of my Boys as sure as thee. Are thee not, William Page?"

"Yes sir," I assured him stoutly. Then Mr Hitchin opened his purse and gave me a penny. I thanked him dutifully and cast a smirk at Will Field, whose face was puce.

"Come, mathematicians!" called Mr Hitchin in regal fashion and shuffled away, surrounded by his small attendants. Will Field ran back and thumped me in the guts and wrenched the penny from me. Taken by surprise I let him do it, and he left me gasping by the sedan chair, vexed at my gullibility. A hand descending from above now gripped my collar.

"What was all that about?" said Pa, glowing from strong drink.

"Nothin', Pa."

"It was Charles Hitchin, as I stand here."

"I don't know who it was. It was just some man who would have words with me."

"It was Hitchin," Evan Bate confirmed laconically, chewing.

"I knew it. I saw the bugger from the window. Words with you, eh, Davy? Those words shall be the last between you and that man. Let's get us home while I am yet upon my feet."

"And Fanny?" asked Evan.

"I could not get her," Pa scowled; and this, and my converse with Charles Hitchin, so inflamed him, that when we reached our house he set about me worse than previously, this time with his belt, and said between his grunts of effort:

"Mr Charles Hitchin! Thinks he's so important in the city. Pah! All know him for what he is, the greatest molly of them all. Now you shall know it too. You helped me put a stone through the window of the molly house. We should have burnt it down. Them boys he has about him — what d'you think he keeps them for? You keep well clear of them. I knew it when I saw your face. Too much like your Ma. If I see you by Hitchin's lads again I'll kick your head in."

Beads of sweat spewed from his crimson face. His beery breath rolled over me in waves. When he had worn himself out with rage and exertion he went upstairs but I did not think he slept. In the morning, earnestly considering the for and against of my situation I enquired if I might after all go to school.

Pa guffawed. "So you'd rather be in the workhouse, would you, than with your dear Pa? Well, that suits me well enough. I've better things to do than keep my eye upon you and your arse away from Hitchin's cods. We'll go see Mr Garrett."

The morning, however, was spent in polishing the chair. Together and in silence Pa and I worked like slaves upon that ornamental monster till the beeswax made me sneeze and my bruised muscles ached and every carved breast, flower, beak and leaf gleamed. For what? It would emerge into the crowded streets, it would be splashed with mud and grime and streaked with dust, it would be knocked and jarred by coach wheel and house wall; the piss from chamber pots, the soot from chimneys and the flour from bakers' loaves would fetch upon it, and come tomorrow this would be to do again. I have polished saddle and bridle in my time, but never like a man at fever pitch nor made myself so red faced and so short of wind. He was a fright to see, was Jonas, all his facial veins a network of raised welts like thin blue slugs. As for his breathing I have heard ancient nags heaving a coach up Alconbury Hill with better.

"Before I go to school," said I, "I'd like my guinea back."

"Your guinea," spluttered Jonas. "That stays here with me." He patted his pocket. "You'll have no need of guineas where you're going."

In asking to be allowed to go to school I had of course no conception of the same. There was an elderly dame in Buckden who taught some children in a back room — you could see them as you passed by, a quiet row sitting on a bench. Mr Garrett's workhouse school in Bishopsgate, close to Pa's house, was not like this.

It was indeed a woman who opened the door to us, not elderly, but manly in appearance, lean and square, with a pale big-jawed face, thin lips and straggly hair that dangled from her cap. I was fair knocked over by the gin blast of her breath. Behind her gaped a dark doorway, with uneven flagstones leading away into the gloom. I heard Pa say in a lugubrious tone:

"It was what his mother wanted."

He turned and bellowed it again in my direction: "It was what your mother wanted!" as if expecting some denial or ratification from myself for an action which plainly caused him a slight pang of guilt.

"Go with Mrs Perkins, son." He bundled me forward, with a thump between the shoulder blades, and thus we parted.

Mrs Perkins ascertained my name, but she said nothing more, and I was left without explanation in a room where twenty or so boys of about my own age were grouped about work benches, making shoes. I stood beside a fat boy who, for all he was an inmate, seemed no more at home than I. We were both ignored by the young man who taught the cobbler skills, but no one spoke or volunteered more information, and by six o'clock a couple of pairs of very indifferent shoes had been made, after which the benches were cleared and a further twenty boys clattered in, and we were fed with bread and lard. Asking my fat companion what was to happen next I learned that next we went to bed. So, still ignored, I slipped away and let myself out of the building.

I went back to Pa's house to tell him I had no intention of learning how to be a shoemaker and would put up with his beatings, for at least with him I saw something of life.

The sedan chair was in its accustomed place, the shadows of evening swathing it in sombreness. Its door was open and someone sat within, a leg out-jutting and the head pressed hard against the glass, distorting all the features to a gargoyle. It was Pa, dead as a fish, his hand rigid about a bottle, and his mouth agape.

I felt in his pocket and found my guinea. I put it in my shoe. Then I went back to school. I swear no one had noticed I had gone.

Chapter Seven

C HANCE threw me straightaway into the close company of the two who were to change the course of my life; and all through the haphazard cosmography of our being obliged to sleep three in a bed.

The big room where the workhouse boys spent their sleeping hours was edged along each wall with shelf-like beds, and in one such upon my first night in Mr Garrett's establishment I found myself cheek by jowl with the fat boy who had stood beside me over the cobbler's last, and with a skinny fair-haired scrap of a lad whose name was Jack. His other name was Bishop. All our other names were Bishop. This was because on entering the school it was assumed that one lost one's previous identity — which some were glad to do — and gave oneself up to the pursuit of labour, industry, virtue and religion, the school's avowed moral intent; and also because no one who had charge of us had wit enough to remember who we were, and with small leap of fancy, named us for the street in which we were now placed. A less eccesiastical bunch it would have been hard to find.

My fat friend had no given name, for he insisted that it was Endymion, the which no one could or would attempt to pronounce;

and he maintained this in the teeth of numerous beatings from boys stronger than himself, of which there were many. He had a round rosy-cheeked face with a button nose, bright beady eyes and straight black hair. About his neck he had a leather string on which dangled an embossed seal. The same was stolen from him time and again, ripped from his plump throat with howls of glee, and returned to him at the pleasure of his foes, or upon the performance of some or other act of personal humiliation. I winced to observe the straits to which he was reduced. I lay abed one night and listened with a mingling of contempt and pity as he grunted like a pig from a position of subservience with his nose and elbows to the floor and his fat bum raised, till the possessors of the pendant deigned to hand it back.

"Why don't he punch 'em?" murmured I to Jack who lay beside me.

"'e finks 'e's a lord," said Jack in the ripe accent of Spitalfields, "'e's too well bred."

"Scared, more like," says I. Then: "*Is* he a lord?" I asked.

"Nah! 'ow can 'e be, in this place? We call 'im Tubs."

Our mortified companion crawled back into bed, thereby causing by his pinguidity much discomfort to Jack and me. We shifted over.

"Are you a lord?" I asked with interest.

"Yes I am," said he. "I should not by rights be in this low place. I am fit for palaces and the halls of the great."

"Small wonder that they beat yer," I laughed. "Don't you know no better than to boast of it?"

"Do you believe me then?" said Tubs.

"Why not?" I shrugged.

"They'll all be sorry one day," Tubs said. "My family will come for me and take me back in a coach of gold. Then I shall do anything I choose. Have anything I choose."

"Eat anythin' yer choose," laughed Jack, "that's what you mean."

"I surely will," said Tubs unrepentant. "And drink, and do all that a fine gentleman may do."

"Ride the best horses," I suggested.

"And race 'em for money," Tubs agreed. "And," he added with magnificence, "my friends won't go short neither."

By day, as we made shoes, he let me see this pendant seal, parting his shirt collar and revealing his podgy neck. Amongst the chubby flesh the object nestled, its imprint in the skin a mottled shadow of itself. It was a regal thing, no doubt, with two crossed spearheads and beneath, some markings which I was to learn conveyed the letters E. V. I traced them with my finger tip.

"That is my name," he said, "my first name and my family name."

"How do you know it?"

"I've always known it."

"But you've been here all your life."

"Yes. But I'm still a lord."

That night some boys dragged him from bed and took the pendant from him and made him take off his clothes and dance if he would have the thing returned. We could all see him, pale and clumsy in the gloom, hopping from one foot to another. We laughed who watched him, not wasting sympathy on one so feeble. I wished I had not to share a bed with him. He came in snivelling.

"Why don't you fight 'em?" I said.

"I don't know how," he said.

"I thought all boys knew how."

"Not with their hands," said Tubs now dignified again. "Lords use swords, or else we order our servants to do the work for us."

"Pity you didn't bring yer servants wiv yer," said Jack.

I could not but observe that Jack — not only in his physical shape — was the opposite of Tubs, for he somehow contrived to remain unnoticed. No large boy tousled him, none teased him for his smallness; he simply went about his day and came to bed and ate and worked, making neither friends nor enemies. He had a small pert face, fair hair and big brown eyes, his manner neat and perky. If Tubs had been a partridge, Jack was a sparrow.

This was a strange business, I thought, to be at school. It never had occurred to me that a day might be divided into segments, or that one day might be in all repects much like another. We rose at half past five, prodded into life by Mrs Perkins' broomhandle. We were hustled into the big room to pray. We prayed till half past six, and then we ate, all in that room, with trestle tables set up, which were later used for work benches. At seven o'clock we set about our tasks, all useless, being sewing, shoemending, knitting stockings, carding wool. At eleven o'clock they tried to teach us book learning. We ate at twelve. They tipped us out into the yard behind the school, where the privies were, and we were left much to our own devices. At two they brought us in and we made shoes till six o'clock; we ate and we were sent to bed.

The yard was contained by the backs and roofs of houses and

there was no way out. There was not much to do. Vexed beyond belief at Tubs's ineptitude I fought with his oppressors, having always been a handyman where punching was required. His pendant being once again detached from his neck and thrown from fist to fist and he red-faced and very like to blubber, I laid into the chap that held the prize, and though circled by his cronies and much bloodied, was able to retrieve the thing and hand it back to him. Tubs was warm in his gratitude.

"When I become a lord again I'll see you right," he promised me.

"Yeah, yeah," I told him disparagingly.

"Why'd you help 'im?" said Jack to me.

"I dunno," I lied.

Jack dabbed my cuts and bruises with his shirt cuff. "You don't know nothin' abaht 'im. Why'd you help 'im?"

"I said I dunno."

But I did know. It was because the silly cull cared for that pendant like I cared about my guinea and I recognized that passion. But I wasn't stupid enough to wave my coin about and boast of it, but kept it in my shoe. And even as we stood there and Tubs began to fix that pendant round his neck a lad came by and snatched it from him and hurled it up into the sky. We watched it rise. It went up graceful as a lark. But down it never came.

"Where'd it go?"

"Up on the roofs!"

"Down a chimney pot."

"He'll never see that again."

This conclusion being the one generally shared by the majority, and a heavy downpour now ensuing, we shuffled round the door to go back inside, heedless of our fat companion's grief. Surrounded as the yard was by the roofs of the encroaching houses, all of different stature, all higgledy piggledy, in various stages of disrepair and the yard wall fifteen feet high, it was plain the treasure was irredeemably lost. There were some forty of us boys to squeeze into the passageway out of the rain. Jack was last in. When he joined us at the work bench, drenched and out of breath, his fair hair plastered to his scalp, he handed Tubs the pendant, surreptitiously, and said: "Now hide it safe, like any chap would do."

It was my turn to question.

"How'd you do that?"

"Climbed."

"What, on the roofs? Up the wall? And so quick?"

"It's easy if you're careful."

"Easy?" I whistled. "It's magic."

"Garn," said Jack, but grinned.

The object of our incarceration in this place was ultimately apprenticeship to a trade of lower order, such as befitted our station as the fairly deserving poor. Particularly the chimney sweeping trade. From time to time a grimy sweep would turn up at the door and any small thin lad would be sought out, cleaned up, and sent upon his way with his new master.

"Nah, not him. He's too broad in the shoulder. Find me a bony boy."

"I try to keep them small and thin," apologized Mr Garrett. "But they will grow!"

He chose one of our number and arranged for the sweep to collect him later that same day. Before the appointed time came round, the boy had sneaked out of the place and run away.

That afternoon it was my turn to be at the elbow of the scrawny youth who tried to teach us how to read and write. This process was a mystery to me still by the time I left that school.

"Will you write something for me?" I requested.

"What would you like?" He dipped the quill into the ink.

I leaned over the table. "'Dear Ma'," I said. He wrote. " 'Pa is dead'."

"Pa is dead?" he queried, pausing.

"That's right. 'Your loving son Davy.' Have you written it?" I watched him write. "Now give it me." He hesitated, frowning. "I said give it me." He shrugged. What difference did it make to him? I folded the scrap of paper and put it inside my shirt.

It had not occurred to me that I would encounter any difficulty in the simple matter of delivering this missive. In this assumption I was proved wrong. When at the close of day I made my way to the door that led into the street I found it locked and bolted, and in attempting to draw back the bolt I brought as if called up by sorcery the most unwelcome shape of Mr Garrett, whom so far I had only seen as one that read our prayers and warned us to be godly in our doings. He now appeared in all too corporeal form and seized me by the shoulder and enquired of me in tones that boded ill the nature of the business that I was about.

"Just goin' out, sir."

"Indeed? Have I given you permission to do so?"

"You ain't given me nothin', sir."

"If I see you again beside that door I will give you that you shall be sorry for. I'll have no more running away."

"I ain't running away. I was comin' back after."

He paid no heed. "Be off with you to your bed. I shall be watching you henceforth."

"He says he'll be watching me," I said to Jack in bed. "How'm I going to let Ma know Pa died, as no one else will do so?"

"Oh Davy!" Jack said, all wide eyed. "'as yer pa died? Must you bear yer sorrow all alone?"

"I ain't sad!" I assured him. "But I must let Ma know. So she can wed her friend."

"You must!" Jack agreed. "I know how it is to lose a pa. Poor Davy, this is bad for yer, and yer ma, grievin' and in despair."

Dancing more like, I thought.

I coughed. "Grievin' or not, she ought to know. And they won't let me go out and send the letter."

"Where does your ma live?"

"Back in Buckden on the Great North Road."

"How did you think to take a message so far?"

"I didn't. I only need to get it to the Saracen's Head in Smithfield where the coaches start. Any traveller going north would take it, or the coachy. I have the letter here."

"I'll go instead," said Jack. "I know the Saracen's."

"You won't be able to get out either. The big door's bolted and makes an awful noise."

"I won't go by the door."

"All the windows are barred."

"Not high up they aren't."

"You'd go across the roofs?"

"Dontcher fink I can?"

"I wish yer would."

"I'll do it for yer ma. I know how mine would be, all sorrowin' and heavy laden."

I had met Jack's ma. Every Sunday she would visit and always brought him little loaves of bread straight from the public bakehouse and still warm. She was nothing like Ma. She was not pretty and blowzy like Ma was, but she was a very agreeable person, little and anxious and very kind to Jack. She always asked how he was and what he had eaten, and then on my being introduced by Jack, including me in her enquiries, in a most touching manner, unlike anything I had ever known.

Jack's father had been a carpenter in Spitalfields, good at his trade and intending Jack to follow in his footsteps; but all suddenly one day he fell forward on his work bench dead, leaving a grieving widow and two sons, Tom who was a Bad Lot and Jack who was an Angel. Now she had to go out to work, and this was the cause of Jack's being here at Mr Garrett's workhouse school. She was a domestic servant in the house of an honest draper, Mr William Kneebone. Wounds, I have heard of some droll names, says I, but that is a droll one, and I laughed my silly head off, little knowing how the cully with the idiot name would be the indirect cause of greatest woe to me in times to come.

Though bolt and key and bars kept us penned in, that very night Jack found a way to quit the building. He took my letter to the Saracen's and gave it to the coachy going north, and he returned all unobserved, and crawled into our bed smelling of rain and chimney soot.

There was a friend, thought I in admiration; there was a very fine friend and possessed of great skills.

The chimney sweeper thought so too. He came upon his rounds in company with Mr Garrett, peering at us boys about our lasts and needles. Jack was the one he wanted.

"Thin and small like that, and bendy. He won't eat much neither. A poor bit of a lad, a scrap. I'll take him."

Mr Garrett shook his head sadly. "I'd gladly let you have him, master sweep; but he has a mother living, who may claim him."

"A curse upon the dame," the sweep scowled, "so to thwart me."

"And on yourself sir," answered Jack at once and took a cuff about the ear.

The chimney sweep's gaze fell upon me, but not for long. I was not worth his attention — "A gangling lad and already growing, I would get no use of him". He turned to Tubs; we all laughed, and the sweep prowled on and finally chose some hapless compromise whose future was most like to be an early grave and until then the sooty warts that caused it.

"You are lucky in your ma," I said to Jack.

"I know it," answered he all soberly. She was his guiding light, was that good woman, and for her sake he did all he was bid at school, and learned and worked and caused no trouble, neither fought nor stole, and said his prayers like one who sees the angels passing overhead.

I thought it strange to see a boy so pious.

"I must be so; it's my duty," answered he. "See, we have Bad Blood in the family. It came out in my brother Tom so maybe I'll be spared. But I must be more than common righteous, and so fend it off. It would break Ma's heart if I went bad an' all."

In the two years that we were together at the school we slept in the same bed and worked at the same bench. Sometimes on Sundays when he was allowed out, I went with him to the house where his mother was in service. It was in the Strand, at the sign of the Angel. The painted angel made me think of Jack.

We did not enter the shop itself, where the rolls of cloth were kept, but came in by a back door from an alley off Drury Lane and thus into a neat clean kitchen where Jack's mother made us very welcome. There were always cakes and biscuits made and a fire to sit by, and they had a bird in a cage twittering by the window, and curtains, and bright pots upon the shelves and pleasant smells of cooking, much more palatable and flavoursome than ever we were given at the school.

And though I was not her kin, Jack's ma was as attentive to me as she was to Jack, and asked me how I did, and of my circumstances, and called me her poor dear boy so much that I was half convinced I was indeed such. I thought that if I spent much time in her sweet company I might grow into a weakling, for she fair made me sorry for myself, the which I never had been. What if I had had this kind of ma, I wondered, homely, caring, making bread and feeding me hot broth and buttermilk? Would I have been different?

I met Mr William Kneebone also, he briefly honouring us with his presence, smiling and beaming and praising Jack's ma's baking and patting Jack and me upon the head, vexing us both by his attentions, and whenever I looked at his knee bones I began to giggle. He was a man of middle years, his hair already grey, his body corpulent, his manner affable enough. I sensed Jack did not like him.

"He is our Benefactor," Jack said; but there is that which does not like a Benefactor, and I guess Jack thought the same.

You may well suppose it most inappropriate a setting for a cull who cherished yet the notion of the highway as a chosen trade on reaching manhood, to be sitting by the little hearth and drinking buttermilk and listening to Jack's ma recalling happier times; and an old clock ticking by the wall.

"He was a gentle man, Jack's pa, so kind and neighbourly and well respected. Why, he was kind to dogs that roamed the streets, and rescued cats from drowning. So good to me and Jack, and Tommy my other son who is gone away from home. Tom took his pa's death hard. So sudden it was — one day hale and hearty, next dead at his bench, and we all unprovided for. If it had not been for kind Mr Kneebone I don't know what would have become of us. We must be grateful. He is so good to us."

I thought kind Mr Kneebone had done all right for himself with Jack's ma housekeeping for him, and he did not pay her much. I thought it wrong for anyone to be so beholden to another.

Touched by her plight and by the almost unimaginable notion of a sweet and caring father I took from my shoe that guinea given me by the handsome highwayman and put it in her hand, and sped away before she could enquire of me how I came by it. It was a stupid thing to do, as I have found are most acts of rash and sudden affection.

"She gave it to Mr Kneebone," Jack told me afterwards. "She said she could not believe that it had come by honest means. She said he could be trusted best to know what to do with it. He has put it in his casket, under lock."

"I did not intend it for Mr Kneebone," I said darkly. "It was for your ma."

I need not have worried. The guinea was that very night stolen by Jack's wayward brother Tom, who was a great trial to his mother. I found this curiously more acceptable than that it should go to kind Mr Kneebone. There was a certain justice in it.

I saw the infamous Tom on one of my visits. He was rough and surly, fair haired like Jack, light boned and lean. He was in a gang. He had left home to live on the streets. He swore at Mr Kneebone and kicked over the log box for the enjoyment. His mother could do nothing with him. He'd brought her some lace, but she guessed it stolen and would have none of it. He swore at her and said he knew those that weren't so fussy. He strode out, slamming the door. He would rejoin his gang in some vile alley. His mother wept but, wretch that I was, I thought him rather fine.

These little forays into warmth and domesticity were not to last, and the more fool me for indulging in the weakness of sentimentality. When I was ten years old, Jack's mother took him from the school to live with her in permanence. He broke the news to me one night as we lay in bed with Tubs, the three of us all pressed close together for warmth.

"It's thanks to Mr Kneebone's goodness," Jack explained. "'e knew Ma fretted for me. 'e says a son should be wiv 'is ma."

"Well, I know differently," I said sourly.

"I asked if you could come and live with us. 'e says one mahf is enough. I did my best for you, and Ma added her pleas to mine, but no good. You can still visit, Davy, any time you like."

"It won't be the same."

"I know. But I'll help you if I can. I'm to be apprenticed to a carpenter and be the same as Pa. And help in Mr Kneebone's shop an' all. And sleep in the attic with the silks and muslins."

"It sounds better than sleeping here, at any rate."

"You'll still have Tubs."

Tubs was asleep and snoring.

"I ain't half sad to lose you, Jack," I said.

"You ain't lost me. We shall still be friends."

I stroked his pretty yellow hair. "I ain't half sad to see you go."

I don't know why, but I grabbed hold of Tubs and shook him hard and threw him out of bed. Endymion! I'd give him names. You may be sure that I considered Tubs poor consolation for the loss of Jack.

And yet this most unwelcome circumstance was soon to cause a strange change in my fortune.

Chapter Eight

ON the day that Jack left Bishopsgate school, that gin-sod den hag who woke us from our beds with the end of her broomhandle, Mrs Perkins, called me to her saying:

"Go with Mrs Peabody, Davy, for today you are her messenger."

It was not uncommon for us to be lent out for a day's duration, and glad to leave the shoemaking I went willingly enough out with my new companion. Not that she was a stranger to me. She was Mrs Perkins's crony and was often in the school, gossiping and guffawing with her, tippling in corners, swapping tales of the street.

Mrs Grizel Peabody was a short female with a square face, little eyes and a big mouth, the which when widened made a hole for a very large laugh. Stories of misfortune caused that laugh, any tale of other's woe, misadventure or death, particularly death by outlandish means. I had heard her weep herself to incoherence at the cull whose foot slid in potato parings and caused him to fall under a cart's wheels; and he that tumbled into the Fleet ditch and suffocated in six inches of mud caused merriment the like of which no jester ever instigated.

It was a cold wet day in early December. We walked pretty

smartly to the place where she lived — the boozing ken called The Goat, in Long Lane, Smithfield. We went by way of Fore Street and Red Cross Street and Barbican. Mrs Peabody would not take the short cut across Moorfields and Beech Lane.

"Moorfields is a filthy place," she told me. "No self-respecting woman goes there." She sniffed and squinted at me intimately, as if I were to understand her meaning. I did not... then.

Nor did I then know that the Goat was a lock for the receiving and disposing of stolen goods — a flash case, as it was called. There were cellars underneath the Goat that could well tell a tale, and I have seen them stacked with movables that by next day were many miles dispersed. I knew nothing of this as I accepted the cup of gin that Grizel Peabody offered and we sat down in the dark parlour on a wooden bench beside the fire to dry ourselves.

Grizel Peabody stretched her legs wide and rolled back her bedraggled skirts. "Let the heat get to me vitals," cackled she.

"My life has not been easy," she confessed, and hiccoughed. "How old do you think I am?"

I did not care to hazard a guess.

"Twenty-seven," she said. "Or as near as makes no difference. Old before my time. Men have been unkind. I was never comely. I had to take what I could get. There have been those who thought me fair, but they were lummocks that I would not look at; I have always fancied handsome men. And handsome men may take their pick and therefore I have had to make do where I might. Ah, Davy, Davy, if you grow to be a handsome man, be sure that you be kind!"

I promised I would be so.

"So young," she marvelled. "And yet I swear that even so you have known sorrows."

I admitted that I had. When pressed I then continued: "Jack is taken from the school to live with his ma and Mr Kneebone. Mr Kneebone is their Benefactor. I still have Tubs," I added fairly, "but I liked Jack better."

"Mr Kneebone?" Grizel Peabody chortled. "I believe I know the man. Nephew to Mr Foot. Uncle to Mr Legg."

I sniggered with her, happy in the gin-induced good humour.

"Jack will be apprenticed to a carpenter, like his pa," I sniffed. "He was my good friend."

"I drink to him," said Grizel. "I drink to friendship."

We drank. Jack's absence seemed less painful.

"We two are good friends now," said Grizel, "and now for friendship's sake my Davy will run errands for me and bring all the gentlemen I send for to this place. Eh? Will yer?"

I said I would. And thus on that day I made the acquaintance of some of the blackest villains in London.

Badger Riddlesdon, who was black of hair and black of heart. He was to grow to fame for peaching his accomplices that did the Whitehall burglaries, and for shooting Tim Dun in the face when Dun lay wounded. But at that time he was a small-time forger with a den beneath the Red Lion in Chick Lane. Here I was sent to find him. I discovered then the fear in which this cull was held, for no one dared disturb him, and I was obliged to seek the man myself.

The Red Lion was an ancient place, all tumbledown and foul, and the descent into the bowels beneath no easy matter. Steps of hollowed stone led down a hole so dark that I must feel my way until I fetched against a thick wooden door and knocked and then again more loud.

"Mr Riddlesdon!"

"Who wants me?"

It was the growl more of bear than man.

"You are wanted at the Goat, sir, if you please."

I heard the door unbolt, then it swung open, and a man erupted, huge as a giant, it seemed to me, holding a lanthorn which illumined his face from below so that he was a mass of shadows, with thick dark hair about his face and a black beard about his chin. I was not a timid boy but I shrank back in fright.

"Out of my way," was all he said. "Be off with you." And off I scrambled, eagerly enough, and out into the rain.

Isaac Rag I next found, who was living then in Crown Court, St Giles. "You will find him near the dead men's place." Wounds, I had never known a stench the like of that. They had warned me, when I asked directions, that his abode lay beside the paupers' burial ground and I would know it long before I reached it.

My stomach heaved as I approached. The streets were no wider than the space between a sedan chair's shafts, and slimy underfoot, the houses tightly packed together, all askew, with overhangs that crowded in and hid the murky sky. Everyone knew Isaac Rag — the woman pulling in her sodden washing on a string through a window, the urchins on the corner kicking the wall — I had no trouble finding him. He came forth from a low door, scratching, a short squat man with a big grinning face and a mass of frizzy hair, and an expression as if he knew a secret and was just about to tell it. He always grinned, but as to whether he was a happy man or a witless it was unclear.

"Grizel Peabody? Would she make a poor cull walk to Smithfield in the rain?"

"I've already done so, sir, and more, and still have yet to do."

"A very Trojan," giggled he. "But why do you shove your fist against your nose?"

"I am half dead from the stink here."

"The old graveyard? You get used to it." And then he added with an even wider grin: "Yes... on quiet nights you can hear the bodies tumbling to and fro in the shifting earth, and the rustle of the dogs rooting for shinbones, and the thuds as a slat gives way and a row of corpses drops upon the row beneath."

My third call was to have been Obadiah Lemon, and I had been given an address in Fetter Lane. But "No," said Isaac Rag, as we walked back along Holborn and the rain slithering down the insides of our collars, "you'll never find him there. He lives in Wood Street now."

"Wood Street? Where is that?"

"That lies between London Wall and Cheapside. But you don't want no dealings with that cull. A darker villain I never did see."

"Indeed I do. Mrs Peabody asked for him most particular. Is he very wicked?"

"The greatest thief of all, my boy. Coaches are his speciality."

"A highwayman?" I breathed.

"Nah! Nothin' so fine. A secret stealer — one who puts his hand into the coach window unobserved and throws ashes in the passengers' eyes so they don't see what he's about, and lifts the baggage from the back. And he'll peach his best pal sooner'n look at him; and very well has he done for himself! Lives in a big tall house with many windows and a coat of arms above the door. Wood Street, that's where you'll find 'im."

We came down Holborn hill, past the church, and here we parted, Mr Isaac Rag setting off for Smithfield and I to Wood street. I walked round and round and up and down that cobbled street with the rain splashing the puddles and me, till somewhat late in the day I understood Isaac Rag's smirking references to mean the Debtors' Prison. Four storeys high it was, and its many windows were well barred, the door also, above the which there was indeed a coat of arms. I stood and stared up at the building for some while, partly scorning those so foolish as to be taken, partly pitying their lot.

All unbeknown to me, there lurked within those walls at that same moment that abhorrent viper Mr Jonathan Wild who was destined to cause me great distress. Even as I gazed, that man was beginning to reach out his evil grasp upon the lives of those within his earthly sphere. His hold upon the cull I sought was even now clamped firm, and Obadiah Lemon was to be his creature.

But sheer vexation was now uppermost in my mind, for I considered myself poorly treated, to be sent on this wild goose chase. A sensation unclear to me, something of anger, something of loneliness now struck me, and without knowing why, I retraced my steps, passing under the great tower of Newgate gaol which spanned the busy street. I was briefly aware of the incongruous and sadly inappropriate statues which adorned it — Liberty, Peace, Mercy, Concord — and I recalled the story of that Dick Whittington who had contributed to its foundation. I wondered whether he anticipated the kind of institution that his generosity was to provide, and whether at that stage in his fortunes he still possessed the cat.

Then, my mind dwelling upon my dear old coachy Humphrey Harvey, a cull I had not thought of these two years, I came along Snow Hill and found myself in front of the Saracen's Head. First of all I laughed, remembering how frightened I had been to see those great teeth in the dark, those turbanned fiends whose grimacing presences betokened the entrance of the coaching inn. And then a sentiment overcame me, so strong I could not put a name to it, but it was truly most disturbing to one habituated to a phlegmatic disposition. There I stood, surrounded by the sound and smell of horses, the clink of bridles and the shouts of ostlers and before my eyes a coach, its sides begrimed with the mud of the road — not the street mud, the pig muck and the slimy offal from the running gutters, but the mud of rut and lane, out where the trees bent in the wind, and the rains blew over open field.

I knew not what possessed me but I turned and started walking, driven by a strange compulsion to be where I knew my essential being lay. I struck out northward, bypassing Smithfield, and up St John's Street where the coaches entered London coming from York, and like a person in a trance I walked until the houses thinned out and ahead of me lay nothing but the road. And there I stopped, of a sudden conscious of my aching limbs and tired feet and inexplicable behaviour.

Muddy, broad and straight, the Great North Road here had its beginning, Beyond the trees, beyond the fields, beyond the village of Islington and over Highgate hill stretched that long and lovely road with all its tribulations and magnificences. I stood and gazed, consumed by a great wish to be upon that road. My entire body was so taken over with this passion that I had no sense of self at all except as a vehicle for this wish. Nothing did I see but the road before me, nor heard sound, nor was aware of passer by.

However, being of a pragmatic nature, when I returned to ordinary consciousness I did not rush forward and embark upon a nameless quest. I knew well enough that to set out on that road I lacked the three essentials necessary — a good horse, a weapon, and the vigour of manhood. I therefore turned and set my feet towards London, somewhat, I mused wrily, as Dick Whittington, but with much less sense of purpose than that illustrious gentleman. It seemed to me that I walked towards nothing. I knew that without Jack the school would own for me no delight, and Tubs was a poor substitute. Certainly a heaviness had overtaken my spirits then, or I might have thought to seek employment as a stable boy at one of the hostelries; this did not occur to me. I merely trudged my weary way into the town, sodden and bedraggled with the rain, deep in morbid thought, oblivious to my immediate circumstance. And therefore when my attention was caught by one patently seeking it, I jumped and gawped like an idiot.

I was standing outside an inn, the Blue Boar in Barbican, and through the whorled glass panes I was staring at the face of Mr Hitchin. This face, because of the glass, was bulbous and distended, like a fish in water. I had last seen this gentleman by flaming torchlight in Covent Garden, and my father had belted me for talking to him, because he was a molly.

Mr Hitchin was smiling at me, and his finger crooked and beckoned me, and without more ado I went inside.

Chapter Nine

"BRING wine for my friend," called Mr Hitchin, and it was brought. I was seated in a high-backed settle, much too large for me, and Mr Hitchin opposite, enormous, filling up his equivalent space with acres of his ample flesh and an elegant coat, braided at neck and cuff, that spread in folds upon the bench. Between us on the table lay some broadsheet. Beside him lay his three-cornered hat.

Mr Charles Hitchin did not at that time hold the high office for which he was to become renowned in later years, Under City Marshall and yet one more corrupt official in our most corrupt society, but he was certainly a person of some authority, and treated with respect in that particular tavern. He divested me of my bedraggled coat and hung it by the fire where it steamed malodorously before the blaze.

"And are thee hungry, boy?"

I confessed myself to be so. Nothing would then content him but that I wolf down several portions of beef pie, the which I happily did, and very much more wine besides.

Mr Hitchin smiled at me, creasing the folds of skin about his jowls, his head fixed at an ungainly angle on his shoulders, his sunken eyes a shrewd and startling blue. He wore a long peruke, its curls abundantly massed about his visage. His thick lips were wet with wine.

"Now, William Page..."

I remembered that I had not told my name. *An alias will stand you in good stead... be Joseph, Will or Jack, and let poor John be hanged...*

"Sir?" said I.

"How may I help thee?" Mr Hitchin said. "And tell me not that thee needs no help; I plainly see thee do."

My plight being difficult to put into words, and if put into words, so pathetic and ridiculous as to merit only scorn — my friend has left me and I am uncared for and too young to take to the road — I said nothing; but to my dismay the excess of wine attacked my reserve and caused my expression to take on a tremulous aspect.

"I see, I see," said Mr Hitchin soothingly, and took my hand and patted it, and there we sat, and there I sniffed and drank, and by and by felt better.

Overcome then by great drowsiness I felt my head drop forward. Mr Hitchin said: "I have a room upstairs," and thence he carried me. I was not a thin scrap of a boy like Jack, yet Mr Hitchin bore me easily up the narrow dark stairway and so into a room above, and there upon a couch he placed me, removing my shoes himself, and wrapping me in his own coat, the braid rough at my chin.

"Get thee to sleep," said he.

To my surprise I did indeed drift off into a wine-warm doze and woke to find that Mr Hitchin was sitting in the chair beside my couch, perusing still the broadsheet by a candle's light, his other hand upon my leg, the which he absentmindedly stroked.

"Awake now?"

"Yes sir."

"Sit thee here upon my knee."

I wriggled from the blanket of his coat and put myself upon his ample knee. He put his arm about me to keep me in position, never ceasing from his study of the broadsheet.

"Can thee read?"

"No sir. They have tried to teach me at school but it makes no sense to me; I can make nor head nor tail of it."

"Thee should learn. I'm much the same myself," he chuckled. "No scholar. But reading's a handy skill, boy. Look at this now, where my finger points. *Stolen,* that's what the words says, *stolen at the Rose tavern... pocket book of no use but to the gentleman concerned... ten guineas reward.* Now all those are useful words to know, else how shall a cull go for the cole and better himself? Thee understands my meaning? A chap must read, or half these mysteries will pass him by. But zounds!" he shook his head. "Reading is no easy matter, I agree. It takes me half an hour to squint my way along the lines of words. But let me teach thee what I know. 'Stolen' you shall know again. And 'gold' — that is a useful word to know. And here — 'reward'. Mark well these words; they are all useful."

I set about to study them, his arm the while holding me close, his hand reposing on my thigh.

"Art warm enough now, boy?"

"Yes thankyou sir."

"And are thee obliged to me?"

"I am, sir, no doubt of it."

"I have a jolly troop of boys that work for me," said he indifferently, as if it were no matter. I recalled that little gang about him in Covent Garden, and Will Field who stole my penny. He continued: "We are always looking to augment our number."

"What work do they?" I enquired cautiously.

"They work about the city," answered he. He put his finger under my chin and tipped my face to look at him. "Can I tempt thee, William?"

"Your offer is most kind," I said.

"Then thee shall take it up?"

"I must refuse," I answered.

"What, mealy-mouthed? I did not take thee to be so particular." He let go my chin. "Is it not the duty of every man to better himself? This is a wicked worldly world and we stand and fall by our own efforts."

"I know that, sir."

"My boys — my mathematicians, in that they deal in numbers, making greater what was less, and less of what was too much — are all good lads and masters of their craft. Nothing vile, dear chuck, but merely an increase of their personal possessions. And is not a cull judged these days by the property he owns? Under my direction they can become rich; and so, my boy, can thee."

"They are pickpockets, aren't they? I saw them at it when we met before."

"Battalions, files, we call 'em such. If thee has high principles I have misread thee, boy, and must end our acquaintance. But I'm not mistaken, am I? Thee'll not run rusty and go snitch on us? Thee'll make rum cole — good money — with me. Don't thee trust me, William?"

"I do! I do! And I am not ungrateful for your care of me. The wine and all... No, it is simply that it is my plan to work alone, work for myself."

"The devil it is!" he chuckled. "And how does thee propose to do that, sirrah?" We were friends again. His hand now rested on my groin.

"On the highway," I answered. I added: "It is my intention to become a Gentleman of the Road, like Claude Duval."

"Ha! Too good for the likes of we, eh? A prancer, no less. And bed old Mother Tyburn?"

"I hope to be more fortunate than Captain Duval," I answered huffily and shifted from his fingers.

"And I was such a brute and laughed at thee!" He ruffled my hair. "Ah, William, I would have thee work for me. I like thee face. But maybe thee does not like mine?"

"Indeed I do," I mumbled, turning away.

"Then show thee fond affection with a kiss."

His arm tightened about me as if he thought that I might bolt. But I had no intention of annoying him who had after all displayed such benevolence towards me. Politely I bestowed a kiss upon his cheek. His other hand then gripped my head and steered it purposefully towards his mouth, and there he held me while his lips had their way with mine.

"There, there, little bird," he murmured. "I'll look after thee. A chap who works for me lives in a feathered nest. I don't ask every Tom or Joe to work for me, thee knows. Will thee reconsider?"

"I shall not change my mind," I answered.

"Ah," says he and smiles. "But what does thee know of the wicked world? How will thee live, and not protected? Think of a stone, a great big stone. Think of lifting up that stone. At once the creatures underneath go scurrying to left and right all in a muddle now the dark has gone — earwig, lice, ant, slug and spider, helter skelter to seek out more dark, another den. London Town, boy, is the dark beneath the stone, and its creatures run hither and yon about their dealings. And I am he that lifts the stone. Think well before thee spurns me."

And he wagged his fat finger at me, like a schoolmaster. There was no menace in his admonition. He was merely stating fact. I nodded. He gave a wide smile, his dewlap piling up in folds above his cravat. He gave me a bear-like hug and chortled into my ear.

"Ah, William, William, I shall have thee in the end!"

Then he set me down and looking at his pocket watch he said: "Put on thee coat and shoes and get upon thee way. The doors of the school will be shut upon thee else, and thee'll sleep in the street."

I came away down the stairs and collided at the foot with Will Field coming up. Our mutual dislike flared instantly; we glowered at each other.

"What are you doin' here?" he demanded.

"I ain't tellin' you."

"You been to see Mr Hitchin?"

"Yeah, and eatin' with him an' drinkin' too."

"You ain't goin' ter be one of us?" he screeched. "Lumpkin! Hobnailed looby!"

"No I ain't. Who'd want to be a common file?"

"Common? We're the cream!"

"Hope the cat gets yer."

He punched me. I returned the punch. He ran upstairs, clutching his pockets, which I saw were bulging.

"One day I'll flatten yer," he promised over his shoulder.

"And apples grow on a cherry tree!" I jeered; honours much about even.

I had not heard the last of my encounter with Mr Hitchin. That following evening, after our bread and broth, I was sent for to present myself in Mr Garrett's room.

However, it was not Mr Garrett who awaited me in the small dark study, but a stranger.

He was dressed entirely in black but for a white cravat, which gave him the appearance of a religious personnage. In this guess I found I was not much mistaken, for he introduced himself as Dr Sylvanus, and from his lugubrious manner and familiarity with the Almighty I understood his doctoring not to be of the bone-setting kind. However, his clothes, though sombre, were not shabby, indeed, they rustled with a certain richness, as though made of taffeta or satin. It was particularly evident when he crossed one thigh over the other, the which he seemed to like to do. It certainly showed off a very elegant leg.

"Come here, boy," he said in a low purring tone, "and stand before me."

He was seated in Mr Garrett's chair. I obeyed him and we looked at one another.

Dr Sylvanus was undoubtedly one of the handsomest men I had clapped eyes on. He must have been quite young then, though his black hair was streaked with a fine silver. He wore it long and tied back with a velvet ribbon. His jaw was firm and square, his nose small, his lips well shaped and sensuous. His brow was broad, his eyebrows thick and curved, his eyes a piercing and metallic grey, his lashes long. His voice was very soft and smooth; he scarcely moved his lips to speak.

"Your name is Davy Gadd."

"Yes sir." No aliases were to be permitted here, I thought regretfully.

"Mr Garrett has kindly permitted us the use of his own room so that we may be private," he continued. "The matter about which I wish to speak to you is very urgent, so urgent that we need to be alone in order to speak freely. You may rest assured that anything you wish to tell me, Davy, will be received in strictest confidence. You understand me?"

His words of course I understood; what lay behind them was as yet a mystery.

He leaned his elbows on the arms of a chair and joined his finger tips together. From behind this bridge he raised his eyes to me and frowned beneath his brows.

"I am told that yesterday you were given leave to absent yourself from school in order to run errands for a female personage."

"Yes sir. Mrs Grizel Peabody."

"And that in the course of so doing you unaccountably disappeared and took up an Assignation." He paused. "You met with somebody. In the street."

"I did not."

"Don't lie to me now; you have been found out. You met with Mr Charles Hitchin."

"Not in the street," I said. "It was in an inn."

"Ah, you do not deny it then."

"No sir. I saw Mr Hitchin at the window and he asked me in and bought me a beef pie. Then I came away and back to school."

"He bought you a beef pie..." He repeated the statement, as if it were the testimony of an Evidence. "There was, I think, a little

65

more."

"Some wine to wash it down," I agreed.

"But you did not, I think, consume this repast and imbibe this beverage entirely in the public gaze. Mr Hitchin took you to an upstairs room."

However did he get to hear of that? I could see now I was in for some kind of trouble, but as yet I could not place which offence I was suspected of and knew not precisely what to deny.

"I want you to tell me, Davy," Dr Sylvanus said, "everything that happened in that upstairs room."

"Nothin' at all, sir," I said, honest as the day. "The wine had made me sleepy and my coat and shoes were wet, so I was put upon a couch and slept, and Mr Hitchin sat and read and I awoke and thanked him and went on my way."

"Remember, God has witnessed all you did, and if you lie to me His Almighty Arm will strike you dead. Now once again I ask you to relate to me the substance of your secret meeting with this wicked man."

"There is no more to tell."

"Do you know who I am?" he asked me then. "I am God's right arm. London is a sinful city, Davy. Every street is crawling with vice and crime. Murder is commonplace. Rapine a daily occurrence. Fortunately for mankind at large, God's representatives abound. The Society for the Reformation of Manners thrives and flourishes. I am one of its leading lights and I shall stop at nothing till I rid our streets of horrible perversion. Worse, far worse than murder and the deflowering of young women" — he licked his lips, and crossed one satin thigh over the other — "is unnatural vice; and I believe you have been subjected to the same in that man's company."

"Truly, sir," said I, "Mr Hitchin was kindness itself."

"Very often," Dr Sylvanus said, perusing me under narrowed lids, "beneath the cloak of kindness the vile deceiver commits his heinous acts. It may be that in your innocence you did not understand the magnitude of his depravity. Come closer to me, Davy."

Most unwillingly I took a step forward. The long white fingers reached forward and took hold of me about the hips. They began to press and play about my privities. I could not help but feel a flicker of astonishment. It surely is not given to many ordinary boys to be the recipient of intimate gestures from two older gentlemen all within the space of twenty-four hours.

"Is this what Mr Hitchin did?" he murmured. I said no; but he continued what he was about, as if further to jog my memory. At length he ceased and turned me round and thrust a hand into my breeches and probed all about. "Did Mr Hitchin touch you here?" he said and pressed and pushed and squeezed, at last removing his hand.

"He did not," I declared robustly, curiously not too much displeased by this unlooked-for handling, rather the while pleasantly surprised.

"Nor did he this?" All suddenly he seized me by the back of the neck and thrust me down until my face was pressed against his belly, and he held me tight against his loins, where I was in no doubt but that there was a pulsating hardness beneath the satin.

"He did not so," I answered, muffled. I was released. We then resumed our original positions, he sitting upright in the chair and I standing before him, somewhat flushed of face.

"Mr Charles Hitchin," said Dr Sylvanus, very calm now, "is a man of whom much is suspected. I am confident that God will treat Mr Hitchin most severely at the Day of Judgement. He will certainly kick him down to Hell with his Almighty Foot."

I did not know the Lord as intimately as Dr Sylvanus did, therefore ventured no opinion.

"Davy," then said Dr Sylvanus unexpectedly, "will you work for God?"

"If I can," I answered cautiously.

"If Mr Hitchin speaks to you again, and if he should invite you to an upper room, go with him," Dr Sylvanus said. He eyed me speculatively. "Now you know what to look out for you will recognize his wickedness when it occurs. Come straight to me, recounting all that happened. We shall have the wherewithal then to put him where he belongs — in prison or in the pillory. We may be lucky and find that these enquiries net us other of his partners in depravity and the pillories shall take 'em all. Then let the mob deal with 'em."

I had seen such a mob. About a pillory those that in the dark may pass for humankind become possessed of madness, a curious mutual ecstasy that makes of them a beast of many forms, without thought or comprehension, fuelled with a strange hatred for one who never has done them harm nor whom they knew not till that day. A little smile played about the mouth of Dr Sylvanus in contemplation of the same.

"But what will Mr Hitchin have done to deserve these punishments?" I wondered. "What crime will he have committed?"

"What crime? Why, a crime against God and man, the vilest crime of all!" expostulated Dr Sylvanus.

"Touching other men?" I asked. "As you touched me?"

Dr Sylvanus became chillingly severe. "I touched you in the manner of an instructor. That is quite a different matter. But God hates that kind of vileness. He has made a law that says one man shall not touch another. Therefore if one man touch another he offends Our Lord and is as the lowest worm, a creature of corruption and decay. Such beasts must be crushed."

"And what about punchin'? Can we touch each other when we fight?" I wanted to be clear about these moral issues.

"What? Oh, fighting? Yes, fighting is all right."

Dismissing this small deviation, Dr Sylvanus leaned back, comfortable and content. "Why," he said, "I myself contributed to the arrest and imprisonment of nine of these vermin last year, when we caught them at a brandy shop in Jermyn Street. A viper's nest of filth! Men loving one another! Would you believe it, Davy, some were dressed in women's clothes! Can you imagine anything more unnatural and repulsive? Ah Davy, it is fortunate that so many of us work for God."

It occurred to me that of my two encounters with older men, it was Mr Hitchin who had troubled me the least, Dr Sylvanus having done with me all that Mr Hitchin had refrained from, and moreover inciting me to involve myself with the crime which he had no doubt God abhorred. And now he turned his attention to other matters.

"Where are you from, Davy? You are not London born and bred."

I mentioned a little of my background. "And so my mother brought me to London, to this school; and she went back to Buckden."

"Your mother... a widow then? She appears to be a well-liked woman."

"Oh yes. There have been gentlemen round her for as long as I can remember."

"A comely woman, I suppose?"

"Very comely."

"Dark haired or fair?"

"Fair."

"And — buxom?"

"Very buxom."

"But unhappy in that jewel in a woman's crown, the love of a good man."

"My mother was never unhappy in that, although I don't recall that there were many good men for her to choose from."

He smiled. His teeth were white and small. "Your mother, like
the meanest sparrow, has not gone unremarked by the Divine Eye,"
he told me. "It may well be that God has marked her out for a
wondrous change of fortune, when the love of a good man may
prove at last her sweet salvation. And remember, if Mr Hitchin
speaks to you again, come directly to Mr Garrett who will send for
me. Therein shall you do great service to the Lord."

I smiled politely. Naturally I had no intention of telling tales
on Mr Hitchin, who, for all that he was deemed a villain, had, as I
believed, a kindly nature, for all his breath was foul.

Dr Sylvanus gave me permission to withdraw.

Lord, how lonely it was in the bed without Jack.

"I can't abear this dreary place much longer," I told Tubs. "This
ain't the life for me, makin' shoes and sayin' prayers, and strangers
lookin' at you for an apprentice to a miserable trade."

"I quite agree," said Tubs. "My own hope in my future prosperity is beginning to wear thin. And yet I refuse to suppose that
good fortune will be so cruel as to pass us by."

Against all odds, this supposition of his lordship's was to be
proven true.

Chapter Ten

AND so, enough of childhood ramblings. It is my intent now
to ride at speed across the next five years, to early manhood; and this more possible because I now possessed the
horse on which to do so.

I have said that my somewhat reluctant friendship with Tubs
was to lead to an improvement in my fortune. It was in effect to
change my life's course, very much, as I first thought, for the better.

Mr Garrett came into the workroom where we shivered over
our needles and leather scraps. He was accompanied by a stranger, a
man in an elegant coat, fine waistcoat and cravat, neat white wig,
black knee breeches and smart buckled shoes. The two came purposefully towards Tubs.

"This is the boy," said Mr Garrett. "Boy! Show Mr Falcutt the
pendant which you wear about your neck."

Thanks largely to my protection of him, none having stolen

the thing from him of late, Tubs was able to do so; and Mr Falcutt stared with widening eyes at it and then at Tubs. He took it in his hands and held it to the light and turned it over several times, and finally he nodded and he said:

"It must be so. Yes, it must be so. This is the very strap, the very seal, and this, therefore, the very boy. His age is right; and now I look at him the face is much the same as one of the family portraits. The wretched woman's tale is true. This is Endymion Vale, heir to Lord Vale and the estate of Ashfield. And I am come to bring him home."

Those nearest to us heard and stared and muttered to their neighbours. The whisper went around the room. Mr Garrett was much discomposed.

"Well, I am glad to say that I have always treated the boy kindly," he said blustering. "Is this not so, boy?"

Even then, I did not think that he could remember his name.

"Oh, kindly, is it?" Tubs replied, pink of cheek. "You have treated me with negligence and indifference and although I spoke often of my noble forebears I was not believed. But I knew that one day the Hour of my Triumph would appear. and here it is. Like a king returned from exile I am come into my own. At last I shake the dust of this establishment from my feet and go to better things."

I grinned. This establishment was very dusty; he would be some time a-shaking. But his next words took the smile from my face, replacing it with a grimace of stupefaction.

"And Davy is coming with me!"

All eyes turned to me.

"You will come with me, Davy, won't you?" Tubs said in a quiet beseeching tone. "You alone have stood by me throughout my Period of Grief and I have grown habituated to your company. I would be lonely without you. Do come. You cannot prefer to remain in this place."

"Indeed I don't!" I hastened to assure him. "I'll very gladly go with you, if he don't mind." I looked at Mr Falcutt dubiously.

Mr Falcutt made a sort of bow or shrug. "I am a messenger, no more nor less. Master Endymion may do as he pleases."

A messenger — here Mr Falcutt underestimated himself a little, as we understood when, as we rode northward in the family coach, he explained to us his own position and the curious events that had led to this miraculous occurence.

Mr Falcutt was old Lord Vale's constant support — his butler, steward, bailiff, gentleman of the horse — and had lived at Ashfield for more than twenty years, indispensable to the smooth running of the house. Old Lord Vale lived in solitary splendour, since the death of his son, also called Endymion. It had been hoped that this Lord Endymion would marry and produce an heir, but it was not to be. Then the scandal of some ten years ago was recalled, and it was decided to pursue the matter further. Ten years ago young Lord Endymion had disgraced himself by a liaison with a serving maid and got the wench with child. Mr Falcutt had been instructed to send her away and pay for her silence; she had gone to London well provided for. Young Lord Endymion who, it seemed, was something of a weak and spineless creature, had not demurred, and the matter was forgotten. But when no heir was forthcoming and when Lord Endymion died, the old man thought of that love child and made enquiries. Mr Falcutt traced the progress of that serving wench, which proved an unhappy one, a path of misery and degradation and a pauper's grave; but his discoveries uncovered Tubs's whereabouts and hence he came to claim him.

And so, that dark December day, we found ourselves inside a noble coach, with velvet seats and polished leather and a crest emblazoned on the door — that same crest as upon Tubs's pendant — and on our way to Ashfield Hall, some twenty miles or so out of London, on the Great North Road.

Our excitement and exhilaration knew no bounds. The pleasure we experienced to be quit of Bishopsgate School and out upon the road was indescribable. We marvelled at everything we saw, even Tubs, who was attempting to assume a dignity appropriate to his new station. We dined at a roadside inn. We could order anything we liked; we had venison pie and porter. It was almost night time when we reached the end of our journey, and the coachman lit the lamps.

We turned down a wooded way and made a slower progress through the ruts and mire for several miles more. Tubs and I pressed our noses to the windows to see the approach of Tubs's mansion. As far as we could see by lamp light, it was a very fine pile indeed. A long wide gravelled drive curved around a green, upon which some statuary showed, its stone pale in the murky gloom. Ahead of us there rose the house, three storeys high, with many windows, lit from within. Steps led to an imposing door. While the coach and horses were led to the stables, Tubs and I and Mr Falcutt entered the house.

Even Tubs was a little sobered as he took possession of his new domain. The door opened into a large hall whence rose a great staircase which we climbed. The balustrade was carved with fruit, flowers and birds, as like the real thing as could be. Paintings on the wall passed by my admiring gaze, and oaken linen chests and casement clocks that ticked with a noise loud as a spoon banged upon a dish.

We were taken to a room whose walls were panelled with dark wood and whose largest piece of furniture was a four-poster bed with massy curtains of a musty blue brocade. A fire burned in the chimney place and we hurried to it, warming our hands.

A mirror showed us two dirty and bedraggled boys still in the brown coats of the workhouse school; but this was to be rectified. Although I had not been expected I was treated exactly as my companion. We each bathed in a tub of warm water brought by servants who stared at us in great curiosity. We washed our hair and dressed in good clothes — old and fusty, but well made — all under the agreeable Mr Falcutt's direction. We had a close stool for what Mr Falcutt called our personal requirements, and it was disguised as a sturdy chair; no one would have guessed its purpose.

Then, still blinking at our change of circumstance, we dined at a little table by the fire. We had roast leg of mutton, and also liver and salted pork, as if it was all perfectly reasonable to eat three meat dishes, and we drank mulled wine and had three kinds of pudding, all very sweet to the taste. Servants brought this food in and took our plates away, and Mr Falcutt supervised it all with an efficient and practised eye.

Warm and well fed — conditions unfamiliar to us — we revelled in our happy state. But Mr Falcutt soon dispelled our mirth with the suggestion: "Now I think is the moment to meet with your grandfather, whose kindness has made all this possible."

Why Tubs should have become so apprehensive, having every right to be here, I know not, yet so he was. Certainly I was so, and quaking in my shoes. To counterbalance such craven weakness I adopted an aggressive stance as, after many passageways of distance, we presented ourselves at a door, and Mr Falcutt announced us as:

"Master Endymion, my lord... and Davy Gadd."

In a sumptuously furnished room an old man was sitting in a big chair by the fire. The many candelabra showed him to be lean and thin with a narrow face and hooky nose, bright eye and pointed chin, with white hair combed in strands across his pate. He got slowly to his feet and came across the parquet floor towards us, holding out his arms.

"My boy!" he said in tones of some emotion. The only trouble was, he reached for me, not Tubs, and held me to him in a fond embrace, the which I wriggled from in some embarrassment, and sneaking a glance at Tubs, caught on his face an expression I had never seen before and which I did not like the look of. In a moment it had passed, the mistake being corrected, and Mr Falcutt hurriedly proffering explanations and accounts, and — that which was of most importance to me — myself accepted as companion for Tubs and not thrown out upon my ears.

Beyond the establishment of a superficial communication, very little more passed between Lord Vale and ourselves that evening, and shortly afterwards we were returned to our own chamber.

One bed only being made up — the large four-poster — it was assumed that Tubs and I should share it. We did so; indeed it was quite large enough for six; and thus I spent my first night in a mansion, thinking no further than the morrow. Tubs, however, had his mind on more distant horizons.

"He is not long for this world," Tubs whispered. "And when he dies I shall be master here."

Lord Vale, however, in spite of his peculiar assumption that I was the scion of his house and Tubs was not, was plainly in complete possession of his faculties, and though elderly, was very much in control of Ashfield and its smooth running. Ten wasted years lay behind Tubs, and he must be made a gentleman, and though the same high goal was not expected of myself, I must acquire a little education by the way. At breakneck speed, it seemed, our formal training galloped forth.

A succession of tutors taught us reading, writing and accounts, and, most important for a gentleman, good manners. Lord Vale was none of your slatternly country squires; he had once kissed the hand of King William. We must not spit or scratch at table, neither lean upon it with our elbows, nor put our nose close to the plate nor gulp food at speed. These were characteristics of the vulgar. We were taught to walk gracefully and incline our heads and bow in appropriate circumstances; these attributes of course being equally of use to Gentlemen of the Road, I was eager to master them. In this refined atmosphere the mysteries of the written word became clear to me at last, and although I always formed my letters with something less than excellence I could make myself understood. A wide and florid vocabulary was also taught us at this time; but common speech was always more comfortable to me and I reverted to the same when I was at my ease.

Tubs had to learn land management and much else, all dull, the which I was spared, it being deemed unlikely that I would ever come into sudden inheritance; but to my elation, at such times I might go riding.

The carelessly mundane manner in which the Vale household fulfilled my wildest dreams has never failed to amaze me. I could ride any of the Ashfield horses. All I had to do was let the groom know in advance, and see that my mount was cared for upon my return. A bay gelding was my favourite: Willow was his name. In the five years of which I am now speaking I learnt everything I might of riding, saddlery and harness, of the forge and farrier, the strange tales of horse behaviour, the right feed for the right beast, the ailments and remedies — matters which are grown so familiar to me now that I am hard put to recall a time when I had yet to learn them. Piecemeal had been my knowledge, scraps gleaned from the inns at Buckden. At Ashfield's fine stable I had my apprenticeship.

We had an old groom there, Dan Carter, who taught me how to jade a horse — that is, to make it stand stock still as if it be enchanted, and later to release the horse from his immobility when none else may, it being all done with noxious scents rubbed into the horse's nostrils or about his body, and then with use of other scents which cancel out the first. When this is well done it can seem like magic, particularly if you stand apart and make pretence that it's to do with the direction of the wind or the boots of a passer by. Stoat's liver and rabbit's liver, powdered — we call it dragon's blood — is a good jader. And for calling a horse on you want a concoction of fennel, rosemary and cinnamon, and the wind to blow the scent of it. Violets'll do it also; violets will keep a horse calm and steady.

Tubs never bothered with this kind of thing; it did not interest him. He'd rather ride in a coach than on horseback; and if he wanted a horse to move he'd lay the whip across the withers.

Tubs, plump in despite of reason on workhouse diet, grew yet more vast on rich fare, bursting his buttons with a reckless abandon. Yet breeding will out, I daresay, and I'll say this for him, he could look the part. Corpulent as he became, there was no doubt which of us was the gentleman. In his fine clothes, strutting and swaggering, giving his orders, striding about his halls and gardens, he was every bit the lordling. Myself I had no natural dignity, and not much elegance of bearing; but I sat a horse well.

We learned how to use a sword and how to load and fire a pistol. It was the pistol that pleased me most, and I was the better shot. Tubs was always nervous at the shower of sparks that seemed to precede by seconds the firing of the ball. It needed a steady hand to hit the mark even when our targets were huge oak trees or grassy banks. The finer skills of duelling passed me by. I always thought the cut and thrust ridiculous; if you had an enemy, I reckoned, best whack him with a cudgel or take your fist to him. But the pistol was another matter.

I practised my aim daily and with my old and cherished ambition still in mind I set about to learn to fire from horseback, a skill in itself. I learned that it could be an uncertain matter whether the pistols would fire or not, especially in damp weather, and therefore it was pretty important always to keep the priming dry. "Stand and deliver," I muttered to the oak tree branches. "Throw down your gold", I told the barn door.

Impressed by my dedication but little guessing the reason for it, Lord Vale gave me my own weapons. Italian pistols they were, about a foot long, fine sleek things with handles of polished wood, barrels of steel, and silver butt caps, ornamented with a flowing design and the name of the maker incorporated amongst the curling patterns. They could be tucked into the deep pockets of a greatcoat yet were long enough to arm a rider. They came in a smooth box lined with blue velvet. They were a pleasure to behold and a joy to use.

He was so good to me, Lord Vale. He let me send a small allowance to Ma, care of the Lion at Buckden. He asked me how I did and talked about horses. Sometimes when he looked at Tubs he sighed.

Tubs and I, with diversion enough, were kept well occupied throughout those five years, and the differences in our natures were largely submerged in the entertainments of the moment. At night we slept in that same bed, and though by then another might have been made up for one or other of us if we had asked, we were content thus to remain. A certain affection bound us, born of shared adversity and relief that the same had ended. We both looked forward to that which we called our Secret, the name we gave to the nocturnal touching of each other's bodies. I knew more about this than Tubs did, having been instructed by Dr Sylvanus and I was happy to pass on what I had learnt. I had never told a soul about the revered fellow's gropings of my person, but I discovered soon enough with Tubs that these, if continued, led to pleasure.

I did not think about the future, content as long as I might ride Willow where I would. Tubs, however, thought very much about it, counting the days till he should be master indeed. This day came one summer, when old Lord Vale died in his chair after a hearty dinner.

Tubs and I were both fifteen years of age. There had been some changes in England then, for Queen Anne had died the previous year, and now we had a king from overseas, George, who could speak no English. However, nothing much had changed at Ashfield, until now.

On hearing the news of his grandfather's demise Tubs swelled with pride and gratified desire, as toads do. He had now learnt from his books that Ovid wrote how 'fortune favours fat folks', and, backed by this respected authority he set about to act accordingly. He sent Mr Falcutt upon his way, with a pension hardly worthy of his years of service. He said he had always felt that Mr Falcutt disapproved of him and was moreover far too old to be of use to him. He said I must now call him 'my lord'. I granted that Tubs was an inappropriate title for one as rich as he — though not for one as fat — and therefore I complied. Small pettinesses then followed, as his ordering the servants to bring him the old Rhenish from the cellars which he deemed too fine for me to appreciate; and for his meals to be brought on silver platters and mine on pewter. He had tailors from London come and fix him up with several suits of clothes but decided that the clothes I wore did not need replacing. I did not mind this, but I minded what lay behind it, as Lord Vale had never been one constantly to show me my place. And sometimes Tubs rode Willow at the times when I had been accustomed to take off on my own, for no other purpose, as it seemed to me, than to be sure I could not ride him; and I did mind this.

He now began a laborious pursuit of serving maids, his noisy conquests echoing through dairy, barn and bedchamber. He discovered that there were any number of neighbouring families to invite to the house, and instigated plenty of occasions for excessive eating and drinking, cards and dice, and in short conformed in general terms to the accepted pattern of a gentleman's way of life.

"What a dreary fellow you are becoming, Davy," says he. "You could have any serving maid you want, after I have finished with her. But you show no interest. We might be having some good sport, all four of us together. But no, not you — you disappear and all you do is ride, or so you say. Dice, the idiot's game, you comprehend, but you are a poor card player and I can drink you under the table. You're hardly fit to be the companion of a gentleman."

Naturally Tubs's criticisms of my character had nothing to do with the fact that the ladies at the Ball had seemed to like me better. I had had propositions from a lady older than Ma; and love letters thrust into my pocket from two young ladies who professed me their ideal. I admit that some devilment made me tell Tubs about it. He asked me what I intended to do, and I said I intended nothing, and he looked at me in bafflement and contempt.

"But these women are all considered Beauties," spluttered he, "and are moreover wealthy. Listen to me, Davy, you and I must have some serious converse. Davy! Where are you going?"

"Riding."

I took Willow northward, further up the road. In my experience there was nothing akin to the great content of setting out alone with a good horse. The whole world opens — I am my own man — I possess a sense of liberation — I am a king, a hero — I may go where I please and answer to none.

I rode onward for several miles. I dismounted and I leaned against an oak tree. It was plain enough that the time had come to quit my curious liaison with the new Lord Vale — a life born of self interest and circumstance — and stand upon my own feet. But where my path lay I was none too sure, and I was purposeless enough to drift, diverted from my boyhood certainties by the easy wealth and general satisfaction of the last five years. Now that the moment of reckoning was here I was unsure of my ground and hesitant to go forward.

The ground whereon I stood was rough and humpy and I kicked at it with my boot. I knelt and spread my hand and moved my palm low over the leaves.

"Look for humps and hillocks," Jerry Dowlan used to say, "and hollows never dug by paw and claw."

I scrabbled in the leaf mould and my fingers closed on something hard and sharp. I knew before I took it out and rubbed it clean that it would be a scrap of gold.

I studied it — a buckle pin, no more, the kind of thing that long ago I used to sense under Jerry's tuition and take to the Collector in the big old house. Lord Staughton. A handsome boy, he called me... *come back and see me, say, in ten years' time... we may be useful to each other.* Little gullible fool I must have been.

I laughed and stood up and pocketed the buckle pin. With a rush of boyish merriment I jumped, and grasped the oak branch just above my head, with my two hands, and swung, elated.

Duval's gold still lay undiscovered, somewhere up the road, this road that stretched away to the north and south, lying there within the grasp of any man who had the skill to seek it out.

I had that skill.

Part II
The Thief-taker

Chapter Eleven

THE Rose tavern, on the corner of Drury Lane and Russell Street, has always been a place of ill repute, and it is there begins the next part of my story.

Entirely for the purpose of witnessing the naked woman in the trussed chicken pose, displayed upon a pewter dish, my lord Endymion decided we should to London, for no gentleman worth his salt has missed this famous sight, nor foregone his turn at attempting to place the candle as the dish spins. Tubs had now realized that there was a wider world than Ashfield, and that much of it was contained between Moorfields, Wapping, Southwark and St James's Park; and with his new-found status he must try a gentleman's delights, and I must go with him, for his lordship was, between ourselves, a little apprehensive about the pursuit of sin and pleasure, novelties both.

The time of year was autumn, the time of day was late afternoon. Our coach deposited us in the piazza at Covent Garden and Dawkins our coachman was instructed to return at midnight. We would then drive to a reputable inn some distance from these meaner streets.

So, Tubs and I set off to walk the length of Russell Street. Innocents as we were, we had not heard the adage that no man may walk the distance between the piazza and the Rose without twice hazarding his life. There were three little alleyways upon the left, each one dim and squalid as the last, and into one we were suddenly thrust and shoved against a wall, surrounded by some half a dozen ruffians demanding money. I am embarrassed to confess that I had no weapon with me, and in that confined space Tubs could not draw his sword. We had thought ourselves safe enough in daylight on so short a walk, and so were easy meat. From Tubs they took his watch and rings, and nothing from myself, since I carried nothing valuable; they were almost as inept as we, for their fingers fumbled and shook, and none of them thought to look in Tubs's coat lining, where his money lay. They ran off towards Vinegar Yard and the dark little lanes behind the playhouse. Tubs was purple in his fury.

"We shall go directly to the Watch. I'll know those rogues again. I'll not rest till I see them all in Newgate."

"You'll not rest then, for we'll leave it be."

"Why should we? Devil take it, we were robbed!"

"I'm sorry that you lost your rings; but did you not see who it was that took 'em?"

"Do you mean you recognized them?"

"I knew the one. It was Jack's brother Tom, who is a trial to his mother."

"Small wonder! But that he is become a villain is no cause for us to shirk our duty. We shall inform the constable and have him brought to justice."

"Tubs, we shall not. It would cause grief to Tom's ma, who is a good woman."

"She may well be dead," Tubs hooted. "It is five years since we knew her."

"In the belief that she is not," said I, "I shan't let you snitch to the constable."

"How will you prevent it?"

"Easily." I took hold of him and twisted his arm and marched him towards the Rose. He spluttered and swore but he sullenly acquiesced, and we shortly arrived at the famous tavern, where anticipation of hitherto forbidden thrills overcame his smouldering resentment. We entered.

A large low room, already crowded, met our gaze. It was dimly lit with candles. Huddled figures pressed about the fire. At high-backed settles and tables men drank and smoked in the gloom; female whores roamed around between them, and a fiddler played in the corner, his tunes half swallowed by the noise of laughter, quarrelling, belching and boozy song.

Tubs's face fell when he learned that the posture woman did not perform till later. However, there would, it seemed, be much to occupy us till then. Tubs and I were no sooner seated and drinking than some women joined us and made much of us. They nuzzled us and draped themselves about us, feeling for our valuables both monetary and bodily, the which occasioned Tubs intense enjoyment, as this, after all, was what he had come hither for. He flashed me many a conspiratorial glance, as if to say: this is good sport — this is the life for gentlemen!

"Will you have our company?" they said, "and shall we pleasure you? We like you very much already," they said to Tubs, "for your fine embroidered waistcoat and your satin breeches and your silk cravat, and you," they said to me, "for your fine eyes and the feel of your prick, the which we hope soon to know better."

I could not fail to notice on Tubs's face that dark look which he gave me when his grandfather mistook me for himself; but thought no more on't, and allowed such liberties as the doxies took, these being new to me and not unpleasant. Then Tubs, a little flustered from the amorous attentions of these women, his cravat askew, said, very dignified: "And so, my dears, it may well be you find my poor companion pleasing. Will you find him so if I should tell you that he does not possess one penny to his name? Whereas I, upon the other hand..."

I sank at once in the estimation of the nymphs, and Tubs it was whom they accompanied from the room, though with, I thought, some disappointment.

"You're well quit of them," said a cull at my elbow, clumsily shoving a jug to me along the pockmarked table. I poured and drank and looked at him. Even in the dim light I could see the oddity of his appearance. He was not much older than myself, stocky and coarse, with a thatch of hair, and a face that was strangely full of shadow. Staring unashamedly I saw that his skin was covered with some kind of dark birthmark, in this mirk the colour of sea-coal, but in daylight, as I was to find, of a curious dull purple blue, like the dye in elderberry.

"Joseph Blake," he said, introducing himself. "They call me Blueskin." It seemed then it was not improper to refer to his deformity. Our age has all the subtlety of a brick wall — we have no scruple to identify a cully for his weaknesses — One Eyed Allsop, Pocky Parker, Skin and Bone Dawson, and the chap who cheated the gallows and came back to tell the tale, Half-Hanged Smith.

"Pleased to meet you. William Page."

We spoke awhile in general terms. He talked of the necessity for a steady income. "Any cull at a loose end could do no better than become a strawman. I've known 'em pick up a tidy living that way and it's so easy. All you do is walk up and down Old Bailey, with straws in your shoe buckles to show your trade. A lawyer comes along and sees yer; you has a little talk about what he'll pay yer, and all you has ter do is go into the court room and swear blind what he tells yer — it's that easy. You've got an honest face — anyone'd believe yer; and everyone turns evidence in these hard times, so why fret about it? What d'yer say?"

"I'd have to think about it."

Blueskin Blake leaned close to me. "What would you say if I

was to tell you that Mr Jonathan Wild himself is behind this offer?"

I preserved an impassive exterior, knowing nothing of the name — O happy time! — but not wishing to reveal my ignorance.

"I don't know what to say," said I in perfect truth.

"If you didn't fancy to be a strawman," said Blueskin Blake, "there are other openings in Mr Wild's service for a chap as wishes to rise. It would be a great honour for you to work for Mr Wild. He's been good to me, I'll tell you. He looks after his chaps."

I was suddenly aware that others nearby were taking an interest in our conversation. I decided to foreclose it.

"Thank you for your offer," I said. "I might be tempted to accept, but that I am already in the employ of Mr Hitchin."

I had found this an effective silencer once before and it was so now, but not in the way I had anticipated. Blueskin Blake spat on the table, and gave a snort which seemed to imply contempt, borne out by the fact that he got to his feet, saying "The more fool you!" and with a scrape of bench he moved away amongst the crowd.

"I don't envy you," said the man next to me cheerfully. "I should quit the service of Mr Hitchin. Mr Hitchin is quite a has-been now he and Mr Wild have fallen out. In this part of the world if you ain't for Mr Wild you are against him, and if you're against him he has fifty ways of getting you to Newgate."

"And molly Hitchin won't be able to save you," added another.

I perceived this to be some kind of insult, and while I was mulling it over, my companion clarified the same with a more specific challenge. "If you work for Mr Hitchin, would you like to tell me something — does he fuck you?"

"Would you like to tell me something — do you want your head punched?" I replied.

It seemed that he did not, for looking me up and down he gave me a wan smile and turned his back.

I stood up and wandered off, with the idea of finding where Tubs was. I went through the far door and found a stairway. I thought Tubs had gone that that way, but I was mistaken, for the stairway led into an upper room, large as the one below, bearing a faded grandeur, being oak-panelled, with some portraits in good frames upon the walls, and lit with candelabra hanging from the ceiling. Several tables were set with gaming devices — cards for Faro, dice for Hazard and Raffle. Players of both sexes sat hunched about the tables, drinks a-plenty at their elbows, and countenances of rapt intensity or despair. Tubs was not there, and I turned to go — then paused.

I had seen sitting over in the corner a man of such grace and beauty that I stood stock still and gawped. Just above his head a three-branched candelabra gave him a halo of gold, and illumined his countenance in a vibrant glow. It also made it possible for me to see him clearly. He and another man were leaning forward, throwing dice, lost to the world. This was plainly a gentleman, vastly different from the ragamuffin riff raff below. He would have been a little over thirty years of age. His forehead was broad, his nose patrician, his lips firm and sensuous. His hair was black — he wore no wig — and tied back with a black ribbon. He frowned. His brows were dark. His hands were pale, with long slender fingers such as might be seen handling velvet or stroking the fur of a cat. A cat? What had brought that to my mind?

I had the shock of my life. Damn me, I knew him! It was Lord Staughton, whom I had last seen in his ivy-covered manor house beside the rooky ash trees when Jerry Dowlan brought me as a boy to offer up our treasures to the Collector. He had had gold displayed on blue velvet, gold which he held in those pale fingers and handled and purred over, taking pleasure in the possession of it, not for its use or for the spending of it, but for the lust of ownership.

And why should it surprise me to find him here? This was where gentlemen gambled, and why not he? He was not frozen in time, like a piece of old gold in the earth, permanently set into that room where I had seen him last. He might move about at will, along that same road that I had taken, the road that linked the northern villages to London. What did I know of him after all? Nothing. Nothing at all.

What was certain was that he would not recognize me, even if he remembered that lad that Jerry brought along with him. Therefore it must be my move if I wished to bring myself to his attention. I went over to him as if to watch his game. I knelt down beside his chair, and let him see the gold pin on my palm, the thing I'd found upon the road beneath the oak. This caught his attention, and now his gaze met mine.

"For your collection," I said; but he now was looking at me and not at the pin, and I had the uncomfortable sensation that it was myself that I was offering and not the pin, and worse, that this was exactly what he understood me to mean. His beautiful eyes were full of amusement. He took the pin from me and studied it most carefully, turning it this way and that, making it seem as delicate as a rose.

"Davy Gadd, sir, at your service."

"So... the boy that was Jerry Dowlan's partner," said Lord Staughton. "And now grown to young manhood. Stay there, Davy. It may be you will bring me luck. Give me a number, under twelve."

"Seven."

They threw the dice. In one of those rare freaks of chance Lord Staughton threw a five and a two; and my own die was thus cast.

My lord decided to quit upon the crest of this coincidence, pocketed his winnings, and squeezed my shoulder.

"I owe you thanks," he said to me. "I should like to bring you where I may express my gratitude. Will you come with me? I want you to think most carefully about this. There is a deeper meaning in my invitation."

"I would be pleased to go with you, sir," answered I; and so we left the Rose together, and went out into the street.

Chapter Twelve

IT was evening, already dark, and Drury Lane's tall houses closed about us, a mass of shadows. We walked for some while, without speaking. We crossed over a broad road and soon entered a street of fine houses.

"Here," said my companion, and paused before a pillared doorway set in one of these high-fronted dwellings. As I had been expecting some low boozing ken I was surprised; this seemed to be a place of some quality. Some steps led to the door. When we knocked, the door was opened and we went in.

We were in a narrow passage, well lit and richly panelled with painted visions in rose and green and grey, very delicate, with images of nymphs floating on swings and dancing in forest glades. But more divine than any of these was the nymph that stood before us, whom Lord Staughton called Lucinda, and who beckoned us towards a stairway.

"And how are you, my dear?" enquired Lord Staughton. "And Aunty Mary?"

"We are both well," answered Lucinda, "and very quiet tonight. Will you dine? We have all manner of festive food, quite depraved indeed. I could bring oysters to your chamber... or we have a ragout of asparagus and herbs, or I could rustle up a nice goose pie..."

I grew speechless, for as we went upstairs I understood that in all the confusion I had been introduced as Delia and nothing had been remarked about the fact, and that now as if it were the most

natural thing in the world Lord Staughton and Lucinda were rapturously discussing the pleasures of the dining table, and strangest
of all, it had become apparent to me that the lovely Lucinda was
male as I was. He was, however, far prettier, and this prettiness was
enhanced by powder and paint and a gown of rose satin and the
daintiest buckled shoes in similar shade, with white stockings that
showed as he flounced his skirts. We were ushered by Lucinda into
a bedroom. He lit the candles and withdrew.

The room was deliciously ornamented, with many gilded mirrors and dainty chairs and an elegant little table and a bed with rose
brocaded drapes. We warmed ourselves at the fire.

"Have you been to such a house before?" said Lord Staughton.

"No, never."

"You find it strange, perhaps?"

"Not so very strange." I had no wish to appear a country bump-
kin. "Besides, I knew such places to exist." I forebore to tell him I
had thrown a stone at one at Pa's direction. "Are there many such?"

"Yes. All havens and no questions asked. This is not, Davy,
like a common whorehouse — more a place of refuge and tranquility
where friends forgather. Each is known. False names are used, usually of the female kind, and thus no identity is inadvertently given
away. Aunty Mary is the most discreet soul imaginable. Not all
houses are like this. Some visitors relish a noisy camaraderie — music, marriages, romps on the stairs — and they will go to other places.
But I hoped simply for a quiet time with you and so I brought you
here."

"But must they all dress as Lucinda who come here?" I asked in
some dismay.

"No, only those who wish it. Are you uncomfortable here?"

"No."

Our hands, warming at the fire, touched. With a most com-
manding gesture he brought me closer to him and enfolded me in
his arms. He kissed me, tentatively, testing whether I might draw
back from his embrace. On the contrary, I pressed closer. The second kiss was longer and more passionate.

"We might undress," he suggested, his lips against my ear.

As I took off my clothes I watched him. Meticulously he began
to divest himself of his beautiful garments. I grinned. He raised an
exquisite eyebrow.

"I thought noblemen could not undress themselves," I explained
mischievously. "I thought they held out their arms and their servants did the rest."

"Impudent brat," said he. "Fold up my waistcoat."

Lovely it was, buff satin, embroidered all over with leaves and flowers.

I stood there naked, holding the waistcoat. "I never done this before," I said awkward.

"Oh," he smiled. "Folding a waistcoat is very easy. Anyone may learn it."

He was himself naked now. He had a fine figure, lean and trim, in no way gone to seed as so many of the gentry go; no, he was sleek and firm, beautiful as the bare sculptured statues they have in rich men's gardens. He thought me good and all. He looked me up and down. He said:

"Davy, you have very much fulfilled your early promise."

Then drawing me closer to the hearth he kissed me much about the body. Our limbs in the flames' glow seemed touched with amber. This lovely lord now knelt and put his lips about my prick and kissed me so that I could not contain myself but must come where I stood and he with plain delight there on his knees caught all he might upon his tongue, and put his face against my belly to our great mutual satisfaction. Then he stood and hugged me, and led me to the bed. Here we lay and kissed and twined, and he turned me face down and lay upon me, holding me with a strong grasp, biting my ears, thrusting his loins against my bum till of a sudden I felt the warm flood of his coming, in the cleft of my arse. Then off he tumbled and lay beside me, breathless and laughing, and his face so close to mine that I could see his perfect teeth and feel his laughter on my face. He held me to him.

"Davy, Davy, that was of the very finest sport!"

Sport, aye, was it so? An odd way to describe, I thought, the tumult of emotions roused in me by that night's doings — the discovery that womankind would have no place in my life henceforth, that having known a lover as beautiful as Lord Staughton I would not easily be satisfied with less — the complete unlikelihood of my ever finding his like for myself — the hope to know his handling of me again — the rational assumption that this same hope would never be fulfilled... so this was sport?

"Yes my lord," I said, and said no more.

And after sport, what was the proper procedure? Lord Staughton sat up and padded over to the wash bowl. He rapidly splashed himself, dried himself, and doused his body with Hungary water from a great glass bottle with a stopper almost as large, and began to dress.

"Bestir yourself, Davy. I shall ring for that goose pie now."

I did as he did, seeing no reason why not to indulge in the generous use of Hungary water either. When Lucinda came in with our dinner and then discreetly withdrew, we were clothed and — I speak for myself — hugely famished, and we put away plenty of pie and much claret beside.

"I saw your mother lately," said Lord Staughton.

I stared. I could not fancy what circumstance should have brought so unlikely a pair together.

"I called in at the Crown," he said, by way of explanation.

"My lord?" I frowned.

"The Crown. The inn near Eaton Socon where your mother is the keeper. And the comeliest innkeeper I have ever seen, if I may say so."

"My lord, I have not been back to Buckden these five years..."

"You should do so, if the alternative is that you have no conception of your parent's circumstance," he said in some amusement.

I fidgetted. "I have provided for my mother in some measure, but... we are not close. We never have been so."

"Then let me be the one to inform you that she is well. However, I have the impression that your presence at the inn would be most welcome — a strong right arm and support..."

"Was there no husband there?"

"Not a one, dear, as far as I could tell," smiled he. "A pretty serving wench and a slow-witted ostler — I cannot suppose him the husband of which you speak, for I know your mother to have always been a woman that knew how to pick and choose. I might add, Davy, that if you were tapster there I should be tempted to drink there again."

Before I had had time to digest, along with the goose pie, the implications of this new development, into the room came Aunty Mary, and Lucinda with him. Aunty Mary was a small sad-faced man, some forty-five years of age. He spoke in a smooth pleasant voice, and, unlike the fair Lucinda, was dressed in garb in which he might have walked unnoticed the length of Holborn — black knee breeches and coat and white cravat. You would have taken him for a lawyer or a clerk. He was neat and precise in his manner. He sat down and took a pinch of snuff. Lucinda spread his skirts and rustled down on to a low stool. Aunty Mary enquired if the food was to our liking. We assured him that it was. He spoke of sauces, knowledgeably and with discernment, as some men speak of weapons.

"This is my young acquaintance Davy Gadd," Lord Staughton

said. "A man from my part of the world. What he does in London I have no idea; but as a boy he was a keen observer of fine horses."

"I am still so," I said. "Good fortune has enabled me to learn to ride instead of merely to gawp. I hope one day to own a good horse myself."

"You have not yet found Claude Duval's gold then, I presume?" said Lord Staughton and smiled.

"No... but I have not been searching. I am certain that it lies out there, somewhere along the north road before Alconbury."

"Davy has promised," said Lord Staughton drily, "that when he finds it he will bring it straight to me."

Both Aunty Mary and Lucinda laughed. "Davy is far too wise to keep a promise such as that," said Aunty Mary. "You teased it from him in his cups, or in your bed, Clarissa."

Clarissa! It was Lord Staughton to whom he spoke. I spluttered into my claret. My lord reproved my mirth. "And you," he said to me, "while you are in this house, are Delia. Who are you, scamp?"

"Delia, my lord," I said contritely.

"Should Delia wish to visit on his own account," said Lord Staughton to Aunty Mary, "admit him."

"It will be my pleasure," Aunty Mary said most warmly. "But you must both return, together, many times."

"Ah, you forget," murmured Lord Staughton, "my plans are made. I shall be... elsewhere..."

"Take Davy with you," smiled Aunty Mary. "I know you mean to journey north. What adventures lie in store in the mists and the mountains... fast horses, wayside inns... the unknown... and he could be a help to you upon your mission."

I believe that Aunty Mary understood the depth of my secret turmoil and my foolish adoration of the noble lord for whom our encounter had been sport. But his lordship was not swayed by his persuasion.

"It would be too dangerous," said Lord Staughton curtly. Then he laughed. "No, Davy has plans of his own — he's going to be a highwayman."

This so plainly being a jest, all laughed; and Lord Staughton, having finished his meal, stood up and said he must be on his way.

He gave me a brief hug and a kiss upon the cheek, and with a careless "See you at the Crown," was gone.

"Stay, Delia," suggested Aunty Mary kindly. "It's late. The streets are no place to be out in after dark."

His sympathy now irritated me. "I must be going," I said.

Lucinda turned and looked up at me from his low stool. He reached out his hand to touch mine.

"I'll keep you company," he said.

He was very pretty, and I wavered for a moment. But like a fool I moved towards the door, believing then that if I could not have Lord Staughton I wanted nobody. A misplaced pride induced me to pretend that better things awaited me outside, a vigorous life of which they could know nothing.

"My friend will be anxious," I lied, "and I don't want to keep the coachman waiting."

I quit that warm and friendly place and went out into the street. It must have been ten or eleven o'clock. I made my way unmolested to the Rose to seek Endymion whom I had left with wenches, after pleasure.

I found the parlour of the Rose a changed place — vibrant, noisy, throbbing with the buzz of lust. Beyond the pushing, heaving throng the posture woman was about her work, naked and up-jutting on a dish, and candles were on sale, and only those who had pressed forward with a killer instinct, stamping on the weak, could see the sight. Having no wish to gaze on aught so nauseous I remained in the shadows, looking for my friend amongst the goggle-eyed spectators. I could not see him. I moved about in the crowd. I had my pockets felt by would-be files. I heard the curses as they found me without cole. At length, thinking Tubs would be already at the piazza where the coach was due to come for us, I turned to go.

"If you're looking for your fat friend," said one beside me,"he left a message. I can take you to him."

I went with him out of the inn. We started off down Drury Lane and had got no further than Drum Alley when I sensed that there were others following behind. I turned, suspicious, but too late. Into the alley I was thrust, and seized by many hands, and taken prisoner.

Chapter Thirteen

DRUM Alley was as black as pitch and narrow as a dagger-sheath. I did not see who my attackers were, especially since my face was flattened against the grimy bricks and with such firmness that I tasted blood. My hands were tied behind my back and I was hustled from the alley, out into the street, and marched up to Long Acre about as far as Dirty Lane. Now in the flickering lights from lanthorns hung above the doors, I saw four raggedy fellows round about me, and if I had been in any doubt about the seriousness of my predicament I was the less so when I perceived that one of them was Will Field, Mr Hitchin's helpmeet, who had ever in the past shown a most pronounced hostility towards me; and I to him.

I would not have known him now, of course — his visage happily forgotten — but for the many clues he dropped me so magnanimously, as: "You'll be sorry now, lumpkin. Where'd you steal them clothes from? Hob-nailed looby! I always said I'd get yer. This is the night when I'm goin' ter make yer very unhappy."

He was still good-looking. Indeed, fresh from my encounter with the lovely Lord Staughton and with the realization still raw upon me that I never could love women, I found my foe Will Field uncomfortably fanciable. He had a pale street-wise face, with spiky fair hair and a wide lewd mouth and those darting lizard eyes. His body was lean as a rake.

"Where are you taking me? What's this about? I haven't any money."

"Who taught yer to speak decent?" he glowered at me, as if I had betrayed some kind of trust.

"Mind yer business, pumper," I replied; and we were back on old terms.

Some boozing ken loomed up on us; we went in at the door, but not into the parlour, no, down into the place beneath, some ancient cellar reached by twisting steps where it was all I could do to keep my balance, likewise they theirs directing me, and slipping and shoving in a tumble of undignified confusion we landed in the space below. A low brick-walled room it was, with vaulted roof and blocked-up hearth suggesting it had been in Gothic times a kitchen. Upon a table burned a lanthorn; at the table there sat Mr Hitchin, a journal at his elbow. He was dressed very fine indeed, in a blue coat richly trimmed with gold braid, and a big cravat, and on the table his black three-cornered hat and more gold braid a-plenty there. His small sleepy eyes made pretence of reading, but he was well aware of our descent and our arrival. He returned to his journal with a studied indifference as false as a strawman's evidence.

"We got 'im, sir," Will Field boasted, "like we said we would."

They grouped about me and we stood, like souls awaiting judgement.

"Davy Gadd," said Mr Hitchin. "Thee has not been kind to me."

A certain apprehension came upon me, for his words, though seeming playful banter, were not so, I knew it. And I was very much at a disadvantage with my hands bound and Will Field straining like a dog upon a leash beside me.

"Did I deserve to be so fooled?" said Mr Hitchin."I who have made overtures of goodwill to thee in past times?"

"No sir; but how have I done so?"

"Were thee not William Page when we last met?" enquired Mr Hitchin pleasantly.

I winced.

"And all the while that I have called thee William I was a fool, for thee were no more William than I."

This being so, I said nothing.

"We do, however, have a William here to show thee how I love to be so fooled. Now show that to him, William."

One, now two, now three punches in the gut from Will Field's fist so doubled me over that I sagged and fell upon my knees and there remained in some distress.

"As if this were not will-full enough," Mr Hitchin paused for his chaps to laugh at the brilliance of his wit, "thee has will-ingly taken my name in vain — willy nilly — making believe thee was in my employ. Yet when I would have thee so indeed, thee told me thee preferred to work alone. Is that not so?"

"Yes sir," I croaked unhappily from the floor.

"How does thee explain as much?"

"Simply I am a liar, sir."

"Come hither to me, Davy Gadd."

I shuffled forward till my face was on a level with his portly thigh. I raised my eyes.

"Ah Davy, they have made thee lip bleed," he cooed over me. "Have they been rough with thee?"

He spread out a fat moist hand and wound his fingers into my hair. Holding me so, he brushed my cheek against his thigh, to and fro, to and fro, and when I turned my face away he chortled and he sharply brought me back to heel.

"What did I say to thee when I called thee William? *William, William, I shall have thee in the end?* I say it to thee now again in thee true person. I am Under City Marshall now. I have no little power. Men come and go at my command. Davy, Davy, I shall have thee; I shall have thee in the end."

Would he so? I very much thought not. I wondered most un-easily whether it were true, the rumour that he took his pleasure with the boys that worked for him. Had those that brought me here known his hands upon them? Will Field? The surly crew that even now stood there behind me, waiting to do his bidding? I grew angry at the notion that I might be seen as one of them — a minion, an ingle, one of a mob.

He lifted my face to look at him. "What does thee say to that? For I don't bear thee grudges, Davy, not like some. And I would have thee work for me. And thee will work for me and be one of my own. Thee were a handsome boy, and thee has grown into a handsome lad. My handsome Davy, my Davy who must do as he is bid, since he is very much at my mercy. We will forget William and let him go; but Davy shall be mine. Eh, Davy?"

"I might agree," said I, "were it not that I am already in the service of Mr Wild."

I knew damn all about the man whose name I so freely made use of. What? He had fallen out with Mr Hitchin and thereby Mr Hitchin was become very much a has-been. *"If you're against him he has fifty ways of getting you into Newgate."* This was a powerful fig-ure, there was no doubt about it, a man it seemed a good thing to be in with. The lie came easily to my tongue. The atmosphere of that room changed instantly.

"What! Zounds! Work for Mr Wild?" spat Mr Hitchin, jerking his frame upright. "Will! Did thee know this?"

"No sir and I don't believe it," Will Field said.

"How would you know?" Mr Hitchin bellowed. "Are you privy to the thoughts of Mr Wild, God damn him? You!" he said to me, and he was much discomfited and vexed, "get up, boy, get up off your knees. Untie his hands. Damnation, this is untoward."

Leaning against the table I lifted myself awkwardly to a stand-ing posture and when my wrists were unbound and I had rubbed some vital spark into them I had to clutch my midriff for the pain of it, instantly to withdraw my hold for the gratified smirk upon Will Field's face.

"Now thee tell Mr Wild," said Mr Hitchin, "that I have no wish to poach upon his terrain. There's plenty room for all in this great cesspit London Town. No hard feelings, Davy, I am sure? Thee made thee choice; thee must abide by it. But as a friend — and I hope that I am so — I have to tell thee I am disappointed in thee. I would have been a better master to thee. Mr Wild! I taught him all he knows. What was he when I found him? Just a bully running a brothel with his doxy in Lewkenor's Lane. I made him my assistant. I took him to the boozing kens. I introduced him to the thieves and rogues. I told the whores to yield up their stolen watches and their pocket books to him or they would find themselves in Bridewell. I taught him the trade of thief taker. Without me he would still be in the Compter running errands for the turnkeys. And he thinks he is become so great!" He turned to Will. "This may cost us dear, this bungle. Get him out of here."

And so, almost as swiftly as I was hustled in, I found myself hustled out again, a free man, into the street.

"Be sure of this, lobcock," said Will Field to me with a parting shove, "Mr Wild shall hear that you are in his employ. I think that it will come as a surprise to him."

I hurried off, hugging my throbbing guts, and limped my way towards the piazza, bypassing the Rose, expecting to meet up with Tubs and Dawkins and the coach, it being about the witching hour. This supposition was confirmed by the bellman on his rounds — "Twelve of the clock and all's well" — as I joined the knots of folk that still milled about the streets on their various businesses of the night.

It became plain enough to me after a very short time that nothing resembling the Ashfield coach with Dawkins standing beside it awaited me in the piazza. Coaches indeed there were, and horses champing at the bit, and coachmen in attendance, but of Dawkins and of Tubs there was no sign, and wherever our coach and horses were, they were not in Covent Garden.

During the hour I waited there I had no less than seven propositions for my services, had I a mind to go with gentlemen for pleasure. Indeed there were not a few engaged in that trade in the shadows of the pillars, young men about my own age, some with painted faces, strolling oh so carelessly, glancing about, presenting their figures to best advantage. From time to time a passer-by would pause and speak and they would slink away together in the encircling darkness. I had refused with great politeness; but when the hour of one o'clock was sounded it occurred to me that I had best make some provision for myself. I was alone, unarmed, and entirely without means. I decided that what I had rejected would be a simple way of earning payment for a room in some nearby inn for the remainder of the night and a fare for the coach home.

After all, I thought with cynicism, I knew now what was expected in that kind of encounter, in that kind of sport. I set about to show that I was now available.

Chapter Fourteen

SOMEWHAT to my chagrin, Fate now chose to send no pleasure seekers my way. Such customers as now came looking were searching for trinkets of the female kind. One fair damosel nearby gave me a most superior smirk as she and not myself was chosen and went off with her catch. A dismal half hour ensued and I was beginning to believe that I must cut my losses and sleep in some alley. But then a man approached me and asked my price.

"In truth I am so new to this game," I replied, "I know not what to answer. Whatever you are accustomed to giving in these circumstances will suffice, particularly if you know a warm place where we may go, as I am pretty cold."

"I do," my friend said. "Come with me."

We walked along together northward and I stole a glance at him. I guessed his age to be about thirty. He was big-built and broad, dark haired, with a pleasant face, large featured, affable. I looked again. There was that about him which seemed curiously familiar but at first I could not place him. He turned and looked at me and smiled. I returned the greeting, but I knew him now. My heart jumped. A warm rush of affection surged in my breast. I laughed out loud.

With a quizzical glance my companion paused. I began to whistle 'It was a lass of Islington'. The jolly tune flew from my pursed lips and I elaborated it with the words: "Fine pears, quoth she, and if it please ye, a taste, sir, you shall have..."

"What do you mean, minx, teasing me with a song?" said he, laughing and frowning all at once.

"Don't you know me sir? You taught me that song as we drove down from Islington in your milk cart. I'm Davy Gadd, the boy you hid in a manger in Henry Yoxon's barn."

"God in Heaven!" Gabriel Lawrence exclaimed. "The Devil you are!" He gripped me by the arms and stared into my face, directing me towards the lamp light. "Well — I should not have known you. A country boy of about ten years old and now a street lad with a handsome face and impudent ways. Oh, Davy, Davy, how are you come to this sorry state?"

I was somewhat put out by his apparent distress. I had thought he would be pleased to see me as I was to see him.

"No sorry state," I answered stoutly. "I merely required the wherewithal to buy a night's lodging. I find myself by chance alone in London tonight, but I have a home; I am provided for."

"A night's lodging you shall have," said Gabriel firmly. "You shall come home with me."

He sounded troubled. Well, it was nothing to me; he must deal with his own misgivings. Myself I believed that all had fallen out greatly in my favour, and I stepped out cheerily.

Gabriel Lawrence lived in a room in a house just off Holborn. Upon entering he kicked the dying fire into life and upon his elbows and knees with a pair of bellows caused the flames merrily to leap. A warm glow began to permeate the room. This and the lighting of candles showed a large bed in the corner, with hangings drawn. There were also two chairs, a stool, a table, and general signs of one who lived not richly but well enough.

"Have you eaten?"

"Oh yes, I dined well." How long ago that seemed!

"A drink then? Buttered ale?" Warmed at the fire and flavoured with sugar and cinnamon! We drank, warming our legs before the blaze.

"Now tell me," said Gabriel a little severely, "what you are about, prancing round Covent Garden by night when you say you are well provided for?"

There was about Gabriel something of kindly didacticism. When I knew him better I learnt that he had not always been a London milkman; he was once a country schoolteacher, but he found that close proximity to the boys he taught provoked a tenderness which he feared might erupt into a stronger passion, therefore he put himself out of harm's way and quit his native village. Gabriel was a man tormented by guilt. He fancied younger men and he despised himself for what he considered to be a lustful weakness. He pursued young male whores but in the morning suffered shame. By nature he was soft-hearted and trusting. The boys he took to bed he tried to convert from their sorry ways; he worked against his own interests.

"I was to meet my friend," I explained, "along with our coach that brought us here from Ashfield; but both are unaccountably absent. We came to London from the country, down the Great North Road, to see the sights, but we went our separate ways. He went after women, and I — "

"Yes?"

"I bumped into an old acquaintance. A gentleman!"

"Who did not treat you well?"

"On the contrary! He took me to a house he knew and dined me royally."

But Gabriel read more into my words. "He sounds no friend if your evening ended as it did."

"Oh, that was my own fault," I assured him. "He is not to blame for that. No, he was very good to me."

"He took you to a house," said Gabriel reflectively. "Do you mean a molly house?"

I knew that Gabriel was well aware of the existence of such houses. I was betraying no secret to reply in the affirmative.

"But Davy," Gabriel sounded puzzled. "You had no need to offer yourself for the price of a night's lodging. You could have gone back to that house if you had fallen into bad luck."

I shrugged. "Why should I expect them to sort out my difficulties? I could not presume upon so short an acquaintance."

"But yes indeed you could," said Gabriel heartily. "Don't you know anything? Any of the molly houses would take in its own from off the streets — it is to do with hospitality, with brotherhood. You could have gone to any of them — they'd have made you welcome; it is understood."

"Well, I did not know that," I replied. "But even if I did, I don't like to ask for help. I'm used to fending for myself. And anyway," I added, "those houses are for mollies."

Gabriel grimaced at me. "Don't tell me that I am mistaken. Your gentleman acquaintance would describe himself so, would he not? And you being in his company — what does that make you?"

"Oh no, I ain't a molly," I said firmly. "I'm someone on my own. I couldn't have asked them to help me just because I'd been there with a gentleman."

"It's plain that you know nothing about living in London," Gabriel said. "Going to a molly house with a gentleman and making love there is exactly why you could have asked for and expected help when misfortune struck. Slight as you may think such a bond, it is the bond which allies us all against hostility and persecution. It is astonishing how dangerous the world perceives the love of one man for another and how violently it seeks to destroy the same."

"I wasn't persecuted," I protested.

"This time," said Gabriel gravely.

"Nor any time," I said irritably. "I can look after myself."

"Maybe," said Gabriel. "But you are safe and warm now and were brought to that happy state because of that selfsame bond, the one I feel for you."

I stared, and, angered by his righteous tone, I said: "I thought you brought me here to fuck me."

96

"Not since I knew it was you," he maintained. "I brought you home because I feared for you."

"You desired me!" I accused. "You picked me up."

"I don't deny that I desired you," Gabriel admitted. "But I would no more take advantage of your present state than I would if you were my nephew or some neighbour's son entrusted to me."

"I only came along because I believed I was to earn my keep," I said a little huffily. "I ought to go then, if you don't want me."

"Oh, be still, Davy. It's dead of night and we both need some sleep. It's surely permissible in your hard code to accept an act done out of friendship?"

I said: "If you had not known me by name you would have been content to swive with me. But all street whores were innocent boys once. Why is it permissible to fuck a street whore? Street whores are somebody's son, somebody's brother. Where's the difference? Is there not some hypocrisy in your argument?"

"I own it, I admit it," Gabriel answered. "It's true that I go with whores, may I be forgiven. That I am in the highest company in the land is no excuse. Man is a sexual creature and I am as weak as any."

I grinned. "It's fair of you to say so. I'm a hypocrite myself. I've lived these past five years without earning my keep, as the companion of a youth I have no high regard for, and for why? Because he keeps horses, and if I stay with him I may ride as much as I please."

Gabriel gave a wry smile. "Let it be agreed between us that it is a corrupt world, and we have our place in it."

"Well," said I, "and I am glad enough to be off the streets tonight. It seems that I have fallen foul of two famous persons and all through my own carelessness. Tell me, Gabriel, have you ever heard of Mr Jonathan Wild? He seems to be an important figure hereabouts. I thought that Mr Charles Hitchin was important, but I understand that even he fears Mr Wild."

"Everybody has heard of Jonathan Wild," shrugged Gabriel. "He's quite a character. A sort of Honest Broker."

"I got into a spot of difficulty with Mr Hitchin," said I, "and when I told him I was working for Mr Wild he let me go without a murmur. It did not sound to me as if he were an honest broker. They all seemed to be afraid of him. Who is this Mr Wild then? What is he like?"

"Well, he's an odd little chap," said Gabriel, "but I don't believe that anyone need fear him. He came up from the country, as I understand; he's not a London man. Got into trouble — debt, I think — and had a stint in one of the Compters, but he seems to have turned over a new leaf and now works on the side of the Law. Used to live in Great Cock Alley near St Giles in Cripplegate. I believe he now lives somewhere in Old Bailey." Gabriel smiled. "The seat of justice, eh? Does that make him respectable by implication?"

We could not say.

"He sets himself to return stolen property to its rightful owner," Gabriel continued. "A chap loses a pocket book — he goes to Wild, gives him a payment, and Wild undertakes to find it. I understand he is generally successful."

"And how does he do that?"

"Now he's made a bit of a name for himself people seem to tell him things. I daresay he's kept in touch with some of his old cronies from the debtors' prison. All manner of folk go to Mr Wild. I heard he is determined to bring all thieves to justice. He is become quite celebrated."

I laughed. "It's odd — you speak of him as if he is the most reasonable of fellows. But at the Rose they speak of him quite other."

"In what way so?"

"As if he should be feared."

"They were perhaps thieves you spoke with. Such would fear him; they have guilty consciences."

"And Mr Hitchin? The mention of Mr Wild's name caused him some apprehension."

"Mr Hitchin keeps bad company. Everybody knows about his pickpocket boys. Perhaps Wild knows some of his secrets. Hitchin was suspended from his high office a couple of years ago. Did you know that? It was on a suspicion of becoming too close with the villains he was empowered to apprehend. I don't think they could prove anything." Gabriel stretched. "But as for Mr Wild, I've always thought him somewhat amusing, both intentionally and unintentionally. He can be something of a clown. I saw him once in the Cat and Fiddle — he was entertaining his cronies by putting his arms and legs out of joint. I heard he used to do that at a fair for money. His brother's something of a fool as well. He once climbed to the top of a church tower and shouted: 'King James the Third!'"

"And then what?"

"Then he climbed down again."

"A Jacobite and so bold?"

"Not really," Gabriel laughed. "More like someone who wanted to be seen and heard. The true Jacobites are either working in secret or have gone north, where the fighting is."

"One king is much like another," I said with a yawn. "None will help the poor."

"Get you to bed," Gabriel said. "You're falling asleep."

"It's true," I said comfortably. "It's real good of you, Gabriel, to look after me, whatever the reason."

"I must be away early in the morning," Gabriel said. "Shall I wake you? I could take you on your way as far as Islington."

"No thankyou. I still have some unfinished business to attend to," I replied importantly.

"Sleep on then," he said. "If you are here when I return, so much the merrier. If not, then it was good to see you."

"I am forever in your debt," said I. We undressed beside the fire. We clambered into bed. It had been my intention to give Gabriel satisfaction as he at first had hoped for; but when my weary limbs were swathed in goosedown and my head upon the pillow I fell immediately asleep.

Chapter Fifteen

JACK was my unfinished business; my dear friend Jack whom I had not seen since his mother took him from the workhouse school. I thought since I had met so many who had been important to me in my boyhood I must not quit London without seeing once again the one whom I held dearest. What was he now become? Was he still watched over by his unlovely benefactor Mr Kneebone? How was his dear ma to whom I had given my precious guinea in my sentimental affection?

I was alone when I awoke, and when I dressed I found to my surprise that Gabriel had slipped a coin into my coat pocket and I had done nothing to deserve it. I would have dearly liked to leave it behind, but I was hungry and it would buy me beer and bread at a Holborn tavern. I stepped out into the morning.

Holborn was so pressed with folk I scarce could move, and as I breakfasted I soon discovered what was afoot — an execution. Did I know nothing? They were today to hang, draw and quarter three soldiers from the First Regiment of Foot Guards. What had they done? They had treasonably enlisted with the Pretender. That which I could not learn from the babble of conversation I might read from broadsheets peddled and sung by the balladeers, ever eager to turn somebody else's misfortune into entertainment.

"In the year of grace 1708
The Pretender reached the Scottish shore.
He saw the English fleet approach
And said I dare no more.
The Scottish lords have sent for him
And raised their banners high
And traitors now do drink his health
And bid him to come by.
And now in Scotland once again
With French gold in his paw
He comes to try his luck again
As he did once before.
We'll have no king but good King George
And loud shall be our cry
And all who do not wish him well
A traitor's death shall die."

I had half a mind to stay and see the deaths, but eagerness to see Jack took precedence, and after I had breakfasted I went cautiously down Fetter Lane, avoiding Drury Lane and its uncomfortable associations, and so by way of Fleet Street to the Strand, looking for the sign of the Angel.

They were building a big new church in the middle of the street, and there were heaps of rubble and stone to climb round. And there was the Angel sign, so apt an indication of the nearness of Jack, and I recalled with admiration his fair hair and sweet nature, his devotion to his ma, and his determination to be good for her sake. Here was Mr Kneebone's draper's shop — I went inside — and there he was, my darling, standing at the counter, and all about him ribbons and silks, and above his head, hanging like sails, billows of linen tablecloths, cascades of starry lace, flowered satins, all dangling from the ceiling beams as light as gossamer.

"Jack!" I cried in great delight. "Do you know me? Davy Gadd, your friend that slept with you when we were boys in Bishopsgate!"

"Davy!" answered that sweet vision, with as much warmth and affection in his face and voice as I in mine. "Of course I knows yer!"

We clasped hands across the ribbons. I perused his visage.

"Wounds," says I. "You ain't half skinny."

Jack was then thirteen, and hardly more grown than when he was a boy. Beside him I felt big and gawky. He had a neat perky little face with a snub nose and wide grin and those bright brown eyes all full of good humour and cheeriness. His hair was yellow and spiky; he had pixie ears. His hands were thin and wiry and his fingernails clean as a whistle. Sorting ribbons and lace they'd have to be, I supposed, and I grimaced a bit, for somehow to me it did not seem employment for a sparky lad. He grinned, watching my gaze alight on the lavish display of cloth behind him.

"Mr Kneebone likes 'em all spread out so you can see 'em. He says rolled up on the shelves ain't no good. Can I sell yer a table-cloth — ten shillings each? A muslin neckcloth for one shilling?"

We laughed. Of course, there were rolled-up cloths and all, stacks of 'em, tightly packed on shelves; and a dainty little ladder to reach the higher ones; but the general impression, because of the spread silks and laces, was of a cave of delight, a lady's dressing room or linen room, the petals of a luscious flower, with Jack there at the centre, where the honey was.

Swiftly we recounted how the intervening years had dealt with us, and Jack laughed heartily when he learnt that Tubs was after all a gentleman.

"And grows daily plumper," I grinned.

"I'd like to see him."

"And so you would have done, but he has flit off home, it seems. But give me news of yourself to take to him."

"No news at all," shrugged Jack. "I stay here to keep Ma company, and Mr Kneebone sees to our welfare and I work in his shop, as you see. We go to church a-Sunday and strive to lead a decent life and are fast asleep by nightfall. Tom left home because — well, because — "

"He could not stand the general goodness?" I supposed.

"Yeah, I guess that must have been it," said Jack soberly. "But Mr Kneebone said it was Bad Blood. I told yer that we had it in our family. 'e says it must come out somewhere."

"Well, as long as you got plenty of bandages it won't matter," I quipped, scornful of Mr Kneebone's grim pronouncements. "But are you happy here, Jack," I wondered, looking vaguely about me, "in all this lace?"

"Oh yeah," said Jack, "I'm well content. We're very lucky, Ma an' me. Mr Kneebone's teachin' me to write in very fine letters, so I do Mr Kneebone's correspondence for him. I am to become apprenticed to Mr Owen Wood soon and learn a carpenter's trade. Meanwhile I roll ribbons. Pretty, ain't they, Davy? Shall you buy one?"

"Ribbons and lace? I ain't got no use for 'em, Jack."

"Not for a girl?"

"What girl?"

"You surely have a girl, Davy, dontcher? You're pretty good

lookin' — any girl'd have yer."

"Well," I grinned, "I could give 'em to Lucinda."

"Who's Lucinda?"

"Someone I met last night, and very pretty."

Rich from Gabriel's gift I chose some ribbons to please Jack, and for myself a muslin neckcloth for one shilling. Jack shouted over his shoulder for his Ma to come and see who was here, and in she came and we all had a good gossip; and when I would not stop to eat, nothing would content her but that I should have a slice of apple pie to take away with me and many good wishes along with it. How long we would have been merry amongst the lace I do not know but that we were interrupted by the arrival of Mr Kneebone, who came in through the shop doorway from the street.

He had grown more severe in appearance, more authoritative, and now stood with his thumbs in his waistcoat, frowning at us. Jack's poor Ma went scurrying back to work and Jack blushed pink as Mr Kneebone's displeasure permeated the little shop.

"It's all right, sir," I protested, holding up my ribbons. "I am a genuine customer, although I know Jack from old times."

"Very well," said Mr Kneebone, "but if we have a quiet moment in the shop there is plenty for Jack to do in the way of sweeping and dusting, without wasting time in frivolity."

"I was just leaving," I replied. "I am already on my way."

Mr Kneebone grunted and went through into the back room. I turned back to Jack.

"I'll come and see you again," I said; but I knew that I would not; at least, not in this hothouse. His little face amongst the lace so moved me that I suddenly went round behind the counter and seized hold of him and gave him such a kiss upon his lips he didn't know what hit him.

"Davy!" he accused, all flushed. "What'd you do that for?"

"Couldn't help it," answered I, and picking up my slice of pie I hurried from the shop, for if he didn't like it I did not want to know.

I was morose and irritable without knowing why. I ought to be pleased that Jack was in work and had a Benefactor who would set him on a path of industry and righteousness. And besides, it was nothing to do with me what he chose to do. But in that shop, I thought, you couldn't breathe.

I cut through Swan Yard and slunk up Drury Lane like a felon on the run. But without mishap I reached the other end and made my way to the house where Lord Staughton had in all senses taken me last night. I stood for a moment looking up at it. It was pretty tall, four storeys high, with rows of neat windows. I went up the steps. On the door there was a lion's-head knocker which I lifted and used. Nothing happened. I knocked again. This time the door was opened by someone I hadn't seen before, an ordinary chap, who looked at me in some suspicion.

"I'm looking for Lucinda," I explained.

"Ah..." He looked shifty, ill at ease. I thought for a moment that I must have got the wrong house. But then he said: "Lucinda isn't here today."

"He was here last night."

"He's now away."

"Is Aunty Mary here?"

"Aunty Mary is asleep. He isn't seeing anyone." He began to close the door.

I grew vexed. So much for Gabriel. So much for the great brotherhood. Always welcome! Havens against a common danger? It looked like it.

I thrust the bundle of ribbons at the fellow. He took it, its pink profusion clustering about his chest.

"Give this to Lucinda," I said. "From Delia."

Then feeling every kind of fool I ran away. I swore I'd have nothing more to do with mollies.

With the remainder of Gabriel's generosity I bought myself a place on a northgoing coach, which I boarded at the Saracen's Head at noon, and I arrived without incident in the region of Ashfield in the dark, while the coach trundled on to its night stop at the Stag Inn.

I walked up to the house squelching through the mud and sodden leaves. I went in at the back of the house where in the kitchen the maids Joan and Bet were still about their work, and they heated up some soup for me from the remains of dinner, with pie and bread besides, and told me, yes, Lord Endymion had indeed come home, and in something of a bad temper. I sat warm at the kitchen table where I was made much of and I responded cheerily. The sound of our merriment must have carried along the passageways, for suddenly into the kitchen came Tubs, in his fine brocaded coat and satin breeches, every inch the landed gentleman. He stood with legs apart, staring down at me.

"So! There you are! Playing about with kitchen wenches!" said he. "And are you going to tell me where you have been all this while?"

"I thought that was the question I should be asking," I replied. "We were to meet in the piazza, as I thought. You were not there; and it was not a friendly thing, Tubs, to go home and take the coach and all, and let me find my own way back."

"You must have found yourself a whore. I know you did. The women were all over you. Even without money on you, you were still a prize to them. You must have taken advantage of the situation wherein you found yourself."

"But so did you. You went out with two of them, and money in your pocket, while I had none."

"That came to nothing," Tubs said pettishly. "They were coarse and dirty and I found that I could not..." He coughed. "I came directly back to where I had left you. You had gone; and someone told me that a Beauty came and took you off upstairs. Why should I stay? Plainly you were set to spend a merry evening."

"But did you ask around? Did you go looking for me?"

"I did not; I was too enraged at your disloyalty."

"So you went home, and took the coach."

"It was no more than you deserved!"

He took a step towards me, bending over me, his eyes quite red with jealousy.

"You were with that woman, were you not? She took you even without money, because she liked your looks. And if that wasn't enough, the first thing you do when you get back is to begin again with my servant girls." He had plainly been brooding upon the matter ever since he left London. "What happened?" he persisted. "Did you spend the night with her?"

Joan and Bet craned forward, gawping shamelessly.

I pushed my plate away and wiped my mouth and squinted up at Tubs.

"I did," said I. "And she did everything I wanted, and said I need not pay her, as my body was so pleasing and my face much to her liking. And after that I went and saw the naked posture woman, and I saw all that she did, and after, she went amongst us all, still naked, and she sat upon my lap and kissed me on the mouth and said I was a Charmer. After that..."

The world was spared more fabrications from my lying tongue because Tubs lunged forward, grabbed me by the hair, and dealt me such a punch full in the face that I saw stars. I put my hand to my nose and found it bloody and my lips began to thicken. I was stunned with astonishment and pain.

"Let's see if all those females you have conquered find your face so pleasing now!" said Tubs, in breathless satisfaction.

Well, I got quickly to my feet, the blood all dripping to my shirt, and I seized hold of him and went for him and slung him to the floor amongst a tumble of chair legs, and I sat astride him and returned the favour with my fist, the maids all screaming round about us. It was so easy to best him in a scrap; he was soft and clumsy and had no muscle strength; he never could have hit me as he did if he had not caught me by surprise. I could have peppered him. I let him go, and clambered off him, feeling stupid. I hadn't meant to quarrel but I was provoked. I wiped my bloody nose with the back of my hand and watched Joan and Bet help him to his feet. Tubs was as bloody as myself, and all his pretty clothes in disarray. I grinned. Odds even. I thought that we would now shake hands.

Here I was wrong. Tubs pointed at me, spluttering with rage. "Get out!" he said. "Get out of my house. Go now. If you don't leave this instant I will have you thrown out, and if I see you here again I'll set the dogs on you."

Much as I knew that Belle and Towzer would take some persuading to run me off I took his meaning plain enough. I knew he was in earnest. I turned and grabbed my coat and went out, into the darkness.

Not far, however. I went and made myself comfortable in the stables, and Willow whickered companionably in recognition. I settled down amongst the hay, with the pleasant company of horses. It reminded me of when I was a boy in Buckden and I slept at the inn stables. I would have smiled at my fond memories but that my mouth was throbbing so. When all was quiet at the house, I crept back inside through a little window and stole silently to the library to retrieve my silver pistols.

I paused for a moment, in the silence broken only by the ticking of the clocks. I was surrounded by objects of value, ornaments that on any market would bring me wealth, something to set me up, presents for Jack, for Ma, for Gabriel. I was tempted, I admit it. But although I many times have robbed, I never stole. I don't know why I make this fine distinction, but I daresay I believe that robbery is more honest, face to face, and that stealing is the thief's way; and your highwayman despises thieves.

I took nothing, and I crept back to the stables, where I slept.

Nearly did I abandon principles when it came to saying goodbye to Willow. I put my arms about his neck, and snivelled like a baby, with my bruised face in his lovely mane, and the scent of him against my cheek; and at that moment I came closer to becoming a horse thief than ever since, and there have been moments. My dear friend, who taught me all I knew of riding and companionship, who brought me from an eager inexperienced boy to a rider of some reasonable skill — how would he fare without me?

But Willow, with the wisdom of his kind, would adapt to change, and he maybe would more easily accept the loss than I.

I gathered up those potions I had made for the calling and jading of horses and stuffed them in my coat pocket, for I did not doubt but that one way or another I would own a horse again.

I wiped my tears upon my sleeve and closed the stable door behind me. As dawn came up, chill and pale, I was on the road north.

Chapter Sixteen

IT was a gipsy tinker brought me on my way along the Great North Road. His name was Nathan Grey.

The tail end of the year is a poor time to be on the road, and though it is true that this particular road is dear to me I wished more than once that I had borrowed Willow for the journey and devil take the rights and wrongs of filching. A carter took me part way for company, and another would have, but he drove on when I said I had no money; while yet another whom I approached as a suppliant whipped his horses to a swifter pace in fear, finding me disreputable and threatening. The mizzle which had steadily bedewed me from early morning now became a sharp rain and after that a steady downpour and before long I became so waterlogged that it was simpler to keep walking than to take shelter and sit shivering. As is the way of things, all vehicles now disappeared, all folk having far more sense than I and staying at home; save for the southbound coach which came at some speed through rut and furrow with good horses and so covered me with mud I looked as if I had lain down in a ditch and rolled in it. Hungry, cold and in sour spirits, and night drawing on, I was less than courteous when I heard the cart approach behind me.

It was a small covered wagon, moving at a slow jog and a clattering of pans that hung at the sides. I stood and waited for it to draw level, then I drew one of my pistols and assumed a menacing pose, wrenching my face into an ugly leer.

"Stop!" I shouted. "I must have your cart."

The cart drew to a standstill. The horse between the shafts was a sturdy big-boned mare with a coat that shone like satin even with the rain and the streaks of mud, and I guessed she fed on oak bark as she grazed; that always makes the coat shine. She fixed me with a baleful stare.

At the front of the cart the gipsy sat, a man with curly black hair and a black moustache. Golden rings glinted in his ears. He wore a red kerchief about his neck, a leather waistcoat over a coarse brown shirt, and well-worn breeches tucked into muddy boots. His skin was dark. His fingers played lightly with the reins; he had no whip. He was perhaps twenty-six or seven. Even in my discomfort, even in my posture of shameless bravado, I could see that he possessed a swarthy beauty, and it caught me in the throat as I tried to speak.

"Either you will take me with you or I must relieve you of your cart," I said, as gruffly as I might.

"Where you going?" he enquired, speaking the clipped English of his kind. Romany was his first tongue, and much of his conversation was in that language. Afterwards he would explain a little haltingly what he had first said.

"To an inn. The Crown near Buckden."

"I know it. You not get there before night."

"Will you take me, or must I — ?" I jerked the pistol, indicating a violent outcome should he refuse.

"Oh, I shall take you," he laughed; and I experienced a curiously agreeable unease.

He gestured me to climb aboard. As I did so, he helped me up. He was broadly built, thick-necked and strong. His eyes were brown and lively. I sat down beside him, still gripping my pistol. He attempted to take us forward.

"Ja!" he said, and clicked his tongue and spoke to the mare. She did not budge. Again he spoke. She dug her hooves in the grass as if he had commanded her to stay. *"Mi dubble eskey!"* he declared. "What ails the mare?" He tut-tutted. "What a *grasni shan tu!"* He turned to me, his brows drawn in a frown. "What a useless mare she is! We shall not go a step today."

He jumped down, light as a cat, and whispered in the mare's ears, all with an expression of great perplexity. He jumped back up on to the cart.

"My friend, we are in trouble. *Bavano.* Broken-winded. No good. No damn good today."

There we sat, I and the gipsy, face to face. Wounds, he was beautiful! His eyes were glittering and very merry, and, as if to vex me further, now he reached into the wagon and took up a fiddle and began to play, a very cheery tune and calculated to annoy. If I hadn't thought that he might have beaten me stupid, I would have dearly liked to thump him for the game that he was playing, and I drenched to the bone.

Still pointing my pistol at him I climbed down and went to the mare's head. I spoke to her. Half turning away, I thumbed a whiff of the calling on potion from my pocket into her nostrils, and she jerked her head about and shifted and took a forward step. I clambered back aboard.

"You'll find she'll go now," I said.

My companion, with an expressionless face, put down his bow and set the mare in motion. We went forward.

"What you do then?" he enquired, business-like.

"As you did," I replied.

We drove on in silence for a while. I sat hunched in my sodden coat, the awning of the wagon keeping the rain off.

The gipsy looked at the pistol resting on my knee.

"Put that away. No need."

I shoved it into my coat pocket. "They're both empty."

"You think gipsy don't take you without you rough?" he said scornfully. "*Kek tatcho* — not true."

"Forgive me. I was desperate, and it made me stupid."

"Today you have no *gry*? No horse?"

"I had to leave my horse in the stable. It belonged to another."

"Take it is better."

"I wish I had."

"Good horse, that one," he observed, nodding.

"How do you know?"

"I see you before."

"You have? When?"

"Oh," he shrugged, as if time were meaningless.

"Then where?"

"On this road." He laughed at my look of bafflement. He gestured about us. "*Brishenesky chiros*... a time of rain. So now we make a fire. Yes?"

I could think of nothing at that moment which I would rather do. Turning off the road along a little lane whose wet foliage brushed the cart's sides with cascades of water drops, we entered a wood, and, pursuing the path, we came at last to a small clearing beside a brook. Unhitching the mare, the gipsy fed and watered her, tethered her and saw to her, slinging up a shelter for her; she was the most important of us three. He knelt and constructed a kind of hearth of stones and crafted a cover of deer skins between forked sticks rammed into the earth and fastened to low boughs to make a shelter round about it. With dry wood from the wagon, helped by a kind of sorcery, it seemed to me, he sparked a fire into life. Crouching there, he looked up at me.

"My name is Nathan Gréy."

"And mine is Davy Gadd."

I crouched beside him beneath the deer skin roof and we warmed our hands. Rain spat intermittently into the fire but the low boughs gave shelter.

Nathan stood up. He found me a big rough towel and a horse blanket and left me to it, disappearing into the wood. I stripped and rubbed my shivering limbs. I sat on a log in the deer hide shelter, wrapped in the blanket, the rain a mere patter somewhere above my head, and began to dry my steaming garments.

Nathan came back later and skinned the rabbit he had caught. That skin came off neat as a glove; he just seemed to turn the rabbit inside out. *Sheshu* was the name for that which he had trapped; *simmeno* was what it became, stewing in the pot. It was delicious.

Darkness fell. The fire burned and glowed, smoking in the thin wayward rain.

"You are very kind to a stranger," I said.

"No stranger, Davy Gadd."

"Where was it that you saw me before?"

"By an oak tree. Horse nearby." He showed me with his arms what I had been doing, swinging to and fro. "As a child," he laughed. "Believing to be alone."

I stared. "You saw me do that?"

"And looking in the grass."

"And where were you?" I demanded.

He gestured to the leaves above us and the earth beneath, as if he had been everywhere, invisible as the wind.

"I saw your good horse. I saw you looking in the grass. Found *sonakey* — gold," he added.

"Aye, a little gold pin, that was all. Hardly a treasure."

"But you have the skill."

"A man taught me."

"Fortunate Davy. Finder of gold," he said, his eyes speculative and amused. "And horsemaster also."

"I am not so, as you well know," I said. "I can jade a horse, and call on; that's all. Many know how to do that."

He shrugged and smiled. "Not so many."

"Have you that skill then?" I enquired.

"Give me a hazel twig and I find water — more useful."

"Gold is more useful in the city," I said. "Gold is more useful in London."

"Ah, London," he spat. "*Bengako tan.* Devil's place."

"Maybe. Not if you have gold. And I shall have gold one day."

"How so?"

"I shall find it. Find it on the Great North Road. A treasure which lies buried. A highwayman's treasure. Golden guineas. With gold, life is an easy thing."

"No," he said, "not with gold, nor without it."

"You say that because you have no gold. If you had gold you would say different. Everybody wants gold. Who says otherwise is a liar. With gold you can have anything you want."

But Nathan just reached for his fiddle and bow and played a tune, and I found myself forgetting Duval's gold, and tapping my fingers, while the smoky fire hissed and the trees hung low, and the brittle leaves shifted in the wind.

"Sleep now, Davy," Nathan said. "Sleep warm and dry."

I stood up and gathered my blanket about me.

The roof of the wagon was made of hide, sewn together, and slung over a framework of hooped spars. In the well of the wagon we lay down to sleep, each in our own blankets.

In despite of my unaccustomed dwelling place and the nearness of my disturbing companion I fell asleep upon the instant, being dog tired; but I was most ungently awakened. It must have been near dawn, for the impenetrable blackness of deep night was gone, and I was aware of contrasting shades of a lighter darkness. A heavy weight lay on me, as if the darkness had taken solid form. Against my throat I felt the prickle of cold steel. Close to my lips Nathan's breath, his voice speaking now into my mouth. He said: "Do you feel my knife?"

Wounds, I thought, he means to murder me!

"Answer me." He was lying full on me now, the knife between us. I could feel it plainly and I dared not move. I croaked out a sort of response.

"Listen to me," then said he. "Never never pull pistol on me, not in play, not in true, and empty or no."

"Well, no," I said. "Why should I have need?"

"You had need before?"

"I thought I did."

"I did not like it."

"I'm sorry. And is there need for a knife?"

He moved the knife away. "Not now."

Suddenly he clamped his mouth on mine. He kissed me, hard and roughly, biting me, purposeful, like a fox on its prey. Belly deep I experienced a thrilling sensation. My body became weak as water. I had no strength in my limbs. Quite as abruptly he ceased his mauling of me and rolled off me. He lay beside me on his back. I heard him sheath his knife. I gave a long deep breath, relief and disappointment closely mingled.

"You have learnt something tonight, Davy," he said.

"I have?" I had; that much was true; but not perhaps what he had in mind.

"You lay down with a stranger. Not wise. Another man might rob you, kill you for your silver pistols. You were easy to surprise. How you know you safe with me? Learn from me — do not take this risk again."

"Right." Devil take me, what was happening to me? I was all of a shiver. Had he known how he had weakened me? I had no defence; he had accused me of the same. He had kissed me; and what he said was true — I had no defence.

"Time for us to be on our way," said Nathan. "I go far, and you also."

"But," I spluttered, "is that to be all?"

"Oh? What would you more?"

"More of the same," I answered boldly.

He laughed into the darkness. "More is maybe trouble."

"But I would have it, nonetheless."

"When I say. Not when you say," he replied.

"But when?" I demanded.

He gave an expressive grunt, suggesting the complete irrelevance of time.

"I go alone," he explained. "Always."

"Why?"

He answered with finality: "*Si covar ajaw* - the thing is so and so it is."

"Where will you go now?"

"North."

"But I will see you again?" I said urgently.

"Soon. Very soon," he promised.

"Will you come to me at the inn?"

"The inn?" He leaned up on his elbow, ready to depart. "You

not stay at the inn, not you."

"I will if Ma needs me," I said sullenly.

"You never will," he told me, pulling the door flap aside.

"Oh? Do you see it in your dark glass?" I said sourly.

I could see him clearly now, dark and handsome, framed in the dawn's light. He turned to me.

"I see it in your bright eyes."

"Soon you'll be telling my fortune," I sulked.

"I could do it; but you'd not thank me."

"Why not? What do you see?" I said alarmed.

"Oh," he said teasingly. "Now you believe, now you don't! These gipsies — we laugh at them but maybe they have power after all, hey? Best not cross them."

"But do you see the future?" I persisted. "My future?" He relented. "Your future," he said, "does not lie at the Crown."

Chapter Seventeen

THE Crown near Buckden was a long, low, timbered building with gabled eaves and a roof of moss-covered slate, set a little way from the road down a grassy incline well worn by horses' hooves and coach wheels. A sign betokening the nature of the place hung upon a post near the road's edge; a further sign hung from an iron bracket above the door. The autumn gusts sent it slamming to and fro.

It occurred to me as I descended to the doorway that I had taken my Lord Staughton's careless assessment of the situation here entirely at face value. What if he had been wrong, and it was not my mother whom he had seen behind the bar of the Crown, the comely tapstress of his tale? Remembering my wayward flighty mother I hesitated with my hand upon the latch. Would she out of choice have undertaken a life of toil and manual labour? What of her gentlemen acquaintance — where were they?

I lifted the latch and entered.

The door gave on to a stone-flagged passageway with doors at both sides. Brief glances showed me a small parlour on the right and the bar room on the left, empty. At the back of the house I found the kitchen. It was a big room, low ceilinged, with heavy beams and an array of hooks whence onions, herbs, and hams hung; and a good-sized hearth with a roasting spit, and a bread oven set in the wall beside the chimney place. A fire burned in the hearth. Beside it sat my mother and a young woman upon a bench, an apron spread across their knees, a carpet of feathers at their feet, and they were plucking geese, freshly killed and still twitching. No, this was not how I remembered Ma, but I knew her all right and she knew me.

We gawped at one another for a moment. Ma looked well, I thought, and certainly had retained her good looks. Pretty wisps of fair hair curled from her linen cap. She wore a plain blue dress with lace at the wrists, quite inappropriate for goose plucking but very pleasing to the eye. And Ma, what did she see? The lad she'd left with Jonas Gadd was now tall and broad and lean, with thick wavy chestnut hair and a tolerable visage, no thanks to the lordly fist that had so latterly thumped it. I could see that she was not displeased with what she saw. She fixed me with an accusing frown.

"I knew you'd do this to me, Davy Gadd," she told me. "I knew you'd just walk in as bold as brass as if you'd never been away. Well, now you're here you'd better make yourself useful."

"I didn't come here to pluck no geese," I said firmly. "I'll carry your barrels and I'll work in the bar, and I'll see to the horses." I grimaced in disbelief. "Them geese, Ma. Did you wring their necks yourself?"

"Yes, and Susan helped me." She indicated the wench beside her, a rosy-cheeked girl of about my own age, buxom and smiling, and very much the sort of person I would have attempted to seduce in the barn if Mr Defoe and not myself had been telling this tale.

"You seem surprised, Davy, that I can fend for myself. Well, I have had to learn to do so, and may I say that the Crown is a thriving establishment and we do very well here and are famed for good food and drink. Unfortunately," she continued with great dignity, "the possession of such a reputation does mean that sometimes we are obliged to pluck geese. Susan, I hope that you'll be good enough to finish poor Horace here, while I attend to my son Davy."

Susan, plainly not best pleased, seemed to be setting herself to conquer my affections, with her dimpling and smirking and the jutting of her ample bosom above the dangling neck and cumbersome splayed feet of the defunct goose. My mother meanwhile most delicately extricated herself from Horace, and stood and washed her hands and dusted herself down. She came forward to greet me and reached up to plant an ostentatious kiss upon my cheek.

"Lord, lord," she said. "Have you been in a fight?"

"Why?"

"Your lip is cut and swollen. Don't you know it?"

Whether this sad state was the result of Tubs's punch or Nathan

113

Grey's devouring of my mouth I was not entirely sure, but I guessed Ma would most certainly prefer the former explanation. I admitted I had been in a fight.

"And your coat is very damp. Take it off this instant and drape it before the fire. Davy, this is very good quality. And your shirt and breeches too; very nicely made. How did you get so damp? Were you out in last night's rain? Wherever did you sleep?"

"A gipsy tinker gave me shelter."

"A gipsy? He would be on his way to the horse fair at St Neots, I daresay. You should have brought him in for a drink."

"I would have, but he would not stop. But he'll be back, he says, and I do hope it, as he was a good fellow and kind to me."

We studied each other, frankly curious. Ma was smaller than I remembered, but she was comely still and her skin clear and fresh, and her lips a little coloured and her teeth yet whole.

"Oh, Ma", I groaned. "You could have had anybody! How'd you end up plucking geese?"

"I'll have you know, Davy, that I've done very well for myself," she said huffily. "I lived for several months in London — London, no less! You remember one of your Uncles — "

"Ma, they were never uncles. I know well enough what they were."

"They were as good to us as any uncle might have been and better!" she said with asperity."When your Pa died I went off to London with my Friend who thought the world of me and mentioned marriage several times. We lived in a smart house and every day we saw a play. I remember some of 'em — 'The Provoked Wife', 'The Beaux Stratagem', 'The Way of the World' — all very good, I'm told. And we walked in the Exchange, and I had any number of fine gowns, and patches on my face — quite the fine lady — and coffee from a silver pot. And there I still would be, but his wife grew querulous and he must go back home to her. But he left me well set up when I went back to Buckden, and I had your allowance which came very regular. And by the way, why did it cease without explanation? But never mind. Another of your Uncles, being of a steady trustworthy disposition, had since bought this hostelry, and desperate for love of me, pleaded with me for marriage, and deeming it best to settle down in comfort and prosperity I accepted and I wed the man. John Shirley was his name. A big big man he was, my dear; you'd swear he was a blacksmith, with great muscles to his legs and arms, and hair from neck to crotch as thick as fur. But who'd ha' thought so big a man to keel over and fall dead carrying an ale cask on his back? But there's the way of it and that was only six months ago, and here I am ever since, carrying on what he began. I have Susan to help me in the house, and two strong lads come by each day from the village to fetch and carry, and we do very well."

She ended her recital upon a somewhat aggressive note, as if defying me to disagree.

"But Ma," I said, "with your good looks you could have got a lord!"

"That's all you know," she snapped. "Your lords are glad enough of company, but they'll always go back to their own kind, and they never marry beneath them out of choice. I am resolved to do entirely without men henceforth and have said as much to the three fellows who have asked to marry me, they all being short and bald and coarse of nature, though well meaning. You've grown good-looking, Davy, ain't he, Susan? Ain't he grown good-looking?"

"Lovely!" Susan answered.

"Leave it, Ma," I wriggled.

"Any girl that I should know about?"

"No, Ma."

"Well, you're still young," she said comfortably, bustling about now, cutting slices from a ham and a shoulder of mutton, and filling a tankard with cider. "And you, Davy? I heard you'd gone to live at a gentleman's house?"

I was silent.

"Davy?"

"Yes, Ma. I don't live there now."

"And — ?"

"And nothin', Ma. I got two silver pistols, that's all."

"You mean after five years you ain't got nothin' to show for it but a cut lip and a pair of pistols?" she cried disbelievingly. "Oh, Davy, Davy! With your good looks you could have had an heiress!"

We looked at one another and then laughed.

"We are a pair," said Ma ruefully.

"I'll stay here with yer, if there's room, and help yer."

"Of course there's room. We only have two people staying at the moment — Mr Throckmorton, who's leaving tomorrow on the southbound coach; and James Goodman, the highwayman."

"Who?" I gasped.

"James Goodman, the highwayman; he has the room above the stable, for an easy getaway if needed."

"A highwayman? A real highwayman? He told you as much?"

115

"And a very pleasant man, dear. As pleasant as you might wish to find. Isn't he, Susan? An Essex man!"

"What does he here?"

"Essex became an unhealthy place for him, and he needs somewhere to lie low. He has a wife and children waiting for him. He'll be going south when things are quieter for him. You know how it is for highwaymen..."

I sat down thoughtfully, chomping my way through the mutton. "Is he in hiding?"

"I believe he is. I don't ask about that side of things. Your pistols, dear... Are they real silver?" She fingered them.

"Hands off 'em, Ma, We aren't selling them." I lightly slapped her fingers. "I'll get you gold enough one day. You'll see."

"Oh? And how will you do that?"

"When I find Duval's gold. It's buried somewhere south of Alconbury."

"Oh, that old tale!" she said. "You were always grubbing in the dirt for something. Ah — that reminds me..."

"What?"

"Wait here."

My mother went out of the kitchen, and I heard her go upstairs. I heard the patter of her heels upon the floor above.

"Davy," Susan murmured. "My room is under the eaves."

I chewed on, silent.

Ma came bustling back. Beside my plate she placed an object, a little leathern pouch. "Open it," she said.

I did so, but before I had opened it I knew what I would find. A pendulum of glass upon a leathern string. Jerry Dowlan's pendulum.

"Ma?"

"He died, dear, in his cottage, in the winter. He must have known it, for he brought this to give to you. Mind, he was always beanpole thin and coughing, so I never guessed; but there you are, it's yours. He never found the gold, he said. He said he wished you luck. He said if anyone might find the gold it should be you. Why would he say that?"

"I don't know. He showed me how to look for gold. We sometimes found old pins and buckles from a bygone time. He used to hold this glass and let it swing. It was his skill. I'm truly sad to hear he died."

She patted my shoulder and poured more cider from the jug. "As must we all, dear, one day," she said, in the comfortable tones of one who sincerely believes her own time not to be at hand.

Later, in the evening, after helping at the bar, I went out to the stables at the back of the inn. One horse only stood there in the stall, besides the old cart horse, a bay mare fifteen hands high, with a white smudge on her forehead, and her saddle and bridle hanging nearby. I chatted to her for a moment, and then with the excuse of a tankard of mulled ale in my hand I climbed the ladder into the loft. With my head and shoulders through the aperture I paused and looked into the room.

A lanthorn placed upon the floorboards showed me James Goodman seated at a table, and his pistol pointing at my head.

"Don't shoot, sir," I said. "I'm your friend. I'm Davy Gadd, sir, Mrs Shirley's boy, and I've brought you your ale."

A couple of mice went scurrying into the shadows. The great beams of the roof sloped to the floor. There was not enough space to stand upright. I saw a low bed and a travelling bag.

Mr Goodman laid his pistol on the table. "Up ye come then, boy, and bring the ale."

"I'll polish your saddle for you, sir, shall I?"

"Bring it up here the while and keep me company, for time is hanging heavy on me."

And there we sat, the highwayman and I, as night fell, in the stable loft. A lean brown-haired man was Goodman, of about thirty, of middling build, with a rough moustache and a small unkempt beard. Brown eyes he had, and a pleasant smile, and, I would say, too trusting a disposition, for, having readily laid down his pistol, he was frank and open with me in his converse, and for all he knew I might have been the worst kind of informer, like Will Field.

"I've been holed up here some three weeks now," he confided. "This far north is way out of my patch, and no one will suppose me here. They'll think I went back to the woods near Aylesbury. We had some good times there when I was younger, going after the deer. We were just like old Robin Hood; there was a gang of us who'd light a fire in the greenwood and roast the deer on a spit and sing our hearts out, with our mouths full of venison and that's not easy!" grinned he. "That was the trouble, the singing. An over-merry heart always causes trouble, don't it! They heard us, and discovered us, and then it was a year in gaol for me. I was a good boy after that, and lived discreetly. Carpentry's my trade. I got wed, and I've three little ones to show for it."

From his pocket then he took one of those miniatures that fit upon the palm. "Wife... young 'uns." He tapped their faces proudly.

I'd have liked to congratulate him on their individual beauty in turn, but even if it had been light enough to see them, I could tell it was a most indistinct painting, and the heads mere blobs, one female, larger than the rest. I grunted admiration, and handed it back.

"'Listen here, Jim,' she would say to me, 'now you steer clear of your old wicked ways and fear the Lord.' And you would laugh to hear me swear I'd do so, but when my pal Stevens came for me and reminded me of the old days I took small persuading to go back on the road. Davy, Davy, don't you know it? The wide road and a good horse, and it goes to your head — maybe it's the wind on the heath, or the clouds that scud across the moon, or maybe it's the promise of gold..."

"I know it," I agreed, all starry eyed.

"We robbed this chap near Ilford, and took off into the forest. We took his spurs, the cole he had on him, the mare he rode..."

"The very mare that waits below? A stolen horse!"

"The same."

"She's a fine mare and I seen plenty."

"Aye, and a white diamond on her forehead. One of these days I'll have to dye that mark. Then I'll go back on the road."

"And are you someone who would rather work alone?" I asked a little despondently.

"No, no, not I," he replied. "I'd sooner work with two or three, an they be trustworthy." He paused. "I love my wife and infants dearly, but there's nothing like the companionship of your pals on the road, the brothers of the King's Highway. There it matters nothing that you're humbly born. On the road you live by your wits — you are princes all."

And then he made me laugh with tales of all the shifts to which these princes resorted.

"You place a pebble in your mouth, Davy, to disguise your voice. And be sure not to choke on it in your excitement! Here, listen..." He took a pebble from his pocket and shoved it in his mouth and spoke to me in a very different voice. "You all have false names, so that when you must call out to one another, no one is given away. And then the false hair..." He showed me monstrous wigs he'd got there — bushes of ginger hair, and others grey as old man's beard on the autumn hedgerows. We tried them on together, squinting, leering, calling to one another in distorted voices.

"And then," he said, "the mask!"

Lovingly, between finger and thumb, he showed the mask.

"May I handle it?"

118

Wounds! A highwayman's mask of fine black velvet, and one moreover that had seen action!

Mr Goodman wore this very mask in Epping Forest when he robbed the man of his sturdy mare and rode away into the night. I put it to my face and looked through the eye slits. I saw James Goodman in the lanthorn light, this highwayman who spoke to me as one friend to another.

I was pretty close to Heaven.

And yet, had I but known it, I was to be closer still, when in a week or so, Nathan Grey came to the inn by night.

Chapter Eighteen

IT was the sound of the gipsy fiddle that awoke me. I rubbed the moist window glass and peered out into the darkness. I could see nothing, but I knew that he was there. I dressed and went downstairs and let myself out of the back door. Now I saw that everywhere was thick with fog. A palpable whiteness hung in the air, scored intermittently by the spiky shapes of bare black boughs; it was the month of November.

I followed the sound of the fiddle. I found Nathan Grey's wagon and horse beside the road. A lanthorn hung at the side of the cart, and Nathan stood beside it, a lean black shadow, otherworldly. The music ceased.

"*Avata acoi* — come with me," said Nathan, climbing up on to the cart. I joined him.

"Not far," he said. "To the stream."

The fingers of mist clawed about us all the way. As the cart creaked forward I admired his skill, to move in the dark and fog by lanthorn's glow, keeping to the road.

A couple of miles or so we went, through fog which, now thick and all-embracing, now wispy and fading away, hung about us all the way. We drew up beside a smudge of trees, and climbed down. Nathan called me over to the lanthorn and took something from his pocket. A brightly coloured silk handkerchief. From this he took an object and held it in his palm.

"Look at this, Davy. What you see?"

"It's bones, Nathan; small bones."

"Toad's bones, Davy. You hang the dead toad on *kaulo cori* — blackthorn bush — till it is dry. You bury it. At full moon you dig it up, and there's the bones and nothing more. Then comes the magic."

"The magic?"

"Good magic, which we do tonight. *Avata acoi.*"

We went between the trees and down a slope where the sound of a fast-running stream came clearly to us. Nathan placed the lanthorn in the wet earth.

"This is the magic, Davy," Nathan said to me in a low urgent voice. "After it you will be master of a skill. *Chovahano.* Watch me. I put the bones in the water. You watch all I do. You see a small bone come away from the others. You take it. But never take your eyes off it. Not for a moment. The magic goes then, so you watch it, watch it always. They will try to stop you, try to take the magic. *Bengeskoe.*"

"Who will?" I said, pretty dubious.

He did not elaborate. "They are strong. They make tricks. They make you hear things. Noises — talking — trees falling. Pay no heed. Bad magic. Keep your eyes on the bone. Take it. You have one chance only. You hear what I say?"

"Yes." Whether I believed it was another matter.

"Good. I put the bones now in the water."

I heard no trees falling, but I watched the bones float on the surface of the stream, while Nathan's lanthorn hung above me, turning the water gold. I took my shoes off and waded into the water, and though it must have been icy cold I was not aware of it being so. I reached out for that little crotch bone from the skeleton of the toad as it disengaged itself and glided upstream separate from the rest. I closed my fist about it.

Nathan heaved me from the water. "Hold it tight in your fist; let no air come to it."

The lanthorn swung with a dizzying flaming arc as Nathan rammed it back into the earth. We were both curiously excited, breathing hard; the moment had been strange, disturbing. We looked at one another. I leaned my back against a tree, and Nathan pressed himself the length of me, fixing his mouth on mine in a hard rough kiss. I flung my arms around him, breathless, winded. He reached down and undid my breeches and brought me to coming, quickly, masterfully. Even while I leaned there gasping, he took my free hand and put it down between his thighs. A kind of ecstasy possessed me — I dropped to my knees, rubbing my face against the leather of his breeches. I took his cock into my mouth. His fingers in my hair pressed me against him. His juices burst into my throat.

I was suddenly aware of the wet leaves in which I knelt, the coldness of my legs and feet where I had been up to my thighs in water. I stood up, wondering dazedly what I had been about.

"Home now," Nathan said.

"But — "

"While the magic is warm."

We trudged back to the cart. My tongue savoured the taste of him. The patient mare was waiting. We climbed aboard; we drove back towards the inn.

"You have the bone safe?"

"Of course."

"When you go in, you burn it; you grind it to powder; you put in bottle. Now, when you jade or call your horse you mix powder with the oils. With your finger you touch horse's tongue, horse's nose. You jade him by a touch on shoulder, you free him with touch on *bul* — on rump. *Gry* will serve you, he will go with you anywhere you say. He is all yours, from his heart."

Bemused I said nothing. We continued our slow progress through the mist. And always in my palm I clutched the crotch bone of the toad that had hung to shrivel on a blackthorn bush, a gift, said Nathan, a gift of horse mastery; but, thought I gloomily, a gift to no purpose.

"A good horse," said Nathan, "will go many miles and not tire. And he is good horse and good for you. He will want to know you well — lick your face — know your hand. At first, go without *boshta* — saddle — show that you trust him. No need *busnis* — prickles. If you think you fall, don't grip mane, but hold on with legs and feet. Never be afraid, for he will know it. Gentle, always gentle with *gry*.

"You talk of horses," I complained. "But what of ourselves?"

"What of ourselves?"

"I suppose you mean to tip me out, and disappear into the mist."

"But I leave you with gift."

"Yes. Thank you." I could see approaching the blurred shape of the Crown. My heart sank.

"Don't you care about anything? Don't you care about me?"

But all he answered was: "I am on the road. You will see me on the road."

And as we came level with the Crown he drew rein and I got down, and with a sense of desolation watched his wagon move into the mist until the wavering whiteness covered it from sight.

"And what the devil do you think you are doing?" Ma asked, coming so suddenly into the kitchen that I jumped. She was in her night gown with her hair down, and holding a candle.

"Davy? What are you doin' pokin' about in the bread oven?"

"Pokin' about in the bread oven, Ma."

"Whatever for?"

I smiled a bit to think how little Ma would relish the idea of baked toad bone amongst her loaves. I did some quick tidying up.

"I was hungry. I was lookin' for bread scraps."

"Poor beggar. Eat is all you do."

"You never got out of bed specially to tell me off, did yer?"

"No. Truth to tell I thought we had a visitor. I heard his horse."

"What horse?"

"I don't know, Davy. Has anyone come in? It seemed to be just below my window."

It was an' all. When Ma and I went out with lanthorns in our hands we found him, tethered to the inn post, with a long woven halter made of reeds and rushes.

"Gipsy knot, Davy, I reckon," Ma observed. "But whose horse is it?" She frowned, pulling her shawl about her, squinting into the mist.

Swathed about with mist the horse stood, sixteen hands. I could see at once he was a strong one, a stallion, half thoroughbred and very sturdy, from an Irish strain, I guessed. He was young, about three or four. His colour was not bay, not black, but something between the two, dark and dusky. He had a noble head and his legs were slender, giving him a graceful stance. His mane was long and thick. He was the loveliest creature I had ever seen in my life.

His eyes glowed from the reflected light of our lanthorns. I went to him and made his acquaintance. I could not credit my personal good fortune nor my obtuseness.

"I believe it may be mine," I said.

"Yours? How should it be that a good horse comes in out of the night and finds itself at our door like a gift of the elves?" My mother looked about us warily. "What am I saying? An elf indeed? It was that gipsy, was it not? He has been by here."

"What makes you think that?"

"Do you suppose I don't know gipsy music when I hear it?"

"He was here, yes. He seems to have brought a horse."

"He will have stolen it. He would have been at the St Neots horse fair."

"If he has stolen it, it will not have been from a fair so close at hand. Grant him more wit."

"More cunning, more like. And how are we going to feed it?

Do you know how much horses eat!"

But she never told me to return the horse nor to discover its owner, but merely said that if the gipsy came by again she'd like to see him and to speak with him. In this, her wishes accorded very much with my own.

The possession of a good horse, no one will dispute it, is tantamount to the possession of a livelihood and personal freedom. Gry — I called him by the Romany name for a horse — and I began to know each other better. We could go where we pleased. Certainly I used the magic brew upon him, crafted on that eerie night of mist, baked in the bread oven, ground to a fine powder, mixed and bottled with the jading oils with which I was already familiar; but I think the magic was of a finer nature, and brewed of qualities invisible.

I marvelled at Gry's fine intelligence and loved his humour. His ears were most expressive. When he was vexed he flattened them and woe betide who stood nearby. He would prick them forward when something ahead had caught his interest or caused him concern. I could always tell if trouble loomed and act accordingly. He assessed, then circumnavigated, breathing heavily through his nostrils; he knew when to stay away. And clear as if he had spoken he would let me know 'that was a close one — we're well out of that!' He never shied, never rushed towards trouble, but was eminently sensible, eminently reasonable; and he remained alert and let me sense through him when danger lurked. He was innately inquisitive. If I worked on his harness and reins, sitting by him in the stable, his nose would be always in what I was doing, a couple of inches from my hands, offering his help; and this nose would be shoved in my ear and down my neck in a companionable way whenever I was close by him.

His coat was soft and silky. I brushed him for hours on end. His mane was long and thick and coarse and I would run my fingers through it for the pleasure of it. On a cold day I would warm my hands there, up under the mane. When he'd been out grazing he'd come in muddy and his coat would feel rough and dusty till I brushed it. He sweated after a long run and there'd be damp patches under the saddle and girth and on his neck. I loved the scent of him, the sweet and sour of it, the hint of grass and hay and leather.

From the first he was dependable and trustworthy. Surefooted, reliable, wise. He stood still when saddled and mounted, obedient to my voice. He loved his food, and became alert and even bossy, nudging with his nose, stamping a front foot, thinking he wasn't getting it quickly enough. I've known him stamp a front hoof in irritation too, but I would say that was my own fault, as maybe I had not been clear enough in telling him what I wanted him to do.

His muzzle was soft, with rough whiskers round it. His eyes are brown. He was in Heaven when I brushed his tail.

I had Jerry Dowlan's pendulum. I had a true highwayman hiding in our stable loft. I had the wherewithal to lay my hands on Duval's gold. My situation at that time was one of greatest happiness.

In fairness to myself I must explain that Ma was right when she maintained that she was well provided for, with Susan, and the two lads who came in to shift and carry, and though I helped with all my might when I was there, I was not much missed when I was on the road.

Of course I went up to St Neots, to the horse fair, hoping I might find Nathan and thank him and repay him in some way; but I found the fair was gone and dispersed, and all there was to show for it were wisps of straw shifting in the wind, and folk collecting horse dung on their spades.

My forays took me only short distances from the inn, but whenever it seemed appropriate I would dismount and try the lie of the land, looking for treasure. Whatever caused the skill, whether it were that same gift that water dowsers have, or fortune tellers, I had it, and the pendulum increased my potency. But never treasure, never any hoard. I had my pick of pretty clasps and brooch pins, ancient coins, shoe buckles and the like, all pleasing, gratifying to discover, but never guineas, nothing to increase my wealth by any magnitude, and never Duval's gold. Or anybody's.

One day I found myself not far from the old track that Jerry Dowlan and myself once took from Buckden, leading to Lord Staughton's old house beside the rooky ash trees. Curiosity impelled me down that path. I recalled my old pal and how he had spoken to me of the Collector, a lord who received such pickings as we acquired, and how that same lord spoke to us of the pleasure to be obtained from handling gold, nay, more, in merely looking at it, beautiful in those cupboards in his upper room. He had said that we would meet again when I was older... well, so we had, and he had made love to me in a molly house and called it sport, and left me in a state of sweet confusion. Or maybe it was sweet certainty, for by his treatment of me I had understood that womankind meant nothing to me, and that only in the love of men would I find satisfaction. I remembered that in the molly house false names were used. No identity was inadvertently given away. Where had I heard that of late? James Goodman... *we all have false names so if we call out to one another no one is given away.* Highwaymen, mollies... men with secrets, men outside the law.

It was a bitter cold day, colder than is usual at this time of year. You would have thought it January. Powdery snow lay lightly on the boughs, and underfoot a thin covering of the same now whitened the frozen mud ruts. I reached the ancient house, which stood much as I remembered it, mossy eaved, the early setting sun glinting on the leaded window panes, a new generation of rooks settled in the ash trees. An air of desolation lay upon the scene. Without dismounting I leaned and rapped upon the door — the little side door by which I had entered in Jerry's company. To my surprise it opened, and a manservant stood there, a big brawny chap, like a prize fighter at a fair, who squinted at me with an air of hostility and suspicion.

"Is his lordship at home?" said I.

"He is not. What is your business with him?"

"I am an acquaintance."

"Then if you are an acquaintance you will know he is from home and travelling."

"I had heard so, but I hoped that he might have returned."

"If you know him, you will know when he will return. And not before."

"Quite." I had no idea to what the servant referred. I remembered that his lordship had gone north and that he thought it might be dangerous, but not being the most astute of lads I had not pieced together what this might mean. I experienced a profound sense of disappointment. I don't think that I had imagined that my lord would have been at home and would have asked me in and taken me to his bed; but I was unprepared for such a sense of loss as now I felt, to see the house so bleak and so unwelcomely tenanted and to learn that my handsome friend was far away, indefinitely, and possibly in danger.

It also occurred to me that it would have been no unpleasant thing to have been invited in to warm myself for a moment; but I was not thus blessed, and taking my leave I rode away and sought my own fire at the Crown.

It was a dreary evening. The wind howled round the eaves. It came rushing down the Great North Road as through a funnel. The weather was turning colder. There were no travellers, no reason for us to bustle.

"The coach will have stopped at the Lion," said Ma. She sat and sewed. Susan sat and sewed beside her, and gave me cows' eyes if our glances met. This dull evening was not the first of its kind. I went out the back and sat with Goodman in his loft. It was pretty cold up there.

"I've been here long enough," he said.

"Will you go south?"

"That is my intent."

"To London?"

"Very likely."

"You were always one that liked to travel in a company."

"There is no companion like the companion of the road," he agreed. And then he saw the drift of my conversation. He thought for a moment. Then he said: "Did you want to come along a-me?"

Chapter Nineteen

THEY reckoned that it was the coldest winter in the memory of man; but cold as we undoubtedly were, I was a happy man as I rode south with Captain Goodman. A hard frost lay on the land — trees, fields and road were dazzling white, and as we rode, the waysides rustled as the melting frost came tumbling from the trees. The Great North Road took us ever nearer to London town, and I believed us free as air; when all the time we were as flies blundering towards the web.

"Your ma was sad to see you leave," said James.

"Not she. Didn't you see it? She clouted me."

He shrugged. "Some mothers weep; some belt yer."

One day Captain Goodman gave me a curious half-squinting glance. "Well, Davy," he said. "Shall we see if you are only talk or if you dare be what you say you want to be? Shall you now take a coach with me?"

But he smiled as he spoke, because he knew what I would reply.

And so came my first taste of highway robbery. A kerchief over my face I waited beside Captain Goodman where a copse of thickly growing ivy-covered trees hid us from view. I felt proud that he had so carelessly assumed me capable. He never asked if I was afraid. He supposed me like himself. We listened in the stillness for the clinking of the bridles, the thud of hooves, the sound of converse carried on the wind — two men on horseback, farmers maybe, advancing all unknowing into range. I thought I might have been fumbling or apprehensive; I was neither. I felt calm and powerful, my hands steady on my silver-butted pistols. Goodman rode forward.

"Stand and deliver!" he said. I watched admiringly, backing him up with my presence. He was pretty masterful. You'd never have guessed he was a family man, with a wife and children.

Obliging them to dismount and walk away from their horses we took from the two men a purse containing five shillings, and two gold pocket watches. The men were stout and slightly tipsy and in no condition to pursue us. We took off at speed. A weird elation rose in me, and if I had been told I flew and had become a winged creature soaring over sun and moon I might well have believed it. Later, in a barn, we shared the pickings, the greater part to Captain Goodman who had taken the greater responsibility.

However, somewhere near Barnet he permitted me to continue my apprenticeship in more active and solitary form. He lent me his own mask, the beautiful black velvet disguiser. I regretted that we had no access to a long mirror, as I would have dearly liked to strut. He laughed at my ingenuousness. He waited for me at a bend in the road, to aid me in case of trouble; but I did not need his help. A gentleman and his lady were riding together, and truly to go so unattended on a quiet road at dusk was provocation enough.

My heart was pounding, but my hand was steady on my pistol. For the first time my lips uttered those timeless words:

"Stand and deliver!"

To which the gentleman replied in equally timeless vein:

"Villain! You'll hang for this!"

Verbally quits as we were, the advantage, however, was mine. Keeping my pistol trained on the gentleman I asked the lady for her jewellery, and before I took off again I had three rings, a bracelet and a necklace, all excellent quality. Captain Goodman said a meaner man than he might turn to jealousy and resentment at the brilliance of my success.

We might not, however, sleep now at the inns as we had been doing, in case we were recognized. Sleeping in haylofts in the coldest winter known to man was no joke, snuggled together for warmth and not for desire; but Captain Goodman said when we reached London we would lose ourselves in its maze and with our new-found wealth we'd find a welcome by any fire.

Once when we lay side by side in one such hayloft James Goodman said to me: "Have you ever heard tell of the Black Dog of

Newgate, Davy?"

"I have not. What is it?"

"It's an old story they tell. There was this chap in the Whit who grew so melancholy that he dashed his brains out on a stone, and the story goes that his cell mates took his flesh and roasted it and ate it. But then afterwards they never had a moment's peace, because a great black dog came after them with dripping jaws; but no one else could see it, only those who were so guilty and afraid. And this dog would sit there, on the stone where that cull came to his end, and the stone was black an' all. The keepers moved the stone and put it in the condemned cell and there it remains, to put the fear into the heart of the man that is to die. And the black dog rises up, with them same dripping jaws, looking for a guilty man to gnash his teeth upon. And that's the story of it."

The wind howled round about us, and the roof tiles rattled. I shifted uncomfortably. I could half believe the selfsame dog was creeping up on us. I listened out for Gry's breathing nearby and felt reassured. Gry was real; the other was a fabrication. Or was it?

"Is it true?" I said.

"By daylight, Davy, I say no. By night all bad things seem possible."

"What made you recall it now?"

"Sometimes I get this dread on me," was all he said.

We spoke no more of it, and in the morning Captain Goodman was himself again, and speaking cheerily of being once again with his wife and children, and eager to be on our way south.

As we came along the Hollow Way, Captain Goodman pointed across the fields to show me an old timbered house amongst some trees.

"Tollentone Manor," he said. "They call it Devil's House, by Devil's Lane. Almost a castle, big, with a great ditch about it. But it's nothing to do with the devil. It's Duval's house, and the ignorant, knowing nothing of the great man, call it Devil's House. It's said that in the olden days it was Duval's hiding place."

"Duval's house!" I said in wonderment. And in my innocence I believed it a good omen.

When we reached London we went directly to the lodgings where Captain Goodman's family were housed. They had a couple of rooms on the upper floor of a mean house in one of those alleys off Turnmill Street; and being close to a brewer's yard and a slaughterhouse it took the stink from either, depending on which way the wind blew.

With shrieks of rapture Captain Goodman was received into the bosom of his family and a warm welcome also followed for his assistant William Page — for Captain Goodman sought thus to protect me, reminding me of the necessity for an alias. We stabled our horses further off, in Holborn, so that they should not be traced to where we were staying. Goodman had used the inn stable before and said our horses would be well looked after. I had a pang at leaving Gry, who had behaved so impeccably upon his first long journey; but I stifled it and went with James back to his lodging.

The sojourn there pleased the captain somewhat more than it did me, since he passed the night in noisy passion, making up for his long absence from his wife, while I slept with his progeny who now, far from being blobs upon a miniature, had taken very solid form indeed, and all possessed of rampant rheumy coughs so vehement you would not think to see the brats alive by daylight; yet they were.

Mrs Jeannie Goodman, with her fair hair and wide smile, was a woman who might well have been good-looking, but she bore that air of weariness which must prevail in those that never know a moment's peace for worrying about the fate of their dear ones. Whenever James went from her door she never knew whether he would return or whether she would hear ill news of him. This week they would eat well for what we picked up on the journey. It was a moment of prosperity, much to be savoured.

Replete from our good meal, Mrs Goodman studied me. "So young," she said. "So young to be on the highway. Take care now, William; don't let 'em catch 'ee. And don't 'ee believe them tales about the Black Dog of Newgate," she added firmly, "for they're all bugbears put about to scare yer. Tales to make yer lose yer nerve." And she glowered at James, who looked sheepish, as if he had been scolded.

Bundling the children down the stairs into the alley Jeannie Goodman closed the door and the three of us sat down at the table and laid the stolen jewellery upon it. How brilliantly it gleamed there! Like stars fallen to earth, the brighter by comparison with the poverty of the scrubbed grained wood, pockmarked with wormholes. There was the emerald necklace, the gold bracelet, there were the two gold pocket watches, and three rings - two of silver, one of gold set with a black stone.

"How gorgeous they are!" I breathed. "It does me good just to gaze upon them."

"Gazing will not get us rich," said James. "We have to turn

them to rum cole, and I am going to ask you to do this, lad. It'll be a good thing for you to try your hand at dealing and I shall know you trustworthy. We'll start with just the watches and the rings and see how the land lies. You'll take them to a bank I know."

"A bank?"

"That's how we call a chap who receives the movables we bring. When I was last in London my man was Sammy Edges and you'll find him at the Cat and Fiddle, Lewkenor's Lane. Do you know where that is?"

"It's near the piazza, off Drury Lane."

"Right. See how you do; and nothing less than ten pounds for the watches, and ten shillings apiece for the rings."

"Right."

"Meet me back here tomorrow night."

"Tomorrow? Where will you be then while I am thus employed?"

"I have to chase up my pal Stevens, who owes me something. I hear he's hiding out in the village of Bow."

I pocketed the rings and watches and went down into the street. First I went to ascertain that Gry was comfortable in the stable. Having been advised by Captain Goodman not to ride while in London "for it is by your horse that they will recognise you", I set out to walk along Holborn, envying the captain his ride amongst the fields of Bow, for London stank.

It was bitter cold weather, with flakes of snow in the air and a sky heavy with more. Turning down Little Queen Street I came by a devious route at last to Lewkenor's Lane, a grim narrow place, all slush and mire, with ropes of washing slung across the street to dry, all stiff with cold and peppered with snow. It was about midday. The smell of soup and ale came sharply from the opening of a door. I found the Cat and Fiddle and went gladly enough into its murky interior and made for the fire. Making enquiries of the huddled spectres there I learned that Sammy Edges would most likely be in during the afternoon; so I sat down with a bowl of that same odoriferous soup, followed by a slice of beef pie, all washed down with ale.

Sammy Edges, nudging my shoulder from behind and coughing meaningfully in my ear, was a small weasel-faced cull with straggly grey hair and the snot from his nose dangling like gristle. His manner was of one that lived in fear. Throughout our entire conversation he was twitching and fidgetting and looking back over his shoulder and jumping at the thudding of the door.

"Is there somewhere we can talk?" I asked.

The greasy landlord jerked his thumb towards a low latched door, and Sammy Edges and I bent our heads and entered. We crouched within, a space no bigger than a broom cupboard, damp and cold, the walls black with mould; and here we squatted, speaking in whispers, by the light of a single candle.

"An acquaintance has sent me, having heard that you take movables."

He twitched. "Who sent yer?"

"There's no need for you to know. I have these with me, and there's more, if you can help me."

"I used to, it's true. Not any more."

"You won't help us?"

"I'd like to."

"Then why not?"

"I duresn't and that's a fact."

"My friend was sure you'd help us."

"I would have. But it's different now. They take their movables to Mr Wild."

"Mr Wild?"

"Mr Jonathan Wild."

"Ah..." I tried to remember what Gabriel Lawrence had said. *A kind of honest broker...an odd little chap...he puts his limbs out of joint for entertainment...he used to do that at the fair.* But then Mr Hitchin had said other. What was I to believe?

"You mean that I should take these things to Mr Wild, and he will serve me as you used to serve folks?"

"Aye, that's the way of it."

I grimaced. "I had a different understanding of the matter. I thought it was the man who had been robbed who went to Mr Wild. He undertakes to find their stolen goods. And now you tell me I should take those goods to Mr Wild. It seems the wrong way about."

Sammy Edges fidgetted and shrugged.

"Is there no other bank to whom you might send me?"

"None," he answered shaking his head vigorously, and the snot from his nose swayed to and fro. He gave a great sniff. It had no effect. He drew his sleeve across his face. "It is all down to Mr Wild these days."

"I see," I said; but I did not. "Then it seems I must go find him. I believe he lives in Old Bailey?"

"That's right. Little Old Bailey. At the Blue Boar, where the street forks from Old Bailey proper. Opposite the Cooper's Arms.

Will you go there?"

"I will; it seems I have no choice."

"You may say I sent yer."

Outside the air was icy cold. The snow was falling thick and fast as I set off upon a mission which I was a fool to undertake.

Chapter Twenty

ST Sepulchre's bell chimed like a warning as I reached my destination. Little Old Bailey was a street of unprepossessing character, pretty narrow, and within the range of the unwholesome airs that blew from Newgate. Somehow all this surprised me, as I understood that Mr Wild had something of a reputation; I had thought his abode would have been grander. I peered through the murky windows of the Blue Boar tavern, but the glass being whorled and dark green I could see very little.

At that moment the door opened and a well-dressed gentleman came out, so smart in fact that I hesitated, wondering if I were out of my depth here after all. I stared after him. A small town coach drew up for him at the corner and off he drove. As my dubious gaze returned to the tavern windows and the street round about, it paused and took in a sudden and most unwelcome sight — a tall man in a doorway opposite, a great dark man, black bearded and broad shouldered, who with three strides crossed the cobbles and bore down on me. I turned quickly to make off, but he had seized me by the arm in a grip so fierce I could not pull away and was obliged to turn and look him in the face.

"And where are you off to?" he demanded.

"Just goin' home, sir."

"You were lookin' in the windows."

"Just nosey, that's all."

"You were wantin' Mr Wild, maybe?"

"No sir. Who's he?"

"I'll take you to him."

"Thank you very much, sir."

This was indeed pretty paltry behaviour from a proven highwayman, a seller of stolen goods, and one, moreover, who carried two pistols inside his coat, I own it. The nub of the matter was that I recognised this man the moment I clapped eyes on him. Badger Riddlesdon, whom I had last seen from beneath, when the lanthorn in the cellar of the Red Lion in Chick Lane had illumined his dark face with a multitude of shadows, so that the grotesque mask thereby created gyrated still upon the pages of my memory and made me once again a child and frightened. If Riddlesdon was now in Wild's employ I was in bad company.

I was hustled through the inside room, a low dark place of barrels and bottles and an inglenook; and through a door we went, into a small room of a somewhat different nature. Here was a bright fire glowing; there was plenty of light from wall candles and a window in the further wall. Near that window there was a table upon which lay a book — some kind of ledger — a quill and inkpot, and a silver tray with two old-fashioned silver caudle mugs upon it, steaming at the spouts. With his back to us, looking towards the window, stood a man.

He was short in stature, stocky in build. He wore no wig, but his pate was covered by a close fitting felt cap.

"Was I to be disturbed?" asked he without turning round. "I had thought not."

"You'll pardon us, Mr Wild," said Riddlesdon, peculiarly deferential.

Mr Wild turned round. Riddlesdon said: "I caught this cull outside, actin' odd."

"And your name is — ?" Mr Wild said looking at me.

"William Page." As soon as I had said it I could have kicked myself. It was time I had another alias. But I was a little discomposed, and said the first thing that came naturally to me.

"And did you have — business with me?" asked Mr Wild.

"I might have," answered I, and took the plunge. "Sammy Edges sent me."

Mr Wild gave a slight nod at Riddlesdon, directing him to withdraw. "Within call," he added pleasantly.

"Now sit down, William Page," he said, all affable. "William Page... somehow it sounds familiar to me. But let that pass. Feel free to warm yourself; and take some caudle with me while you tell me of your business here."

With a sinking feeling in my heart I prayed that if he had any memories concerning William Page they would rest dormant till I was well quit of Little Old Bailey. I sat down upon a stool beside the fire, toasted hands and feet and gripped the caudle mug further to heat myself, and sipped the hot spiced wine through the silver spout with extreme relish, for it was very good indeed.

He had an odd way of talking, Mr Wild, an accent from somewhere I did not know. He came up from the country, Gabriel said.

I sneaked a glance at him. He was about thirty years of age, maybe a little older. He had a hooky nose and clever eyes, a broad brow, large ears and a pointy chin. I will say later what was most grotesque about him, as I do not know if he had it then, his head being covered by the fitted cap. But I could never look at that fitted cap in days to come without a sensation of nauseous dread, imagining what was beneath.

Mr Wild sat down at the table and placed his hands upon it. He turned them palms upward. He had short stumpy fingers. It seemed like a gesture indicating that he was ready to receive something.

"Sammy Edges, you say?" he prompted.

"Yes sir. A friend of mine sent me to Sammy Edges on a business matter and Sammy Edges said he was no longer in that business and that I should come to you. But I don't know anything about it, being as it were a messenger, and may have been misinformed."

"But Sammy Edges is a rascally fencer," said Mr Wild. "What should I have in common with him?"

I shrugged. "I only know what I was told."

"What were you told?"

"It was all down to you."

He laughed. "That don't mean nothing, do it? Though I think I should feel good about it, as it seems to mean that I am taken notice of. Mr Page, I am an honest fellow and I live by helping others. You may find me here any day of the week. I have nothing to hide. I am a servant of the community. In the course of my Enquiries I am obliged to mingle with the dregs, but I know how to remain pure, and I am held in high regard."

"No doubt of it," said I.

"Did you see the fine gentleman who just left? He tells me he has lost a silver-edged pocket book. I shall enquire about, and if Providence is good to me, by accident and chance I may hear something whispered in a tavern or a market place. Maybe an honest pawnbroker will bring it to me, fearing it stolen. I may be able to let the gentleman know a little when he returns within the week. I am only here to serve."

I shifted on my stool, thinking I had better leave.

"But..." Mr Wild said firmly, sensing my intention.

"Sir?"

"But maybe I have even now a gentleman who's looking for the very things your friend would like to lose. If that be so, pray name the objects to me, bearing in mind that you yourself are a mere messenger and in no way blameworthy, but, like myself, an

Honest Broker."

"The gentleman would then pay money for their return?"

"He would. What are the objects in question?"

"Two silver rings. One gold ring set with a black stone. Two gold pocket watches."

I offered him a sight of them.

"Where were they taken?" he enquired.

"I am not at liberty to say."

"And is that the sum of the goods in question?"

I hesitated.

"Is there more?"

"There is." I knew the emerald necklace would fetch the greatest reward of all. The rings and watches were pigfood by comparison.

"An emerald necklace," I said, "containing one dozen emeralds, each set in gold. And a gold bracelet. But the necklace is a beauty."

"I'll tell you what I'm going to do," said Mr Wild. "Here's the price of a meal. Go and eat; I suggest the Baptist's Head in Great Old Bailey. I'll make some enquiries and look at my lists. Then you come back to me here and I will let you know what I have decided."

I took the money and agreed to come back. Then I went out into the snowy dusk and wolfed my way through a couple of beef pasties and a fair amount of beer at the Baptist's Head. Naturally I thought about Mr Jonathan Wild as I munched. For all that Gabriel Lawrence said he was considered praiseworthy, for all he gave donations to the poor fund, and for all he dealt with gentlemen and swore he lived to serve, I knew Mr Wild was crooked. Anyone who used Badger Riddlesdon as a doorkeeper was crooked. By this same token, I reckoned he'd be unlikely to get me into trouble with the constables, and I wanted the money; so I went back.

Little Old Bailey looked about as inviting as a tomb. It was pretty dark now, but here and there a lanthorn hung above a doorway, casting a feeble strand of light and revealing flakes of falling snow. Outside the Blue Boar a shivering huddle of female whores touted for trade, and they had plainly had no luck tonight for I was propositioned several times before I got to Mr Wild's door; one wretched drab said she would take me for nothing if I liked, just to get off the streets. Several more of the same were gathered inside, crouched about the hearth and drinking noisily; again if I had been so inclined I might have had my pick of beds that night.

Mr Wild received me in his little back parlour and sat me down beside the fire as before, enquiring heartily if I had eaten well. I could not say exactly what it was, but I found there to be a subtle change in his manner towards me. It was lighter, less wary, and though I could in no wise imagine why, there lay beneath his attitude now a mild touch of amusement.

"Tell me, William," says he then. "You're not a London-bred chap, are you?"

"No; I was born in Huntingdonshire."

"Ah! Just like Oliver Cromwell," chuckled he. "So maybe you are also born to upset the apple cart."

See, I was not mistaken — he was laughing at me; I could see no reason for it and began to feel uncomfortable.

"No, you don't speak common like the culls I have to deal with hereabouts," he continued. "You speak well but I hear a country burr come now and then. It's the same for me, you know. I daresay you can tell I'm not a London man?"

I fidgetted.

"I come from Wolverhampton," he explained. He looked at my blank face. "You don't know it, do you? Why should you? — it's a nothing place — nothing going on, nothing doing for the chap as wants to get on. I've had an interesting life, William, and it's all down to leaving Wolverhampton behind, all down to my own cunning. We men of wisdom have to leave these little humdrum holes, don't we, William, and come to London? I daresay Oliver Cromwell thought so too. London is the honeypot that draws us all. And have you lived here long?"

The question came abruptly.

"No sir."

"And therefore you perhaps don't know London well?"

"Only in part."

"Which part?"

I found the catechism odd. "Holborn," I said, my feet still aching from traversing that highway twice.

"Moorfields?" then he asked, most carelessly.

"Moorfields?" I shrugged. "No, I never went there."

"That's a pity," answered he. "But as it's not so far from where we are and if I were to direct you, I daresay you could find the way?"

"I could, but what would be the purpose?"

"I have been busy," said Mr Wild, "while you were filling your face. No time wasted here! I have been making enquiries, as I promised, and I have, as we might say, struck lucky."

I waited for him to continue. He did so, in the tone of one sure of my gratitude for what was to follow.

"Now it happens that I can put you in the way of a gentleman who will give you the cole for your movables, and he is to be found walking in Moorfields this evening. You understand — he wishes to remain anonymous and does not wish to exchange goods with you here."

"How will I know him?"

"He will find you. All you have to do is stroll about, keeping your eyes open for his approach. You won't be fearful, will you, out in the fields with darkness falling? I don't think so. You have the look of a lad with spirit."

"And how do I reach Moorfields?"

"Up Giltspur Street to Smithfield; then Long Lane and Barbican..."

"I know them."

"Past the watch house and along Beech Lane which is just nearby. Anyone'll direct you. Cross over White Cross Street into Chiswell Street, and at the end of Chiswell Street you'll see the approach of Moorfields, or at least you would do so an it were daylight. You'll see trees, you'll see the marshy meadows. You'll see a well-trodden path along a wall and folk that use it tramping to and fro. Walk up and down, that's all. Can you do that? It will be very much to your advantage."

"Have you settled with the gentleman the payment I am to receive?"

"We thought twenty-one pounds fifteen shillings. Each gold pocket watch ten pounds apiece, the gold ring fifteen shillings, the silver ten shillings apiece. He will have the cole about his person; you take the movables with you."

I could barely contain my excitement. I had never handled so much money. I nodded my agreement.

The tavern doxies were well gone in inebriation as I tried to weave my way between them. They grabbed at me as I passed, reaching for my privities and cackling in great good humour. I felt, as I struggled to attain the door, much like Hylas with those nymphs that pulled him down into the pool and drowned him.

"Come back if yer change yer mind; we know how ter please yer."

"See how 'e wriggles; yer can tell 'e likes it."

Their raucous words still buzzed in my ears as I stood by the wall that separated Moorfield's meadows. The speckled lights from windows and doorways twinkled in the darkness further off, but ahead of me the snowy fields stretched, and the bare-branched trees soughed in the wind. The night was cloudy, thick with unshed snow.

To my surprise I found myself by no means alone. There was no small amount of to-ing and fro-ing, with many gentlemen abroad, it seemed, yet not hurrying towards town to seek their household fires, but lingering in the cold night air, and passing and repassing, retracing their tracks. Most carried lanthorns and some brought a link boy along with them; there was plenty of light therefore, though intermittent. Each one as he came alongside me peered closely at me, as indeed did I at him, and some gave me a smile or a nudge, with the air of a fellow conspirator. This puzzled me.

Then came one who paused, and stood beside me. He was a man of middle age, well built, well dressed, and as he spoke to me I could see he had a pleasant face, a little marred by nervous apprehension.

"May I make so bold," said he, "as to ask whether you have something to trade?"

"I have," I said in some relief. So this must be the gentleman I had been sent to meet. "And you have something for me in return."

"I have indeed," he said. "Step this way, where the wall is darkest."

I followed him to an angle of the wall, where a small nook made a place for two to stand together, partly hidden; and here I must admit I was not a little baffled when he pressed me back against the wall and put his arms around me and his lips sought mine. The matter being quite agreeable I did not resist, but willingly enough opened my mouth to his, speechless both from surprise and from his thrusting tongue. And now his hands lifted up my coat and clasped my buttocks, gripping each cheek with a fervour so intense I felt his fingernails upon my flesh. My cock always swift to participate in pleasure leapt; but his was in advance of mine — I felt it thick and firm pulsating hard against my belly. My companion now gave himself up to excitement, biting my ear, sucking my neck, moaning and gasping, digging his fingers into my posterior, till he came into his breeches with a lengthy sigh.

"So beautiful!" he breathed. "Your arse — so perfect! Will you be here again tomorrow, sweetheart?"

"I don't know," I gulped, a little overwhelmed.

"I'll pay you twice as much tomorrow," whispered he, and pressed a coin into my hand — a guinea, I could tell! Then he gave me a brief kiss upon the nose, and scrunched away through the settling snow. Two passing gentlemen, their arms about each other, whistled at me, and I felt my neck redden, guessing they had been watching what I had been at.

I stood in my aperture, frozen like a Roman statue, feeling stupid. What a simpleton I had been! What a gullible lubbardy blockhead! There was no gentleman to give me twenty-one pounds fifteen shillings for my stolen goods. I had been set up by Mr Wild for his amusement, sent out to a pleasure ground where men who looked for men made assignations. No wonder Mr Wild had asked me if I knew London well. Had I done so, I would have known that Moorfields was such a place, like the piazza and the Exchange 'where boys sold their arses for a shilling'. A shilling! A treacherous flicker of pride passed through me — I had not even sold my arse, but had been considered worth a guinea!

A sudden recollection then succeeded, as I recalled Mrs Grizel Peabody who would not cross Moorfields, saying it was a filthy place, and no decent woman walked there. So this was what she meant.

But why had I been so trifled with? Why had Mr Wild so fooled me?

I stumbled from the wall niche. Yes, I was well and truly filched, for when I felt in my pockets for the rings and watches I found them gone. I did not suspect my lecherous gentleman, for I knew where his hands had been; but I suspected those same doxies at the Blue Boar, no doubt in Mr Wild's employ. I cursed myself again for a lumpkin, just as Will Field said I was.

It was at that moment that a sweet voice spoke beside me.

"Delia!" it said. "Clarissa's Delia, as I live!"

And I turned to see a lovely youth of my own age standing in the snow, with snowflakes tumbling all about him.

Chapter Twenty-One

LUCINDA! The lovely boy who had received Lord Staughton and me in Aunty Mary's molly house! Then he had been dressed in a rose taffeta gown and been painted and powdered like a fine lady. Now he wore the coat and breeches of his own sex, but his face was white and painted and his lips dark with a burnished gloss, the which became him very well.

"But Delia! What are you doing here? I've not seen you here before."

"I might well say the same of you," I said.

"Me?" he laughed. "Need you ask?"

"I thought you lived at Aunty Mary's."

"So I do. Aunty Mary is my uncle."

"And he looks after you?"

"Indeed he does," chortled he.

"But have you no parents?"

"I am fortunate in the possession of both parents. They live in comfortable circumstances in the city of Lichfield. Aunty Mary offered to give me a home in London. My parents believe him to be a respectable lawyer, and certainly he is well connected to the legal profession and was able to find me a situation as a lawyer's clerk. We share a pleasant existence and we want for nothing."

"Then why are you here?"

"I like to contribute to the smooth running of the household. A shilling here," he said with a flutter of the eyelashes, "a shilling there."

"I don't like the idea of you going with strangers," I said.

He pouted. "I can't bear disapproval. Don't be severe with me, Delia."

"My name's Davy," I said irritably.

He ignored that. "Do you still see Clarissa?"

I was even more vexed to hear Lord Staughton so called. "I don't like these female names," I said. "I haven't seen him since that night. More's the pity. He's away on business."

"Is he your lover?"

"No. I wish he was. He's the handsomest man I know."

"He is handsome," conceded Lucinda. "But I could show you any number of others equally so. More so." He smiled. "Do you like muscles? Men whose work has made them well shaped? Blacksmiths... and sailors."

"I might," I said warily.

"Would you like to come to a wedding party," then said Lucinda, "at which such would be present?"

"Where?"

"Holborn."

"Are you going?"

"Yes, and I was hoping to find a partner here to bring with me. I'd be very glad if it was you."

"Won't they mind? A stranger?"

"The more the merrier."

We began to walk back towards the town. Lucinda looked at

me confidentially. "How much did you make tonight?"

"A guinea."

"Very good! Did you have to do much for it?"

"Not a thing. It was enough for him to grope my arse and kiss."

"Lucky you. It's pretty cold for taking your breeches down tonight."

I marvelled at the strange convolutions of my evening's course; now to be squelching through the mucky snow of Long Lane, passing the Goat where Grizel Peabody had brought me as a boy and sent me thence in search of London's rogues and villains; circuiting the edge of Smithfield, taking Chick Lane cautiously, with one hand upon my pistol and one upon my nose because of the stink; and chatting the while about taking breeches down, in the company of a youth as male as myself whose only name I knew to be Lucinda.

We reached the dark gap where the narrow street of Saffron Hill meandered off into the darkness to our right, and to our left the even narrower murkiness of the inappropriately named Field Lane teetered down towards Holborn.

Lucinda took my arm and squeezed it, nestling against me for a moment. We were of equal height.

"I want to thank you," Lucinda murmured, "for the ribbons. They were lovely."

At first I had no notion to what he was referring. When I remembered I felt guilty, as it had meant nothing to me when I had pressed the ribbons into the arms of the doorkeeper at Aunty Mary's. My head had been full of Jack, of kissing Jack, and of his lack of interest in my kiss, as he had stood there in a bower of lace. *Have you no girl to give a ribbon to? You should do, good looking as you are...*

I grinned. "Who should I give 'em to but you?"

We picked our careful way down Field Lane, more gutter than street, slimy with unidentifiable objects, slushy with muddy snow, obscurely lit from wavering lanthorns, shadowy with folk who did not wish to be seen. At the far end we could see the jutting shape of an inn sign. Later I would know it as The Bunch o' Grapes. A surge of light now shone against the gloom. A doorway showed; above it not one, two, but three lanthorns, and one at each side of the door. Light showed from behind a window shutter, and above, in the upstairs rooms. As we approached we could hear music.

"Who lives here?" I said.

"Mrs Margaret Clap," Lucinda said. "We call her Mother."

A waft of warm air and strong perfume enveloped us as the

door opened. Everywhere was alight. I saw a narrow well-lit hall-way full of people, noisy and laughing. The doorkeeper was a middle-aged man in a white peruke and a suit of grey satin. He had a thick-jowled handsome face, something of a beauty when he was young, I shouldn't wonder; but now a little gone to paunch.

"Mr Eccleston," purred Lucinda. "This is my chap, the lovely Delia."

"You're both very welcome," said Mr Eccleston. "Go in, go in;" he gestured us past, and we were in the throng, and the door was shut upon the cold and darkness.

I once heard a street ballad about a man who wandered into Elfland by entering a door in the side of a hill. He left behind a gloomy grey world and became part of a land of gaiety and pleasure. Inside the hill were lights and music, food and drink and strange company, all beautiful, all dancing. I felt like that man.

The company, as far as I could tell, were all men, and yet I could not swear to it, for so many were dressed in wonderful gowns, with hair piled high upon their heads, and gorgeous jewels, their faces painted white, their lips flaming, their manner very merry. And while some were dressed to deceive and might well have passed for women, others had made no attempt to do so, but were palpably male, flauntingly so, with stubble on their chins, or beards, and bull-like necks above the lace and frill of bodice, as if the feminine attire was worn for jollity and good humour, with mockery and ebullience, for laughter's sake. Other men were in conventional attire, as might be seen in any street or tavern. There must have been some forty or fifty there, pressed tightly in the room and on the stairs, the buzz of converse very loud and pierced with shrieks of mirth and deep guffaws, so that the fiddlers in the corner must play for all that they were worth to get a hearing. A table was laid with food and drink, replenished intermittently and as rapidly devoured; some pretty lads in satin ambled to and fro from the kitchen, plates shoulder high and swaying.

Lucinda proved a popular addition to the festive throng and would have been absorbed into the mass, propelled by eager hands, but that he was determined to introduce me to the lady whose establishment this was; and he led me upstairs, skilfully weaving a path between the silks and satins and the sculptured coiffures and the smiling mouths and the invitations which we received and parried.

In an upper chamber upon whose air hung a loud perfume we found a group of folk about a dressing table, a tableau with a purpose clear enough — the preparation of a bride. Upon a stool before the mirror sat a lovely boy with curly hair dressed in a crimson gown and simpering at his reflection. Three people acting as handmaids patted his hair, pulled at his bodice laces and dabbed him with powder, praising him the while. One now turned and came towards us smiling.

"Mother!" said Lucinda. "This is Delia, a good friend of Clarissa. Davy, may I present you our dear Mother Clap."

In the brief moments since we had entered and climbed the stairs I had somehow formulated the idea that a hostess with a name that brought to mind an ill-visaged disease must be a pocky old hag. I was very much mistaken.

Mother Clap was a tall and well-made woman. Yes indeed, there was no doubt about her gender, and it was this which caused me most surprise as I stood there dumb and gawping. She had a sweet face, oval in shape and small, with hazel eyes and a charming smile, with reddish hair and curls about the brow and temples. She wore a gown of cream-coloured silk. Her skin was pale, and much in evidence, and upon the cleavage of her ample bosom lay a single gold chain with one pendant pearl. She enveloped me in a warm hug, but she also looked me over, welcomingly and measuringly all at once, revealing behind her affable gaze a palpable astuteness.

"You have come to us on a lucky occasion, Davy," she said. "Helena is to be married. We have been expecting the good news for weeks, and tonight shall be the night. I want you to enjoy yourself, my dear — and any other that takes your fancy!" she chuckled. "They are all charmers and any one of them will look after you; but if Lucinda is your favourite, you could not have chosen better. Now Davy — we'll leave Davy out of doors, shall we, with all his griefs and questions and confusions, and we'll say Delia for convenience' sake; and first of all, pray let me take your coat, for it is grown excessive warm downstairs, and you will be too hot; and with your coat we'll put away your pistols, for you will not need those horrid things tonight, and I shall put them safely in this cupboard and lock it with this little key and no one shall know that they are there, and they will be as safe as the King's jewels; and when you leave, you ask me for the key and here it will be about my waist upon this little thread, and so, go mingle, dear, and love with all your might; and enjoy, enjoy..."

Before I knew it she had thus disarmed me in so pleasant a fashion I might make no objection; and I found myself back on the staircase with Lucinda; and a dark and handsome fellow was handing me a plate of syllabub and offering me wine from his own glass. I took a sip.

"Harry Radley," whispered Lucinda. "Isn't he a treat!" Then the press of people separated us. I made my way to the table, where I munched my way through all manner of dainties, till finally a voice said at my ear: "Davy Gadd! Will you be leaving any honey tart for latecomers?"

It was Gabriel Lawrence. Pleased as I was to find a face I knew here, I was also a touch embarrassed. What was it I had said to him — disparagingly as I now recalled — "Those houses are for mollies"? And here was I in the thick of 'em, stuffing my face.

Gabriel was not in woman's garb, but much as I knew him, and he was here with — "You remember my friend Peter? You saw him in Henry Yoxon's barn, I believe, on the day that you and I first met."

I had indeed — naked. I had lain aloft, a hidden boy, peering down at my first sight of a grown man undressing for another. Peter Bavidge, beloved of Gabriel, and also of his own self; for I well remembered how this good-looking cull had pranced about, so comfortable in his nakedness, and with good reason.

It was plain enough from the gaze of rapt adoration in Gabriel's eyes that he still loved Peter Bavidge, plain enough also from the way Peter's eyes ran over me that Peter was a rover yet.

"We call him Petronella while we are hereabouts," said Gabriel.

"And you?" I asked.

"Gloriana," he said modestly.

I laughed. "A great Queen," I observed.

"And yourself?" he then enquired.

I scowled. "Delia. But I am only passing through. You won't see me here again."

"I hope otherwise," said Gabriel soberly.

"Gabriel," I murmured. "Who are they all? They don't all live here — nor you yourself, a milk seller. How did you hear of this? Are you a wedding guest?"

"Tonight we are all wedding guests," he answered. "Another night it may be dancing or converse or drinking, as in some tavern. These men are all good citizens, working by day, tradesmen — any one that you might meet about the streets. We come here to be merry and to cease pretence. She is a wonderful woman, Maggie Clap. She understands. She earnestly desires our happiness; and more, she has as merry a time as we — it is her pleasure to see us pleased."

A group of chaps somewhat the worse for liquor now began to

144

shout for the bride and stamp their feet and call for Helena. Now I saw the bridegroom, a great brawny fellow all bedecked in greenery, like the Green Man, with garlands on his head and neck and calling for his bride.

"Joseph Chicheley, a cooper from Wapping," murmured Gabriel in my ear. "We call him Stella Sweetbeer."

The fiddlers ceased their tune, and down the stairs came Mother Clap, strewing dried flowers from an urn, like Flora, rollicking, luxuriant, abundant; and behind her Helena in saintly pose, hands clasped together; followed by two nymphs more, with beribboned periwigs and gowns of taffeta, and farmboys' boots as big as barges. Now stepped forward a man made to seem a priest, and there by the table did he read fine verses from a book, and took the hands of Helena and Stella Sweetbeer and pressed them together, and we crowded nearer to hear all, pushing and nudging and, yes, groping and squeezing.

" — to love her and frig her all the days of my life..." And there, it was done, and Mr Eccleston opened up a door, and the fiddlers started up the music again and the contented couple went into the room beyond the door and there within was revealed a great bed. Mother Clap went briskly in and turned the coverlet back and beckoned, and the fortunate pair embraced, to cheers and a variety of suggestions and advice, far bawdier than the song about the nag so stiff and warm with his bags of provender underneath his chin. Then Stella Sweetbeer very pointedly closed the door, to howls of disappointment.

Now some began to dance and some to eat, and many who had lighted upon one they liked, to kiss, and sit together fondling, and Mother Clap wafted to and fro like a summer breeze, encouraging all: "Enjoy, enjoy..."

"Davy!" said Lucinda, appearing as it seemed from nowhere. "I've been looking for you. Your big friend is with his lover — see, you'll get no further converse with him tonight." It was Gabriel to whom Lucinda pointed, locked in the arms of Peter Bavidge, oblivious to all. "Will you," said Lucinda, "pass the time with me instead?"

"Where?" I murmured dubiously, casting a hesitant glance at those couples so seemingly careless of observers, who were embracing, handling each other openly, blatantly inviting comment and envy.

"Upstairs," said Lucinda, and I followed him there. He led me into a bedroom, where behind a curtain lay a narrow trundle bed, and here he put his arms around my neck and kissed me. As I responded I was startled by the surge of pleasure that rose up in me. Why it should surprise me that this very pretty youth should thus engender lust in me I know not, except that he had not the beauty of Lord Staughton nor the roughness and mystery of Nathan Grey, who up till now had been the ideals of my fancy. We clung together, pressing our bodies close, then stumbled down upon the bed, tugging at the hindrance of our clothes. In the darkness we could see nothing, but there was a thrilling excitement in the touch of skin on skin as our limbs entwined and we felt the rising hardness of each other's cock. Lucinda lay upon his belly and I sprawled across him, moving against the warm globes of his arse. My eager juices flowed; and from his most contented moanings, so, I guessed, did his. We lay close in one another's arms, sleepy now; and shortly drifted into slumber.

It never crossed my mind to think of Jonathan Wild who had played me such a prank, nor of Gry my precious steed whickering in his stable, nor of James Goodman my companion of the road, who was gone to Bow upon a stolen horse, with stolen goods upon him.

Chapter Twenty-Two

LUCINDA'S given name was Ralph Marchant. He was sixteen years of age. He had dark hair — a fine chestnut merging into auburn and smooth to the touch — and blue eyes. His nose was perhaps over large but it was not unbecoming. His lips were full, beautifully shaped. He had a mole a little to one side of his mouth. His ears were very pretty; his eyelashes were very long. He was slender in build. All this I saw as for the first time, as the daylight caught us and I watched him wake, his face framed in the softness of his hair.

He smiled at me, and as our eyes met we both saw the flames of lust arise within. I lay upon him, kissing him, stroking the warm hair at his crotch, handling him. I gripped his buttocks and we moved against each other, belly to belly, taking our pleasure till we were both sated. Our eyes met closely once again, and we saw there shared satisfaction. I lay back and let my breathing calm itself.

"I have to be away," I said.

"Oh Davy, so soon?" he pouted.

"I have things to do."

"What things? Where will you go? When will you be back? When shall I see you?" He clutched at me. "You were carrying pistols, Davy. You will not put yourself in danger?"

I laughed, fending off his solicitude. Truth to tell, I felt uneasy at his questioning; it made me think it must be thus with anxious wives, always to be called to account.

"No, no," I shrugged, reaching for my discarded clothes.

"I'll get some water for you; you can wash and eat before you go."

It was well into the afternoon when I quit Mother Clap's house; we had slept all morning. I did not see the good dame, but the cupboard where my pistols lay was unlocked and I retrieved them. In many a room and on the stairs there were sleepers awakening, and people to and from the necessary house; and in the kitchen there was the wherewithal for a good breakfast. Lucinda was attentive to me, and I kissed him a swift goodbye and promised not to leave London without seeing him; he would be found at Aunty Mary's.

I stepped out into the cold daylight, trudging through the filthy snow to the little street where Gry was stabled; all was well. I gave further payment to the innkeeper. I nuzzled Gry about the neck and told him he'd soon be upon the road; and he gave me a wise lugubrious look, as if he knew otherwise.

Then off I strode to Little Old Bailey, and made straight for Mr Jonathan Wild's den. I entered the tavern. Two doxies, ghastly by daylight, were sharing a jug of gin. They eyed me blearily and lifted their cups to me as I passed. I knocked upon the door of the parlour where I was received yesterday and Mr Wild's voice told me to enter. I was relieved he was alone; this would be easier than I had anticipated. I closed the door behind me, and stood, leaning against it.

"Mr Wild," I said, "I am come for my reckoning."

Mr Jonathan Wild, seated at his table, writing, closed the ledger smartly and smiled at me, as pleasant as if we were on the best of terms.

"Mr Davy Gadd," says he. "What a delightful surprise."

This salutation took the wind out of my sails well enough, since I had been William Page when we parted. However he may have come by my name it boded no good to me.

"A surprise I do not believe it to be," I countered. "I am come to enquire of you why you have so mistreated me and to regain my property, which I daresay you know something about."

"And how have I mistreated you?" said he, most affable in

147

manner.

"You know very well how, sir," answered I. "You sent me to a place known to be one where gentlemen seek others of their own sex for pleasure, persuading me the while that I would find a buyer for my valuables."

"And did you so?" he sniggered. "Did you find a buyer for your... valuables?" He was consumed with enjoyment at his own wit. "I believe that along the Sodomites' Walk there is much to do with buying and selling."

"It was an ungallant act to play such a trick. I wonder at your reasoning, Mr Wild."

"Malicious mischief, purely," grinned he. "Tit for tat. Did you not spin me a yarn concerning one William Page? I thought I recognized the name. I never forget a name — to the misfortune of some! When you were gone to dine, at my expense, I made enquiries of one known to you and me, and learnt a pretty tale. Will Field is close with me. Will Field is, you might say, in my pocket. I see from your expression that you recall Will Field."

"I do. A pocky little swine."

"He holds your good self in equal regard," chortled Jonathan. "He had much to tell concerning your past exploits, Davy Gadd. It seems you have more than a nodding acquaintance with my old crony Under City Marshall Hitchin, but that you pull yourself clear of him by boasting that you work for me. Is this a happy premonition on your part, I ask myself? Be that as it may... Any lad with a comely face and a trim figure, both of which you have, who has been one of Mr Hitchin's boys, will find himself at home on the Sodomites' Walk, and I lose no sleep over having sent you there. Why, I might even have done you a favour thereby, and put you into the path of an eager lusty lover. I was no little pleased at the aptness of my prank. No one, Davy, fools with me."

"Very well," said I. "I was not honest with you. But I was never one of Mr Hitchin's boys. Though he did ask me to be," I conceded.

"And you refused so tempting an offer?" he mocked. "Davy, you surprise me — what, has he never buggered you? I had no idea. I believed you were no stranger to the joys of buggery. Virgin even? But perhaps not so, now that you have been... trading?"

"I know nothing of buggery," I said tetchily. "But I would like to know more of the goods of mine which the drabs in the next room stole from me and I suppose handed to you?"

"Which goods could those have been?"

"Two silver rings, one gold, and two pocket watches. We agreed their value to be twenty-one pounds fifteen shillings."

"I don't recall."

"No? I have these shall remind you, Mr Wild."

I pulled a pistol on him. "You have played enough with me. Give me my dues and have done."

A look of pure astonishment crossed his face. "Come now, Davy, there's no need for this!"

"The money, Mr Wild."

"Well, I have never disputed with a chap that holds a pistol at me. I must do as you suggest. How fierce you have become, Davy!"

Opening a drawer in his desk Mr Wild took out a handful of cole and he counted out the sum that I required. He slid it across to me and I grabbed it. I filled my purse and pockets.

"Davy," Mr Wild said, "I could do with such a one as you."

"What for?"

"I know you work the road, Davy. You'll do well there. But I'll say to you as I have said to others: as trade goes at present you stand but a queer chance; for when you have taken anything, the fencing culls and flash pawnbrokers will hardly give you a quarter of what it's worth, and if you offer it to a stranger it's ten to one you'll be arrested, so that there's no such thing as a man's living by his labour. If he don't like to be half starved he must run the hazard of being topped or, as they say, made to dance from a ribbon of hemp, which, let me tell you, is a damned hard case." He leaned back in his chair, pretty comfortable with himself and not much like someone who thought it likely he'd be shot at. "Now if you'll take my advice," he said, "I'll put you in a way to remedy all this. Next time you have gold rings and silver and two pocket watches, let me know all the particulars and I'll engage to pay back the goods to the cull that owns them and raise you more cole by doing so than you can expect from the rascally fencers. And more, I'll undertake that you shall be yet more successful in your chosen craft. Trust me, I know what I am about."

"You are mistaken," I said cautiously. "Why should you think I got the movables upon the road?"

"Did you not speak to me of an emerald necklace? One dozen emeralds set in gold? And a gold bracelet?"

Mr Wild spoke in a kind of surprise, as if he may have been absent minded and needed confirmation of what he supposed.

"I believe I may have done. But they need not concern us, for another has them, and he may have other plans." I was uneasy now and blustering foolishly, standing there with my pistol, feeling nothing like as masterly as the weapon should have made me.

"My proposition stands," said Mr Wild. "I have all London at my fingertips. All the best men. A brotherhood. Loyal to the death. You would be a fool to turn your back on such an offer, which is not made lightly. And Davy, it seems clear to me that who does not work for me, works against me."

"Mr Wild," I said, "I will be honest with you. I am not insensible of the honour you do me in asking me to join with those who serve you. But I have to say to you what I once said to Mr Hitchin. I don't work in a gang. I work on my own. I don't like being obligated. What you call brotherhood is like chains to me. I can't be beholden; it don't suit me. I like to break away when it pleases me. I am no good to you, see. I would not be what you want."

"Let me be judge of that, Davy. Must I ask you once again?"

"My answer will be the same. I must refuse."

"You'll not survive a month without my patronage, I tell you bluntly," said Mr Wild a touch unpleasantly. "I tell you as a friend this time. At another time perhaps not so."

"Pardon me, I shall take my leave."

"Do so, by all means; I care not," Mr Wild said with studied indifference, opening his ledger. He waved me away with a careless gesture.

"Oh, and by the by..."

"Sir?" I turned, on my way to the door.

"James Goodman the highwayman was taken last night at Bow. His horse was recognized — the one he stole and had not the wit to disguise. There was a brief pursuit. There being no doubt of his identity he was taken at once to Newgate, where he now resides. Found upon him was an emerald necklace and a gold bracelet. The necklace was a beauty — a dozen emeralds set in gold." Mr Wild fetched a long sigh. "He was a chap who thought he could do without the protection of Jonathan Wild —just like yourself. Good day to you."

Chapter Twenty-Three

"IS this another trick?" I said, and stood there stupidly with my pistol at half mast, as useless as a hedgerow twig.

"There'll be no more tricks between us two," said Jonathan shortly, dipping his quill and beginning to write. "Of the kindness of my nature I'll grant William Page the credit for being James

Goodman's companion of the road. William Page has fled. But Davy Gadd is known to me and if I find him sniffing around Newgate I'll be obliged to reconsider who exactly Goodman's thieving pal might have been. And now be off with you before you further waste my time."

I went, tucking the weapon back under my coat. I was consumed with guilt and remorse. While I had been romping at the molly house my companion of the road had been taken, had been dragged to Newgate and incarcerated. And if I had been there with him, as I might well have been, there now would I be. Or, maybe my being there would have made the difference, and together we might have beaten off his assailants. In a state of great agitation and a prey to morbid thoughts I walked the frozen streets for hours, wary, fearing to be robbed or followed. I slept that night in the stable loft above Gry's stall.

Next day I went to Captain Goodman's lodgings. I found his wife there, her face gaunt and tear-streaked.

"You shouldn't have come, Davy. It's not safe here now."

"I want to help. What can I do?"

"Nothin'. He wouldn't want it on his conscience if you ended up in there with him."

"I can't just stand by."

"It's all right, Davy. It's all in hand. His old gang will get him out, his gang from Essex days. They're here in London. Don't you go anywhere near the Whit. You stay well clear. You promise me. Your ma's been good to Jamie. Jamie and me we won't repay her with a bad turn. So you stay well clear; you don't go near the Whit. And don't you fret, I tell you; it'll all work out."

"Take this then. It's our pickings. Take it all."

She gasped at the sight of so much wealth, so rudely strewn about the table, as my pockets disgorged their contents. But she said: "I can't take it all."

I laughed wrily. "It weighs me down. I'm scared I'll be set upon; any thief of quality could see my pockets stuffed a mile off."

Jeannie Goodman scooped the bulk of it away and I took enough to content me.

"His mask," I said hesitantly. "I still have his velvet mask. Would you like it?"

"Like I want a black eye," said Jeannie darkly. "Keep the whoreson thing; I never want to see it again."

I loafed around London, waiting to hear the news of James Goodman's rescue. Instead I heard the news of his being brought to trial. I went hurriedly to the Old Bailey Justice House which stood in a courtyard at the end of an alley called Sessions' House Yard. The prisoners, all in their chains, would be standing in the Bail Dock, which lay open to the air, ringed about with a wall of iron spikes. When I got there a great crowd was dispersing, still buzzing with the excitement of what they'd seen. James Goodman had escaped! Chained as he was, he had overleapt the wall, and willing hands had eased him over the spikes and hurried him into the press of people. He was out.

The flood of relief that overtook me warmed me from head to toe like a draught of mulled ale — no mean achievement on that bitter icy day. So! James Goodman had escaped. His Essex gang had seen to it. He would be free to ride the highways once again. Where would he go? If that were me, I thought in gleeful contemplation, I would have taken off along the Great North Road — I would be out through Islington by now, and I'd not stop till I'd put fifty miles behind me and this place. Fifty? No, a hundred. Up past Alconbury, cocking my fingers at the gibbet, I'd not sleep till I made Grantham.

I was so elated I must celebrate. I strode off towards Aunty Mary's house and I knocked upon the lion's-head knocker with all my might. That same gloomy fellow who had opened it before when I had thrust a bunch of ribbons into his arms, now let me in, but this time I was not to be gainsayed, and his morose manner did not hinder me.

"I must see Lucinda."

"Ah," he grumbled tolerantly, "that young wench is such a heartbreaker..." and he called Lucinda for me, who came tripping down the stairs, all in a gown of pale blue velvet.

"Davy! Wicked!" He flew at me. "How could you be gone from me so long?"

"Not so long," I maintained defensively.

"My arse in a bandbox!" he cried flamboyantly. "Eternity!"

I grinned at his particular oath. "If you will have it so. But I am here now and I want you to rejoice with me. I have had good news. Where shall we go?"

"Take me to the Frost Fair," said Lucinda. "I am all ready; I was intending to go out."

"What, in your female gown?"

"Indeed. I often do. Do you think I can't get away with it? Believe me, no one will know."

"Agreed," I said with a light heart. "To the fair."

Lucinda and I took a coach down to the frozen river. Between the Bridge and Temple Stairs the great fair spread, a village of stalls and shops and entertainments. Gaudy tents showed gaily against the street of ice, their pennants fluttering in the wind. We picked our way cautiously, tumbling over more than once. Some folk had made a long glittering slideway, others had sleds and big flat shoes made out of baskets. We ate roast chestnuts and hot pies and drank mulled wine. There was a wooden effigy of the Pretender James Francis Edward Stuart, who had arrived in Scotland and declared himself King of England. It was painted like a grinning goblin, with a box of coloured balls nearby, which you could shy at it and knock it down. I knocked it down half a dozen times and onlookers cheered; but neither I, nor, I believe, they knew much about the fighting in Scotland, nor cared which king sat on the throne.

Lucinda wore a velvet cape and hood, and hugged my arm, and walked as daintily as he might, and a pedlar offered me a phial of Hungary water 'for the lady' and I purchased it and gave it to Lucinda.

"It's Ma Clap's favourite," he said; so we bought some for her as well. We were merry in a pleasing careless kind of way. I thought of nothing more serious than how to keep upright.

It was not until we walked back towards Drury Lane that we spoke of matters dear to us.

"You never told me, Davy, what your good news might be, that we have been so amiably celebrating."

"James Goodman has escaped."

"James Goodman?"

"The highwayman. Don't you know anything, rosebud?" I teased.

"I believe I did hear something."

"He was to be tried at the Old Bailey. While he was waiting in the yard he leapt to freedom. With his fetters yet upon him he broke free. His old gang smuggled him away. It's most marvellous. But then, that is the way with highwaymen. Their deeds are always heroic."

"I'm pleased to hear that he is free," Lucinda conceded. "But — ?"

"Any man that goes upon the road knows that the end is always Tyburn tree."

"Not so!" I protested. "He has a fair chance of long life if he has a good horse and a brave heart."

"They all die young," Lucinda insisted.

"The unlucky ones. But Goodman is free."

"Till he is captured once again."

"Why are you so dreary on this matter?" I cried. "Don't you count the highwayman's life a merry one? A Gentleman of the Road, his own master, respected by all common thieves, a romancy adventurer?"

"Since death comes soon enough to all I think he is a fool that courts it before his time."

"You disappoint me, sweetheart. You are a huswife at heart and have no fine spirit."

"Why is this matter so important to you?" said Lucinda curiously. "What is a highwayman's life to you?"

"It is the one that I have chosen."

"How can that be? You are here in London with me, not on some far highway."

There was something of the braggart in my reply, I fear. "I was with James Goodman."

Lucinda stopped short and looked at me in horror and dismay. For a moment I was afraid. I had boasted like a swaggering soldier, to impress him. What an idiot I had shown myself to be!

"Lucinda," I said, "I have put my life in your hands by that confession."

"Oh yes indeed," he shrugged dismissively. "Don't talk of lives and hands. As if I would speak of that to anyone! But what a waste — to hazard your youth and beauty for so pointless a cause. How did you come to cherish such an unworthy ambition as to become a highwayman?"

"Because of Claude Duval," I said.

"Oh? He came and asked you?" said Lucinda with sarcasm.

"Naturally not; he is long since dead. But his memory calls me to be like him. A short life and a merry. And afterwards a name, a reputation."

Lucinda gave a snort of exasperation. "Claude Duval? Let me show you something."

"What?" I said ungraciously.

Lucinda darted down a sidestreet and I followed. We were close by Covent Garden; I could see the pillars of the piazza as we drew near. Lucinda splashed prettily through the miry snow ruts towards the portico of St Paul's church.

Cold as it was in the street it was yet colder inside the church. Gloomy too, for dusk was fast approaching. Lucinda boldly took a candle and stepped along the aisle. He stopped and knelt and showed me by the candle's light a white marble slab, whereon I saw engraved a coat of arms and verse.

"What does it say?" I squinted at the jumble of words.

"You can read, surely?"

I knelt. A little haltingly I read it out:

"Here lies Duval. Reader, if male thou art
Look to thy purse. If female, to thy heart.
Much havoc has he made of both, for all
Men he made stand, and women he made fall.
The second Conqueror of the Norman race
Knights to his arm did yield, and ladies to his face.
Old Tyburn's glory, England's illustrious thief,
Duval the ladies' joy, Duval the ladies' grief."

"Oh Ralph!" I said awed. "His grave!"

"I brought you here," said Lucinda implacably, "to show you what he is, this cull you so revere. A skeleton beneath a slab, and worms and creatures picking at his carcase. And stinking the while. In short, dead."

"But naturally he is dead," I said irritably. "He lived fifty years ago. All those which were young men when he was are now dead, or at least very old. But unlike them, he has Passed into Legend."

I was silent, moved beyond belief. I stroked the words of the verse most tenderly.

"Did you know," I said, "he lay in state, like a king, with a bodyguard at each corner of the bier, and candles lit, and women came in droves to weep for him."

"An exercise in futility," said Lucinda firmly, "for I daresay that all their tears did not cause him to jump up again."

"How can you be so heartless who in other ways are full of sentiment?"

"If he had done as others do he would perhaps have lived to a good old age and pleasured many and enjoyed a useful life. But no, he must take to the road and rob and thus make enemies and end his days a spectacle and dangling from a noose."

"He made death glorious," I replied. "He was brave to the end. His cart was covered in flowers. The cheering crowd threw nosegays. Ladies of high quality went with him to the gallows, masked, to hide their rank and station. Everyone was weeping. It was all very beautiful."

"What flowers?" said Lucinda.

"Eh?"

"I said what flowers covered his cart?"

"How would I know?" I said testily. "Roses, I daresay. Lilies, lavender, that sort of thing."

"But I have heard he died in January," Ralph remarked. "So, which flowers? Who told you there were flowers?"

"It's in the Legend," I said stubbornly.

"You tell me of the Legend," said Lucinda. "I tell you what is true. What is true is that they all die, highwaymen, before their time; and come to this."

"I shall come back here alone," I said huffily, "and pay my respects without your profane cackling."

Lucinda shrugged and flounced, and the heels of his shoes pattered on the stone-flagged floor, and his petticoats swished and rustled.

"My own ambition," he said over his shoulder, "is far more reasonable than yours. I intend to become indispensable to a great nobleman. He will look after me during his lifetime and leave me a fortune in his will. And many such come to Aunty Mary's. I shall almost certainly be fortunate." Then he added, half in earnest, half in jest: "It will be useful, will it not, if ever I need to ask for a pardon for anybody."

I went home with him to Aunty Mary's, and we spent the night together in a lovely feather bed, Lucinda's own. We sank into its all-embracing warmth with rapturous delight. Aunty Mary warmed it for us with a warming pan. As he removed it he wished us good night, sweet dreams and many hours of love. I had never slept so comfortably since I had slept with Tubs. We made love swiftly, superficially, and fell asleep.

Next day the talk upon the streets was all of how James Goodman was recaptured. He had not ridden off along the Great North Road. He had gone to his lodgings to be with his wife and children. I blanched at his stupidity. On Jonathan Wild's instructions Will Field had followed him from the Old Bailey and found where he lived. With a posse of turnkeys from Newgate, Mr Jonathan Wild arrested him; and he was hanged at Tyburn.

I saw it. It was not glorious at all.

Chapter Twenty-Four

TRUTH to tell, I was more shaken by the nubbing of Captain Goodman than I cared to admit. I was not a particularly reflective boy, as must be apparent. Things happened to me; I received them; I moved on. I was not one to take a notion, mull it over, play with it and make a philosophy. I had known poverty and riches, but I tolerated the one and did not sigh overmuch at the lack of the other. I had known the indifference of both parents, the demise of one and the waywardness of the other, all without the need to make a song and dance of it. I had committed highway robbery with enthusiasm and no dwelling whatsoever upon the rights and wrongs of it. On the whole I acted generally without too much thinking. When I saw James Goodman hanged I turned my back on London without more ado, and, unlike Dick Whittington, when I reached Highgate I kept going. All the bells in London could not have chimed me back. Who has heard the bells of St Sepulchre has heard enough of bells.

The night before he is to die, the condemned man hears in his cell the bellman ringing his handbell, a horrid high-pitched jangle like enough to give a man the shivers, and this same eerie messenger calls out a gloomy warning in poetic form, thus:

"All you that in the condemned hole do lie,
Prepare you, for tomorrow you shall die.
Watch all and pray, the hour is drawing near
That you before the Almighty must appear.
Examine well yourselves, in time repent
That you may not to eternal flames be sent,
And when St Sepulchre's bell tomorrow tolls
The Lord above have mercy on your souls."

This grisly bellman has come down from St Sepulchre's church along a secret passage leading to the condemned cell of Newgate and there he stands, a-ringing of his bell, a-telling of his message. St Sepulchre! The name of a tomb! No homely saint, not a Thomas nor a Stephen nor the gentle St Mary, nor even St Alban a martyr of our nation, but a tomb — that is the church that nourishes the prisoners in the Whit.

In the morning from the four pointed turrets of the tower comes the sound of St Sepulchre's bell, deep and sonorous, carrying across the cold clear air to let the world know one is to be hanged.

Then comes a carnival, then is the highwayman a hero. Crowds throng, women blow kisses, soldiers with pikes force a way, pedlars hawk ribbons and ballads and trinkets with the face of the hero painted on them. Off goes the cart with the hero and his coffin and the prison chaplain, who till the last pesters the highwayman for lewd salacious titbits from his wicked life, to sell that evening on a broadsheet. Down Snow Hill, up Holborn, along the Oxford road, towards the fields of Marylebone, to the mother and father of all gibbets, Tyburn Tree, a three-armed monster so big that there is hanging room for twenty-one.

A man of sensibility would never have tumbled into the muddle in which I found myself then. Believing all my life that hanging was a hero's death, that Claude Duval went from the world in a whirl of glory and his bold spirit ascended with a laugh on clouds of gold, I never thought what it might be like to see the nubbing of a chap I shared a hayloft with, or a piss in a ditch, or a laugh over a jug of ale. The ordinariness; the complete absence of glamour. To be sure, I'd grown up accustomed to the anonymous carcase swinging in the gibbet cage upon the heath beside the road. I was unprepared for the effect upon me when it was a cull I knew, whose saddle I'd polished, whose wife and brats I'd lodged with. The purpling of the visage, the jutting of the tongue, the gyrating of the shins, the time it took to die... the coach that waited to receive the twitching corpse to hustle it away to be slit open in the cause of knowledge. And you heard such stories — the corpse in the hands of novices, the yards of gut escaping across the floor like wet rope, the limbs that fidgetted and dropped upon the floor and crawled about, the eyeballs on threads like baubles on string.

I abhorred myself for this unmanly frailty. What kind of weakling was I, to have looked upon a hanging — an everyday occurence —·and become so agitated? What had become of me, who all my life had wanted nothing better than to ride the Great North Road, a shadow black against the moon, like Claude Duval, like Jamie Whitney, like the highwayman who counted out his guineas in the Saracen's Head and carried me with him riding through the billowing darkness?

Rather than put these thoughts into words at the time I pushed them from my mind, and much else beside. I know I felt a curious loathing of myself for escaping the noose, for chance had played me fair and Goodman foul. If I had gone with him to Bow... if Jonathan Wild had been of a different humour on the day he sent me packing... I had left the good captain to his fate, albeit unwittingly — and for what? To cavort with mollies at the wedding of one chap to another... to romp and swive with a boy who painted his face and wore a woman's gown, and slippers with rose-coloured ribbons. And therefore, entirely unjustly, I included poor Lucinda in my loathing, not in the way of words or logic, but in an all-embracing onslaught of disgust and shame, violent in its intensity.

There seemed to be nothing left for me in London; and I took off up the Great North Road and put the city behind me without regret. My dear pal Gry at least was pleased with the outcome. The spring wind on my face, the wild woods and faraway fields, the wide clear skies seemed wonderful to me. It was to be a full five years before I lived again in London; though London remained very much in my mind, as you shall hear.

I arrived at the Crown unannounced. My mother was in the kitchen, slapping a piece of meat upon the well-scrubbed table, thumping it with a mallet to soften it, pausing merely to observe: "So you're back."

"Captain Goodman is hanged."

She clenched her fist on the slippery gobbet. "Oh Davy! Was there nothing you could do?"

A question I had never ceased to ask myself, and one I did not wish to hear upon the lips of another. Guilt! A dark and useless emotion, eating away at the innards. Could I have done something? Traced his Essex gang, joined with them, taken tools and weapons into Newgate? It was too late for that. Now I was alive and he was not. But why? What purpose was behind it? What of the working of chance in all this? How could it all be explained? What responsibility was now laid on me alive, he being dead?

I opened my mouth to voice some of this mental turmoil. But pragmatic as always, Ma wasted no time upon what she had no part in.

"It's as well you're here. Those lads from the village have gone to be soldiers, and I need your strong right arm. I have half a dozen barrels in the cellar to be brought up here."

In the doorway Susan stood, plump and starry eyed. "Davy!"

Humping casks of ale and assaying female kisses... If I wanted it, here was a way of life laid out for me.

I had tried to avoid a formal parting with Lucinda; but he had found me in the stable, where I was making my preparations for departure.

He was clad in male attire. He looked pale and pretty, sleek as a tabby in tawny and grey, with a little white knot of lace at his chin.

"How can you leave me so easily?" he had demanded. "Are you so heartless? You would have gone without a word. Have I no rights upon your consideration? Don't the times we shared together count for anything?"

There it was again — rights, sharing, the obligation to belong, all chains upon a traveller. It was true that we had been together upon many an occasion on those miserable days between Goodman's recapture and his topping. But on the day that Goodman left this earth it was the reassurance of Gry's presence that I sought, not Lucinda's, and it was into Gry's rough mane that I wept my hidden tears, not against Lucinda's painted cheeks.

"I wish that you would remain in London, Davy."

"I shall go back to my mother's. She needs me."

"I need you."

"No, you don't; you are well provided for at Aunty Mary's."

"Since I met you I am not so happy there as previously. Has it not occurred to you, Davy, that I am become fond of you? That I shall worry about you in the life that you have chosen?"

"You need not," I said bitterly. "There is small danger for a potboy at the Crown."

"May I write to you?"

I never thought that he would do so. It came as a great surprise to me when I received a letter handed to me from the stagecoach. Indeed, so rare an occasion was it for anyone amongst us to receive a letter that we all gathered round in a group, standing on the grass outside the inn, and nothing would content them but I read the missive aloud.

Haltingly I did so. Beginning with good wishes for my health, Lucinda thus continued: "Here in London all the news is of the Jacobites. They say the fighting in Scotland is all over, and the Pretender has gone back to France. Some noble lords have been beheaded, but one, Lord Nithsdale, who was imprisoned in the Tower, had a miraculous escape. His wife and two of her friends visited him and in his cell they dressed him in women's clothes and painted his face white and powdered his cheeks and smuggled him to safety. They say he is fled to Italy. Do you believe it possible, Davy, for a man to dress in women's clothes all unperceived? And yet they say it is so! I can scarce believe it, can you? Others also have escaped from Newgate, one by locking up the gaolers, and one by cutting through the bars of his cell, and one by bursting out with a gang of other prisoners in the excercise yard. But I think Lord Nithsdale the most piquant. Jonathan Wild has moved his office to a bigger house but still in the same street. He has a bodyguard of the blackest villains you are ever likely to see. One would think that he expected violence to be directed against himself, a surprising belief for one who only lives to serve. I must away now, as I am invited to a Masquerade. Your friend Lucinda."

Ma sniffed, and said that was an odd letter, all about Jacobites and men in women's clothes; and who was Jonathan Wild? Susan screeched at me for having made the acquaintance of a person named Lucinda.

"Who is she?" she demanded. "What does she mean by calling herself your friend? And have you kissed her?"

There it was again, the shriek of possessiveness. It was true that I had tentatively kissed Susan in the cellar, but it meant nothing; it was only to try woman's lips. And now it seemed she had the right to question me and expect explanation.

"I did kiss Lucinda," I admitted.

"And who was better, she or me?" said Susan, hands on hips; but I went off at speed to shift the casks, glad to sweat under the weight of them rather than under the weight of Susan's displeasure.

Being curious to try what women had to offer I admit I had not resisted Susan's advances. When I first quit London I could think of no better way to expunge Lucinda from my mind and all that he represented, which had so treacherously delighted me on the night that Captain Goodman was taken. I lay with Susan in the hayloft and found it pleasant, though passionless, and in no way comparable to the rapture I had experienced with Lucinda. But Ma then gave me such a talking to about how necessary Susan was to her about the house and how we could not afford to be overrun with infants, which so alarmed me that I let Susan alone, and endured much abuse thereby.

Never easy with writing, I found it difficult to reply to Lucinda's letters, but when I indicated that I was curious to hear all he could glean regarding Mr Wild he responded with enthusiasm.

In the five years following, while I served behind the bar at the Crown, lugged ale casks, plucked geese, dodged Susan, fed and watered strangers' horses, and rode out upon the road alone, Lucinda kept me carefully informed about the happenings in London which he guessed would interest me — and all of the most indiscreet nature and possibly libellous.

"Jonathan Wild and Mr Hitchin have quite fallen out and now rail at each other from public broadsheets. Mr Hitchin says that Mr Wild is a king among thieves, and Mr Wild says that Mr Hitchin is Beelzebub in human form and is hand in glove with all the Houses of Lewdness in the city, and no stranger to a molly house. But nothing is come of all this, and both continue at large. Mr H- was in here last week and not a whit dismayed. He is grown yet more portly. I would not have him if he paid me a fortune. It is my intention to land a gentleman. We had a very renowned gent in here yesterday; but more of that anon, I hope."

"Mr Wild has moved into an even bigger house, in Great Old Bailey — and Great being larger than Little, one assumes his star is in the ascendant. It is understood that the proximity of the seat of so-called Justice is to give credence to his own respectability; and curiously enough, many seem to consider him to be a most proper man. Ladies of quality come to him, praying he will find their lost goods, and you see him bowing and smirking and escorting them to their coaches, when everyone supposes that he has a hand in the stealing of the very goods they come to him to find. He is wed again, though it is said he has three wives living and a dozen or so doxies; he has married a niece of one of the Newgate turnkeys, a great oaf of ill repute, and this was done on the very day that a gaggle of his victims were topped at Tyburn and the wedding celebrations continued for a week. Mr Hitchin told me that if one of Mr Wild's thieves outlives his usefulness he is informed against, and with all that Mr W- knows about him, he stands no chance of being saved. This intermittent feeding of the gallows keeps his reputation high and his own thieves in fear. Mr W- has a coach and six now, Davy, and liveried footmen and lives like royalty, they say, and has taken to carrying a silver staff, and I have heard there be a knife blade within, which makes a spearhead should he be attacked. But the bodyguards are like to prevent this eventuality, as evil a crew as ever you did see aboard a pirate ship. And yet he is generally assumed to be an honest man and gives large sums to the poor..."

"I am reading a fine tale by Mr Defoe, concerning a chap that lives upon a desert island and must survive by his own skill... By the way, the Earl of Sunderland is the gent I mentioned who has visited our house and been entertained here. He is First Lord of the Treasury. He is a man of great sensibility, who loves books and paintings and the encouragement of artists. His first name is Charles. He has large beautiful eyes, fine eyebrows and exquisite lips. He smells divine. He is in his thirties, or so he says. But he is very charming, witty and ambitious, very proud and arrogant, but reasonably so, say I. So you see, we deal with quality. But more of that anon..."

"Davy, did you know that Jonathan Wild has not an entire skull! In the dangers which he has encountered he has been so foully injured that his head is broken into in many places and the missing parts are composed of polished silver plates which join the remaining parts together. And for this reason he is never without a turban even when he sleeps, for fear his deformity should become visible. And yet he is reputed to have many mistresses... The reward for the capture of a highwayman is now raised to one hundred pounds. I therefore hope and assume that you have given up your foolish ambition on that score. By the way, have you heard of the South Sea Company? It is something to do with politics, and it has gone wrong, and the lovely Sunderland has had something to do with it. He is distraught, and needed much of comfort when he came here yesterday. I was able to minister to his needs. You recall that I said I hoped to find a man of quality for myself? I believe I am as Ganymede to Jove here and may prove useful in my lord's hour of need. But more of that anon..."

"A new church is to be built, St Martin in the Fields. A highwayman named William Spiggot was captured at the Blue Boar and hanged. Jonathan Wild has sworn to capture every highwayman now upon the road. Davy, you are not still about that old desire, I earnestly hope? The Society for the Reformation of Manners is suddenly grown very strong and vociferous. The Earl of S- is fearful that they suspect his secret life. It would mean the end of his brilliant career if it were known."

"The E. of S. has been accused of sodomy and must resign. Robert Walpole who is ill-favoured, dull natured, short and plump, is to take his place. Lord S- swears that the King will stand by him. It must be good to have friends in high places. The Society for the Reformation of Manners is become both powerful and obnoxious. It is said they mean to work to destroy the molly houses. But more of that anon..."

Part III
The Road

Chapter Twenty-Five

ONE spring morning, when the century and I were twenty years old, and before I had received Lucinda's letter concerning the danger to the molly houses, a southbound coach drew up outside the Crown, and as the passengers tumbled out, their talk was all of Captain Sable.

"We were robbed in broad daylight near Alconbury Hill."

"The fellow is as bold as brass."

"We handed over all we had."

"What is this nation coming to?"

Now there is something perverse in a chap like myself which cannot entirely sympathize with such folk whose dress and bearing manifest every appearance of enough wealth easily to make good the loss of that which presently concerns them. I don't know why this should be so; maybe it is the times we live in, when the rich are excessively rich and the poor excessively poor. A detached and dispassionate redistribution of wealth seems to me no bad thing. I would no doubt feel differently were the wealth in question mine own; and I daresay our position in society colours the stance we take upon the matter.

Later, pacified and refreshed, the affronted company sat around the parlour and we learnt more about this same captain.

"Well spoken in his manner... quite the gentleman."

"His coat was as fine as my own."

"Dear, he was not a common footpad. His horse was pure thoroughbred. His hat was trimmed with sable."

"The highwayman is held in high regard by his own kind, as I understand it. Have you never heard of Claude Duval? They dance with ladies in the moonlight, and kiss them even as they rob them."

"I found him very gallant. When he helped me from the coach, his hand was strong yet gentle. Behind his mask he had the most beautiful eyes."

"What hope is there for law and order," spat the head of the family, "when foolish females praise the very one that robbed them of their finery?"

After that, we heard pretty regularly of the mysterious captain, both from parties he had robbed upon the road and in the farms and villages where we got our supplies. I determined to discover more of him. All my dormant longings were rekindled. I was envious of his reputation. What had become, I thought, of my brave hopes to become a Gentleman of the Road?

I sat amongst the hay in the loft above the stable late one evening. Here I first had met James Goodman, polished his saddle for him, talked about the road. From a box which I had hidden amongst the old stones of the wall I took James Goodman's velvet mask and put it on. I wondered whether after all I'd lost my courage and was fated to work all my life as a potboy and an innkeeper. It was an honest trade, yes, but it was not what I wanted.

That selfsame night I took Gry and rode some twenty miles north. It was a warm and cloudy night, wonderful to be abroad. Somewhere up near Stilton as I paused beside a copse of raggedy hawthorn I saw the lights of a small coach some way off and took a sudden chance. I stopped the coach and obliged the passengers to descend — a man and a woman and a lady's maid. They had no guard but a single coachman and though he had a musket to one side he could not reach it and remained cowed by my pistol. The maid at my direction opened the lady's jewel box. I took a couple of necklaces, and from the gentleman his gold watch and ten guineas. Remembering the illustrious Captain Sable I was careful to be most courteous and polite and as I quit them I said:

"You may say it was Captain Fox that robbed you."

I took off at speed, northward to the second crossroad, and turning left then, into the obscurity of the drovers' roads, through hamlets I had known in childhood when I dowsed for gold with Jerry Dowlan. My sentiments were entirely inappropriate for one who had performed so unsociable an act. I was elated; I was as one that rode a moonbeam, light as air, in every sense alive, pulsating; I owned the world. In that short interchange I had made some irrevocable choice, some statement, some committment. I was once again Duval's disciple. The old glory was unblemished and intact.

I was further gratified the following day to hear some gossip outside the Lion at Buckden.

"And they said that it was Captain Fox that robbed them. It seems we have two captains on our road now."

So many spoke of Captain Sable as the spring progressed that I could not but suppose that some accounts were fanciful and that a legend was in the making here. The heroic captain was now at

Stamford, now at Stevenage, now at St Neots, now at the Caxton gibbet, and always the gentleman, always well spoken, always with his hat trimmed with sable.

But then we heard a story of him which put something of a different complexion upon his activities.

A party came into the parlour of the Crown — an older chap, one Mr Benson, and his wife, and their niece and nephew Lydia and Stephen; and as we brought their food and drink to them we heard what had befallen them upon the road. They had been held up by Captain Sable and obliged to climb down from their carriage.

"We had already heard something of the villain," Mr Benson said, "and were debating whether we should fear to meet him or if his reputation of politeness would protect us from severe harm. We were particularly concerned for Lydia..."

We looked at her. She was a pretty girl, but at the present moment seemed a little discomposed. Flushed and scowling even.

"We had heard such tales," continued Mr Benson. "Everyone has heard of Claude Duval. We thought that Lydia might be required to dance with this Captain Sable upon the heath. Or worse."

"'Stephen,' I said," Mrs Benson then chimed in, "'Be prepared to defend your sister's honour. The rapscallion may mishandle her. After all, Lydia is a Beauty.'" She looked round at us for verification of her surmise. We responded enthusiastically. Yes indeed, Lydia was a Beauty; no one could deny it.

"Captain Sable was a gentleman, no doubt of it," said Mr Benson. "When we were gathered outside the carriage he surveyed us from his horse. He could see that contrary to his first expectations we were not as rich as he had hoped, but honest country travellers. 'I shall permit you to continue upon your journey,' said he, 'but first...' And he looked closely at us, and we thought: 'Ah, now it is, the kiss from the maid's lips which the highwayman always demands.' I strode forward to protect her, flinging my arms out, so..." He paused, arms akimbo.

"Yes?" Ma said impatiently. "And — ?"

Mrs Benson gave a little shriek and buried her face in her hands. Lydia snivelled into her handkerchief.

"It was Stephen whom he kissed!" expostulated Mr Benson.

"No!" cried Ma. "The villain!"

"Disgusting!" Susan sniffed.

We all looked at Stephen, who fidgetted and blushed and lowered his eyes. Lydia burst into tears.

"There, there," said Mrs Benson, comforting Lydia as best she might, and Ma cried: "Davy! Fetch more wine! Poor Mr and Mrs Benson, please drink up at our expense. My, what a fright you have had. Ad's blood! What a rogue, to be sure, and at loose upon our highway!"

We sent the injured party upon their way, restored a little. Ma and I watched their carriage depart.

"What a great fuss over nothing," Ma remarked. "That Stephen was every whit as pretty as his sister, and 'tis no surprise a man may fancy him. More to the point, 'twas plain for all to see the lad enjoyed it, and dared not admit as much!"

As for myself, I became more than ever obsessed with that mysterious captain, shirking my duties at the Crown to ride in pursuit of the rumours of his deeds. Whenever I heard that he had made a picking I rode round about and up and down, across the fields, along the road, no thief-taker more meticulous, no hound more tenacious.

From the location of his robberies I felt pretty sure he must live nearby and know the terrain as well as I, a man no doubt born or raised not far from the Great North Road. Indeed I studied him so closely and so constantly that it was not a great surprise to me when one afternoon in May, following close upon the news of his latest encounter, I caught my first glimpse of him.

I knew that it was he — a fine figure of a man, and all in black, his hat trimmed with the blur of sable, his horse a black thoroughbred. He was some way ahead of me upon the road, going at a slow pace, but some instinct making him aware of me, he turned, saw me, and urged his horse forward into a gallop. I followed. There ensued a merry chase, hither and yon, across many a field and ditch, along winding lanes, through smudges of woodland, with doubling back and circling about, with losing sight of him and regaining it, with listening for the sound of hooves and returning to pursuit. A freak of chance brought me upon him at last. Ahead of me, beside a knot of trees, he turned in the saddle, and seeing me, spurred forward suddenly, and a branch caught him across the chest and knocked him from his horse. He lay sprawled upon his back, in the grass.

I hurried forward, slithering to the ground, and threw myself upon him, kneeling astride his supine form, my face close to his own. He opened his eyes. We stared at one another in a gaze of mutual recognition.

"Lord Staughton! My lord!"

"Davy Gadd! If it isn't Davy Gadd!"

"My lord — you are not hurt, I hope?"

"Small thanks to you if I am not so. You follow me with all the determination of a hunter and now you press the breath from my lungs. Whatever would you have of me to use me so?"

I did not move. I had forgotten quite how beautiful he was, how melodious his voice. After so long I could well believe it was my own over-heated fancy that recalled him as the epitome of manly perfection, the fond dreams of youth that knew no better. But no, it was no dream. Here lay perfection — the dark eyes, the patrician nose, the sensuous arrogant mouth, the dark sleek hair. This was the man whose image ruled my heart, preventing me from loving any other. I gazed at him, the blank glazed stare of adoration. Then he reached up his hands and pulled my head down towards him, and our lips met in a long and fervent kiss.

When I came to my senses I said urgently: "My lord, we must remove hence. You may be recognized. But what brings you here and are you home to stay? I heard that you went north. But for so long? Are you now once again at Staughton manor?"

"Will you permit me to rise?" Lord Staughton enquired quizzically.

I did so, helping him to his feet. He dusted himself down, winced a little, straightened his cravat. I handed him the fur-trimmed hat.

"I did go north," Lord Staughton said. "But all that came to nothing. These past few years I have been living in France. I am at Staughton and shall be there for a while. Come with me there now; we may be of use to one another."

We rode over the fields, and by the quiet pack roads made our way towards the ancient house beside the ash trees. The air of desolation which in winter hung about this place was quite dissipated in early summer by the flowering of abundant nature. As we rode, the hedgerows were lush with cowparsley and elder blossom, and white and rose hawthorn; these grew right up to the door of the old timbered building. I recalled Ashfield where I had lived with Tubs, its well-trimmed lawns and geometric hedges, its neat borders and the herbs which grew to hand as if one had filed them away with the same precision as had been used for the books in the well-stocked library.

Staughton manor was a wilderness, abundant and unkempt. It rose from amongst its luxuriant foliage like an enchanted place, forgotten, timeless. Also — the eye of love must own it — dilapidated. The upkeep of the manor was plainly not Lord Staughton's overriding passion.

We dismounted, and a servant led our horses to the stable. As I watched the groom about his work I noticed that it was a different matter here — there was more than one fine horse to be seen. The beautiful black mare Bella whom Lord Staughton had been riding that day was treated with far more care than the house; and Gry no less was handled with all proper attention.

We entered the house through that same side door which as a boy I had entered with Jerry Dowlan. I remembered how we had been led to an upstairs room where by the fire in the gloom had sat a gentleman, half in shadow, with a black cat on his lap. I recalled his long white fingers against the cat's black fur. Into that selfsame chamber now we went, and as if recollection sparked response, a black cat ran to meet us and rubbed itself against Lord Staughton's black leather boots. My lord picked the creature up and nuzzled it and it wound itself about his neck and settled on his shoulder, with its face against his ear. It purred.

Lord Staughton lived alone, except for Scorby the brawny sour-faced doorkeeper whom I had met before and, besides the groom, an aged manservant George Fellowes, who plainly cared for him with much affection. This George, however, being stiff in the joints and not a little deaf, was not the most useful servant I had ever met, and I soon realized that to spare George inconvenience Lord Staughton looked after himself as much as possible; and it was his lordship who now poured us wine. The day being warm, there was no fire in the upstairs hearth, and the sunlight slanted through the small paned windows on to the dusty floorboards. We sat and drank, and the cat sat purring on Lord Staughton's lap.

I guessed that Lord Staughton must be thinking about the last occasion we had been together in this room, for he said then: "You are old enough now to know something of my circumstances. The truth is, I am pretty well penniless." He laughed. "Whenever you have encountered me you have found me either at the gaming table or about the act of highway robbery. Not a pretty picture. I do not present an inspiring example, I fear."

"There I disagree," I murmured.

He smiled deprecatingly. He could not have been unaware that he was gorgeous. His next remark surprised me.

"What are your politics, Davy?"

I blinked. "I haven't any."

"Seriously, lad. You must at least know the name of the chap whose fat bum has sat upon the throne these past six years. That is, upon the throne when it is not in Hanover."

"Yes, my lord." I grinned as it occurred to me. "He has the

same name as your old manservant."

"And would you die for him, Davy?"

"Wounds, no. Why would I do that?"

"Is it not the duty of the true-born Englishman to hold himself available for that eventuality, usually upon the field of battle?"

"I do not consider that I have a duty to anybody other than myself, to see that I survive," said I.

"Unnatural and amoral boy. What of your duty to your parents?"

"My father is long since dead. As to Ma, I wish for her happiness, of course, and if it is in my power I shall see that she remains in comfortable circumstance. But between us there has never been a close bond; it was always thus."

"Is there no creature upon this earth to whom you feel an obligation... to care for and protect, whose interest you would put above your own, in short, whom you love?"

"Yes — Gry, my horse."

"Well! That is a start then! There is some hope for you."

"A gipsy gave him to me. He is faultless."

"But is there nothing else? You care for nothing else?"

"No. Why do you ask?"

"Merely that in my estimation it is good to have something other than oneself at the centre in the pattern of one's life. A brotherhood — an ideal — something larger than oneself. Such, I am told, distinguishes mankind from the inferior creatures and gives purpose to our sojourn upon earth."

"Well, I do have a purpose. I still want to be the one that finds Duval's gold."

"Ah, yes," he smiled. "So you have not found it yet?"

"I keep looking, when I have the time. We are pretty busy when the coaches come in, and the daylight hours are needed round the house. I take off when I may, or when I can't take more of it or Susan. Susan," I added ungraciously, "thinks we should be wed."

Lord Staughton was not interested in what Susan thought.

"And have you the skill you once had?" he enquired, leaning forward. The cat, disconcerted and annoyed, jumped to the floor. It took up a watchful position in the corner of the room. Lord Staughton said:

"Jerry Dowlan used to reckon that you had a knack, the same as he. He often spoke of it."

"I have it still," I answered. "And besides, I now have Jerry's pendulum. He left it to me."

"You have the very pendulum," Lord Staughton said in a tone of wonderment and surprise.

"Yes," I patted my pocket. "I usually find something when I use it."

"Better and better!" said Lord Staughton and his eyes glittered. "Davy," then said he, "if I were to find a chap to take your place at the inn, it would leave you free to work for me, if you were willing."

"Willing? Of course I am. What kind of work?"

"Looking for gold; what else?"

"What, give up helping Ma?"

"Yes. You would live here with me. Each day you would ride the road and search. If we took it yard by yard... How does it go?

'Twixt Tollentone Lane and Alconbury Hill
Duval's gold lies buried still?'

The furthest northern point then is Alconbury — it has never been suggested that the cursed Frenchman went beyond Alconbury! Begin there and work southwards. If you had nothing to do but search, no claim upon your time, how could you fail?"

"There is nothing I would like better," I responded. I hardly gave the matter thought. Live here, with him, the figure that had dominated my dreams for so many years — ride the road at his direction — and the summer coming...

"So you agree?"

"I do."

"Good." He stood up and came across to me and grasped me by the shoulders firmly, warmly. "Davy, follow me."

He whirled about and opened the door into the adjoining room, where long ago his great Collection was housed, beautiful treasures from the road, all cleaned and polished, useless and inert, like pinned butterflies. I stood up and followed him.

The cupboards were still there, but when he opened them I saw at once that most of them were empty. The sunlight came in long dusty shafts and caught the gleam of what remained, here a brooch, there a cloak pin.

"All sold, " he shrugged. "All to no purpose."

Lord Staughton led the way towards a door at the far side of the room. It opened into a dark wainscoted passage. He ran his hands over the panelling and soundlessly a small door opened. We had to bend our heads to go through. His lordship lit a candle, set in the wall, then another and another. We were in a little room with no window, lit by the dancing glow of the candle flames. One entire wall was covered by a thick curtain. Before it, upon a table covered with a blue silk cloth, stood two very fine glass goblets and a tall glass container. Lord Staughton drew the curtain aside and revealed a painting which hung behind it.

It was the portrait of a handsome man wearing a suit of armour which was tailored to his body as elegantly and close fitting as if it had been velvet. He wore a lace cravat at the throat and a blue sash about his person, with a jewel at the waist. He wore a long curled periwig; his face was sombre in expression. Lord Staughton watched me closely.

"Do you know who that is?" he asked.

"No, my lord."

"It is the King of England."

Apolitical I may have been, but I was not so stupid as to suppose this King George, whom I knew to be unprepossessing and fat.

"James Francis Edward Stuart," said Lord Staughton, "son of King James II. Now does that not, I ask you, cause him to be King James III — and King of England?"

"I suppose that it does, my lord."

"You suppose correctly; but there is that small hitch," said Lord Staughton ruefully. "that he is not recognized as such. However, his day will come."

"Yes, my lord."

"You don't believe me?"

"I know nothing about it."

"Davy," cried he then in some exasperation, "I am pleased you are no rampant Hanoverian, but your general ignorance is a little to be regretted."

I agreed, and waited to be enlightened.

"I was amongst those that fought in Scotland in Fifteen, " said Lord Staughton. "I am one of many that wait upon events. The army in Scotland never surrendered; it will rise again. We hoped for French aid; vain hope. They have abandoned us. But we have the promise of Swedish aid now. Politics, Davy. The Hanoverian steals Swedish territory; the Swedes will invade on our behalf in Scotland in retaliation. Then there is Spain... Spain works with us. Spain has already sent troops to Scotland. It is true that they were not successful. But they will come again."

"When?" I asked.

"It is not decided," he said grandly, as if it could be so upon the instant, if one but chose.

"And where is... the King now?" I wondered.

"In Italy. He bides his time."

Myself I did not think that I would be alone in lacking enthusiasm for a parcel of Spaniards and Swedes in London sorting out our politics, but then, what did I know?

Lord Staughton poured us both a glass of fine claret. The goblets in this hidden chamber were exquisite, with long stems, and white roses carved into the glass.

"To the King over the Water," said my lord, and I echoed the words and drank. Lord Staughton replaced the curtain and snuffed out the candles.

"We do not of course speak of this matter outside this house," said Lord Staughton. "I have noticed in Buckden a certain very regrettable toadying to the notion of the Hanoverian succession."

"Naturally not." I had seen the crowds that had lined Holborn to witness the quartering of the Jacobite soldiers, and I knew that the penalty for loyalty to the misplaced king was death. But this secret room in Staughton manor seemed a far cry from the streets of London and the baying mob that shrieked for blood and knew as much about the rights and wrongs of it as I.

Lord Staughton put his arm about my shoulders.

"We have been too sober, Davy. Do you recall the last time that we were together?"

"Certainly I do."

"We suited each other well, as I recall."

"Yes sir, we did."

"What do you say then, Davy? Shall we make love?"

"I thought that you might never ask."

We left the secret chamber, locking it behind us, and continued along the dark passageway, which led into a bedroom. A big old four-poster bed with amber-coloured hangings filled the room.

I hesitated, suddenly uncertain in the face of the fulfilment of my dreams.

"Come here," said Lord Staughton, and enfolded me in his arms. We shared a warm embrace.

"Tell me," said Lord Staughton smoothly, "has anyone conveyed to you the mysteries and delights of that which Aunty Mary would call the Pleasant Deed?"

The name itself was a mystery to me. I said as much.

"We will discover together the extent of your knowledge," said Lord Staughton with a smile. "It is fortunate for you that I am the one to initiate you. I think you will agree the matter is well named; but your partner must be a man of skill and tenderness... such as

174

myself. Let us now undress."

My lord was right; I found the deed well named. That night when I went to sleep beside Lord Staughton in that great bed I accounted myself among the most fortunate of mortals.

Chapter Twenty-Six

AND so I began to search for Duval's gold in earnest. At first Lord Staughton accompanied me upon these journeys. We rode out along the road. He questioned me closely about Jerry Dowlan's methods. True to his intention, we rode up as far as Alconbury hill. From a long way off you could see the gallows on its summit. There was always some wretched soul a-swinging there. They must bring the condemned from miles around, I thought, just to make sure an occupant hung there, to spread fear and dread over the wide lands round about. It was impossible not to look at it as you approached; the eye was drawn to it. The carcase hung in a cage of close-fitting iron, dangling from a chain. The chain creaked as it shifted in the wind, and the wind was always bleak and wild at Alconbury. In winter time the snow lay in great drifts high as a house wall. Even in summer this was not a good place for a traveller, very open, and a great strain on coach horses.

We paused, beneath the gibbet.

"Davy, look," said Lord Staughton, and his lip curled in a movement of repulsion.

A bird was perched upon the corpse's head, and there under the ear inside the collar had built a nest, and there were young ones in it, screeching.

"It were no bad thing for such as you and I who like to flirt with danger," said Lord Staughton, "to meditate upon the likelihood of what we all may come to."

I shrugged. "I lost my nerve once; but I'm over it. It does no good to think of these things."

"Dismount then; prove it. We'll begin with a dowsing here on Alconbury."

I crouched there in the wind-blown grass, and took the pendulum from its pouch.

"There is too much wind..."

His lordship dismounted and knelt beside me. He cupped his hand around the trembling glass. We waited.

"No," I said. "There is nothing here."

But he would not be satisfied, and ordered me to try again at many points upon the hillslope, and I did so, and the wind soughed and the horses fidgetted and the hanged man creaked and swayed above our heads. But we found nothing.

I began to realize that because of Jerry Dowlan's undeniable success in gold digging, Lord Staughton placed an almost reverential belief in the power of the pendulum of glass which I now owned. Because of his straitened circumstances and his devotion to the Jacobite cause — that bottomless pit into which he had sunk all his money — it had become a matter of great urgency to him to find the legendary treasure. I dared not even contemplate what would happen if, finding it, I demanded half. He was like a man possessed. He had some old maps in his library and he would spread them out over the table and peruse them as closely as if he thought the intensity of his gaze might draw the secret from the parchment. Copses, spinneys, woods that hugged the road, these he marked out and showed me.

"This is where we try tomorrow."

And he would turn and say to me: "They say it is more than a thousand guineas, Duval's gold."

"It must be buried in one of those woods and copses then," I said. "A man would need to be well hidden burying so much money. It would take him a long time. And folk would hear the chink of coin."

"It must have been buried in a wood, yes, but not far from the road. The legend says on the road."

"The poem does not," I reminded him. "'By stem and root, as we are told...'"

"But it is understood," he frowned. "It must mean near the road. Otherwise it could be anywhere in the southern part of England. The thought is frightening. Between Tollentone and Alconbury. The straight road binds the two. It must be on the road, or very near it."

And therefore, as soon as it was day, we would rise from slumber, take a hurried breakfast, and set out, winding our way by packhorse roads to join up with the great north road towards Alconbury, till, returning, we had probed as far as possible upon that day. Sometimes we slept at a wayside inn, sometimes returned to Staughton.

A strange way of passing time, I thought more than once. Two grown men and a pendulum of glass, two patient steeds, and the summer leaves and the ferny glades and the dips and hollows of the earth. If we had been mere searchers for the golden scraps of past ages we had not been disappointed, for the pendulum and I found curiosities enough to satisfy the most eager gold-seeker. Rusty spurs we found, and broken swords, snake-like bracelets, shoe buckles, an old pouch with a few pence in it, and much more of the like.

Each find caused us to lose all track of time, our entire being concentrated in sharp expectation. The pendulum would seem to breathe, then quiver, and then circle widely. You would swear a force had entered it. At the close of the day my arm and wrist would throb, and yet I had felt no discomfort as I held the thread. We would grab and scrabble at the soil, excited, panting, laughing; and beneath our blackened fingers would emerge the cause of the pendulum's vibrations. As we passed the object from one to another our disappointment would be palpable, and yet we never said as much. The thrill of the chase had been justification enough; and though we had not found our heart's desire today, there remained tomorrow and again tomorrow.

The vibrancy of the quest we were upon permeated every aspect of our existence. Time and again as we pushed our way through the bushes and bracken we would catch each other's eye and reach for one another. The leaves rustling about us we lay down on beds of moss or flowery banks or flattened fern and took our pleasure. We bathed in woodland meres where trees hung down low and spread their leaves in the water, and lilies lay golden along the surface. Sunlight came slanting through the quivering foliage, dappling our naked bodies. We stood waist deep in water and embraced. We ran in the sunny glades to shake ourselves dry. Then back to the task in hand, the pursuit of gold.

Then in the evening as the twilight thickened about the old timbered walls of Staughton manor and the candles were lit, we'd pore once again over those maps. Lord Staughton marked off the places we had attempted. He divided the maps into squares, running ruled lines across and spoiling the drawing beneath. Each square was then shaded in. It was a methodical and foolproof way, Lord Staughton said. If anybody were to find the gold it should be us. And we deserved it for the care that we were taking. We were artists in discovery.

Lord Staughton seemed now to have lost interest in the storing and displaying of the metal objects that we found. When I first knew him there had stood stack upon stack of objects of polished beauty which had once graced a woman's body or been taken into battle by a warlord. Now it was the gold or nothing. What we found, presumably of value in itself, lay heaped as carelessly as earthenware. Nothing was as important now as to discover Claude Duval's hoard.

At night we were lovers in the great bed with the amber-coloured hangings; though rarely did we indulge in the Pleasant Deed — which was as well, no doubt, since we spent most of our days in the saddle. Teasing out the finer points of pleasure Lord Staughton led me to delights that I had never known possible. I felt obscurely grateful. He could have had any lover, gentle or simple, but it was me he chose to share his bed. For him love was something of an art. It made me think of horse jading. Just as I knew gipsy skills to draw the best from a good steed, so did my lord understand the subtleties of love — ways to make the pleasure linger, to ease out excitement to a crafted conclusion. He had special oils to rub on the skin with fragrances unlike the natural odours of wayside and cottage flowers, and some with a kick like a wild stallion which you breathed in at exactly the right point for highest stimulation.

Sometimes by daylight I thought that between folk who loved each other, simple fumbling affection might have been enough, but he would have called that common, prudish even. And what had that to do with our peculiar intimacy anyway — for befuddled as I might be with sensation and his presence I was never so confused as to suppose that he loved me. I believed that I loved him, but it was more with a dog-like devotion than the proper love of equals; these of course we were not, he being a lord and I a gentleman only when upon horseback with a mask upon my face and a pistol in my hand; and since joining my lord in our shared search I had not been even as much as that.

Visitors he received from London — lone riders whom he spoke with in private, who stayed overnight and rode away without more ado. Sometimes he was from home, and I understood his journeys were to do with the same business as his receiving of visitors — in short, another plot was hatching, similar to the Fifteen. On the tenth of June we drank a loyal toast to King James, it being his birthday. I understood that King George's government was in difficulties, and no better time than now could be envisaged for changes. It was to do with that same South Sea Company which Lucinda had mentioned, which was later to be known as the South Sea Bubble. I heard names spoken of in connection with the Jacobite business which have since become notorious — the Duke of Ormonde, who was supposed to sail up the Thames; Bishop Atterbury of Rochester; and Christopher Layer a Norfolk squire, a barrister of law. Now more than ever was the fabled hoard deemed necessary.

As the year went by Lord Staughton was from home more

than before. But my orders were clear — I was to continue the search. Scorby would be there to make sure I did not shirk my task. As soon as daylight woke me I was to set off, and not return till darkness fell.

"You need set no menial to spy upon me," I said angrily. "I will gladly do your bidding, as you know."

"Forgive me," said Lord Staughton, all sweetness. "I am grown desperate. Time is short, and our great cause is woefully supplied."

I did as he said, even though he was away. I searched as diligently as I could. It was my ambition to discover Duval's gold myself while he was away, and present it to him. I pictured his homecoming. Tired and dispirited he would stumble from his horse, and George would take his coat and boots. I would have spread the gold upon the blue silk cloth before the portrait of King James. I would lead my lord to the secret room and light the candles. Each flame would illumine the glinting heap of guineas, each separate coin a winking glittering brilliance. Moved beyond words, my lord would take me to his bed.

"There is no one like you, Davy," he would say.

But there was some way to go before the realization of this splendid dream, not least in the traversing of actual miles. And how I knew it, as, with autumn's approach I went out each day upon that mission. Without the pleasure of Lord Staughton's company I at first was content enough with the task itself, possessed by the hope I had to be the one that handed him the treasure. I had, I think, even given up the idea of the satisfaction I would experience on my own account, so eaten up was I with the desire to please and offer to Lord Staughton his cherished goal.

This ambition kept me going for several weeks before my glowing ardour faltered. Jerry Dowlan's pendulum and my own curious talent never let me down; I always found some oddity or other from the distant past, and even a lost coin or two of the present age, the which I had no qualms in pocketing.

I became one with the solitary creatures of the quiet road — I saw badgers amble to their holes, I saw the timid deer drink at the meres; hares ran across my path. I conversed with foxes, surprised as I to see a fellow loiterer in the quiet glades. The owls of the dusk in silent flight were my companions as I made my way home. I could take any number of rabbits for the pot.

And then one morning early, my faithful Gry and I came slowly into a clearing. The autumn days were full upon us now, the air smelt dank and rotten, and the toadstools lay rich among the hoary tree roots. The dark trees gave way suddenly to a golden daylight, and warm sunlight fell upon us, speckled with yellow leaves. We drew rein. The grass was wet with dew, the brambly thickets shook with water drops, and every bush was laced with spiders' webs. The sunlight caught them all. The glade was like a mass of jewels. Everything sparkled and was gold.

I could have laughed or cried, had I been given to emotion. It was the first time that the thought occurred to me: what if this were the only gold to be found by root and stem 'twixt Tollentone and Alconbury? Reach out a hand and there would be of all this glittering brilliance nothing to show.

Was Duval's gold as insubstantial? Was there nothing for the dedicated seeker more than this?

Chapter Twenty-Seven

LORD Staughton was in no mood for failure. In early spring he returned from London in a dark humour the which, while hugely suiting his saturnine beauty, did nothing to alleviate the circumstance of the observer. As watched him kick off his mud-stained boots and slam his tankard down upon the table I understood that the life of a plotter against the safety of the realm was not an easy one.

"What, nothing, Davy?" he repeated, hoarse with disbelief. "And did you really search as I commanded, every inch of ground, and every day?"

"I did, my lord; but don't lose heart — there are many miles as yet untouched, and I'll set off at first light to continue what we started."

"Time grows so short," said he, despondent now. He sank wearily into a chair. "Each link in the chain dependent on the other, and all moving forward, supporting one another; and never enough gold. Important people, Davy, are counting upon our success. Men are putting their political careers in jeopardy. The highest in the land, Davy, are committed to our cause. If we fail they lose everything."

"The highest in the land?" I doubted. "That's the King himself."

"The highest of his noblemen," said Lord Staughton irritably.

"What?" I said, boasting of my knowledge, gleaned entirely from Lucinda's letters. "Do you mean the Earl of Sunderland?"

Lord Staughton went as pale as a ghost, and I thought: Wounds! I have hit upon something here! Is the Earl of Sunderland a secret Jacobite? As well as a frequenter of the molly houses? There is a gentleman who is treading on eggshells!

"Never," said Lord Staughton soberly, "speak that name again."

"No my lord."

"His very life may depend upon the discretion of his friends."

"Yes my lord."

"In what connection did you hear his name spoken?"

"In another one entirely." I drew up a stool and sat beside him. "Lucinda, Aunty Mary's nephew, informs me by letters — which come to me at the Crown — of events in London. He said that the gentleman of whom we spoke sometimes visits, and Lucinda comforts him."

"Ah yes, Lucinda." His lordship frowned. "I had forgotten that you and he were friends. If you write back to him please urge him to be discreet and never mention names in full."

"My lord, if you are acquainted with the earl," I said, "perhaps you know whether I should warn Lucinda against too close an intimacy. Is the earl a worthy man who will provide for Lucinda's well-being?"

"The earl is very worthy," said Lord Staughton. "But like us all, he is at the mercy of events."

We drank a health that night in the little secret room. We drank to the King across the water, who last December had become the father of a son, Charles Edward, thus continuing the Stuart line and giving hope to his adherents. This reminder of political optimism caused his lordship a brief return to good humour; and that night we made love with an exquisite tenderness and passion.

Studying his handsome features as he slept, in the early light of day, I was consumed with great affection for my lordly benefactor and I vowed to do all in my power to bring him cheerfulness.

As I dressed and buckled on my belt with its silver-mounted pistols I swore I would not return without some gold to bring him.

North I went, and the road hard going with the boggy mud, but we plodded on, and I never could fault that good steed of mine; be it speed or endurance he would give all I required. Thus by evening we were well clear of our usual haunts, and the air much obscured by the dusk of a bleak and overcast day. Few travellers were upon the road. From a long way off in the grey gloom I saw the approach of what I took to be a small coach.

I looked around swiftly: I was unobserved. A light rain was

falling. I waited behind a thicket of bramble. I tied James Goodman's mask about my visage and I took a gamble which paid off; luck, as they say, sitting on my shoulder that day.

The coach was poorly defended. A gentleman within, fearful for the safety of the lady that accompanied him and plainly in a state of fright, threw a small casket from the window, and begged to be allowed to continue unharmed. Naturally, having no intention of harming them, I permitted it. Indeed, I was a touch embarrassed to have been the cause of such inappropriate terror on the man's part, though of course he was not to know that I was pretty peaceable. The rattler trundled off; I watched it from sight, dismounted, picked up the casket and took off down a side track, never stopping till I was well clear of the place of robbery.

Beneath an oak I paused and, the rain trickling down my collar, I opened up the casket — and near tumbled from the saddle. Damn me if the casket was not full of golden guineas — fifty at a guess; this was the most I'd ever taken on the road. A certain modest pride now overcame me. I could hold up my head with the best of 'em. Fifty guineas! No small thing, and so easily got. And all it took was a daring heart and a pair of silver pistols.

Much cheered in spirit I whipped off the mask and stuffed my treasure in my saddle-bag, and so by circuitous ways returned to the road. The darkening now upon us, it was with pleasure that I saw the lights of a wayside hostelry ahead. A big inn it seemed to be, with plenty of stables and barns, and standing on its own, fronting the Great North Road, with fields and woods and heath its only neighbours.

There was merrymaking within: I could hear it from afar.

"We be soldiers three
Lately come from the Low Countree
With never a penny of money..."

Voices; and a fiddle also. Only pausing to be sure that no small coach was there before me, I dismounted. As I led Gry into the stable the words rang clear and plain:

"Here good fellow I drink to thee
To all good fellows wherever they be
With never a penny of money..."

I gave a small fee to the ostler but saw to Gry's welfare myself. With the fellow gone, I buried the casket in the corn bin of Gry's stall, and crossed the cobbled yard and entered the inn.

I saw at once that I had again struck lucky. It was a haunt of thieves and swivers and here I would be much at ease. Drunk and cheery, the disreputable company were far gone in revelry, each singing louder and wilder than the next.

"I cannot eat but little meat
My stomach is not good — but —
Back and sides go bare, go bare,
Both hand and foot go cold.
God send my belly good ale enough
Be it new or old."

All attention was now centred upon the hero who stood, one boot upon the table, comely of countenance, muscular of arm and thigh, a flagon in his fist, and his golden curls gleaming in the lanthorn light that swung drunkenly above his head, and he singing his heart out:

"Her yielding lips he gave a good wipe,
And gave her nelly a damn good gripe..."

Gazing up at him adoringly sat any number of wenches, grasping his legs, reaching up to his crotch with eager hands, bawling at him to leave off singing with the lads and take the girls to bed. A fine sight — Macheath himself, he seemed, with Polly Peachum and Lucy Lockit, Betty Doxy and Dolly Trull no less, caught in a moment of time, and living in truth the tale that Mr Gay was later to blaze abroad upon the London stage.

Benjamin Child! The greatest highwayman of our day. Famed in song now, Passed into Legend. I was on hallowed ground. Some of the culls sprawled across the table were his cronies. I pressed them for stories of his prowess and they willingly divulged them.

"There was this one time on Hounslow Heath..."

"Hounslow Heath... we know every blade of grass there..."

"Women would die for him..."

"He could have any one he chose, high or low..."

"But always a gentleman, kind, courteous..."

"In his company you are warming your hands at the fire of life!"

I am proud to say that I shook the hand of the great man before he finally made his choice and took the fortunate female up the stairs.

"Davy Gadd, sir, and I'm honoured to meet you."

"The honour is all equal between us," smiled he; and his hand was warm and strong, his eyes as blue as cornflowers.

So brilliant was his presence that after he had gone the room seemed darker. A sensation of loss engulfed me. I leaned back, downing another mug of ale. A couple of drabs, cheated of Ben, sloped over to me, cajoling me, feeling my pockets for coin and my crotch for the assessing of joys ahead. For the first time I now saw the fiddler.

He was standing in the shadows and he changed his tune now from the bawdy jig that accompanied the singing, to a whining mournful air that called to mind the wind upon the heath. My heart lurched. It was Nathan Grey.

I stood up. There were howls of accusation from the trulls who held me, and I crossed the floor and stood before him. Without relinquishing his bow he eyed me.

"Have you still the horse?"

"I have."

"Wait by him. I will come to you."

I went out of the warm noisy tavern parlour and crossed the yard. In the stable I sat down upon a hay bale and obediently waited till the gipsy chose to come to me. I would have waited till the crack of doom. I was breathless with elation. He had recognized me. He was coming to me. I had even forgotten to make sure that in the corn bin fifty guineas waited in a casket.

When Nathan entered the stable he took no more heed of me than if I had been a post, and straight to Gry he went, and handled him and crooned into his ear and spoke him fair, and only when he had assured himself that the gift was in good hands and I thus worthy of the same, did he crook his finger at me, and I followed him out of the stable.

He paused and looked at me.

"*Sar shin?*" he said. "Well with you?" I nodded.

Pitch dark it was now, and away from the lights and noise we went, walking through wet mulchy grass, between the soughing trees, while the owls hooted, and beyond the tangled branches rode the black and moonless clouds. There was a stream nearby, trickling over stones.

Suddenly we were at the steps of Nathan's wagon. He lifted the cloth and all in the darkness we clambered in and lay in the blankets. We tugged off our boots. He took me in his arms and nuzzled me, sensing me, as he had with Gry. Then kissed me. Eagerly I responded. There was a certain perfection about the lack of question and account — what have you been doing? — where have you lived since I last saw you? All this was irrelevant. It was as if we had only just met by the stream when he had given me the toad's bone, cast the spell, made love to me.

"Unfinished, yes," he murmured, understanding. "Now to do

so."

More of the same... It was what I had asked for, the first time we met, when I had lain in this same wagon, warmed by him and his coney broth and his wood fire, when he had kissed me roughly and shown me that he could have knifed me if he chose.

I undid my breeches, eased them from me, lay upon my belly, spread my thighs. He lay upon me, handling me with knowing fingers; then he was in me, greased and hard, and moving to our pleasure. May it never end, I thought, may he do all he will.

"*Kushto*," he murmured. "I am content." He wrapped the blanket around me, and we slept.

In the icy chill of early dawn I washed in the stream. Nathan was already making preparations for his departure. His horse was between the shafts, snorting, flexing itself, ready for the road, breath steaming in the bitter air. I slapped my bare shanks dry, shouting with the cold of it. He laughed and slung me my breeches.

"Listen," I urged, dressed and decent. "Where may I meet you? When see you again?"

He grinned. "Travel the road. I am always on the road."

Disappointment made me silent. He patted my shoulder. "If you stay with the Great North Road, chance will always bring us together. Now, *Ja Develehi!* Go with God!"

Small consolation did divine protection seem to me as I watched Nathan Grey turn his wagon from the glade away towards the road. His pots and kettles knocked against each other, and the cart shafts creaked and in his passing grasses bent. Soon they would spring up again and nothing would remain to show that he had passed this way.

I trudged back towards the inn and ate a hearty breakfast.

Chapter Twenty-Eight

IN a little spinney down a drovers' track I knelt amongst the wet ivy leaves and scooped up a fistful of earth. I smeared it all over the casket, taking care that every inch of it should show some signs of having been long buried. I surveyed my handiwork with cautious pride. Was it grimy enough? I pressed it once again into the soil, twisting it round, blackening its pretty exterior. That should convince my lord that we had found Duval's gold. That should cheer him.

A couple of hours later I was standing before him in the upstairs parlour, and he had the muddy box in his elegant white hands and was turning it about and about, his brow drawn in a thoughtful frown, his lips pursed.

"Not a thousand, as we thought," said I apologetically. "A mere fifty. But buried as it was, amongst the roots of a great oak tree, and containing guineas as it does, it must surely be the gold that Captain Duval hid all those years ago. The pendulum swung so hard and fast it nearly pulled my wrist out of joint. We're in luck, my lord. You can send it to the King Across the Water and he'll pay his soldiers, and he'll praise you to the skies. I'll take a dozen or so for myself and buy some clothes; but you can have the rest and welcome."

Lord Staughton turned his chair and presented his back to me and set about to count the guineas upon the table. I smirked a little, and ground my boot along the floor, modest in my generosity, awaiting confirmation of my success.

Lord Staughton stood up, crossed the room and opened the door and called for Scorby, who came thumping up the stairs.

"Scorby," said Lord Staughton smoothly. "Do me the kindness to take this boy by the ear and throw him downstairs and out of this house."

Scorby's face lit up with unexpected pleasure as he hurried to comply.

"But — " I began, and got no further, being halfway down the stairs. Hustled and shoved with over-zealous enthusiasm by Scorby's great arm I found myself ejected through the door and fetched up in a bank of violets beneath the dove cote, their sweet perfume the more intensified for having been expressed by the vigour of my landing. There I sat for a moment, marvelling at the unfairness of the human lot until, bespattered once again by the pittering rain, I stood up and rubbed my posterior and limped towards the shelter of the dove cote.

No plump cooing bird had graced this edifice for many a long year. It was an old brick building, with a roof of lichened tiles. Its door swung to and fro on uneven hinges. Inside, a creaking ladder led to a place beneath the conical roof, where small box-like partitions marked the dwellings of its long-departed occupants. I sat morosely there upon the boards, hugging my knees, and the rain came trickling through the gaps in the roof. He had not, of course, believed me.

I was spared the necessity of having to decide upon a course of action, for within a short time the door below thudded more violently and Lord Staughton's head and shoulders emerged as he climbed the ladder. I saw with some relief that he was smiling.

"How did you guess?" I said.

"In the lining, which is of a remarkable freshness for something fifty years buried, is a letter dated the fourth of last month."

"Ah..." I said sheepishly.

"Why did you indulge in the subterfuge, Davy? Have you grown tired of seeking for gold?"

"No, my lord, not I. It still remains my greatest wish in all the world. But you were sad at heart. I knew that finding Duval's gold would cheer you."

"And so it would, my dear," he assured me warmly. "But I had rather never find it than find fools' gold. And Davy, you should know better than to trifle with an ideal."

He eased himself up and sat beside me on the mouldering boards.

"Duval's gold," he said, "is a hope, a dream. Oh yes, I don't deny the usefulness of a thousand guineas. But the search, Davy, the seeking... that's a part of it. If we did not find it, we should not deserve it. The joining in spirit with the highwayman hero... time slipping between our two ages, binding us, this giving significance to each day. Pitting ourselves against his cunning, a mystic conjunction. A Holy Grail which, when discovered, lets in self-discovery also. Not to be degraded with tricks." He slung his arm about me. "You've no idea what I'm talking about, have you?"

"Yes I have," I answered stoutly.

"Where did you find the fifty guineas?" he then asked me.

"Robbed a coach."

"Where? Not nearby, I hope?"

"No, no," I said impatiently. "I must have been the other side of Stamford."

"What a risk, Davy!" he said severely.

"I knew what I was doing, and," I added sulkily, "you have done the same yourself."

He was silent. The rain eased, plopping rhythmically now, through its roof-gap runnel.

"Davy," said Lord Staughton, "it might not be such a bad idea."

And so Lord Staughton and I turned highwaymen in earnest, and all that summer long we worked the road.

We lived by night; we rarely saw the sun at noonday. The setting of the sun was our call to rise. With the coming of darkness we saddled up. The creatures of the night were our companions. We saw the fox on the prowl and heard the badger lumber through the woods, the snake rustling in the grass. We saw the ghostly white owls with their wide-spread wings and heard the pounce of their kill. The starlight caught the tree boles in a pale grey light, and the streams were speckled with stars.

Into this vibrant darkness came the lamp-glow of the coaches that risked travelling by night. We saw them from miles away. From any of the hills and inclines over which the Great North Road ran you could see anything that carried a light, and mark out its progress. And since most of these high places bore a gibbet at their summit, there would be a silent witness to our waiting, one that swung and creaked, bound about in his iron cage, grey-silver in the starlight. You could almost hear him call out to us: "Good luck, my beauties. Better luck than I had." And at the right moment down we would ride and stop the coach and take what we might; and it was easier with two of us than it had been when I had worked alone.

Now to hear the tales of Jamie Whitney and Mulled Sack and of Captain Duval himself, you would think that the life of a highwayman was entirely composed of narrow escapes, constant danger, breakneck chases and merry banter exchanged with the victim, all adding to the legend of the gentleman in question. It was not so with us, and so much not so as to make me doubt a little the veracity of some of the stories I had been brought up to believe.

For me it was a trade like any other, and I applied myself to it with all the dexterity and competence of any that has undertaken to follow his chosen profession. Though I say it myself, I was pretty good at what I did. Beyond the risk of the trade itself — which is no greater than the smith risks of burning himself in the forge, or the slater of tumbling off a roof — I took no risks. We avoided the coach which showed itself to be heavily armed; we avoided the full of the moon, and the rainy nights when we could not be sure our pistols would fire; and afterwards we made a quick departure down a network of byways, a route planned in advance. We never stayed in one place, so never built up a reputation. We were now in York, now Grantham, now in Royston. I regretted that we had no ballads sung of us; but the successful highwayman has no ballads to his name — none knows it. He is now here, now gone. The ballad that celebrates a hero of the road ends with his death.

Once, we called in to the roadside inn where I had heard Nathan Grey's fiddle, where there had been drunken merriment and song, where Ben Child had held court. I was telling Lord Staughton about the handsome highwayman.

"Big and broad, with yellow hair. And so good to look at. The women thought so too."

The innkeeper put down our drinks upon the table.

"Ben Child?" he said. "Haven't you heard? They caught him and topped him. If you want to see him now you can see him on Hounslow Heath and hear the rattling of his chains."

"I don't believe it!" I said angrily.

"It's true. I never thought they'd outwit Ben. But I'll tell you who it was — it was Jonathan Wild the thief taker — he was behind it all. And he put Ben on Hounslow because that was where Ben had his triumphs."

"I know of Jonathan Wild," I said grimly. "A two-faced double dealer who grows rich on men's misfortunes. He has sworn to capture every highwayman upon the road. But I never thought he had it in him to take Ben."

"He is patently no fool," Lord Staughton observed.

"I remember when he took James Goodman," I said. "But poor James was small fry. He made mistakes; and I believe he half brought his fate upon himself through loss of nerve — he used to dream about the Black Dog of Newgate. But Ben... It would seem that Jonathan has grown in stature."

"It will be a feather in his cap having taken Ben," said the innkeeper. "Ben was a Gentleman, a hero. Everyone admired him."

"A health to him," said Lord Staughton soberly; and we all three drank.

I came away subdued and thoughtful. Lord Staughton said: "Now then, Davy, don't be downhearted. It happens. Ben Child knew the way of it. He was unlucky."

"We are so carefree on the road," I said. "But down there, where the road begins, sits Jonathan like a great spider, with men that do his bidding, and then out he bounds and pounces. My lord — I saw again that carcase in his cage and the bird that made its nest amongst the rotting cloth, and I remember how alive was Ben, and the women begging for his love; and now..."

"And now he's dead, and there's an end," Lord Staughton said firmly. "And you and I will ride the road this very night and take ourselves a fat coach in his memory."

"He would expect no less," I said, my spirits rising.

And we did so. We took twenty guineas and two gold watches from a coach just south of Retford, and our nerve held, and we got clear away unscathed. It made me wonder about the impartiality of justice, for it seemed that night that justice was a friend to highwaymen; or maybe it was simply that luck sat upon our shoulders.

In January Lord Staughton went on business connected with

the evolving plot, to London.

"I shan't take you with me, Davy," he said, "for it would be dangerous for you and a burden to me. I have some people to see and some journeys to make, some beyond the seas. You and I must part company. I shall close the house; so best if you go back to your mother's place the while. Or wherever it is that takes your fancy."

"Anywhere, indeed; it makes no difference to you," I laughed derisively.

"It is the wisest course," said Lord Staughton, "considering what I shall be about."

"Will you be coming back?"

"Oh yes," he said easily.

We sat together at the table in the upstairs parlour, counting out the pickings we had amassed over the previous summer. It was a pretty good haul, no doubt about it. Besides the guineas, there was a fair amount of jewellery, which Lord Staughton planned to take to France for disposal. He certainly had no intention of involving himself with Mr Jonathan Wild, which would be the case if he tried to shift the stuff in London. It had been understood from the start that we were robbing for the cause of the King Across the Water, and I didn't quibble about the fact that our cole was not divided equally. I had more than enough for my needs for a good while to come.

I told myself that I had no particular regrets about our parting. I knew our friendship was not meant to last; but it had been a good partnership on the road, and, more, I felt privileged to have learned love's skills from a gentleman so skilful in the same, and so beautiful.

I managed to persuade myself that it was no matter to me if the handsomest man in the world was going off to London and was so easily detaching himself from me. What use could I have been to him in his so important plot against the safety of the realm? Why should it concern me if the King Across the Water took up all his time and devotion and a lover close at hand did not? I put from my mind that reproachful voice which suggested to me that I could have gone with him if he had so chosen. I could have held his horse while he lurked in darkened rooms with fellow conspirators. I could have watched out for the soldiers who were bound to discover them sooner or later. I knew Lord Staughton: I did not think he was the kind to tumble down a monarchy.

"Davy," said my lord then, "are you still receiving letters from the pretty boy at Aunty Mary's place?"

"Lucinda?" I said. "Well, he writes to me at the Crown."

"Ah, yes, the Crown. And how is your good mother, by the by?" enquired his lordship absently.

"Well, thank you," I replied; though in truth she had been somewhat low of spirit when I saw her last. "She is tired of inn-keeping. I am amazed she has endured it this long; she was never one liked drudgery."

"And she keeps Lucinda's letters for you, at the Crown..."

"I daresay there'll be a stack of letters waiting," I said cheerfully. "He seems not to grow tired of my unequal response. I never got into the way of liking writing," I confessed, "but Lucinda is a real scribe, and all his letters evenly shaped and in a straight line."

"When you write to him," said Lord Staughton, putting his fingertips together and regarding me from behind the resultant steeple, "I would suggest it should be put to him that his acquaintance with a certain man of high repute should cease, for his own sake."

"You mean the Earl of Sunderland, the First Lord of the Treasury," I said at once and somewhat provocatively.

"Davy, try to develop discretion," frowned Lord Staughton. "You will find it is so useful when mingling in company. I happen to know that there is trouble brewing for that unfortunate. Lucinda would do well to extricate himself before the storm breaks. He could be damned by implication."

"If I know Lucinda he will stand by his friend," I said stoutly. "He won't leave him if he is in trouble."

"Some of the trouble is political," said Lord Staughton carefully, "but some of it is... personal. An old scandal, with letters... love letters... has come to light, and his lordship will find it difficult to steer a course through it undamaged. The letters are likely to be made public. The knives are out for Sunderland." He took a long deep breath. "The times are inimical to pathick love... even more than is usually so. I fear a witch hunt. At least write to warn Lucinda and let him make up his mind."

"Pathick love?" I said, fidgetting at my ignorance. "What is that?"

Lord Staughton shook his head and laughed exasperatedly. "You have been indulging in it all summer."

While I considered what seemed to me an odd notion — that my particular friendship with Lord Staughton should bear a label — his lordship ceased to smile, and said: "I suggested that you warn Lucinda... I wonder now whether you risk some danger to yourself should you ever go to London."

"Danger? From knowing pathick love?" I said scornfully. "Not me. Besides, I shall deny it."

I wrote my letter of warning to Lucinda, and I helped his lordship make his preparations.

We parted most politely, outside the house, with an affectionate kiss and a grasp of the hand. But a sharp pang about the heart warned me that I minded losing his company far more than I had admitted to myself. He had said he would be back; somehow I did not think so. Whichever way his wretched plot went I could not foresee his living quietly at Staughton, after its outcome. I did not think that I would see him again.

"Take care, my lord," I said and could not help myself from hugging him.

"Take care yourself, Davy," he replied.

I swung into the saddle and turned Gry away from that ramshackle manor which had been my home; I did not look back.

As a boy in London I had once stood at that point where St John's Street peters out and joins the Islington road, where the Great North Road has one of its beginnings. I had looked towards the distant fields in great frustration, for that I was young and weaponless, without a horse, or the strength of manhood to defend myself, and therefore could not leave my pain behind and ride myself into oblivion.

It was a different matter now. With no clear purpose, reason or plan, but simply knowing that the road for me would always be the salve for griefs and disappointments, I took off, northwards.

Chapter Twenty-Nine

IT was the merry month of May when I called in at the Crown on my way south. You might not have recognized me; I was got up very smartly by courtesy of a tailor in Lincoln. Doeskin breeches tight across the hips and a well-cut coat of claret velvet, with thirteen embroidered buttons, and six of the same upon the cuffs, with side pleats and a fashionable split at the back. I had an embroidered waistcoat over a shirt with ruffled wrists, and a lace cravat, and a hat with wide turned-up brim; and a wondrous pair of leather wedge-toed riding boots.

The day was sunny, and the hawthorn flowering in the hedgerows, and I was in good spirits as my faithful Gry and I came ambling down towards the roadside inn.

But I was to find a deal of change at the Crown.

First of all there was no inn sign, and all indication obliterated that the Crown had ever been a tavern. I stabled Gry and entered, only to find more startling changes within.

Gone the brass and pewter and the stink of ale and tobacco. Upon the parlour walls hung pictures in heavy frames, which upon closer inspection seemed all to be scenes from the Bible, which I recognized from my days at school in Bishopsgate. Interspersed with these hung improving texts, sewn by a careful hand —

"The Lord sees all we do. Fear the Lord, O sinner."

Further, I found Susan all in sober garb and sitting sewing by the hearth, demure as anything, and simpering as she told me: "I am become a lady's maid."

The greatest change was the change in Ma. I had left a tapstress — albeit a discontented one — in a blowzy yellow gown and apron edged with a frill, her gown cut low enough about the neck to give clear indication of her comeliness. I found her dressed in black and reading a book — *The Sermons of Jeremiah Wortley.* The apron was still there, but plain and unadorned, and as for a bosom it was left entirely to the fancy as to whether she possessed one, for she was encased in drapery from hem to chin, and here a small gold chain hung bearing a bulky pendant with embroidered lettering, which to my surprise and dismay read 'Repent ye of your sins'. All her hair was contained within a linen cap, with not a curl or ringlet showing, and she lacked all paint and powder. And yet because Selina was a Beauty still, the severity of her garb in no way hid her essential charms, but only brought them into sharper relief, the black gown emphasizing the creamy whiteness of her skin, the cap her wide full lips and lively eyes. I suspected this fact was not lost upon her.

However, she had chosen to cultivate a forbidding exterior and a manner suitable to an abbess. Quite lacking was that merry banter in which she and I used to indulge. No pert remarks concerning sons that turned up when they would with not a thought for grieving parents, and no teasing admiration for the fine clothes I was wearing.

"Don't you like 'em, Ma? D'you see the neat buttons and the leaves and birds embroidered on my waistcoat? And feel the lace of my cravat! And Ma, what about my boots!"

"Gaudy finery don't please the Lord," said Ma severely. "Honest cloth is what He likes."

"I never knew the Lord had views on fashion," I said laughing. "I thought He only dealt in souls and sins."

193

"Davy, do not mock," she said. "We dress only to cover ourselves for modesty's sake and to keep warm in winter. The rest is all frivolity."

"And a health to it!" said I. "I'm disappointed in you, Ma. I thought you'd like my fine things. You won't want the yellow kerchief I bought you then. Silk an' all. And what about my beautiful buttons and each one sewn on so careful? You used to have an eye for a good button, and you'd never have let go by a pair of polished leather boots like these without a whistle. What is it, Ma? What's changed? You look pretty grim in black. You look like one of those Puritans."

"And you sound like a sinner of the first degree," said Ma. "I know how much it costs to sew a coat of that kind, and the buttons that you boast about. And boots so finely turned as would amount to a God-fearing worker's monthly wage. You never got those clothes by honest means."

"I did so," I lied indignantly.

"Will you add subterfuge to thievery?" said Ma.

"I never stole 'em; I bought 'em with earned money."

"Earned how?" she demanded.

"My wages, working with the gentleman who gave me bed and board."

Not entirely satisfied Ma said: "Well, Davy, if you have come to live here you must abide by the rules now set in this house."

"Rules, Ma? You have made some rules for us to live by?"

"Not I. This house has a new master and — I am wed to him."

I received the news with equanimity. "He is a rich man then?" I assumed.

"We live comfortably," she agreed. "But more to the point," she added piously, "he is a good man."

My heart sank. The miserable truth got through to me.

"Ma! Have you been converted?"

"It was about time, son. I was a sinner of the greatest magnitude. It will take the rest of my mortal life to make up for it. I must atone. And I shall do so under the guidance of dear Dr Sylvanus."

"What did you say his name was?" I frowned.

"Sylvanus, dear. He is a very learned man, and reads and writes and makes pronouncements. To hear him talk, you'd swear he was a preacher."

"Would you indeed?" A horrid suspicion was dawning upon me. "Is this Dr Sylvanus one who used to live in London?"

"He did."

"And visited schools where poor boys lived, and told them to be dutiful and serve their betters?"

"Dr Sylvanus has always had the welfare of the poor at heart, and that would include poor boys."

It must be him! It must be that handsome cull who came to Mr Garrett's school and talked about morality. That same man who had sent for me when I had been with Mr Hitchin. That man who asked me questions about whether Mr Hitchin laid a hand upon me, and to bring the matter home to me with greater clarity had touched me himself. *Did Mr Hitchin do this? Did Mr Hitchin do that?* Mr Hitchin had not done so; but Dr Sylvanus had. I twitched with anger at the recollection of what boyhood must endure through its weakness and with good manners at the hands of those who purport to be its moral guardians. Dr Sylvanus had seemed to be on familiar terms with the Almighty. He had talked of loathsome and unnatural vice and then stuck his fingers into my breeches. He had said that men who dressed in women's clothes were repulsive. This of course I knew to be a lie since I had seen Lucinda. And then he had enquired about my mother. A comely woman?... Buxom?

"Ma," I said accusingly. "Is this same Dr Sylvanus devilishly handsome?"

"Davy!" gasped Ma. "Blasphemy!"

But she had not been quick enough to hide the look that crossed her face. Two crimson spots burned in her cheeks. So! Prim and proper as she might appear, it seemed that Selina was not so much changed as she would have the world believe.

"Is he good-looking, ma? And does he wear black satin?"

"Dr Sylvanus is not ill favoured," conceded Ma with dignity. "And he dresses as befits a man of fine discernment."

I heard the sound of a horse and carriage outside and saw through the diamond panes of the window the dark clad figure that climbed down.

"Here he is now, Davy," Ma said with a brightening of the eye. "Be kind now, Davy; you must like him."

This man of fine discernment now stood framed in the doorway. In he came. The briefest of glances sufficed to show that my new stepfather was indeed the figure of my boyhood recollection. Although it was more than ten years since I had last beheld him I found small alteration in him. His hair was more silvery and his face more lined, but this gave him authority and a certain masterful obduracy which was not at all unattractive. Why beat about the bush? He was as handsome as they come! His jaw was firm and square, his brows dark and his eyes bright, his mouth sensuous almost to the point of lewdness. He favoured still black satin. His breeches rustled as he stepped towards me. I had considered myself something of a beau in my new clothes; now I felt graceless and gaudy.

Ma introduced us.

"Davy, my dear son," he said, in that soft purring voice which once had spoken to me of ridding the streets of horrible perversion. "How pleased I am to meet you at long last!"

It seemed that he had made no mention to Selina of his previous encounter with me. For a moment I wondered whether he had forgotten it, an incident no doubt trivial to a man who was God's right hand; but he had specifically asked me about Ma and with something of the flavour of a traveller seeking unknown terrain to explore when chance and time might be appropriate; and surely she had spoken of me and the workhouse school in Bishopsgate. With these cogitations in mind I enquired: "How was it that you first happened to meet my mother?"

"I rode up to the doorway and I paused to quench my thirst. The dear lady was within. I knew at once that she was too good for a life of toil in uncouth company. I determined to raise her to a life more suited to her gentleness and beauty."

"I needed small persuasion," smiled my mother. "But I only marvel that one as worthy as Dr Sylvanus could so demean himself as to have dealings with a poor and shabby widow, ignorant and sinful and unaware of the Lord's great mercy."

"Selina has undertaken to put herself completely into my hands," Dr Sylvanus murmured modestly. "I read works of morality to her and she studies to my direction. It is my delight to teach her and instruct her and if necessary... to correct her."

Selina lowered her eyelids rapidly. I fidgetted, heartily embarrassed. I believed I understood the situation very well. I daresay that it would not be an altogether dull business to receive correction from the worthy doctor. I felt sure he would administer the same with all diligence and fervour.

"Do you intend to favour us with your presence for any length of time?" enquired Dr Sylvanus in the tone of one who hoped for a negative reply. I gladly gave it.

"No time at all. I am on my way to London."

"That Sodom and Gomorrah," he observed disapprovingly.

"Yes sir, that's the one," I answered briskly.

"You will stay overnight at least," said Ma.

"I will; and tell me, Ma, there must be some letters for me.

Have you got them safe?"

"I'm sorry, Davy, but you are mistaken. I have no letters; none have come for you."

"Are you sure, Ma? I would have sworn Lucinda would have written."

"No, dear, nothing."

I was astonished at this, and I noticed further that I was more disappointed than I would have believed possible. How carelessly had I taken for granted Ralph's willingness to supply me with the London gossip and his generous affection for so small response! I wondered if he had grown cool towards me with the passing of time — or worse, had Lord Staughton's forebodings proved correct, and could it be that Ralph had got into some kind of trouble through his friendship with Lord Sunderland?

I was vexed, moreover, for I felt a fool in front of my stepfather for having my expectations so dashed, and so I scowled and went off to the stable to oversee Gry's welfare, and found his company more tolerable than my relations'.

Susan was sent to bring me to dine.

"What do you make of it?" I enquired. "This is an odd business, ain't it?"

"Davy, it's a great improvement," she replied. "We don't work half as hard as we used to and we live in comfort. Two servants pluck the geese and scrub the floors, a stableman attends the horses, and your ma and I sit and learn to read, and go to church by carriage. We are soon to have a harpsichord and learn to play! I must say God is a little too much with us for my liking, but if He must come along with the present life of ease then I am pleased to make Him welcome! Now, come and eat — we don't stint at mealtimes, for all that Dr Sylvanus is so holy!"

When the candles were lit and our meal finished and the night closing in about us, Dr Sylvanus told Ma that she looked tired and suggested that she went to bed. But to my surprise he asked me to sit down with him and take a further glass of wine, and I agreeing, we sat each side of the hearth in the parlour which used to be the inn parlour and where merry conversation had often taken place in times past. Merriment, however, was not to be the issue here.

"Davy," said my stepfather, handing me a glass, "how old are you now?"

"Just twenty-two, sir," I replied.

"You were a boy of — what — eight years old when we last met."

"I was not sure if you remembered that we had met," I said guardedly.

"Oh yes," he answered smoothly. "After all, it was thanks to a chance remark of yours that I made the acquaintance of your mother. My life in London kept me busy all those years, but I had never forgotten that you spoke of a charming widow living near Buckden, in sadness and toil, praying for the love of a good man."

I had not the impression of having so described Ma to him, but no doubt he had formed his own conclusions from whatever I had said.

"It happened," he continued, "that I was passing through Buckden and I wondered whether against all odds the lovely widow would be still available. I made enquiries. Everybody remembered your mother, it seemed. I was told that she had married but was a widow once again and kept a hostelry upon the Great North Road. I had no difficulty finding her. I was afraid that she might have already sought solace under the protection of another; but I was fortunate."

"Yes. She told me she had no great opinion of men and was resolved to live a widow."

"I was able to persuade her to change her mind."

"No doubt," I said caustically. It was the damndest thing that I should find him so attractive when I found his moral stance repugnant and his paternalistic attitude to Ma a matter of some irritation. But every time he crossed one satin thigh upon the other I had a curious dryness in my throat not unlike hunger.

"I myself am a widower," said Dr Sylvanus. "My former wife was a very saintly woman. She believed that the touch of a man's hand upon her flesh was sinful in the Lord's eyes even within the sanctity of marriage. I could not concur with that opinion. And sometimes I was obliged to take what was rightfully mine. By force. Our time together was not a happy one. Your mother now... your mother has no such disinclinations." He coughed. "Quite the converse."

I put down my glass upon the table with every intention of quitting the room.

"You are disturbed to hear me speak of such matters," said my stepfather. "But it is impossible to deny the power of carnality in the human condition, and it is discipline and self-control that curb this dragon. It was my intention to warn you of it in yourself and others, and warning may not be inappropriate since you so rashly purpose to go to London, which, believe me, is a city full of vice, and when I spoke of it in Biblical terms to you you answered flippantly."

"Sir, I do not consider it your place to warn me about that or any other matter."

"When was it that you last went to London, Davy?"

"I have not been there for several years."

"Let me inform you then, that London is composed of two halves, Davy, one good, one evil. The good is the respectable, the family, the church. The evil is the life of vice and shame as personified by the female harlot and the sodomite. Speaking of the latter, your friend Mr Charles Hitchin is still very much — in all senses of the word — at large. If you should for old times' sake meet up with him you will be greatly at risk. You are a comely lad, Davy, and young. He will certainly desire you."

"I am convinced that London town is large enough to contain us both without us ever meeting."

"Pah! London is a village," said Dr Sylvanus dismissively. Then he returned to his favourite theme. "I fear that you have no conception of the magnitude of the wickedness contained in London. There are sodomites in every street, preying on the young, perverting the godly, acting against God's Holy Word. They must be rooted out — destroyed — utterly crushed. It is the duty of the righteous man to make this his aim. God wills it. Did you know that there are houses set aside for sodomites to meet and indulge their depraved appetites only a short distance from where matrons and virgins walk to church?"

"Good Lord!"

"They must be stopped!"

"It would empty the churches, alas."

"Do you mock me, sirrah?" it occurred to him.

"Forgive me. I never knew a father's care and was not raised to honour my elders with all due respect."

"A good whipping would have done the trick," he growled.

"No doubt it pains you that you were not there to administer it," I said drily.

"It is not too late," he panted.

I laughed out loud. "Shall you attempt it?"

He would not; I would have slung him to the ground. Instead he set his face into a supercilious sneer and said: "But perhaps you do not share the ordinary man's aversion to unnatural practices? Your careless response to my proper admonishment suggests to me that you perceive an affinity with these Pathicks — it may have been that Mr Hitchin did indeed debauch you when you were a boy, for all that you did strongly deny it."

"He most certainly did not," I said; but I guessed that he would have liked to. I could hear his voice quite plain: *I shall have thee in the end, Davy, I shall have thee...*

"I must assure you, sir," said I, "that I have no close kinship with anyone at all. In my experience, folk will be close with you for as long as it suits 'em and then they move on. I have learnt to expect nothing and trust nobody."

If I had perhaps recovered from Lord Staughton's rejection of my close acquaintanceship I was still smarting from Lucinda's aberration. "I am my own man and shall be so," I insisted. "After all, in essence we are all alone, all solitary."

But Dr Sylvanus would not be drawn into a discussion upon the nature of the human condition. His mind was fixed upon the condition of the Pathicks, as a cat that watches at a mousehole.

"It used to be that they lived in fear and dread, and of necessity kept their vile ways secret. But they are grown bold. They flaunt themselves upon the streets, and now with these abominable haunts of vice they may meet whom they choose, and eat and drink and worse — as if their *modus operandi* was most natural. They wear women's clothes — they dance — they marry! Well! Not for long. Their days are numbered. Our Society for the Reformation of Manners is strong now, very strong, and the Law is for us. The net is cast and will be tight drawn. Then let them do their dancing from the gallows!"

"You mean that you would hang a man for what he did inside his own house and with another that consented?"

"It is the Lord's wish," answered Dr Sylvanus calmly, "and Heavenly vengeance will fall upon us if we permit buggery in London."

I said nothing, being unfamiliar with the workings of the Almighty mind. Dr Sylvanus continued: "Hanging is the only sure remedy. We have the pillory of course, and I am pleased to hear that Pathicks are caught now every week in London and made to stand in that place of shame; but in despite of the righteous wrath of the townsfolk they usually survive, though very much the worse for wear, and will no doubt pollute the town with further bestiality when they have recovered."

"We must admire their perseverance," I observed. "But my own wears thin, and I shall go to bed."

In my room under the eaves I lay thoughtful and warm — Ma

had left a warming pan between the sheets — and wondered if there were indeed others like Dr Sylvanus in any quantity in London. I had not had much experience of the godly, knowing only rogues and wastrels, except for Gabriel Lawrence and my schoolfriend Jack and his kind-hearted mother.

My own now unlatched my bedroom door and, with all appearance of great secrecy, crept in and placed a lighted candle on the floor beside my trundle bed.

"Under your mattress, Davy," whispered she. "Letters did come for you. But Dr Sylvanus insists on reading everything, so I hid them as they came. I did not think that he was ready for the London gossip of a lad that dresses as a woman." She winked at me. "Sleep well. Oh, and Davy, leave me the yellow silk kerchief you spoke of. Tuck it under the mattress." Then she was gone.

The pleasure I enjoyed upon the reading of Lucinda's letters was partly caused by the discovery that he had written at all. I had so carelessly accepted his devotion, and had surprised myself by the strength of my sadness on supposing that he had grown tired of writing to me. I lay on my stomach, propped up by my elbows, and read Ralph's letters by the candlelight.

"I am sorry to say, Davy, that there is not a pillory in London which does not contain some wretched fellow accused of mollying. It seems to be the fashionable crime. If a man bear a grudge toward another he shouts Rape and the accused must hurry to defend himself. It is no use to plead a drunken stupor; the magistrates, whom we suspect of being leading lights of one or other of the Societies for Reform, are very eager to prove sodomy, for it improves their standing in the eyes of the Lord and pleases the unthinking populace. It is no longer safe therefore to swive in the back room of a tavern or the Lincoln's Inn boghouses, for here it has been known for constables to wait all night on pretext of a lengthy piss and then cry sodomite to anyone who looks down at their Member from Cockshire for longer than a moment..."

"Hell Fire clubs are being discovered almost with as much frequency as molly scandals. It seems the noblemen of our land are all now to be found by night in caves and cellars where strange rites are performed by candlelight and naked virgins of both sexes, slaughtered hens, black candles, monkish cowls, and curiously carved Spanish daggers are the accessories. I have never met anyone who has attended such a ceremony, but I hear they are all the rage, and I believe my social life a little lacking in richness by comparison..."

"Badger Riddlesdon, who was sentenced to transportation, escaped and was seen living riotously with lewd women somewhere in the north. But he was caught and now is in Newgate once again..."

"A man that was hanged at Tyburn said from the gallows that he believed that there were so many sodomites in the city and the suburbs that they would bring down that same judgement from Heaven as fell upon Sodom and Gomorrah. The speech is published and is circulated and will no doubt start a panic among the good folk of London town. Flame, flood and pestilence in whatever form will no doubt be ascribed to us henceforth..."

"My dear Lord S- was very much disturbed today. He fears that an ancient scandal which occurred when he was a young man may be revived by the publication of some letters. I have never seen him so distant and withdrawn. He was not at all himself. His mind was patently elsewhere. I am very troubled, Davy, and I wonder what I might do for the best. He has been very good to me..."

I blew out the candle. It seemed plain to me that events were closing in upon Lord Sunderland. But Lucinda? Was there any need for him to be caught up in whatever trouble was to follow? Lord Staughton had known something of the matter and he had thought it best I warn Lucinda; I had done so. I now thought that maybe I could be of use to him if I were there beside him.

As to Lord Staughton's misgivings as to my own safety should I go to London I dismissed them with a shrug. I did not imagine for a moment that I would be in any danger.

But in this supposition I was to find myself mistaken.

Part IV
The Masqueraders

Chapter Thirty

AS soon as I arrived in London I became embroiled in strife. The white waysides thick with hawthorn flower and cowparsley which had been my companions upon the road gave way to the narrow streets and closely packed houses of Clerkenwell and Smithfield ; and the scent of may was dissipated by the well remembered smell of gutter filth, smoke, butchery and roasting; and the chorus of birdsong in the windy trees gave way to the clatter of carts and the noise of humankind. This latter sound now became more pronounced — so much so that I drew rein to see what caused the clamour, which was of truly exceptional proportion.

I must have been expecting trouble, because I stopped to load and prime my pistols. I now drew rein. Where St John's Street joined with St John's Lane and Peter's Lane there stood a pillory. A motley crowd some thirty strong in various positions of hostility was ringed about it, hurling missiles and abuse at the poor wretch pinioned there. Whether the object of the fury was a creature male or female, young or old, it was impossible to tell, for it was so besmeared with mud and worse that its features and shape were obscured entirely, but it stood knee deep in offal and sir-reverence, the stench of which was enough to make a fellow puke; but not the righteous citizens, whose efforts to obliterate the criminal redoubled themselves whenever there had been a momentary flagging of enthusiasm.

I leaned towards a chap and shook his shoulder. It was all I could do to engage his attention, so engrossed in his task was he. He turned a glazed gaze upon me, his hand in a claw-like grip upon a clod of mud.

"Lord save us, whatever is his crime?" said I.

"A molly!" said the man and flung the clod.

Now I was come a stranger into London from the Great North Road where the air is clean and the wind blows free, and maybe if I had been long habituated to the city's ways I would have seen no perverseness in the ritual before me, for after all, upon the road we have our justice and our punishments; but at that moment it occurred to me that even the dead highwayman swinging in his chains at a crossroad with the crows a-pecking at his eyes possessed a certain solitary dignity; but this...

I swear it was a natural revulsion and no more that made me at the next lull in the communal blood-lust draw my pistol and fire a shot into the air. In slow degrees the mob turned gawping eyes to me, blinking like folk coming to a bright light from the dark. Gry reared up; we were a monstrous impressive pair.

"What? Would you kill him?" I shouted.

"He deserves it," one growled in reply.

"Are there no officers of justice here to prevent it?"

"They're boozing in the White Hart across the road. They said he was all ours."

"Then you shall take better care of him. Any man that would do otherwise goes home with a bullet in him and I never miss my aim. You — go bring the officers forth. And you — go fetch a pail of water and douse him down. Do it, I say!" I jerked my other pistol in his direction and he ran off.

It was fortunate the crowd gave me no trouble as I could not have reloaded in the saddle; but the threat of the remaining bullet seemed to do the trick, and though they glowered and grumbled they became reluctantly obedient.

More than one pail was needed, slung at the heap of dung that hung there. The form of a young man emerged at length, more dead than alive it seemed to me. The intensity of their passion a little abated by the check upon its course, the crowd grew sullen and resorted more to speech than baying.

"Who are you, anyway?"

"Why spoil our sport?"

"Don't you know his crime?"

"He was caught in buggery."

"He denied it," said another. "But they proved him guilty."

"He denied it?" jeered the first. "So he would. Wouldn't you?"

"Where are you from, not to know the story?" said the cull I spoke to first.

I did not reply, maintaining my position of alertness, watching for the officers' return; but I sensed their curiosity. Keen eyes assessed my riding boots, my pistols, Gry, who waited patiently, but tense, as I was.

"I'd swear he was a highwayman."

No particular hostility in his tone. Admiration, even envy. Of rogues and villains your Gentleman of the Road is the cream, no one will deny that. Over the heads of my observers I saw the officers in charge of the pillorying now coming from the White Hart.

I laughed. "Me? I am a passer by."

I stuffed my pistols into my belt and turned Gry's head. In order to make myself less conspicuous I dismounted, having no intention of discoursing with the officers. I made for the obscurity of Peter's Lane.

"Mr Davy Gadd!" A voice spoke from the darkness of a doorway. A shadow disengaged itself. "Mr Davy Gadd — I invite you to drink with me."

Devil take me, it was Jonathan Wild. My expression must have shown something, I know not what, for "You remember me, I see," he said.

"More surprising yet," I answered, "you remember me."

"I never forget a face," said Jonathan, "even one I have not seen for seven years. Since Jamie Goodman danced his way into eternity, and all because of a necklace set with emeralds."

"I'll drink with you if you like," I said, "But I need a good stable for my horse."

"Let us cross over to the Windmill Inn." He gestured regally, as if he were in league with Providence and had procured the inn and its decent stable for this especial purpose.

We sat there, I and Jonathan, in the dark inn parlour. He bought us a bottle of Burgundy and two glasses were set down for us. It was in my best interests to preserve at least the appearance of amiability; this was a man with influence, and if I was intending to be long in London I could do without his enmity.

I watched him. He was much as I remembered, though plainly more prosperous. He must have been then a little under forty, not tall, broad-browed, big-nosed, square-faced, with eyes of great alertness. He kept his hat tightly in place over a neat wig, and I recalled Lucinda's gossip: *he has not an entire skull, and his head is kept together by polished silver plates...* It was all I could do not to let my eyes stray in a curious manner towards his pate. His face was not ill-favoured. The lines about his mouth were cynical, but showed amusement. I knew to my cost that he considered himself a man of humorous notions. Was this one, treating me to good Burgundy at six shillings a bottle, and equivalent politeness? He carried a silver staff. His stumpy fingers gripped the end of it and he laid it across his knees. It did not escape my attention that there was a company of villains grouped about a table not three yards from where we sat, great hulking brutes no man would wish to tangle with. One of them was Blueskin Blake. A bodyguard, it seemed, for Mr Wild. They drank and diced, but their eyes never left us. It was not a comfortable sensation.

"Did you know him, Davy?" Mr Wild enquired.

"Know who?"

"The sodomite you saved. Was it for old times' sake you held off the crowd?"

"I don't know him from Adam," I shrugged.

"You took a risk there. I admire that. You had courage."

"Nah — I had pistols," I grinned.

"Let me understand you. You didn't even know who it was beneath the slime? And still you thought him worth saving?"

"It's for punishment, the stoop, not murder, ain't it?"

"With sodomites..." He scratched his chin, as if suggesting something implicit and left unsaid. "Did you know he was a sodomite?"

"No," I lied. "But he was a fellow creature."

"The brotherhood of mankind, then, not the brotherhood of buggery."

"That's the way of it," I said and swigged my drink.

He was watching me, looking at my clothes. "You have got on well in the world since I saw you last," he observed approvingly.

"Not bad," I agreed warily, putting my empty glass down carefully upon the table.

"The north road has been good to you."

My eyes widened. How did he know that?

He gave a little laugh, without opening his mouth — it was a laugh that came from his nose.

"Davy, I know everything," he said affably. "About everybody. And what I don't know now I will have found out by the time you next see me."

"I have no secrets," I coughed.

"Then you've nothing to fear, boy, have you?" he said comfortably, not believing me. "Let me tell you how much I admire your skills. The de Lacy coach outside Stamford now, that was a good haul. I would have thought to have seen you in London before now with your pickings for disposal. I have to suppose that you got them out of the country instead. But I don't bear grudges. You'll come to me in the end."

I grinned in spite of myself.

"Was I amusing?" he enquired, raising one eyebrow.

"No sir. Only that Mr Hitchin once said the same to me, or

words to that effect; though I daresay he meant other."

"Mr Hitchin is a has-been," Mr Wild said. "He lets his appetites — all of them — rule his life. They'll be the death of him, one or other of them. Steer clear of him, Davy, he'll do you no good."

"Whereas you, sir... ?" I supposed.

"You've got to work in my employ, Davy," Mr Wild said conversationally, as if he were observing that it rained. "You must. I can't protect you otherwise."

"I don't need protecting. I can look after myself."

"They all say that, to begin with," he smiled tolerantly. "But I always have them. Sooner or later. Davy, I could crook my little finger and bring any number to the hanging tree. Someone no longer useful — someone too ambitious. Small fry, Davy, small fry." He shifted in his seat and carefully laid the silver cane across the table. With one hand he slowly rolled it to and fro, never losing touch of it. I wondered if it were true that there was a blade within. I watched the rhythmic rotation of its knobbed head. He said: "I take a chap who's in a gang. I persuade him to peach his mates. I get a new chap to peach the first — everyone's got something on everyone else. And down they tumble like a row of ninepins, for they've all committed felony, the dears. Sometimes I have to throw one to the wolves to keep the good citizens happy, to show them that I'm working for their interest and well being. They see me bringing offenders to justice — it reassures them of my good faith." He smiled modestly. "I learn much from Madame Spider — a little tug at the links of my web and one fly or another goes tumbling to oblivion. I can get forty pound a man. I don't boast," he added. "I state the facts."

"You've got nothing on me, Mr Wild," I said. "You're only guessing."

"I don't want to threaten you, boy. I want you to come to me willingly because you can see that's how you'll prosper. Look at my successes. I got Goodman, didn't I? I got the gang that murdered Mrs Knap in Gray's Inn Gardens. I won't tolerate murder, see," he told me disapprovingly. "I got the Whitehall gang. I got White," he said, and, snapping the fingers of his free hand, one by one, with a noisy cracking of the joints, went on: "drunk in Lewkenor's Lane and easy meat. I got Chapman in White Horse Alley. Then we found Isaac Rag hiding in the alleys round St Giles and he peached twenty others. We got Thurland at the Bell; and Riddlesdon got the last of that batch for me, Tim Dun. Shot him in the face."

"I remember Isaac Rag."

"One-eyed Isaac now. He had his eye shot out."

"He used to live by the paupers' burial ground. He used to grin a lot."

"His grin is twisted now," said Jonathan sardonically. "But what's it to us? He grins the other side of the Atlantic! He was transported some two years ago. It's down to me who goes, who stays." He paused, reflective. He brightened. "Hawkins I got. Awaiting hanging even as we speak. A man after your own heart, Davy — fifty coaches he took last year and where did it get him? Hawkins' gang, Shaw's gang — all nubbed now or rotting in the Whit; and all down to me. You see, they weren't working for me. So they had to go. I'm telling you this, Davy, so you know the way it is."

"I appreciate your frankness, Mr Wild."

"Davy, I can get a cull out of Newgate, one that looks as though there's no way out for him but past St Sepulchre's and along the Tyburn road. The Newgate turnkeys are in my pocket, see. I know them all. I can get a doomed man out of Newgate. Or in," he added.

"I see that you are much to be admired," said I.

"I live in Great Old Bailey now," he said. "A good big house, close to the source of justice and of retribution. I have my office there, for the recovery of lost and stolen property. They all come to me, you know, the quality. I'm well known for my charity, and my successes on behalf of law and order. They say that supernatural powers assist me," he chuckled. "Perhaps they do. Perhaps the Devil sits upon my shoulder."

I found myself looking, just to make sure, but reminded myself that were he to be present Old Nick would no doubt be invisible.

"You see, Davy," Mr Wild confided, "you're looking at success. And them as comes along a-me will share it all. I'm offering you the chance to be one of that number. You're fresh in London — you don't know how it is. You could through being unwary land yourself in any kind of trouble. But with my guiding hand, well, it's another matter. So, what do you say?"

"Mr Wild," I said, "why do you want me?"

"From the kindness of my heart," said Jonathan. "A charitable spirit. I want what's best for you; I want to see you thrive. I don't want to see you step into a pit and wake up one morning in the Whit and find yourself listening to St Sepulchre's bell and the bellman telling you tomorrow you die. That would be so dreary, Davy, such a waste, and your young neck in a necklace of hemp and your fine boots kicking at the air, and your pleasing young body stripped by strangers who'll cut you up like a piece of cloth and poke about in your insides; no, that isn't what I want for you."

"There we are much in accord, sir," answered I, "and I am sensible of your kind concern for my welfare. But what do you need me for, Mr Wild? I am a country boy with few skills, new to London, as you say, and you are by your own admission already well furnished with many loyal servants, however rapidly they seem to be diminishing."

"I am well furnished with loyal servants," he cried emotionally, "and every one as dear to me as if they were my own children. And I have always thought it proper to take care of my chaps. You would be well looked after, Davy. You would do as you have done before, but all your pickings you would bring to me, that is, to a place of safety under my direction. You would be recompensed for your trouble. And you would be safe, because you would be one of mine. No worries; no fear of betrayal. A brotherhood. Now, what d'ye say?"

"I think you suppose me more worthy than I am."

"I think that you are lucky, and I think that you believe yourself to be so, which is halfway to being it. I know you for a brave young sprig; oh yes, there'd be enough in it for me to make it worth my while and yours."

"Mr Wild," said I. "I am most heartily aware of the kind offer you make me but I cannot go along with your suggestion. I think that you mistake my trade — I've worked as groom and ostler, tapster, stable lad — my skills lie here and nowhere else. But whatever I embark upon, I prefer to work alone, favouring neither one nor another. Trouble comes from getting close, or so it seems to me. While I wish you well, sir, I would sooner keep myself apart. It does not suit my nature to be part of a brotherhood, even one where a man as mighty as yourself cares for us all."

"Ben Child believed that he could best work alone," said Jonathan, not a whit impressed with my tales of respectable employment. "And look what happened to him."

I said nothing. There was no denying it. I hardened my heart against the thought of that golden-haired hero with the women at his knees and the singing in the air about him, who now hung in his chains on Hounslow Heath and the crows pecking at his eyes. Mr Wild had been instrumental in that; Mr Wild had been behind his capture. I fidgetted in my seat. I would have jumped up and got well clear of that place in the instant; but the bodyguard had pistols too and there were half a dozen of them.

But Jonathan made it easy for me. He stood up.

"Our conversation is at an end," he said, and tapped his silver cane upon the bench in small jerky movements of intense vexation. I stood up too, relieved, and when he offered me his hand to grasp I took it, having no wish to be on bad terms with him, and hoping, if somewhat fondly, that the case was closed upon the matter. He put his arm about my shoulder in a possessive affability, veering me thus in the direction of his heavies.

"Let me introduce my friends to you — Mr Hell-and-Fury Sykes... Mr Quilt Arnold and Mr Abraham Mendez my particular helpmeets... my brother Mr Andrew Wild... and Mr Blueskin Blake... Gentlemen, this is Mr Davy Gadd," he said to them as if he and I were the best of friends, and adding in a no way reassuring tone: "You'll know him again."

They would, I knew it. Feeling somewhat of a marked man I quit the inn parlour and went off to the stable.

"Oh Gry, lad," I murmured into the mane of my trusty friend. "This is a bad place for us; we were best to get back on the road."

But I had come to see that all was well with Lucinda; and such was still my intention.

I found that there were soldiers in the streets of London. Their regiments were encamped in Hyde Park. They were assembled for the defence of the realm against a suspected Jacobite conspiracy. Soldiers, hundreds of 'em. There were knots of 'em on street corners. They were jumpy and carried muskets. I wondered not for the first time what had happened to Lord Staughton and what would happen to him and his kind; and what chance did they stand against a city that was ranged against them?

Or any of us — what chance did we stand that went — for whatever reasons — against authority?

I thought that London seemed a place of menace.

Chapter Thirty-One

A HEARTFELT warning to Lucinda about the trials of too close involvement with a member of the nobility who might trifle with the affections of a simple boy and bring him down in the toils of his misguided political entanglements proved superfluous. Lord Sunderland was dead.

I was ushered through the portals of Aunty Mary's. I didn't know the chap who let me in, but he went to fetch Aunty Mary when I said I knew Clarissa.

"Who shall I say is here?" he asked me. I hesitated.

"Delia," I said most reluctantly; but I didn't think they'd know me otherwise.

Aunty Mary came into the parlour. He looked much older than I remembered him — he must have been in his fifties — small and slim with neat grey hair and a plain black suit of clothes and the shiniest buckled shoes. His face, even smiling, had an air of marked desolation; in repose it bore the expression of one who had just learnt his entire kin had died of the plague.

"Delia," he said and took both my hands in his.

"You do remember me then," I said dubiously. "It has been seven years."

"I have not been permitted to forget you," he said ruefully, gesturing me to a seat. "Lucinda has been determined not to let you go, and the gathering of snippets for his letters has engrossed us all. Letters which, may I say, have not been as enthusiastically answered."

"I was never handy with a pen. It's all I can do to write a straight line. As to spelling words so folk can understand 'em, it takes me all day. I was taught, but my heart was never in it. I'd sooner see a chap face to face. That's why I'm here."

"Lucinda has been in a sorry state since his lordship died, only last month. I fear he cherished hopes of some permanent outcome to their friendship. Of course, this would have been highly improbable. And the circumstances of his lordship's going were so very odd..."

"I know nothing of them."

"Well, the suddenness..." Aunty Mary said helplessly. "He was here not two days before, a well man, not elderly or infirm. Forty-seven. Well, that's no age... though of course he told us he was younger."

"But what killed him?"

"Oh, there is some talk of lungs and kidneys and any number of those grisly internal organs that we all possess and never know it till they seize up on us." Aunty Mary shrugged dismissively. "It is common knowledge that he took poison."

I could not help a smile. "Common? Where did you hear it?"

"It is Whispered on the Streets," said Aunty Mary huffily, as if that were the definitive method of purveying all truths.

"Something about love letters to be published," I recalled.

"My dear, it is much more intricate than that." Aunty Mary drew up his chair closer to mine, with the air of one who abandons decorum and settles to the pleasure of a gossip. "There is an old scandal about to break, something from his lordship's distant past. All I know is that his lordship in his youth was passionately in love with the Beauty of his day, a young man of incredible charm and no fortune who lived extravagantly at Sunderland's expense. This young man was killed in a duel in mysterious circumstances after a quarrel with his lordship; and he who killed him fled abroad; but is now returned with a royal pardon under his belt and certain letters which passed between the lovers. The question that is being asked is why return now? Why now, when there are so many moves afoot utterly to discredit Sunderland?"

"Well, why?"

"The finishing touch, dear. Whatever else is contained within these letters — and I have heard the murkiest whispers — they will certainly reveal his lordship's true inclinations. He would have been ruined. Ruined! No, believe me, he took poison."

"That is a sad tale you relate, sir, that a man must die for fear the world hears that he was in love."

"The world has its own views on whom it is proper to love and finds nothing so agreeable as to see a great man fall for deviating from them."

In truth there seemed no more to say. I stood up. "And now, if you'll permit it, sir, may I see Lucinda?"

Ralph tear-stained and gin-sodden was not a pretty sight; and yet he was, for there was that about him which was curiously appealing. He was sitting on his bed eating gingerbread and reading. He flung down his book and gawped at me. I stepped into the room and kissed his cheek, cautiously, like someone visiting the sick.

"But this is wonderful, Davy!" he exclaimed brightening. "Why didn't you say you were coming to London? Why are you here? Is it just to see me?"

"Exactly that; just to see you." I sat beside him on the bed and helped myself to gingerbread.

"And you received my letters?"

"They were waiting for me at Ma's, so I know all the news, and think I've never been away."

"But you have. Bad boy! Seven years! How could you bear to be away from London for so long? What could you find to do, away from London? What is there, outside London?"

I laughed. "There's the Road," I said.

"What road?" he said grumpily.

"The north road, Ralph, the one that goes to York and further."

"But what can you do with a road except go along it from one place to another?"

"Numbskull! It's a whole world. It's the sky and the rain and the sun, it's the people you meet, and it's the wondering what's around the next corner. Sometimes it's danger, but not if you keep your wits about you. It's stabling your horse in a good stable, and the lights of the inn beckoning, and the singing and drinking, and hearing where people have been and what happened to them — through their own fault or the fault of the road. And there's the chance you might find gold."

"Oh Davy!" He looked at me very pained. "You aren't still hoping to find that crock of gold the highwayman buried? Claude Duval? Have you been looking all this time?"

"Yes, mostly," I said defensively.

"And you haven't found it, in seven years?"

"Looking for it could take a lifetime."

"But is that how you want to spend your life?"

"Yes it is," I answered stoutly.

"But isn't that a little... pointless?" said my pragmatic friend.

"Duval's gold is special," I said. "To find it would be like taking on Duval's mantle. It would mean you were as good as him. Worthy. I'd count my time on earth well spent if I could find his gold."

"What would you do with it?"

I shrugged. "I don't much think about that, Ralph. I'd live like a gentleman, of course, with a big house in a park, and a stable big enough for any number of horses. Go to horse fairs and buy the best. Race 'em against the nobility. Win, of course. And clothes... I'd have new clothes — good shirts, good boots; and several pairs of pistols, all silver-butted."

"You're halfway there already, Davy — look at you! That's a new coat, and that's a lace cravat. You haven't done so badly for yourself without the finding of buried treasure."

I put on a modest face. "I've been lucky."

This made Ralph despondent. "I haven't," he said. "You heard about my loss."

"You mean his lordship."

"What else? I've lost not only a certain way of life but also something of the future. I thought that we might be together, he and I. And I did hope that the love of those who held him dear might have moved him to lay hold on life in spite of circumstance.

It seems he did not hold me in as high regard as I believed. Not even a letter of explanation, something to cherish and remember him by."

"I dare say he thought writing letters had got him into enough trouble already — and maybe would have done you no good neither. Best forget him, Ralph. Now he's gone they'll say all kinds of things; men do when the chap can't answer back."

"Forget him?" sniffed Lucinda. "How little you understand."

"I won't let you sit there getting the vapours like a lady. I do know something of your trouble, so there. Do you remember who we called Clarissa, the handsome lord who first brought me here? I lived with him and we travelled the road together for a while, and he shared something of his secrets. But I knew he'd be off sometime and sure enough he was. A quick goodbye and that was an end to it — nothing about missing me or joining him in London, or wherever it was he was going. Though I knew he'd drop me one day I can tell you that it wasn't easy. Not that he died and caused me that kind of grief as yours is; but I haven't got him any more and he was very dear to me."

"How did you bear it then?" Lucinda asked all tremulous.

"I took off up the road."

Ralph looked at me in such utter blankness that I laughed.

"That was my remedy; and now you must find a road, and that's the way of it."

Aunty Mary, who had been listening at the door, said: "Persuade him to go out tomorrow night, Davy. His road need not be a long one — just about the length of Holborn. There's a masquerade at Mother Clap's and all are invited."

The full thrust of his grief being already somewhat abated by the passing of a month, I did not find it too difficult to convince Ralph that it would be more agreeable to be among folk on pleasure bent than alone with a jug of gin. I did not stay at Aunty Mary's that night, but returned to the inn at whose stables I had left Gry, and rested well there and saw Gry comfortable.

When I returned to Aunty Mary's in the morning Ralph was looking cheery, sitting at a table sipping chocolate and eating toasted bread and honey and perusing sheafs of drawings, the which seemed to be a series of extravagant costumes, all female.

"Davy, it is a masquerade; I must dress up; they will expect it; and so must you."

"Indeed I shall not."

"I shall find something to suit you."

"Not from amongst those beauties."

"Everyone dresses as something they are not."

"I'll go as a sturdy beggar then; the more raggedy the better."

"What a spoilsport, Davy; and I shall be so tasteful."

"What will you be?"

"A shepherdess. But I am short of ribbons. Look!" Lucinda stood and opened up a tall cupboard door. A wealth of silk and taffeta burst forth, and from amongst these he took a blue and violet striped skirt, a layer of petticoats, a chemise and a bodice.

"Have you not still the ones I gave you?"

"Yes, but they are all bedraggled now; I wore them so much."

"Then I'll buy you some more, and we'll go out together and you shall choose them, from the very shop where I bought those."

"Oh, Davy, lovely!" said Lucinda. "And where was that?"

"Mr Kneebone's, in the Strand."

"I know it," said Lucinda gleefully. "And we'll have a further treat, for there's a pretty chap who serves there, with yellow hair and teasing eyes."

"Is there?" I grinned. I did indeed hope so. "Then make yourself smart and off we'll go and have our satisfaction. But Ralph," I added warily, remembering our day at the Frost Fair, "put on your breeches, not your skirts." I envisaged Jack's mother — whom I heartily respected — seeing through Ralph's dissembling and calling for the constables.

We set off merrily enough, the weather fine and warm, a ballad singer on every street corner. The place of danger and foreboding through which I rode after having quit the company of Jonathan Wild was miraculously transformed into a kind of Arcady, where everyone we passed seemed pleasing — pretty women, pretty boys, hawkers of baubles, orange sellers, persons of quality in lace and satin, liveried footmen, painted chairs, fine horses, flower sellers thrusting ribboned bunches under our noses. Yet it was the same city, and the muck and smoke were still there did I but choose to notice them, the gutter offal ever present, and the soldiers prowling, ready to rid the nation of Jacobites; and the ever present threat of Mother Tyburn and the Whit, like dark presences behind the gaiety. But inexplicably they were not in my thoughts as I steered Ralph down Drury Lane, past the wicked portals of the Rose and so down Bridges Street and Catherine Street into the Strand.

Taking my bearings I looked out for the sign of the Angel. The new church they had been building, St Mary's, was finished now, with a fine steeple, and Mr Kneebone's shop was just nearby. I slapped my hand down on a pickpocket reaching for my purse, and we made our way to the door and so within.

The interior of the shop had been a little altered. The memory of Jack standing there amongst the billowing laces, like the honey at the centre of a flower, faded rapidly; for it was Mr Kneebone who stood beside the counter, folding away a roll of silk. Behind him shelves of silks, muslins, serges, taffetas, and cloth of silver; to one hand a vast array of ribbons. Ralph began to handle them assessingly.

"Can I help you gentlemen?" Mr Kneebone said in a voice which bordered on the suspicious.

"We wish to see some ribbons," Ralph began.

"I was hoping to see Jack," I said. "I am a friend from his childhood days."

"Jack no longer lives here," Mr Kneebone said unhelpfully.

"Has his mother gone and all?" I asked.

"His mother," said the draper in the tone of one who plainly considered her whereabouts no affair of mine, "is at present far too busy to receive a caller."

"Nonetheless," said I, with a careful hint of menace, "I'd like to see her."

Sucking his teeth in irritation — I was after all younger and stronger than him — Mr Kneebone put his head around a door and with the remainder of his person firmly planted in the shop — a vantage point from which he hoped to witness us when we snitched an armful of silks — he called:

"Mrs Sheppard!"

Jack's ma came scurrying from the back room, paused, and said: "Davy? Is it Davy Gadd? You have grown so smart and comely! Well — you was always comely..."

"But you have known me when I was not so smart," I grinned. I hesitated to give her a hug; Mr Kneebone's disapproving presence lent a dampener to the procedings, and I thought he might reprove her afterwards. I asked if she was keeping well; she was. I introduced Ralph; we spoke briefly about changes in the city; and I asked her about Jack.

"Jack lives in Wych Street now." She was plainly very proud of him. "He is apprenticed to Mr Owen Wood and learning carpentry and house joining and lock making. He has his own room and is doing very well."

"I'd like to see him while I am in London."

"He'll be pleased to see you, dear."

I thanked her and turned to go.

"Davy!" cried Lucinda with black brows. "We came here for ribbons."

Chastened I attended to that business, buying everything Lucinda asked for, as a penance for forgetting. He was very sulky as we came away, scowling over half a dozen rolls of cloth.

"Why didn't you tell me you knew Jack? I feel a fool. When did you know him? You never intended to buy ribbons, did you? It was an excuse. Why do you want to see him? Was he your lover?"

"No indeed," said I with some regret.

"But you wished it?" persisted Ralph.

"If I did, much good may it have done me, since he told me I should be going after women. The same, I guess, as he was."

"Then why do you want to see him?"

"For old times' sake, that's all."

"You fancy him, I know it. And why not? He was very pert and personable."

"I told you, he likes women. But that has nothing to do with anything. Don't be so sour; you've got half a shopful of satins. Since Wych street is so near and on our way I see no reason why we should not visit it. Go home if you don't want to."

But I knew he would not; his curiosity was too strong.

The sound of Mr Owen Wood's carpentry workshop came to us from the open windows in the narrow cobbled street. Squinting through the windows we could see work benches and lads hunched over them, using lathes, long-handled gouges, chisels.

"That's him," I said; and without more ado we went in and made ourselves known to Jack.

"It's midday," I said. "Why don't you leave this work and have a drink with us?"

"I ain't supposed to leave the house," said Jack. "But you can come up to my room; there's bread and cheese and beer."

We followed Jack up a dark and winding stair to a garret room with a small barred window, its ceiling shaped by the angle of the roof, and the joists thrusting across it. A mattress lay upon the floor.

"Small but cosy," Jack said with a laugh.

The place was stifling hot. I was loosening my cravat throughout our conversation, tugging at my collar.

We squatted there and shared the warm beer and the steaming cheese. Jack spoke about his work. Lucinda preserved a dignified silence. We recalled old times. Something I had never noticed before — Jack spoke with a stammer. 'S-small but c-cosy,' he said. It was disconcerting.

"I'm really glad to be quit of Mr Kneebone," Jack said. "I never liked 'im, yer know. 'e was so friggin' good to us. Can yer think what it's like always bein' beholden? Gotta be grateful, Ma said, and polite, 'e's took us in all out of charity; we'd be on the streets else and you'd end up like Tom. You be good, Jack, and always do like what you're told and one day you can get a trade and stand on your own feet. So I bin good for years. It's worn me to a frazzle."

"Yeah. You was always skinny and pale. I reckon you got worse'n I remember. Don't they feed you here? It makes me think of Bishopsgate."

"It's givin' me a trade, see. When I quit here I'll be my own man, earn me livin'."

"What did your ma mean, end up like Tom?"

"My brother took to crime. You remember as 'e joined a gang."

"Yeah, he was always wild, was Tom."

"We got Bad Blood in our family, see. It must've all gone into Tom, Ma says." He laughed. "She don't know my dark thoughts. I reckon I got some of it. But I can't stand to see her disappointed. She's got Tom to put up with. She don't need me to let her down and all. Tom never could have stood the life I had. Tom never could have been so dutiful. And it wasn't friggin' easy."

"But things are better now?" I said doubtfully.

"Oh yeah, I'm learnin' locks now — makin 'em, takin' 'em apart, fixin' 'em on doors an' cupboards."

I grinned, trying to mask my discomfort. He was so pale, Jack, dead white and thin and little, and he stammered so — cu-cu-cupboards was what he said, on the s-streets, he said, s-see her disappointed.

"I better get back to me work," he said. "Mr Wood will be back; I don't want 'im to catch me skivin'."

We stood up. I winced at the notion of a man giving orders to a friend of mine. It wouldn't do for me. I wouldn't have it.

Then Jack said: "Davy — how'd you get them decent clothes?"

We looked down at my coat and its embroidered buttons.

"And do I see a silver-butted pistol not quite hidden there down at your waist?" he continued. "What's it all abaht then, eh?"

I stared at him. What should I say? Did I know him well enough to trust him with the truth? I thought I did.

"I got 'em... on the road," I said. "The one helped me to the other." He knew what I meant.

We clambered noisily down the twisty stairway, holding on to the wall, as it was pretty dark. We left Jack at his bench.

"He's not as pretty as I remember," said Lucinda waspishly.

"No, you're right, and all his spark's gone. I wish," I added roughly, kicking at a stone, "I wish I'd never bothered seein' him."

"Trapped," Lucinda said. "That's how he looked. Trapped."

"I don't want to talk about it," I said.

As we came up Drury Lane. somewhere in the region of Martlet's Court, we heard the sound of running feet behind us. I spun round, a hand to my pistol, the other arm thrusting Lucinda clear, for I assumed that we were about to be robbed. Not so, as it proved, but yet we were the object of the pursuers.

"Davy Gadd! Stand! We want to talk to you."

"Blueskin Blake!" It was the one man in London any chap would recognize at a moment's glance, he with the dark blue-shadowed visage. That I had seen him amongst Jonathan Wild's heavies at the Windmill tavern was a further cause of my instant recognition of the man. His corpulent shape was heaving with the effort of his running and for a moment he was unable to speak, coughing with exertion.

His companion, being lean and fit, sufferered no such incapacitation. He was tall with spiky tawny-coloured hair, and him at first I did not recognize nor pay much heed to, a mistake I would be sorry for. I waited, and my hand stayed on the pistol butt.

"Davy Gadd," said Blueskin, "I have a message for you, from Mr Jonathan Wild."

"Yes?"

"You are invited — cordially, he said — he said to tell you it was cordially —"

"Yes? Cordially?" I said impatiently.

" — invited cordially to breakfast with him at his house in Great Old Bailey tomorrow morning."

"What for?" I said ungraciously.

"You're new to London, ain't yer?" Blueskin Blake said scornfully. "Mr Wild gives breakfasts to his friends and pensioners. He calls it a levy. There was a king in France who did the same — his courtiers stood around his bed and watched him gettin' up and puttin' on his clothes, and they had breakfast and the king gave them their orders. It was called a levy. Anyone'll tell yer. Mr Wild has levies, and you're asked to come along."

"Now why should I want to see Mr Wild in bed and putting on his clothes?" I laughed derisively. "And breakfast I can get anywhere."

"You don't understand," said Blueskin. "It's an honour."

"It's an honour I can do without."

"You don't understand," Blueskin repeated dully. "We call it an invitation so as to do the thing proper. But it's like an order, see. You have to go."

"Damn me, I do not."

"All kinds of folk'll be there," Blueskin wheedled. "Thieves and scamps and creditors and people beggin' for his favour. It's a foot in the door, Davy Gadd, a step up the ladder. No one refuses."

I was vexed and disgruntled because of Jack's plight and I had not the wit to frame my words with any diplomacy.

"Here's one that does," I said. "Mr Wild has no cause to give me orders. I'm heartily sick of Mr Wild. Tell him to leave me alone and stop bothering me. I said I would not work for him and there's an end. Tell him to give his breakfasts to the poor and needy. Or stick them somewhere else."

Blueskin Blake's face creased slowly into a frown as it began to occur to him what I had said. "You want me to tell that to Mr Wild? Them very words?"

"Why not? I ain't afraid of Mr Wild. He ought to learn that not everybody comes and goes at his dictates."

Blueskin looked disbelievingly at his companion. The tall fair fellow's face broke into a wide smile of pure malicious glee.

"We'll tell him, Blueskin, won't we? We'll tell the most powerful chap in London about Mr Davy Gadd telling him where to put his breakfasts!"

Will Field! How could I have been so stupid! I could be sure that my careless reply in his hands would be magnified a hundred-fold and much embellished. He grinned at me. "Not very wise, Davy," he said. "Perhaps you'd like to think how much Mr Wild's feelings will be hurt when we tell him how you refused his offer, and him so generous and good-hearted."

"Well, you was only ever fit for that, Will Field," I said sourly, "takin' messages for other people."

He made a fist and jerked it at me, but backed off, neat as a dancer; he knew I had weapons. "Come on, Blueskin," he chortled. "We got a message to deliver."

They ran off down Cockpit Court and I whistled through my teeth and swore at myself for being such a lummock.

"Davy?" said Lucinda.

"Forget it," I said irritably. "I've been a fool, but nothing will come of it."

"That was Blueskin Blake."

"Yes; there are no two chaps with a face like that."

"Why should Jonathan Wild ask you to breakfast?"

"You heard nothing, Ralphy, put it from your mind."

"Davy, you told Jack you were on the road. I thought you'd left that trade. I thought you worked for Clarissa. On the road? Is that how you were able to buy me the silks? Two guineas a yard and you never turned a hair."

I clouted him, but gently. "A well-bred lady asks no questions. And no more peevishness either, my sweet, if you're coming with me to Mother Clap's masquerade!"

Chapter Thirty-Two

THE interior of Mother Clap's molly house had been transformed into a woodland glade. A young tree with its roots in a barrel of earth half filled the parlour, and the ceiling was decorated with green boughs and bunches of wayside blooms that hung in raggedy profusion. Flowers were twined in the tendrils of the tree. Amongst the leaves hung lanthorns, and the same about the room, so that there was no light but such glowing flames as burned within. A band of fiddlers played continuously but for the pauses when they drank. The room and hallway were crowded with a press of folk, some dancing and some kissing, and where the darkness was greatest was the kissing most intense, and more besides. Amongst it all went Mother Clap, all dressed up like a lady, in a sumptuous shining gown, and her hair a mass of ringlets, making certain all were well provided for, which meant carrying dishes of ham and beef and custard tarts to the hungry, or leading a possible partner to such chaps as stood alone; for love was very much the business.

When Ma Clap embraced me I was touched to note that she remembered me with no introduction from Lucinda. Her perfume was like enough to knock a person out, and her face was powdered, soft as a budding apple, and dotted with black heart-shaped patches.

I returned her embrace with enthusiasm.

"My, ain't you grown so tall and handsome, Davy!" she declared. "If all sturdy beggars were as good-looking as you they'd have no cause to beg."

"Lucinda dressed me to his own requirement. He has judiciously torn the shirt for me."

"Ah yes, I see, to show your pretty nipples."

"And the breeches also," I admitted.

"Ah, let me feel! Here, at the bum?"

"No; in the leg — but be pleased to feel me wheresoever, ma'am!"

"So I am and very pleasing it all is, my love. Now off you go and find your fellows. There are many of your old friends here tonight... all in disguises," she added conspiratorially. "You'll be hard put to recognize them. Zounds, it was all I could do to recognise you and Lucinda — Lucinda with his cap of ribbons and you with your wicked eye-patch!" And she led me straight to one that drank, and it was Gabriel Lawrence, who had brought me singing on his milkcart into London when I was a lad, and now all in a scarlet coat, dressed as a soldier.

The fiddlers being close beside us, there was little opportunity for converse, but there was mutual delight in recognition and in default of words we simply kissed with warm and tender friendship. Then we were jostled by the press of folk about us, and Peter Bavidge hooked an arm in mine to prise me away from Gabriel. I found myself jammed against another, and, as if it were the kiss I shared with Gabriel continued, our lips met; but I was startled to discover how different in essence this same act now became.

This fellow was a big man and muscular, and as our bellies pressed against each other a flame of desire so sparked in me that I wanted more and knew it was the same for him. Without more ado he grabbed my arm and hurried me to a little latched doorway under the stairs. Two chaps emerged as we arrived, pulling up their breeches. We bent our heads and went inside; a dark enclosed nest it was, scented with lust. He kissed me roughly and buried his face in my neck till his stubble burned my skin, and then he was on his knees and his face was in my crotch. He pulled my breeches down and cupped my bare arse in his hands and had his lips about my prick all in a moment. I pressed him to me and there he knelt, I hanging over him. He sat back, his knees apart, and I was instantly down there with my face in his groin as on my knees and elbows I unlaced him. So roused was he that at once I was well washed all about the face and had not even time to remove the eye-patch.

"Whose lovely arse is that?" cried voices; and a fistful of candles shone upon us. I made haste to cover up and pull my breeches over my exposed posterior. Out we came, and two others took our place.

All I knew about the identity of my companion in pleasure was the curious coincidental fact that he was wearing an eye-patch too. I was laughing at the oddity of the business as I fixed my tattered clothes in place. What was I about, I marvelled, happily bemused, thus without word or explanation to have behaved so, all suddenly, with one I did not know? And how agreeable the self-same act had been...

As I blinked my way from the darkness of the cupboard into the dusky glow of the sylvan parlour, to the great amusement of those about me I had my face slapped by Lucinda, whom I had not seen by virtue of the cursed eye-patch.

"Faithless wretch!" Lucinda cried, and aimed a kick at my privities with his dainty slippered toe.

"Leave me be — I haven't done anything."

"My arse in a bandbox! I felt on your face what you haven't done. I felt it all over your face!"

"A lovers' quarrel!" said our observers gleefully. As Lucinda was now clawing at me with his nails which were of the consistency of scissor blades, I was obliged to seize his wrists and hold him still and shift him back against the wall, where I held him locked against me till I felt him calmer; then I stopped his mouth with kisses. His resistance ceased and under mine his lips opened and I drove my tongue within. We shared a deep long kiss. Its passion and intensity surprised and confused me. A need to dominate and silence him had prompted my action, that alone; but like a predator entrapt by its own prey I now stood weak and baffled.

It occurred to me that I was somewhat in deep waters in this bountiful company! Whatever had become of me, so to forget myself? What had happened to the cool detachment that I prided myself upon? I should be on my guard; I was well on the way to any number of close involvements.

Lucinda softened in my arms. "Davy, let's not quarrel."

"I never wanted to quarrel. I'm sorry you are vexed. I don't know what came over me."

We both heard what I had just said and both began to laugh.

"Speak with whom you please, and more if you must," Lucinda said, "and so will I; but sleep with me tonight."

"I will and gladly. After all, I brought you here to cheer you up and if it's in my power you'll go from here content."

I went in search of wine, and sat down with a glass of Rhenish. I found myself in the company of Peter Bavidge, Gabriel's close friend, not in disguise, but merely as himself.

Mr Eccleston the door-keeper then banged a hammer on a table top and shouted for silence. We looked towards him.

"And now the prize-giving!" he bellowed.

"What prize?" I asked Peter.

"Oh, that remains a secret!"

A blaze of lights careened across the shadows as candelabras were carried in; and now all who wished to display their finery came forth and made a line and walked in turn, twirling and whirling, bowing, blowing kisses.

"May I present Gay Belinda!" Mr Eccleston announced. "A flower seller."

("Billy Griffin," murmured Peter in my ear. "Thirty-nine years old; an upholsterer. Lord, how fat he has become!")

"His hat is marvellous; more ribbons than Lucinda's! Real flowers and all!"

"Cider Mary!" said Mr Eccleston. "An emperor!"

"Hadrian," whispered Cider Mary loudly.

("Tom Wright," said Peter to me. "Ale seller. Aged twenty-eight. Thinks he is the answer to prayer — look at him strutting. If he has his way Orange Deb will be his Antinous tonight.")

"Sweet Lucinda! A shepherdess!"

("Ralph Marchant, clerk to an attorney. Twenty-three.")

"That one I know," I laughed.

"He's very pretty — if a little over-painted. My congratulations."

"Dockside Betty, a Good Fairy."

("Matthew Broad, a coal heaver from Shadwell. Hairy as a bear. Forty-five, would you say? What a buffoon! Dainty as an old sea-going tub. He lifts his arm and you'd swear he had some furry creature in his armpit. His skin by daylight is murky and grey from his trade. Close by he stinks of coal dust. But I've heard his wand's a big one.")

Matthew was making no pretence of daintiness but was playing for laughs, the which he got, in good-natured abundance.

I thought Peter's remarks less than charitable. He had a sour nature, and no good to say of any of the beauty queens.

"Dairy Cream Sarah! Her Majesty Queen Anne!"

There was a cheer for this royal personnage,

("George Page, a butcher," Peter translated. "Forty-two. He takes the pretty alias from his sister who lives in the country and keeps cows." He snorted. "There is no sweet name for a cull who chops the heads off beasts. Bloody Mary we should have called him.")

"He's very splendid and statuesque. I suppose he grew so big and broad through wielding a cleaver."

"He is big, isn't he? And see how he lifts his skirts to show his thighs. Pure muscle. It takes an ox to slaughter one."

"Lovely ringlets... every inch the queen..."

"Henrietta May — a pirate! A fine eye-patch, Harry!"

("Henrietta may!" sniggered Peter. "Henrietta will, no doubt of it. It's Harry Radley, a coachman. Somewhat under thirty.")

I was all eyes now, sitting up straight and staring ahead, my eye- patch lodged waywardly against my forehead. This was my encounter from underneath the stairs. This man I knew most intimately.

Now with the lights on him I had leisure to peruse him as he deserved. He had a rough honest face, with a wide firm good-humoured mouth, dark eyes, dark brows, and thick black hair. He was very well built, as you would expect for the work he did, with a thick neck, broad shoulders and great muscles in his arms and chest. In his piratical gear he was a joy to behold, with crimson breeches tucked into a very fine pair of boots; no shirt, and a gaudy braided waistcoat; and the black eye-patch that I well remembered.

Just as I was indulging in the secret pleasure of my recollection of his lips about my cock, Peter added: "He's the one who had you under the stairs;" and I coloured up like a fool and made no reply.

"Orange Deb! Queen of the May!"

("Martin Mackintosh... sells oranges round Covent Garden. Twenty years old. A real Titania, eh? Goes with anybody.")

"Great Gloriana! A soldier of the king!"

("Gabriel Lawrence, thirty-nine years old, though he tells you thirty-five. Milk seller. But that's another one you know, isn't it, Davy? You were busy kissing him earlier."

"Not me," I said hastily.

"I hope you haven't got your eyes on him," said Peter. He spoke with apparent carelessness, but I sensed more beneath the surface. "Gabriel's devoted to me. Absolutely devoted. Always has been. Follows me around like a dog. Always has done. He used to have a fondness for the Covent Garden boys but I won't have that. I told him — I said if it's me he wants he keeps away from riff raff; I won't share him. And he does as he is told, I'm pleased to say. So don't be hoping he'll come after you."

"I don't. You warn me needlessly."

"Aha — you have someone else in mind. Confess now — what takes your fancy here tonight?"

"Me? Oh, I take what comes."

"Golden Lavinia! A highwayman!"

("Georgie Whittle, innkeeper. Keeps the Royal Oak in St James's Square.")

"He's a handsome brute," I observed. "But no highwayman looks like that. He is very much overdressed; more like a gaming beau."

"Take my word, he dare not cry Stand and Deliver to save his life and can no more aim that pistol than you or I. His evil leer is entirely false for he is affable to the point of folly, and thus pretty well liked by folk of all gender and persuasions; and therefore frequently cheated. Are you not tempted to display yourself and try for the prize, Davy? We have had no sturdy beggar yet, and you are a tasty sight in your tattered shirt and torn breeches. I am sure many think so," added he with a sugared smile.

"Oh no," I said diffidently, "these are old clothes of Lucinda's and not worth a prize."

"Nonetheless," said Peter meaningfully, and he put his hand upon my bare knee which jutted from the rent cloth of my breeches. His other arm had crept along the chair behind me and lay against my shoulder. His fingers idly toyed the curls of hair at my neck.

"And Gabriel?" I enquired sharply.

"He understands that I may go with whom I choose," shrugged Peter comfortably. "It has always been so."

I thought it seemed an odd arrangement that they had between them, and desired no part in it. I stood up and moved away, the better to hear the judgements.

"And the winner," said Mother Clap, "is Dockside Betty, the fairest of them all."

There were cheers and boos as Matthew lumbered over to her, gauze wings and starry wand and all, and a great curiosity now prevailed as to what the prize would be.

"Come in, the prize!" called Mother Clap, and into the middle of the room came a young man wrapped in a sheet. We all peered around the foliage and the lanthorns swayed vigorously as the tree branches were shifted about in the pushing and shoving. The youth threw off the sheet and stood there stark naked. Cheers and whistles from the assembled throng. Illumined by the candelabras this young man began to flaunt himself for our delight or for his own, for it was plain that he thought much of himself and had no qualms about parading naked before a crowd. He bent and stretched and jutted his behind, played with his privities, kissed the hand of Mother Clap and, as she led him towards Matthew Broad, he pretended an attack of modesty and hid behind her.

"It's Tommy Newton," someone said. "Very nice!"

"Our neighbourhood whore," said Peter in my ear. "They say

he is an unforgettable experience. But he picks and chooses whom he goes with. Gabriel fancies him most dreadfully."

Now Matthew Broad with whoops of glee, bedraggled gauzy wings, and an erect wand, took Tommy Newton off to the marrying room, accompanied by a surge of well-wishers fighting to keep the door open and watch the proceedings.

Queen Anne approached me, stately and sweating beneath his wig of abundant glossy chestnut curls. His bosom was padded to enormous proportions. A lace frill edged the neck of his flowing crimson gown. Above that lace, the hairs of his chest showed thick and matted. His neck was red and knotted with muscle. He had a beard and all. You never saw a Queen Anne like this one.

"I'm George Page the butcher," he said without preamble. He looked enquiringly. "I haven't seen you here before."

"I'm Davy Gadd," I said.

"I hope I wasn't out of turn in taking you from Peter Bavidge?"

"Not at all; far from it. He was only telling me who everyone was."

"Now tell me if I'm wrong," said George, "but weren't you the cull that kept the crowd off Jemmy Boyle? You were on a sturdy horse and in a fine claret coat and carried pistols? Now was that you?"

"What if it was?" I answered cagily.

"I want to shake your hand, that's what," George answered warmly. "I was in a doorway watching. To my shame I did nothing; but I didn't know what I could have done and not been dragged up there beside him. I thought what you did was the bravest thing I ever saw."

"Not at all," I mumbled in embarrassment. "I had all the advantages. And I was lucky; they were docile."

"Lucky you may have been; I call it courageous. They could have rushed you and turned on you, and you had one other bullet and no time to reload."

"That's true," I grinned. "But like I say... lucky."

"Did you know Jemmy Boyle?"

"No I didn't. I just thought it was wrong."

"You're new to London, aren't you? If there's a molly in the stoop they try and lynch him; it's understood. A thief's a hero to them... a poisoner they tolerate... a cull who broke his wife's head open, he gets their approbation. Let a chap be accused of sodomy — accused, I say, the same not proven — and they'll not rest till they've crippled him."

He took off his Queen Anne curls and mopped his broad brow with the ruffles of his sleeve.

"It's wicked, Mr Page," said I.

"Call me George."

"And how is the cull that was in the stoop? Did he live?"

"Aye, but badly marked about the head and half his teeth knocked from his jaw. Bricks, stones, they don't care what they throw. It was a great risk you took, for it may seem you showed yourself to be a man of like persuasion and in some danger thereby; and so I say again you are a brave man, howsoever you deny it."

"I hope a passer-by may make a stand for common humanity's sake without any particular slant cast upon his character," I answered. "I have to tell you, George, I did not help the man because he was a molly, but because he was in trouble."

"I am proud to know you, Davy," George said as if he had not heard me, "and when I tell the others, you will be welcome wherever you go."

"Wounds, I pray you, enough of this," I said alarmed. "I want nothing said further and I insist on your assurance that you'll speak no more of it to folk."

But he clasped me to him in a huge hug and gave me no such assurance, and I was the object many times that night of gratitude and admiration such as I in no way merited as one or another came to me and praised me for my service to the brotherhood.

I was much ill at ease in the role of saviour, having no great opinion of myself and knowing myself to be much less than they would have me. Somehow the tale had lost nothing in the telling. From what was said to me, it seemed that singlehanded I had fought off an angry mob that came at me with stones and staves. Gry had become a horse of myth and legend, now pure white, now raven black, rearing and plunging; I daresay at last he grew wings and took off above the roof tops. At all events we had made our escape by the skin of our teeth and Jemmy Boyle was saved to swive again.

Then came a moment of some noise and confusion, for with the heat and throng Ma Clap had swooned, and we all gathered round and she was lifted on to a couch, and fanned with George's Queen Anne fan while smelling salts were brought, and water.

"She is not a strong woman for all she seems to be," said Mr Eccleston. "She is all heart."

She revived and told us all was well, and how excitement always brought the same upon her, and no harm done. The fiddlers struck up anew and there was dancing — jigs and reels — and singing, and those with best voices sang out the verses. There was, to the tune of 'Now is the Month of Maying', one that began:

'Now is the time of swiving
when all to fuck are striving...'

and there was to the tune of 'Greensleeves':

'Alas my love you do me wrong
to kiss my lips so daintily
when I have wanted all along
your partnership in buggery...'

Then there was a ring dance where two rings of dancers met and you must take the partner that stood facing you. Harry Radley shoved Orange Deb aside to bring himself to face me, and took hold of me, and held me firmly by the arms and stood me still, and we looked at one another, and both began to laugh, for we were both in eye-patches still, and both moved at the same time to lift the patch and see the other better.

I rid myself of the encumbering thing and hung it upon a jutting twig.

"So," said Harry with merry eyes. "It seems I tumbled with a hero under the stairs tonight."

"What, as well as me?" I retorted.

"I've seen you here before, you know," he said.

"You have?"

"I handed you a glass of wine on the stairs; you drank it; you were with Lucinda."

I remembered him, a darkly handsome face, a taste of sweet wine.

"How do they call you?"

"Delia. My name is Davy Gadd."

"Harry Radley. Henrietta. The story goes you ride a good horse."

"A gipsy, half thoroughbred. He is the hero, not me."

"I have six horses, three leaders, three wheelers, all pretty strong."

"I heard you were a coachy. Who do you work for?"

"I work for no one. I'm my own man."

"I knew a coachy once — Humphrey Harvey, he took his coach from Buckden to the Saracen's — a great big chap, built like a house."

"I knew him, I knew Humphrey Harvey. I have drunk with him at the Saracen's. He's dead now, alas; drink, they say, was the cause. He could drink us all under the table and took pride in it."

"He was a hero."

All around us, little by little, one chose another and together slunk away; and little by little all the candles in the lanthorns were blown out, and a warm provocative darkness descended.

"Well, Davy," Harry Radley said, eyeing my torn garments. "Did you come here on purpose to unsettle a chap?"

"I did not mean to unsettle anybody," I said, myself unsettled. "It was for the masquerade; Lucinda tore these holes in my clothes."

"I would like to finish what he started," Harry Radley said, "and rip off what remains."

My mouth being unaccountably dry at the contemplation of the same I was unable to reply; and when Lucinda sidled up to me and nestled against me in a movement both coy and possessive I had not wit enough to clarify my position.

"I see," said Harry tersely. "Still with Lucinda; my mistake."

"Come upstairs with me," Lucinda said, all ogle. "I'm ready to be cheered. You promised."

Harry was gone; and I went upstairs with my arm around Lucinda.

We found a mattress in the corner of a bedroom, under the window, at the front of the house. Plenty of others had the same idea, and we stumbled over bodies both inert and heaving, and we lay and made ourselves comfortable. I was still aroused from my swift interchange with Harry, and pretty muddled. I was like a lyre that night, I thought, anybody might play upon me; but the result-ant confusion, though disturbing, was startlingly pleasurable. I unlaced my friend from his bodices and petticoats and white stock-ings, eager to lose the sheperdess and reach the man beneath. I lay upon him, taking his face between my hands, and kissed him. Per-plexing sensations rose in me — desire, bewilderment, tenderness and greed, an irritation with Lucinda who tried my patience to the utmost with his pert ways and his excessive love of ribbons, and a curious wish to watch over him and see him safe — all these mingled with vivid fleeting images of Harry Radley. I still tingled to imagine him ripping the shirt off my back as he had threatened. This added to my befuddlement, for I would certainly have resisted him had he attempted it.

I shook my head of thought as a dog emerging from a stream shakes water, and set about my satisfaction, which by his reciprocal warmth was Ralph's also. We moved together close entwined, belly to belly, mouth to mouth, till both at once in pleasure erupted, panting and gasping, tightly clamped together; but we said nothing. Afterwards we lay in one another's arms and I stroked his hair about his ears.

I had taken no notice of the other people in the chamber. Now I did, and listened, slumbrous, to the sounds of pleasure and of sleeping. Through the window as I drifted off to sleep I heard the sound of people leaving, setting out in the darkness up the narrow thread of Field Lane or into broad Holborn, with wavering lights, and singing their merriment somewhat drunkenly out into the wider world.

"Now is the time for swiving...
now is the time for swiving..."

As I fell asleep I could hear the singing, distant and indistinct, isolated and discordant notes loosed upon the air, as a broken tawdry necklace scatters bright beads.

Chapter Thirty-Three

AROUND noon I came downstairs, and, climbing my way over those who had fallen asleep on the stairs, made my way to the kitchen.

Matthew Broad, out of his fairy gown now, in breeches and shirt sleeves and munching cold beef, asked me what I would eat; I took bread and beer and asked him how his night had been. He chuckled ruefully.

"I'll say this for Tommy Newton, he gives full measure. I'm near exhausted and can scarcely stand."

"But?" I prompted.

"But it was worth it!" he declared. "And yourself? Where's your pretty companion?"

"Still preening," I said. "Lucinda cannot face the day without making himself beautiful, though he is pretty enough as nature made him. I shall prove an unworthy escort and am half regretting the poorness of my disguise — that which seemed merry by night seems by day a sorry thing."

He laughed. "I won't be the first one to say this to you, but if all sturdy beggars had a body as good as yours it would be others that would be begging — for their company in bed."

I looked down at myself. In the remnants of my torn clothes a good deal of that selfsame body was revealed. Matthew was looking at it also. He asked casually, as if on an afterthought: "Are you with Lucinda, permanent like?"

A swift memory of Harry Radley disconcerted me.

"No," I said, suddenly irritated and not knowing why. "No; I'm on my own."

Matthew began to speak, and I stood up abruptly and moved away.

"Oh! Huffy!" he said after me.

I made my way to the parlour to retrieve the foolish eye-patch, which I had left hanging on the tree.

The parlour had a melancholy air this morning. The curtains were half drawn, giving the room a curious half light of shifting shadows, for the tree was still in place, though drooping somewhat. Entwined in its branches hung the bunches of dead wayside flowers that had seemed so sylvan by lanthorn light, their petals idly dropping to the floor, their woody scents rank in the dusty air. A tangle of discarded garments lay in a heap, as if someone had hurriedly gathered them up, for tidiness or propriety.

Mother Clap sat in a low chair near the window. She was this morning dressed most soberly in grey, her bosom covered, and her hair her own — wispy, with the auburn colour of her dye a startling brilliance. She was not alone. In a high-backed chair sat a cumbersome bulky figure, half obscured by foliage. I saw his buckled shoes, white stockings and the thickness of his calves before I saw his face, which now turned to me, and, leaning round the leaves, showed him to be Under City Marshall Hitchin.

"Davy dear, come in; we have a guest," called Mother Clap.

Most unwillingly did I step forward. In an age as ours is, when the clothes upon our back proclaim how well or otherwise we are faring in this wicked world, I felt much at a disadvantage to renew my acquaintance with Mr Hitchin in torn breeches and a ragged shirt. My memories of my previous meetings with him were tinged with some embarrassment, moreover, and it was no comfort for me to recall that he had sworn to have me in the end, a prospect which however I might interpret it was not one that I relished. But perhaps he had forgotten who I was?

"Zounds! Davy Gadd!" said he and eyed me up and down.

"You know each other?" Mother Clap enquired.

"I have known Davy since he was a little lad," said Mr Hitchin.

"Is this so, dear?" Mother Clap said dubiously and with interest.

"Yes, ma'am," I admitted.

"And was I good to 'ee?" boomed Mr Hitchin. As I paused he said: "Come now, Davy, thee must tell this good lady. Did I not give thee wine and pie and put thee to bed wrapt in my own coat?

Did thee not sit on my knee? Did we not kiss?"

Ma Clap's eyebrows were so raised now that they almost disappeared into her fringe, and her eyes were quizzical.

"We did not, sir," I answered stiffly. "That is, as I recall, the kissing was done by yourself and I received it with politeness." Ungallant of me, but I was riled by his teasing of me before Mother Clap.

Mr Hitchin chuckled throatily, but I did not think he was amused. He was as gross as ever, all flesh and jowls. His sunken watchful eyes gazed out from their lopsided pouches. His podgy fingers stroked one of his chins.

"So — thee did not get to be a highwayman then?"

I winced to recall that I had boasted of my boyish longings to him in that upper room at the Blue Boar.

"A Gentleman of the Road, like Claude Duval," he said to Mother Clap, as if the idea was a quaint one and he had humoured me the while. "By the looks of thee, my sweet, thee has a little way to go yet."

"Lord love you, sir," chortled Mother Clap, "Davy is quite the gentleman and wears a coat of claret velvet. These rags you see are for the masquerade."

"These rags," drawled Mr Hitchin, running his eyes very slowly over me, "become him very well."

"Mr Charles Hitchin," Mother Clap explained to me, "has come today upon a serious mission. He is here to reprove us, Davy. We are in disgrace."

It did not seem to be a matter for concern. Plainly she was unperturbed by Mr Hitchin's being there, in whatever capacity. Her tone was lightly mocking.

"It seems, dear, that some naughty boys went from here singing, late last night. This wicked music reached the ears of one of our more righteous neighbours, one who went directly to Mr Hitchin with his grumble. Mr Hitchin has come on purpose to reform our manners. Shall you start with Davy, perhaps?"

"Me? I was fast asleep," I said alarmed.

"Fast asleep?" said Mr Hitchin lightly. "Here?"

"A friend brought me. I was keeping him company."

"Exactly," said Mr Hitchin, "and with no idea what kind of place thee friend was bringing thee to."

"Mr Hitchin!" said Ma Clap affronted. "Whatever do you mean by that? This is a most respectable lodging house."

"I merely ramble," Mr Hitchin smiled. "I am a peacemaker, as thee knows. I have told thee neighbour I am come here; I tell thee to quieten thee more exuberant cronies; and justice is done. Fortune has smiled upon me, however, for I did not think to see my old acquaintance Master Davy. I would like to talk to thee, Davy, about thee being here at all, and what it might mean as regards our future friendship."

"Indeed sir, it means nothing at all," I said. "I slept in this respectable lodging house overnight and now I take my leave of it and there's an end. I'm pleased to find you well this morning, ma'am; and now if you'll permit me I must seek out my friend who will be waiting." I did not wait for a reply, but shot out of that room and hurried to find Ralph; and quit the place without more ado.

"You have nothing to fear from Mr Hitchin," said Lucinda panting to keep up with me. "He is a friend of ours. He has the interests of the molly houses much at heart. He often visits at Aunty Mary's. Socially, you know. He keeps in with the Holies so that he may keep us informed of what they do. If there was trouble he would let us know. He's ugly, isn't he, but cuddlesome, I think."

We slowed to a more sedate pace. "There are folk I would sooner cuddle," I laughed. "I didn't like the way he was looking at the rents in my breeches."

Then the smile came off my face as it occurred to me that I was walking along Holborn dressed as a beggar beside a man dressed as a woman, and I felt more apprehensive than ever I had waiting in a woody copse for the arrival of a coach, with the intention to divest its passengers of guineas. How could the passers-by not see through Ralph's disguise and run at us and tear him limb from limb? I marvelled at their obtuseness and his daring. Yet we were not accosted. Folk see what they want to see, and all concerned with their own cares and toils they have not the time or curiosity to go peering in the faces of each passer-by; and though Lucinda received polite acknowledgement from gentlemen, apprentices, and street traders, so convincing was he, so assured, that we went unmolested to our destination.

I saw Lucinda to the door of Aunty Mary's; then I turned back towards the stable yard in Great Queen Street where I had left Gry. I busied myself about his welfare.

"Poor lad," I said as I combed out his mane. "I know that you would sooner be upon the road. And truth to tell you, so would I. What'll we do, lad? Shall we quit London after all?"

But Gry, however, munching on his oats, now seemed content, and merely blinked his wise eye and flicked his tail. Myself was not so easily satisfied. A restless discontent was on me, an unease I found it difficult precisely to define. I left the stable and went out into the yard, a straw-flecked cobbled court, with a hay wagon propped upon its shafts, and squawking hens scrapping and pecking, and an old mare with her nose in the water trough. It was late afternoon.

Leaning against a water butt was Will Field, chewing on a straw. He was so plainly waiting for me that I paused in a curiously pleasurable anticipation. The prospect of a scrap with Will Field suited me down to the ground.

"I'm bringin' yer a message from Mr Wild," he said.

"Another one? And you can take one back to him."

We circled round each other measuringly. Messages and Mr Wild were incidental. We just rubbed each other up the wrong way, always had and always would. We had fought each other as soon as we had met, in the yard at the Saracen's Head, eight years old.

We lunged at each other and went down in a tangle of limbs. We rolled over and over on the muddy cobbles, clamped together firm as lovers. When we stopped short I was astride him, holding him by the wrists. He twisted clear and clawed up for my eyeballs. I laid a fist into his face.

I hardly knew what happened next but I was roughly lifted off him, heaved up, planted on my feet, my arms twisted behind me, the lust of conflict all unsatisfied. More in surprise than anything I found myself held in the grip of Blueskin Blake and Andy Wild. Wounds, but Blueskin was odd this close, his mottled purplish face two inches from my own. However, surprise flicked rapidly to alarm as I watched Will unwind himself from his recumbent pose and clamber up, his mouth all bloodied, and his darting lizard eyes full of intentions.

Even as I flinched in resignation I experienced his anticipatory pleasure with a grim sympathy. I felt an inexplicable admiration — how very neat of him not to have come alone — how very astute of him not to demean himself with playing by the rules. Thought of any kind then ceased. His bunched fist drove into my face and again, so that I saw an explosion of stars, I heard my teeth crack and I swallowed blood. He laid into my midriff then; I sagged and grunted; I was held upright; and when my head dropped forward it was pulled back by my long thick hair so as not to impede Will's punches. When they let me go I crumpled in a heap; I lay, my knees drawn to my chin, my hands about my head, my face pressed in the straw. I saw through half-shut lids the heel of Will Field's boot but I could no more move than fly, and next I saw his face close to mine; he must be crouching down beside me.

He smoothed my hair back from my face and said close to my mouth: "You had it comin'; you had it comin'." He surveyed me with some satisfaction. Then he said: "I was to teach you manners. If you ain't at Mr Wild's levy before three days have passed you'll get another." Then almost apologetically, almost with solicitation, he added: "I could have done you worse. Only Mr Wild said be sure as not to cripple yer." Then he was gone, and the other two, as I supposed, along with him.

Whatever Mr Wild's precise instructions I found that I was unable to stand and was obliged perforce to lie where I had fallen, and in a good deal of pain. Moreover I could barely see, my eyelids being pretty well closed up. Comings and goings about me there surely were, but seeming far away and unrelated to myself. Therefore it was with complete incomprehension that I found myself raised up and lifted bodily off the ground. My mumbled protestations and groans of distress went quite unheeded. I was carried along by a pair of strong arms, against a broad and manly chest. For a moment I thought that my situation had taken a turn very much for the better, until a voice close to my ear said:

"There we go now. We'll soon have you on your feet. The watch house is just nearby; and I am Constable Willis."

Chapter Thirty-Four

NOW never let it be believed that the city constables were a race of gibbering idiots fit only to be jeered at and despised and merely one stage up from the night watchmen, who were indeed beneath contempt. Any man who makes his living on the other side of the law must cherish a healthy respect for his opponent, must know his ways and guess his moves. Constables there were who would have been more use growing turnips than catching villains; but even those had the wherewithal to shout for aid, and every one of them had behind them the weight of the law in all its corrupt mightiness, the apex of which is the triple tree at Tyburn, whose judgement is irrevocable. It was no joke for me to find myself borne aloft by the brawny hands of the law's embodiment and our destination the watch house. But I could not do a thing about it.

I was sitting hunched up on a bench, clutching my sides; I ached from head to toe. Constable Willis was bathing my face. I squinted through my pain. I saw a big broad man with a strong and craggy face, with straight black hair tied sharply back from his thick neck. His brow was knitted in a frown of concentration.

"Ah, now we can see you," he declared, dabbing and smoothing. "You have lost your looks for the moment, but you'll recover. Now let's have your name."

I told him, as stupid a thing as ever I did, mumbling through swollen lips. Gingerly I verified that all my teeth were still in place.

"And who's been disagreeing with you, Davy Gadd?" enquired Constable Willis pleasantly.

"Nobody," I answered, beginning to recover my wits.

"Of course," said he, and prodded and listened to my moans. He pressed my ribs and ascertained that none were broken. He poured some wine down my throat and smeared my bruises with an ointment.

I looked about me at the inside of the watch house. There in the corner stood the staves and lanthorns which the Watch would take out later, to patrol our wicked streets at night. There was the locked door to a cell for some unfortunate. An ancient fellow, one of the Watch, sat upon a stool and stared at us. He looked simple, cackling from time to time, sipping gin from a spoon; the smell of it came over to us. I looked at Constable Willis.

"Why have you brought me here?" I said.

"The charity of a God-fearing man," he answered severely. Then he added: "At first, that is. And now I've grown curious about you. I thought at first you were a beggar, but I saw your fingernails were clean, and you have shoes, and they well heeled. Now I've seen the eye-patch bound about your wrist. You're one of those culls as make pretence of being beggars, with your false bad eye. By rights I ought to haul you in for that."

"If I was that, maybe you should; but I ain't. I wouldn't stoop so low," I said indignantly.

"I'm glad to hear it. I hate to hear of a man that's sound in wind and limb turn to falsehood and decit to make his living. So what's your trade then, Master Gadd?"

"I used to work in an alehouse. But I'm new to London and I haven't found work yet."

"I may be able to help you there," said Constable Willis, monstrously alarming me with his rampaging goodness. "When you are fully recovered come and see me here. I know a chap who needs a gardener; or if it's alehouse work you want I can find you a place in any number of our hostelries. There's no need for a sturdy fellow to be on the streets if he don't mind hard work. Have you any money?"

"I left it with a friend."

"I'm going to give you five shillings."

Five shillings! Half a week's wages for a labourer — the cost of a good quality hat — a pair of cloth breeches — a silver buckle.

"Repay me when you can. Or put it in the poor box for one who truly is a beggar. And now let's see you on your feet."

I lurched stiffly about the room.

"Very good," he commended me. "Now off you go, Davy Gadd, and next time keep out of trouble. We have some scoundrels on our streets, so it would be no bad thing to stick a cudgel in your belt."

"Yes sir; thank you very much." I needed no persuasion to be out of there. I hurried away, wincing with every step. I bought a pitcher of gin from a chandler's, and some bread and cheese, and went back to the stable yard. I took my repast up into the hay loft and delved my way into a corner like a hedgehog in a nest, and there I passed the night.

The hay was meadow-sweet, musty and embracing, and below me Gry slept in his bed of straw, and those other stable companions of his with him, snuffling and whickering. Though I was feeling pretty sick I slept, if fitfully.

I awoke stiff as a board and aching. I came down the ladder, saw to Gry, and so out into the morning.

I bought my breakfast at the Claypot and sent a lad to Aunty Mary's for me with a message. "And when you've brought him, you'll get tuppence."

All the talk was of Hawkins and Simpson, who were to be hanged in the morning. Everyone, it seemed, knew the awful details of their history. Hawkins used to be a tapster in Hounslow; then he was footman in a gentleman's house but was kicked out for filching silver. He took to the road and led a gang that worked the heath. Robbing postboys was their speciality, because they carried banknotes. They knew that notes were often sent in two halves, to foil such as themselves, so they used to rob the post boys twice and catch the second half of the note; they were caught with two halves of a twenty-five pound note and half of a fifty; but they had already burned the rest. When they were caught they all split on each other to try to save their own skins. It was Jonathan Wild who was behind their capture. It seemed that these days any highwayman taken, any gang broken up, it was always down to Jonathan Wild.

"Hawkins? He won't make a good hanging," said one doxy. "He's so fat and short."

"You like 'em tall?" her companion asked.

"I like 'em pretty."

"He'll go the sooner, with his weight. It's the little skinny ones that take a time to die. Hawkins'll be so heavy his friends won't have to pull his legs down to make him heavy against the rope."

"I say chubby or no, Hawkins'll make a good end," said another. "They know what is expected of 'em, the Gentlemen of the Road. And any cull in his best coat and the nosegays round him and the doxies weeping will make a good showing."

"Will you go watch?"

"I surely will. I love a hanging day."

My messenger returned with Ralph who was looking, to my relief, extremely male in his coat, shirt and breeches. I resigned myself to his gasps and commiserations while he peered at my bruised visage — which I had not seen, so did not know how justified his horror. We sat together in the inglenook, the table between us, shadowed by the high-backed settles.

"Oh Davy! Whyever did you not come home? Your cheek is quite purple and your lip all swollen up!"

"I had no intention of obliging you and Aunty Mary to look after me. It was not your quarrel."

"Oblige?" he cried. "It would have been a pleasure. I did not sleep for worrying. I would have come looking for you, but you did not say where your horse had been stabled. But what happened? Quarrel? Was it someone you knew?"

"Yes, Will Field. You saw him when we came away from Jack's place. He was sent by Mr Wild, as he says, to teach me manners. When he finished I could hardly stand, but he was not alone or I'd not have come out of it so lamely. Have some beer and a dish of ham — Constable Willis is buying it."

Ralph helped himself and waited with an air of saintly patience.

"I guess someone went and fetched him; he must have been nearby. He carried me to the watch house and cleaned me up and gave me red wine and advice. He means to see me into honest work and gave me five shillings to get off the streets and out of trouble."

"You may laugh," Ralph said reprovingly, "but you need tending. You must come back with me and rest and I'll look after you."

"No, Ralph," I said. "I'm getting out of London. That's why I asked you here, to let you know I'm going."

"Oh," Ralph wailed. "Why?"

"It's plain enough. Too many people know me. Either for love or hate. I feel as conspicuous as if my name was written up for all to see on some wall or tree — Wanted! I can't come and go as I please; I have to look about me. It don't suit me."

"But what's so menacing about being known by folk who care for you?"

"I've always got by on my own. It puts me under obligation, kindness. I like to know I can just take off, get out, ride away. I don't want people grieving, asking where I'll be."

"In touch with folk, that's to be human, I'd have thought," Ralph said.

"Well, I don't want it."

"But what do you want?"

"To be like a shadow, now here, now gone, something you can't nail down."

Lucinda made a noise of irritation. I protested.

"I can go on the road and no one knows who I am. But I come to London, the mollies claim me as kin for an act of impulse. Mr Hitchin wants to talk about our further acquaintance — Mr Wild wants me to work for him and sets his creatures to spy on me; they knew where I had stabled Gry and waited for me there. London's like a big glass bowl and everyone sees all you do. I'm getting out. Copses and woods, heath and track, you know where you are with them. And now look what has happened to Simpson and Hawkins and how the crowds are gathering already. Who'd stay in London out of choice?"

"It sounds to me like running away."

"Well may you judge it so — you run no risk of having your head slammed against a wall."

"Why don't you simply go to Mr Wild's breakfast and have done?"

"I wouldn't go there looking like this and have them all grinning and saying I hope you've learned your lesson; it would be pretty humiliating. No, I've had enough of London. Besides..."

"What besides?"

"Besides...there's folk." I ran my finger round the rim of my tankard, thoughtfully.

"What folk?" Lucinda demanded.

"Well, you for a start," I laughed, and ceased my fidgetting.

"Me? What have I done?"

"I might be likely to get fond of you."

"So what? I care about you — you know I do. I don't mind if

240

you know it. Though why I do I don't know, you being so ungrateful and perverse."

"If you care about folk and want to see them again it's a burden to you. You aren't free and easy, but always wondering how they are. On the road you need no baggage; and that's baggage. I'm quitting before I get in too close."

"Just as I told you, running away."

"All right, I'm running. Why should I stay here? I'll never find the gold I'm looking for in London streets."

"Dick Whittington believed them paved with gold!"

"It's odd you said that. I used to like that story. But they weren't, were they? He found that out soon enough. And he ran off, same as I shall."

"And he came back."

"But I won't, you can count on it."

"How will you live?"

"My old trade."

"I detest you, Davy," said Lucinda viciously. "You come plunging into my ordered way of life so carelessly and leave it as soon. You cheered me from gloom and now you leave me in it afresh. Then you tell me you are dealing still in that dangerous business and a prize of a hundred pound if you are caught."

"I won't be caught."

"How do you know that? How can you be sure?"

"Because I'm good at it and careful. I don't take risks. And besides, I'm lucky."

"If I write to you..?"

"Don't say much if you do. My new stepfather is a Holy. If he gets the letter first we'd be done for."

"There's no pleasure in writing a letter without scandal and gossip," Ralph pouted.

"Just send me news."

I quit London, in my own clothes and with two black eyes, but looking once more the gentleman. I rode along Holborn and dismounted at St Andrew's church to put five shillings in the poor box, for Constable Willis' sake.

Early as I was, I was not early enough to escape the preparations for the hangings. In awful fascination I paused, holding Gry steady, where Seacoal Lane joins Snow Hill, at the head of Turnagain Lane. Already the streets were filling with folk. Ballad singers chirruped the tale of the Hawkins gang, already much embellished. The God-fearing bawled against them, warning us all to take note of the fate of the wicked. Piemen took up their positions. Flower sellers pressed nosegays into the hands of girls who would later throw them into the coffin cart.

Hawkins would ride backwards in it, down Snow Hill, along Holborn, to the Oxford road, and so to Tyburn, his rope about his neck, his coffin with him.

I saw Under City Marshall Hitchin arrive by coach, splendid in his gold-braided coat and three-cornered hat. I saw the smudge of scarlet as a group of soldiers moved towards the arch of Newgate. If I waited any longer I would certainly see Mr Wild, the cause and perpetrator of the spectacle. I turned up Cow Lane, making for St John's Street. There was a fiddler playing on the corner, and folk were dancing.

I thought about Dick Whittington as I reached Highgate Hill and I heard bells and all, but I kept on riding. It would take a most astonishing piece of news, I thought grimly, to make me turn again to London.

I was on the road for many months. It was a wet summer but a dry mild autumn. I went as far north as I'd ever been, eager to put distance between Jonathan Wild's spy network and myself. You might have found me about Scarthing Moor and Barnby Heath, and trailing up Crockley Hill, where Gry cast a shoe, and we had the devil of a search for a smithy; and so into York by Fishergate, and sleeping at the Old Angel or at Eel Pie House.

I was careful, as I told Ralph I would be. I chose my coaches as a hawk might pick out the fattest, most foolish field creature, and I hovered at the roadside, pouncing when the time was best. Two narrow escapes I had. Once I made the cardinal error of holding a coach in the rain. I was obliged to try and fire a pistol when it only sparked. The coachman started to unwrap a musket... Another time I missed sight of a mounted guard and was pursued, but I shook off those who followed me and put forty miles between us in no time at all.

And I looked for gold. Most often at sunrise or at sunset, when the world was quietest, and the tree boles golden red in the sun's rays. I never lost hope of it. I knew that one day I would prove the old saying to be true —

'By stem and root as we are told
Duval hid his crock of gold.
Twixt Tollentone Lane and Alconbury Hill
Duval's gold lies buried still.'

And as before, I found buckles, pins, broken blades, dagger hilts, ancient rings and coins. I threw them all back; the coins were of a bygone age, the trinkets no use to me except to make me wonder who owned them, how they lost them, how they died; except to make me feel part of a strange disjointed fellowship — the travellers who in their day took to the Great North Road.

And I lived well. I had new clothes made — fine white shirts, cravats, breeches, gloves, waistcoats, a smart coat of dusky blue velvet, a greatcoat with good deep pockets. I had a den in the back room of an inn, like James Goodman used to. A man with a good horse and two good pistols is never hungry, never ill clad; wayside hostelries are his, with company if he needs it, and all the ale he cares to drink.

My hope was to find Nathan Grey who haunted the road as I did, with his horse and wagon and his lean pleasure-giving body. I prowled the horse fairs, where they squint at your horse and scratch their chins and try to sell you cholic balls, purging balls, cordial balls, cough balls, blistering ointment, mange ointment, eye water. I listened for the gipsy fiddle. I never found him. Was this the essence of the road, I wondered, the isolated encounter, always full of meaning, but nothing of permanence?

One day I rode into the yard of the old Crown, and Ma made me a vast meal which we ate together while her husband worked upon a holy tract in his study; and she smiling slipped me a letter from Lucinda.

I said it would take most surprising news to make me return to London. This letter contained it.

"Everyone you know in town is well. This letter, being free from gossip, is a short one, but I thought that you might like to know your saintly friend Jack Sheppard has now turned to crime."

Part V

A Hero of Our Time

Chapter Thirty-Five

"I GUESS I'm weak and easily led," said Jack comfortably.

"Must you sound quite so pleased about it?"

"I told you there was Bad Blood in my family," added he triumphantly.

I might well have believed myself asleep and dreaming. When I remembered Jack, the angelic vision framed in lace in Mr Kneebone's shop — when I remembered him dutifully going back to work at Mr Wood's carpentry establishment — I found it hard to reconcile the image with the one before me now.

We were in the back room of the Black Lion, as low a boozing ken as London could offer, hard by the dark insalubrious back alleys of Lewkenor's Lane, where every other house was a brothel and every chap upon the street a villain. Jack had a tankard in one hand. His other arm was round a big blowzy female with a cheerful face and a mass of auburn curls. He was dressed in a smart blue coat with buff-coloured piping. He was able to dress in such a suit because he had just filched it. I could not believe his foolhardiness.

He had at that stage two successful housebreakings to his name. He had used his locksmiths' skills to pick the locks. It seemed he had a natural talent. Suddenly he had become a valuable commodity. In a further corner sat as dastardly a crew of ruffians as you might care to meet, who seemed to regard Jack as a bit of a trophy, a pretty child to be spoiled and gratified, a boy who had put on man's attire at last.

His brother Tom I recognized, and Hell-and-Fury Sykes; but the lean fair-haired youth with the jagged teeth — Ned Burnworth — I had yet to know, and the lad Kit Leonard who had twice done murder, and the simple-minded John Allen with a voice like a honking goose — these were joys to come. And like some kind of predatory pander, Joe Hind the landlord of the Black Lion leaned against the wall, overseeing it all, with a fixed proprietory smile.

"It was your fault, Davy," Jack grinned. "It was your fine clothes as did it. I wanted decent coats and shirts an' all. An' shoes wiv buckles."

"And very smart you now appear. But what are you about, with your booty on your back? What if the owner of the coat should see you? Where'd you be then?"

"I'd be where I am now, cuddlin' Bess," he laughed, "because if he came dahn 'ere, someone'd filch 'is other coat an' someone else 'is shoes, an' 'e'd 'ave ter go home sharpish. Or if 'e stayed, someone'd crack 'is skull an' sell 'is hair for a wig."

Bess leaned forward till her breasts half spilled out of her bodice, and she put her hand on mine.

"It wasn't your fault, Davy. It was mine. There were so many things I wanted. Jack said I oughter have 'em."

"I seem to 'ave a natural skill," Jack said modestly. "When I did Mr Baines's house I took up the iron bars at the cellar window an' I nailed 'em down again. They never knew the house was broken into!"

Bess chuckled. "We got silver spoons, we got gold rings, we got some beautiful flowered silk. Like he says, our Jack's a natural. He makes stealin' easy."

"But Jack, your ma," I groaned, "who thinks so much of yer, whose heart'll break to see you turn to crime. Who sorrows over Tom already."

"Yeah, I know," Jack said. "But there's no need for her to know. She thinks I'm with a carpenter in Fulham. And Tom won't tell her. Tom and me are goin' into partnership."

"What kind of partner can Tom be for you?" I said in a low angry voice. "Wasn't he in the Whit? Didn't they brand his hand? He's known, Jack. It's no good once you're known."

"'e may be known, but 'e knows pretty much 'imself. 'e knows the houses for keepin' things safe. 'e knows the Carrick gang. They're all set up; they've got it all worked out. I know who to take my stuff to. I know who'll get rid of it for me. It's all goin' very nicely. And I don't need to get involved. I mean to use 'em when I need 'em, and for the rest of it, to work alone like you do."

"Wounds! You don't mean to try your hand upon the road?"

"I might. I'll see what takes my fancy."

"If you must work the road, Jack, you must promise me you'll do so in my company," I said with a sinking heart. "I know something about the business. I learned what I know from a good chap who knew the way of it; and so should you."

"And who was this good chap?" Bess said provocatively.

"James Goodman."

"And where is he now?"

"Well, he was topped."

She chortled: "So, what kind of a teacher was that?"

"He was unlucky."

"Jack can look after himself," Bess said. "To hear you talk, Davy, you'd think he was a baby."

Why did I think him so? Stupid of me. Those days in Bishopsgate school were long gone, and it was no business of mine to bother about the finer feelings of his poor ma. He was twenty-one. He was old enough to know what he was about.

A black-haired wench of unsubtle charm joined us.

"Now Davy, look, here's one for you!" cried Jack entirely eager to please. "Have you met Poll? Poll Maggot?"

No, I had not. Somehow in my dealings with the lower portions of the city's reaches I had happened to steer clear of the vast array of drabs and doxies that frequented every alehouse and were to be found on the arm of every cull with a reputation to maintain. Luscious wenches, skinny and unwholesome jades, blowzy queans, goatish crones — you could find them in any boozing ken. In Jack's company at the Black Lion and at the Cat and Fiddle in Lewkenor's Lane just nearby, this celestial banquet was there for the tasting — and I was to be offered a bite.

Poll Maggot glided into place, her bosom contriving to brush my shoulder as she settled beside me on my bench.

"Jack — who's your handsome friend?"

"Davy Gadd's been my good pal since we was boys," Jack beamed. "I'd love to see you two get together, like me an' Bess."

"What about it, Davy?" Poll suggested amicably.

We shared a good-humoured desultory kiss. I think Jack was a little disappointed at its lack of passion, but maybe later? Maybe in the privacy of some upstairs room? And Poll was no doubt something of a catch — any man would tell you.

"Davy's one of the best," Jack told her, starry eyed. "A gent of the road — a bridle cull — and pretty good at it. Ain't yer, Davy? Tell Poll all about it."

"While I'm in London I'm sticking with honest work," I told him firmly. "I'm keeping out of trouble. Last time I was here I got into Jonathan Wild's bad books and now I'm living whiter'n white. I'm hoping he's forgotten all about me. So no talk about my wicked ways."

"Honest work?" sneered Jack. "Fuck honest work. And you'll never stick it, Davy. What can the likes of you an' me make doin' honest work? You won't keep your doxy in ribbons, doin' honest work."

I laughed, thinking of Lucinda. "True. I know a bit about doxies and ribbons."

"Where are yer stayin, Davy?"

"At a friend's house," I said carelessly.

"With a woman?" Poll asked.

"No."

"Is it the lad who was wiv yer when you came to Mr Wood's workshop?"

"Yes."

"Quiet, like, and sulky."

"That's him."

"Ralph."

"That's right."

"Is he in honest work?"

"Not half. He's a clerk by trade and writes a good hand."

"A married man?"

"Wounds, no!"

"Bring 'im dahn 'ere; we'll soon find 'im a girl. An' then we'll lead 'im orf the straight an' narrer!" Gales of laughter at the prospect. "And I know what that's like," said Jack, "and I'll tell yer, bein' led orf the straight an' narrer was the best fing I ever done. I never knew what I was missin'. I've learnt about women, Davy. I've learnt about Vice. Yeah, vice," he added. licking his lips. "Vice is real jolly, Davy. I'll show yer some vice one day. All them fings I never knew. All them wasted nights when I went to bed early on my own so I'd be able to wake in time to be up early. You can keep it. Vice is much more to my liking!"

He was holding court like a little prince, noisy and perky, his brown eyes merry and his yellow hair glimmering, and the villains in the corner raising their ale mugs to him, as if in earnest of good times to come. I must have been the only one there with misgivings. I felt horribly wise and about a hundred years old.

"Where are you livin' now, Jack?"

"Wiv Bess. But I got so many pals now wiv me new trade as I'm welcome in any number of lodgin's. Our fence has put me up a couple of times. He lodges wiv my pal Blueskin Blake."

"Blueskin Blake?" I must be hearing things. "You know Blueskin Blake?"

"Yeah, everyone knows Blueskin. He's a pal o' Tom's. Tom made me his acquaintance, thinkin' we would be good partners, me an' Blueskin. He wants to go on the road an' all, does Blueskin. We thought we might be partners on the road, see. Blueskin's ma lives in a brandy shop in Wapping. And the chap who'll sell our disposables for us lodges there, and so he puts me up."

"You have a fence already! What foresight! You and Blueskin have been most methodical. However did you find one who was not in the pay of Mr Wild? Or wait — perhaps he's known to Mr Wild. Oh Jack, steer clear of that one. You've already got one of his heavies sitting over there, Hell-and-Fury Sykes. You wouldn't surely be so reckless as to get into Mr Wild's clutches? Who's your fence?"

"Will Field. Why?"

"Will Field has agreed to sell your movables for you?" I blanched. It grew worse and worse.

"Yeah. What's wrong with that?"

"You must be joking," I prayed.

"What's wrong about Will Field?"

"What's right about him?"

"He seems to know what he's about."

"But with a fence — you put your reputation in his hands. right? He can snitch on you if he chooses — he's seen your face — you can't deal with a fence unless you trust him, either because he's dependable or because you got some hold on him. Will Field? I'd sooner trust a cat to mind a day-old chick. He's anybody's who'll pay him, and he'll lead you straight back to Mr Wild."

"I've nothin' against Mr Wild," shrugged Jack. "I met him in the street and he was very civil to me. 'e said 'e hoped 'e might do business wiv me when I became better established."

"Is that what you want?"

"Nah. I said I met 'im, not that I liked 'im. I didn't like 'im, as it happened. That's neither 'ere nor there. I want to work alone, like you do, Davy; but I'd take a partner if I needed one. It's useful to 'ave a chap on lookout when you're pickin' locks. I'd ask you if I thought you'd do it, but you're too grand to be a lookout to a newcomer."

"I might have to, Jack," I replied, "as I shan't sleep for fretting about you. From being a hard-working innocent you've landed right amongst the wolves and seem determined to go further."

"I ain't no lamb," he assured me with a grin. "I'm slippery as an eel. I'll always wriggle out of trouble."

Bess cuddled him. "Don't worry, Davy. I'll look after him."

I believed it. She was bigger than him. I wouldn't have liked to tangle with her, unarmed.

"And Davy," Poll said. "Who's lookin' after you?"

"The angels," I grinned.

"If you take me upstairs," she told me, "I'll be an angel to yer."

I gave her a swift kiss. I said: "I got one waitin' for me, darlin', and she's as much as I can deal with."

"Do you mean she kissed you?" said Lucinda outraged. "With her lips?"

"I had to let her; it would have been unkind to refuse."

We lay in Lucinda's bed at Aunty Mary's. Understandably, Lucinda had received me coolly when I first arrived in London, a knowing smirk about his pretty mouth.

"I guessed that mention of your friend Jack would bring you scuttling down to London, rat."

"So you were right."

"But what is it about Jack? I grant he has a certain something. It must be the yellow hair. But he'll never let you fuck him. You're running after shadows."

"I don't want to fuck him."

"Liar."

"No, I don't. I want to make sure he is alright."

"Why?" Ralph asked reasonably.

"I don't know," I shook my head. "When we were boys together he was so little. They wanted him for a chimney sweep, he was that thin. The sweeps used to come round squinting at us and they'd pick him out and piss themselves with excitement when they saw him — oh, he was chimney-sized, they said; but they couldn't have him because he had a mother. They only dared take the orphans. Jack's ma was real good to me. She used to bake cakes. She always asked me how I was."

"Well, you're easily won over!"

"Jack was the same as her, always helping, always a pal. He took a message for me once, sneaked out of the school to take a message when my pa died and I had to let Ma know."

"Why didn't you go yourself? Why send a runner?"

"They locked the doors. But Jack knew this way out, see, climbing walls and wriggling through holes. Only a skinny boy could have done it. Jack did it. Yeah, he was good to me. You don't forget."

"I don't want you to see him," said Lucinda then.

"Why not?"

"You fancy him."

"I don't, Ralph, truly."

"Why not? Is it because you fancy me?" he added archly.

"Yeah, that's it."

"Then when you come back from seeing him, will you show me which of us you prefer? With interest, for my having told you about his fall from grace?"

"Of course I will."

I did and all. Here we were, together in Ralph's bed, and the pleasure in each other's close company that we had always known was in no way diminished from our having been so many months apart. We were comfortable together, no doubt of it. But beast that I was, my mind was not entirely on Lucinda as I held him in my arms tired out from lovemaking. I was uneasy about Jack. He was deep in trouble. He had thrown himself into bad company with an enthusiasm I could scarcely credit. If he had years of purity to make up for he was in the right place and with the right associates. I could not leave him to muddle through it; I dared not leave London while he pursued this crazy course. It was, I told myself, only what any caring friend would do. I owed it to his mother.

The damnable thing was that his new wayward life suited him immensely. He seemed to have come alive. He was all merriment and sparkle. He talked a lot of gibberish but he was pretty appealing the while. He had lost almost completely that debilitating stammer. He looked very much at ease.

I thought about Ralph's accusation: You want to fuck him. And I thought about how I had lied in my reply.

Chapter Thirty-Six

"RED taffeta!" said Bess. "It's beautiful. Jack, it's beautiful. Drape it round me. Let's see what I'd look like if I was a lady." We were in Poll Maggot's lodgings in Lewkenor's Lane. February it was, and pretty cold, but Poll had got a fire going in the hearth, inflaming Jack's brother Tom when she kneeled down on her elbows and knees with the bellows. He and I now sat scowling at one another each side of the fireplace, toasting bread on brass forks, while Poll lounged on the bed and Bess paraded, and Jack in justifiable pride revealed the results of their latest foray into the profitable world of the housebreaker.

Drapers' shops he liked. You could get a good return on cloth — damasks, poplins, serges, and the silks from India with outlandish names — but I reckoned Jack in his choice of plunder was paying Mr Kneebone back in indirect fashion for years of sugared slavery.

His modest successes had not yet filtered down to the improvement of the quality of Poll's apartment — that she was in Lewkenor's Lane at all was indication that they had yet some way to rise. The peeling plaster showed the bricks beneath; the bed curtains were flecked with mildew. From a beam hung a line of washing draped above the hearth; and the toes of two white stockings teased Tom's ears when he leaned back.

Tom Sheppard was a lout. He had left home when Jack was a boy and joined some gang or other, living off the street. Fair-haired like Jack he was toughly built and clumsy. He it was who had undertaken to lead Jack to greatness in his new-found trade; but in the past he had shown a poor record of excellence, since he had been caught at least once, and suffered the punishment of being glymmed in the paw — that is to say, branded in the thumb. There he sat, picking at the boil on his ear, belching over his beer. He knew that I thought little of him, and he thought as much of me.

"Why'd you let him come here?" he complained to Jack. "He ain't even on the road no more."

"Davy's my best pal," said Jack. "He can visit me any time of the day and night and welcome."

Tom Sheppard had a point. I was then in honest work. It was as if Jack and I were heads on the same coin — flip it one way and I was the law breaker, toss it the other and he was. I had some small wealth put by, in a casket under a floorboard at Aunty Mary's, which was for him and Ralph if I became unlucky. But day to day necessities I earned from working at the White Hart in Long Acre, where I stabled Gry. I was tapster, potboy, ostler, anything. I left my fine clothes and my pistols at Aunty Mary's, and in my homespun shirt and plain breeches and dun cloth coat I reckoned I would not draw much attention to myself. I had a slim cudgel for a weapon, and I moved between the White Hart and my lodging at the top end of Drury Lane unobtrusively, as I hoped, offering no temptation to the likes of Mr Wild as a potential source of revenue.

My lodging — well, I had a room above a butcher's shop in Drury Lane; and the butcher in question was George Page, who had so much admired me at the masquerade at Mother Clap's. When he heard that I was looking for accommodation he offered me this at a small rent, still cherishing the memory of what he would call my heroics when I stopped the mob from murdering poor Jemmy who was now, but for his broken teeth, recovered from his grim ordeal.

I got on well with George. It is a pretty easy business to get on well with one who already thinks you admirable. He was a man in his forties, big, brawny, hirsute, strong. He drove a cart between Drury Lane and Smithfield. Where his slaughter yard was I never asked. On the cool side of his house ran a stone-flagged passage. Here there were carcasses hanging and you were like to find yourself of a morning face to face with a pig's head and to endure his reproachful glassy gaze. The servants of the mighty called into George's shop and gave their orders, and he stood beside his marble slab, his apron bloody and his fearsome array of knives and cleavers at the ready. You would never think he was as mild a chap as anyone could meet.

He liked my living there. "The son I never had," he cried, embracing me, "I would that you were kin of mine indeed." He told folk I was his nephew; and I said yes, I was his brother's son, up from the country — William was my name — and I laughed to think the wheel had come full circle, for it was my old alias William Page whom I had now become indeed, in George Page's house.

Aunty Mary would have had me stay with him and Ralph, but I would not — I would be part of no deal which included being asked where I had been each time I rambled back late, or oblige me continually to counter Ralph's inevitable accusations — you were with Jack! — with falsehoods.

I was with Jack, but not in any sense Ralph need have feared, unfortunately. I drank with Jack at the Black Lion and at the Rose, and he was become a prodigious boozer. Women were drawn to him. He was always with some drab or other — Bess, Poll Maggot, Molly Frisky — and as often trying to pass one or other of them on to me, like some kind of benign potentate but newly come to power whose good fortune must be shared with one who had once been a companion in the leaner times.

"If you won't take Poll or Molly," he said, "why dontcher bring the girl you said you'd got, the one you said was as much as you could deal with? She sounds all right."

"Because there ain't no girl," said Tom scathingly. "He's making her up. Else why ain't she here?"

"Her aunty doesn't like her coming to the Rose; and she'd have words to say about a naked woman squatting on a plate."

Jack grinned happily. "To think good times like these have been goin' on for years an' I was just nearby an' never knew! I fort a candle was just for givin' light."

"What's her name, Davy, this girl of yours?" said Poll.

"Lucinda."

"We'd call her Lucy. She sounds a snotty little bitch."

"Sometimes she is."

"Is she prettier than me then?"

"About the same."

"Is her hair better than mine?"

"About the same."

"Has she got lovely eyes, like me?"

"Oh, much the same."

"Then for Heaven's sake," said Poll in exasperation, "what has she got that I haven't?"

While I judged how best to answer that Bess, all draped in crimson, intervened. "Tits," she pronounced sagely. "All men like 'em big. That's what it'll be. Ain't it, Davy? Ain't your Lucy more finely formed than Poll? More like what I am?"

"There's no contest, Bess; you win stupendously."

Jack jumped across to her and cuddled her possessively. "Yeah, Bess is a big bonny wench, an' I ain't sharin'."

There was a knock at the door. We all jumped. Tom pulled out a pistol; and Bess and Jack, entwined in taffeta, froze where they stood.

"It's all right," Jack said. "It'll be Will Field."

"Here?" I said.

"Yeah. You know, I told you he was goin' ter be our fence. He's come to look at the stuff. 'e said 'e would."

"I should be off," I said, and stood up.

"No, stay, you don't 'ave ter mind the likes o' Will Field."

In he sloped, whom I had last seen from beneath his fist in the stable yard in Great Queen Street, my mouth tasting of blood and straw.

Tom Sheppard moved forward, taking charge, claiming all the credit.

"You got some cloth for me," said Will.

Tom heaved the taffeta from Bess and cast it forward; Will caught hold of it.

"You don't want ter let yer whores play with it," he remarked. "You'll get a poorer price for stained goods. Yeah," he said, handling the taffeta,"I can get you a good price for that. Show me what else yer got. Was this the stuff from Clare Street?"

Jack perched on the table, and we watched as Tom and Will talked prices.

"I'll be back next week and bring the cole," said Will.

"Not here," said Poll. "I live here. I don't want no trouble here."

"I'll meet you at the Cat and Fiddle."

"Agreed," said Tom.

Will Field turned to me. "So, you're back. I heard you was. Couldn't keep away, huh?" He frowned. "Are you in this?"

"No he ain't," Tom interrupted irritably. "Jack and I did this ourselves, with no help from anyone."

"I'm back, but I'm reformed," I said.

Will laughed scornfully. "You never are."

"I'm in honest work."

"You'll never stick it. No one does. You'll be back to yer old trade."

When he had gone, Poll said: "Like I say, I don't want him back here. I didn't take to him, Jack."

"Ah, he's all right."

"He's got shifty eyes."

"He seems to know you, Davy?"

"We can't stand each other. And I'm surprised you trust him to do business with. He's a two-faced weasel."

"Don't tell me who to do business with," growled Tom.

"He's on the end of a thread that leads straight back to Jonathan Wild."

"So what?" said Jack. "We ain't been caught. He's got nothin' against us."

"If you get successful he'll want you in his employ, that's what."

"Well, if you must know, Mr Wild's already asked me if I'd like to work for 'im. An' 'e asked me to his levy to take breakfast wiv 'im."

"The devil he did! What did you say? You surely did not go?"

"I did. It was pretty odd. The room was full of villains buzzin' round 'im, and in the middle of it all sat Mr Wild in a dressin' gown and funny 'at, drinkin' chocolate from a silver cup. 'e was pretty kind to me, an' said I was too good to flounder on my own, an' I'd do better wiv 'is might behind me. 'e said the law was pretty rough on housebreakers. But I told 'im I 'ad no fear of the law." Jack smirked. "I told 'im it was good of 'im to ask me but I must decline. 'e didn't like it much. 'e kept on smilin' but 'e wasn't much amused. What does 'e fink I am? I know somethin' of 'is ways — I ain't the stupid boy I was. I heard about what happened to John Filewood."

"What did?"

"'e came back secretly from transportation an' got protection

255

in Mr Wild's employ. 'e was a pickpocket, an ordinary thief. 'e stole this sword an' Mr Wild took a fancy to it and would have had it for 'imself, but Filewood sold it to a fence, without telling Jonathan. So Jonathan had 'im arrested; not for that, but on the charge of having returned from transportation. One of 'is own chaps! 'e didn't stand a chance; they topped 'im. Jonathan don't value 'is own. 'e says 'e does but it's a lie. 'e 'as the names of all 'is chaps in a ledger, an' 'e puts a cross by their name if they're expendable, an' when 'e wants to keep in with the law 'e peaches one and hands 'im in, and puts a second cross beside 'is name, which makes a double cross; an' that's 'im gone." Jack stuck a finger and thumb around his throat and jerked his eyes skyward. "Think I want ter work for 'im? I ain't givin' 'im no chance to double-cross me! Not friggin' likely!"

"In my experience," I said, "I have found that Mr Wild does not take happily to anyone who refuses his offers. You take care, Jack. Don't go down any dark alleys; or take Tom with you."

"D'you think Jack needs a nursemaid?" chortled Bess, and plainly tired of hearing about Mr Wild, said: "A chap was in the Rose last night with Mr Defoe's new book. He read some of it to me. Have you met Mr Defoe, Davy?"

"That Mr Defoe ain't half nosey," Poll laughed. "Always askin' questions. *How much do you make livin' on the streets? What's it like to be transported? How did you feel when you was in Newgate? Were your spirits much afflicted?* — that's how he talks, elegant. You should see the book. It's all about Moll King, though he don't call her that. He gets her to say: I was in a dismal and disconsolate case — there was a heaviness upon my spirits — I was lost in fancies and imaginations — and I was possessed of horrible apprehensions! Did you ever hear Moll King talk like that? He said it wasn't Moll King's story, but made up of women he had known, and out of his own head."

"How can it be hers? She must be nearly sixty now!" Bess cried. "Did you ever meet her, Davy? She's transported now, for the second time; she went last summer. She used to wear a cloak with false hands, so her real hands could be busy pickin' pockets. It looked real odd when it was hangin' on the peg. I heard she'd had two hundred lovers!"

"No!"

"Yeah, and she had John Stanley when he was sweet seventeen and she was old enough to be a grandmother," Poll said admiringly.

"She got caught and put in the Whit," Bess continued. "She had one of her brats in there. When they sent her over the seas she came sneakin' back, and Mr Wild looked after her — she did her pickin' an' stealin' for him. Yeah, he looked after her, but she got unlucky — she got caught again, housebreakin', so back to the Whit, and overseas again."

"An odd kind of looking after," I observed. "Couldn't he save her? I thought his power was absolute."

"He did look after her — she got transportation, didn't she? She could've gone to Tyburn."

"She got unlucky," I agreed. "Once you get unlucky you might as well pack up."

"I don't worry," Jack said. "I'm lucky. I've got plans. I'm goin' ter make a fortune. I never knew it was so easy. I'm goin' ter buy a big house out of town for Ma and me to live in. Servants an' all, an' she can spit in Mr Kneebone's eye. I'll look after her. I got all the skills I need an' I ain't afraid of no one."

That evening, in Lucinda's company at Mother Clap's, I voiced my gloomy thoughts aloud. Like Mr Defoe's heroine Moll Flanders I was possessed of horrible apprehensions; I was in a dismal and disconsolate case; I was lost in fancies and imaginations.

"Lucinda! He makes me feel old and wise, and goodness knows I am neither. Have you ever heard sprats playing in the gutters chasin' each other with sticks and stones and yellin' Get me, Get me? That's what Jack's like. And those drabs encourage him and push him on and he laps it up."

We had a big old tom cat at the White Hart, kept to catch mice, a fat striped thing with one ear bitten off. He used to sit in the yard where the sparrows came for the crumbs. I once leaned on a pitchfork, watching him. He used to make believe he was an idiot, like he had no idea what birds were for. He had the patience of Job. He could wait all day, inert as an old loaf. But when he pounced he never missed. You had forgotten he was there. The sparrows used to come right up to him and dance between his paws.

Chapter Thirty-Seven

I HAD always considered it an amiable notion to Pass into Legend, but as my highwayman friend from the Saracen's Head had pointed out to me as he counted his guineas, to enjoy this state of bliss one should have let one's name be known to ballad singers and have quit this world in public circumstances, preferably in the arms of Mother Tyburn. Jack, however, contrived to Pass into Legend in his lifetime.

"Davy!" he hissed at me from the hay loft of the White Hart. "Over here!"

"Jack? What in hell are you doing here?"

"Hidin'." He scrambled down and brushed the straw from his clothes. "I'm on the run. Just came to tell you where I'll be. Don't follow me; come later. Listen — me an' Bess are at the Queen's Head, off Thieving Lane, King Street. You was right about Will Field," he added. "What a shammock!" He shook his head and grinned. He thumped me in the chest. "Davy," he boasted, "I got a price of forty pound on my head!" Then he dashed off, to Pass into Legend.

Poll Maggot came round shortly afterwards. My standing at the White Hart increased by a mile. She leaned against a post provocatively, chewing on a straw.

"Will Field?" she snorted. "I knew he was a wrong 'un. No, it was frigging Tom that was the villain. He took the stuff round to the back of the Cat and Fiddle and met up with Will Field. It was a set-up. There was constables there, and they took Tom to the Whit. He only told them everything they wanted to know! Peached Jack, peached Bess — Ad's blood but he's the kind of pal you want, ain't he? Mouth as wide as where the Thames meets the sea."

"Will Field, Tom — they're small fry," I said. "You know who the real villain is. I knew there'd be trouble when Jack said he'd been asked to work for Mr Wild and he'd refused. I knew it wouldn't be the last of it. Will Field's his creature. Anything Will Field does has Mr Wild's hand in it. He was out to get Jack. We'll have to make sure he don't."

"Listen here, Jack," I said at the Queen's Head. "Don't you trust no one, not anyone at all, and in particular anyone you think might come from Mr Wild."

"I won't," he agreed, all solemn eyed. He had such big brown eyes, all open and honest looking, with hazel lashes. I was distracted for a moment by how beautiful they were. Then he grinned. It was what we call a fleer. It's that kind of sweet smile a chap gives you when he doesn't mean what he says. "Come on, Davy — I can look after myself!"

My arse in a bandbox! He only went and trusted Hell-and-Fury Sykes. Short of wearing Jonathan Wild's livery James Sykes could hardly have made clearer where his loyalties lay. He was a chairman, same as my pa had been. You know how they are, shoulders like house rafters, an endless capacity for ale and a comfortable familiarity with every oath known to man. I thought everyone knew he worked for Jonathan. And with this angel in went Jack to some boozing ken in Seven Dials to play skittles. The place was stuffed with constables, pretending to be innocent skittle players. Of course they arrested him.

"You have ter help him, Davy," said Poll Maggot, tugging at my arm. "He's in St Giles lockup. Bess will meet us there tonight; she's bringing weapons."

"You mean there's just us three to get him out? Where's all them others who were drinking at the Black Lion?"

"Bess don't trust them. She said you'd know what to do."

We set out smartish for St Giles. It was dark and cold. The usual idiot watchman was trundling up and down bawling: "Ten o'clock and all's well."

"They'd shout that if the world was ending," I said scornfully.

Bess was waiting in a doorway, opposite the Roundhouse where Jack had been imprisoned. She was muffled in a cloak. She reached into its depths and handed us each a couple of daggers, all unsheathed, which we received with due solemnity.

"I've already tried askin' if I could visit him," she said. "I was goin' ter hand him a knife. But they said no, he was locked in for the night now and would receive no visitor till morning. He's on the top floor."

"How many guards did you see?"

"Four."

There we stood, irresolute and stupid, clutching our knives. It was plain enough what should be done; but knives are for use, and the likely outcome was the killing of a guard, and I hesitated.

"Wait! Look!" Poll croaked. "No, don't. Look quickly, then turn away. Jack's on the roof."

A tile came clattering to the ground and smashed upon the cobbles. A light in the upper room of a neighbouring house illumined Jack's small figure, scrambling up amongst the chimney pots. He carried a bulky bundle; it was composed of knotted sheets and blankets.

"He's making for the church," whispered Poll. "He'll come down in the churchyard. Plenty of tombstones for cover."

"There's someone on the roof!" a man's voice shouted behind us.

"Yes! Over there!" we all said at once, pointing in any kind of direction but the true. We fixed upon a spot far to the right, jabbering excitedly at nothing. We had a small crowd soon about us, jumping up and down, squinting upwards.

"There he is, behind that chimney — look!" said one amongst us. It was Jack. He was down. Bess hustled him away, and Poll and I stood pointing, calling, keeping the crowd riveted with sightings on the rooftops of this dark elusive roof dancer.

"He's going to jump! There he goes! Oh no!"

I swear they ran off at a great rate and may even now be picking at the ground for smashed and gory fragments.

I thought our troubles were all over, just as I did when Jamie Goodman got out of the Sessions House and I believed him halfway up the Great North Road, and all along he'd gone home to his missus. It was pretty neat to have escaped from the Roundhouse. I felt a surge of relief and joy and a pleasant amusement at the thought of the Roundhouse guards going into the locked cell in the morning only to discover a hole in the ceiling. Our Jack must have had a razor on him. And we with all our knives, standing below!

Poll seemed to feel a similar content. She grinned and caught my eye.

"Come home with me, Davy," she said. "Why not?"

We must have looked a gruesome pair, our hands full of daggers, staring at one another in the lamplit gloom. In the unaccustomed intimacy brought about by our sharing in Jack's rescue I would have liked to have been honest with her; but I recalled the screaming fishwives at the pillory.

I coughed and answered sheepishly: "I have an indisposition," and she took the answer in good part and said that she would ask me again.

When I got back to Drury Lane and eased my way round the dark alley that led round the back of George's house I was surprised to find a light showing.

George was sitting in the parlour, at the table. A single candle burned. In its glow I could see plates of ham and bread, some slices of pie in a dish, and the ale jug with two tankards nestling about it.

"Oh, George," I said in dismay. "You surely have not waited up for me."

"I have; but as it was my pleasure to do so, you have no need to reproach yourself. Now eat."

I sat down at the table. "This is most welcome."

He watched me fondly.

"You look after me so well," I said. "You shouldn't."

"That's for me to decide."

"Thank you for not asking where I've been."

"It's none of my business. I'm just pleased to see you. The streets at night are not all they should be."

"George," I said. "I've a wayward friend who gives me concern. Tonight I went to try and get him out of the Roundhouse at St Giles. I needn't have troubled, as he burrowed his way out and scrambled up on to the roof."

"The devil he did!" said George admiringly.

"And then he climbed down into the churchyard where a friend took him to safety. The whole town will be talking about it in the morning."

"I don't doubt it. And now he's on the run?"

"He has as many bolt holes as a fox, I now believe."

"If he needs to hide here," George said, "that's all right by me."

"You're a good pal, George."

George watched me eat.

"He's not one of us?"

I winced. There was always that in me which resisted the implication that I was one of a brotherhood, however fair the assumption. It was a shackle. I didn't want it.

"He's become the greatest womanizer of our time," I answered. I had meant to sound amused; I sounded bitter. "You can't get near him for females, and it's to them he goes for help."

George slid me the ale jug and I poured. "He used to be the purest creature upon earth. He has a sweet kind mother who would die of shame if she knew how he had turned out; and he used to sell lace and ribbons in a draper's."

"And why do you mind so much about it all?" said George; and it was a very reasonable question.

"I frigging well don't know," I answered. "Six months ago, George, I was on the road, as free as a bit of wind-blown summer dust. I was looking for gold, and the rumours of gold. Now I'm marking time with stable work and my good horse is getting fat and lazy; and all to keep an eye on a chap who pays no heed. I've known him since he was six years old and I'm just drawn to him, I don't know why. Not so strange, perhaps, as all the women love him too, on account of his yellow hair and big brown eyes, and I daresay he gives 'em a good time besides. Not that I'd know anything about that," I added morsosely.

"And that's what rankles, eh?" said George.

"I guess so," I said ruefully.

"Finish your pie," said George.

We stood up. He put his arm round me in a comfortable hug.

But — whether it was the night or the curious closeness brought on by our conversation — a sudden lust rose as our bodies touched, surprising us; at least, surprising me. We kissed. I laughed with pleasure at the rough tickle of his beard. I pressed against him greedily. He held me to him.

"Shall you be with me tonight, lad?"

I hesitated. "If you will leave me free."

"What is so fearful to you about drawing close?"

"I don't know, except that it is so."

"I will respect that; but I think you are wrong."

We went upstairs, the candle streaming in the draught. He unlatched his bedroom door and set the candle down. We undressed, and his eyes never left me.

"What?" I said.

"It isn't every day a gorgeous young man takes his clothes off for me," said George frankly.

I felt uneasy then, and gawky as a colt. "I'm nothing special."

"Leave me to disagree."

He blew out the candle and we got into bed. He was good to lie against, big and firm and warm, and he treated me so well, lying me upon my back and kissing me all up and down my body, and his beard brushing and nuzzling my skin. Shaking and gasping I lay back and waited for my heart to quieten. Pretty roused himself he rolled me over on my belly and he lay on me, his hot breath in my ear, his beard rough in my neck, and the warm flood of his juices in the hollow of my back. He ruffled my hair, and because he knew I wanted no words of love or niceties he gave me a swift hug and told me to go to sleep. I did so, well content.

The following evening we went round to Mother Clap's together, as there was to be a marrying, and fiddlers; and I spent the evening with Lucinda, except for one brief moment when I asked Ma Clap if Harry Radley ever called in these days; and she told me no, not lately.

Apart from all the talk of the amazing escape of Jack Sheppard from the Roundhouse, the gossip was that Gabriel Lawrence had grown religious, and from too much contemplation upon the work of the Holies, was asking whether it were true that God would punish those of a mollying disposition; thus he proved dull company. Yet folk were gathered round him, all eager to offer their pennyworth on the nature of God.

When I went past with a drink in my hand, being one who never gave the matter thought, I caught snippets of the conversation.

"If you live well and do no harm to others, how may you offend the Almighty?"

"The Lord forbade that one man lie with another."

"Gabriel, He forbade that one man lie with another man's wife, but that hinders no man!"

"He also said, 'ye shall not round the corners of your heads, neither shalt thou mar the corners of thy beard!'"

"What does He mean by that? Has He an interest in fashion?"

"He said, 'ye shall not steal', but all would if they thought they could get away with it, and many do, both small fry picking pockets in a crowd, and the statesmen of our nation, taking bribes."

"He said that those that curse their parents shall be put to death. But who has not said 'a pox on the old fellow!' from time to time; and must he be put to death for it?"

"And how is Jack?" Lucinda asked me with a smirk.

"I hope that a narrow escape from the arms of the Law will have taught him to lead a blameless life henceforth."

"That would be too dull for words," said Ralph. "Let's watch the marrying. It's Orange Deb and Susan Sweetlips. I heard that Susan's cock was fourteen inches long when roused! Do you believe that? I do not."

We looked in awe upon the happy couple, wondering if it were true. Into the marrying room they went, with paper garlands in their hair, and nosegays of violets, and the fiddlers following them closely, playing fit to burst, and Mother Clap embracing them and throwing cascades of paper petals.

"How pretty Susan looks," said Ralph, adding waspishly: "from the left-hand side. How pleasant it must be to have your partner care so much about you that he says as much before all the assembled company. I would rather fancy to be married and go off into the marrying room. What do you think, Davy?"

"I think Gabriel's problem is that he is attracted to street boys."

"I beg your pardon?" Ralph said huffily. "What has that to do with marrying?"

"Nothing, except indirectly. It has more to do with religious doubt. If he had one partner whom he loved he would find it easier to seek God's approval."

"He is a slave to Peter Bavidge; that is enough to give anyone religious doubt!" sniggered Ralph. "By the way, did you know that under his wig, Petronella is becoming almost bald? I often think that is at the root of his bitchiness, and that he seeks to dominate

Gabriel out of a fear that he is losing his good looks. How Gabriel can fancy him I simply fail to understand."

"I believe he cares for Peter but I guess he is butter in the hands of the Covent Garden whores and cannot help his fascination for a neat arse in tight breeches. Or out of tight breeches, come to think of it."

"He wants Tommy Newton," Ralph said sagely. "You remember, the prize at the masquerade? But Peter would have apoplexy if Gabriel ever achieved him. He likes to think that Gabriel is under his thumb. I think Gabriel means to be faithful, but he longs for dirty swiving."

I agreed. "So guilt is at the root of his present questioning."

"Fury is at the root of mine," Lucinda said with asperity.

"Are you furious with me, by any chance?"

"How quick you are, my dear, how astute!"

"Because I said nothing about marrying you?"

"I please you, don't I? Everybody says we make a lovely couple."

"You know you please me."

"But not enough."

"I don't know," I said, uncomfortable at the directness of his questioning.

Suddenly Ralph kissed me. "Oh Davy, I'm a petulant beast. I won't pester you. It isn't meant to be, is it? We'll keep our separate dreams. I'll pursue my quest for a rich nobleman to look after me — I have one in mind, you know — and you'll pursue your quest for gold."

I stared at him, startled by how curiously hollow a prospect that rich goal appeared. But I had not time to dwell upon the matter further for we were hustled into the dancing and grew merry and made new verses to 'Come let us bugger finely'; and Orange Deb and Susan Sweetlips came out of the marrying room with flushed faces and disarrayed clothes, and Ralph asked Deb if the rumours about Susan's cock were true and Susan clipped his ear — he was a hefty chap, a farrier by trade — but Orange Deb said nothing and looked well content.

Then Ma Clap who had been dancing vigorously caused us once more alarm by falling in a faint upon the floor and there were cries of 'Give us room, make way' and those with knowledge on the subject set about burning twisted rolls of paper and thrusting smelling salts under her nose, and she revived. We lifted her, no easy business, with her skirts and petticoats and she a well-made woman.

"Boys, boys," she panted. "I am no longer young, no, not a young woman!"

"Ma, you are in your prime!" we told her, and brought brandy by the glass.

"I think," said Gabriel, in the lugubrious tones of one who has been loosening his mental processes by drink, "that it all depends upon whether the Lord God is a jealous god or a kindly god. If He is a kindly god then He is all understanding and forgiveness. I believe Him kind."

We all cheered at this happy conclusion; and I went home with Lucinda.

"You know, Davy, don't you," he said as we walked, "that when I say things at Mother Clap's — silly things and such, about going into marrying rooms and personal remarks about anatomy, I only say them because we are at Ma's, where folk may be as foolish as they please. I have to spend all day copying out legal documents. A person may act foolish in the evening. It does not mean that a person *is* foolish. At least, no more than anyone."

In the dark bedroom overlooking the street at Aunty Mary's we helped each other out of our clothes.

"I never saw such a good body as yours, Davy," Ralph said. "So lean across the chest, and so strong in the arm! And the muscles of your thighs... It must be all that horse riding! And you have the loveliest bum in all the world!" He went down on his knees against me, pressing his face against my belly. I moved my fingers through his thick smooth hair.

"Ralph, I'll come into the marrying room with you whenever you like when you do that, and let folk gawp at us and make lewd jokes and peer into the room and see all we do... now take me all the way..."

When we sank into the feather bed and drew the sheets about us, Ralph curled into my arms, well pleased with himself.

"Tell me what I'm good at," purred he.

"What you're good at? You write a lovely letter."

He snorted. We dozed in good humour. Some time in the morning we were awakened by a great commotion in the street below.

The day was well advanced; it was daylight and we could see quite clearly when we looked out through the glass.

A young man had run amok. He was throwing stones at the windows. Some glass had been smashed. Mr Brewer our doorkeeper was there and shouting: "Be off with you! Come back here and I'll have the constables on you!"

But they were here already. I recognized my old acquaintance Constable Willis who had patched me up after my encounter with Will Field and Blueskin Blake. He took hold of the young man and hurried him away.

"Looks like he's been thrown out for causing trouble," Ralph said. "Aunty Mary will be vexed. We deal with the quality. They detest a disturbance."

He was very young, sixteen maybe. He was thin and rangy with dark brown raggedy hair, dark brows and a big mouth. He had pointed ears — goblin like — and an oval face with a jutting jaw, and there was a deal of noise coming from that wide mouth. He was yelling at Constable Willis. He was calling him a wide variety of names, none complimentary.

I laughed. "Constable Willis'll deal with him," I said confidently. "Who is he? He's pretty tasty, ain't he?"

"Who is he? He's Ned Courtenay," said Ralph.

"Ned Courtenay?"

Ralph shrugged dismissively.

"A nobody."

Chapter Thirty-Eight

I SLIPPED the turnkey a guinea at the Clerkenwell prison and he let us in. Poll Maggot was got up to look as if she was far gone with child, and I her solicitous husband with, of necessity, a limp, and both of us heavily overdressed for the month of May. It is a happy truth that many of the prison guards are stupid; and the rest are amenable to bribes.

Jack was sitting on the floor of his cell, fettered and manacled, weighed down with double links and leg irons, and chained to a ring set in the wall. Bess was sitting on a bench. She jumped up and hugged us both. She was as tall as me and twice as wide. It was like the embrace of a coal heaver but not so exciting. I daresay they were pleased to see us, but it was what we had brought with us that most pleased them.

Jack had not remained long at liberty. He had gone straight to the likes of Burnworth and Leonard, as hardened a crew of villains as a chap could care to meet. They were the successes of the moment, bloody and heartless throat-slitters — no self-respecting bridle cull would have gone within an inch of them. And what good

266

were they to Jack now? Who was it smuggling in the tools that he would need for his escape?

He had been picked up in Leicester Fields. Bess like a fool had gone running to the gaol armed with a halberd spike when she heard of his recapture. She had got herself caught breaking down the cell door, and they put her in there with him when she said she was his wife.

"Five minutes only," said the guard to Poll and me, and locked the door. From Poll's false belly came a lengthy coil of rope; from my coat cuffs a file, gimlet and piercers, and from my boot a slender saw in a leathern case. We put them all under Bess's skirts and she arranged them about her person. I looked at Poll. I thought: we'll never pull this off. The guard returned and Poll and I were escorted out. There were some gardens near the prison and when it got dark we hopped over a wall and waited, sitting under some apple trees, whose blossom blew down into our hair whenever there was a wind gust. Our conversation was monotonous.

"They'll never do it."

"Maybe they will; no, it's impossible."

"It's impossible; maybe they will."

And then Poll groaned: "But Bess is built like a brick wash-house. However will she get out of a window?"

"It's impossible," I agreed morosely.

Just before dawn we saw two shadows slip away and creep off towards Pear Tree Court and Rag Street. We jumped to our feet in relief and disbelief.

"Leave them," I said. "We'll draw attention to them." We stood motionless, squinting into the darkness.

"It was impossible," we agreed in awe.

All London spoke of it next day. You could even read about in the news papers.

"Miraculous escape! Sawed off fetters! Cut iron bar from window! Gimlet used to weaken beam! Twenty-five foot descent into yard! Outer wall twenty-two feet high! Gimlets and piercers to make a scaling ladder! Sharp spikes! Rope tied around gimlet! Jack Sheppard and his Fair Companion at Large! Keepers asleep!"

What a hero, I thought, envious and proud.

It seemed he could not put a foot wrong. There was the robbery at the master tailor's house. He got notes and bonds to the value of three hundred guineas; and clothes. The chap he took along to help him was later caught, charged and transported; but Jack was free. Free and elegant.

"Look at me suit," he told me, upstairs at the Goat. "Know what it's made of? Paddy soy. Real silk, my tailor tells me. Comes from Italy. You didn't know I got a tailor, eh? When I acquired this suit it was big enough for Bessie. It was made for someone who was pretty fat. But I had it altered to fit me, and now ain't I smart!"

Pale green it was and nicely cut.

"Yes, pretty smart," I said. "And pretty recognizable. You won't go strolling about in open places?"

"Don't fret so, Davy. I got secret dens all over London. I'll show you one."

There was in Chick Lane, next door to a dilapidated boozing ken, a chandler's, which you reached by descending some half-dozen steps below the street. The shop was in darkness — fusty, filthy, smelling of tallow, gin and piss. There was no one within. Jack tweaked aside a curtain of sacking, and we felt our way up a ladder, which brought us on to a landing. Faint light from a hole in the brickwork showed us a low latched doorway. We went through.

"Now," said Jack. "Try and catch me!" He darted off. We were like boys climbing round an old barn; it was a game to us. We could hear each other laughing as I hunted him and he hid. I ran up a stairway; the top stair sprung a secret spring and the floorboards slid sharply back and made a hole I nearly stepped into, over a pit of blackness. I climbed round the edge of the hole, I came flat up against a wall, I leaned against it, it gave way, I stepped out into thin air, I landed winded in a heap of straw, I scrambled up, and from above my head Jack pelted me with — what? Wounds, I guessed it must be stolen goods — a length of cloth unrolled about me, and pocket books and snuff boxes and a very fine feathered hat. I put my arms about my head and looked for a way up. A ladder teetered against the wall. I went up it cautiously. Jack at the top teased me by moving it outwardly from the wall and back again. When I got to the top he was gone. I climbed over a rail, pursued him along passages that curved and dipped, became dead ends, and led me through a low door where I saw Jack on a ledge above a dark place and the only way to him a long beam laid across the abyss. There was a disgusting smell coming up out of the darkness. I went on hands and knees across the beam, and Jack rollicking with laughter tipped the beam's end and I dropped and clung on by my hands and then my feet as I swung my legs up. I gripped the beam like a monkey and Jack lit a lanthorn, holding it towards me, laughing fit to burst.

"Do you give in? Or shall I rock the beam again?"

"I give in. I'll never catch yer. Where in hell's name are we,

Jack? By the stink of it I'd say the Fleet ditch."

"You'd be right. You're balanced most unsteadily above the Fleet. If I was not your friend I'd see you tumbled in it."

"I give thanks to heaven that you are my friend then; though if this treatment be friendship I'm the Queen of the May. Are you going to let me up?"

"I could've spiked you any number of times when you were running after me. This place is made to trap your foes. It goes on for miles. No one'll catch me here."

"Jack, will you frigging well let me off this beam?"

"You ain't afraid of a dirty old ditch with all them dead dogs and sir-reverence?"

He leaned carefully forward and took my shoes off and tickled my feet. I was wriggling and laughing and pleading and he was consumed by such merriment he nearly fell in head first himself. And I kept thinking: this is a man with forty pound reward on his head, who if he's caught will be lucky to get transportation, and he's tickling my feet.

He paused, squatting there, surveying me.

"Blueskin Blake has asked me to go on the road wiv 'im."

"That is the stupidest idea I ever heard."

"Why so?"

"Jack, being on the road's a skill, a business. You don't pick it up overnight."

"Gerroff — you take some old nag and a pistol and you bawl Stand and Deliver. Any fool knows that."

"Some old nag!" I groaned. "It's got to be a horse that you can trust with your life. It takes years to be that close."

"What if I went on the road with you?" then Jack said tentatively.

"You'd be a liability. I'd have to watch you every step of the way."

"So you don't think we should do the road together?"

"I can't talk about it dangling on a beam. My arms and legs ache."

Jack slithered snake-like back into the darkness. Gingerly I moved forward and he helped me off the beam and on to firm ground. There we sat, backs against a wall of tangled cobweb, while I put on my shoes.

"Jack, I'd love for us to be together on the road. There's nothing I'd like better in all the world."

"But?"

"For your best safety you should leave off lawlessness. Don't make it any worse than it is now. Think of your ma."

"You are becoming such a killjoy, Davy. I thought the world of you when you was bridle cullin' an' you wore that coat an' them tall boots an' carried silver pistols."

"Yeah, I miss it," I agreed."But it'd be asking for trouble. You're so... I don't half love yer, Jack, but you don't have no sense at all. I don't know what it is — you're foolhardy — you take risks you shouldn't. It's partly what makes you dear to folk, but on the road it would be frigging stupid."

Jack stood up. He sniggered. "Looks like it'll have ter be Blueskin Blake then," he said.

I darted after him. I grabbed him, twisting his arm behind him, pressing his face against the wall. I held him there, my face in his hair, my body tight against his. My loins responded instantly to the firm shape of his arse. After enjoying it for a moment I backed off.

"Promise me you'll not take to the road with Blueskin Blake."

"I promise," said Jack dutifully, and I let him go, with a shove of exasperation.

Lifting a flap of wood he led the way into what proved to be a store shed in a dyer's yard. We emerged into the street. Jack pressed a purse into my hand.

"Take this to Ma," he said, "An' tell her I'm doin' very well." Then he looked about him cagily and nudged me in the ribs.

"Look to hear of another famous robbery," he said.

I was walking towards Drury Lane in the mid afternoon when a coach came up alongside me. I noticed the good quality of the horses as I stepped clear; but the vehicle slowed down to walking pace until the passenger within drew level with me. I saw that it was Mr Jonathan Wild. Our eyes met in recognition and I decided it would do me no good to run off, and so I let him have his say.

"Mr Davy Gadd!" he said, as if we were the greatest friends and had only quit each other's company yesterday. "How agreeable to see you! Are you keeping well?"

"Very well, thankyou; and yourself?" said I with no particular interest in the reply.

"Excellent!" said he. "I hope I do not find you in straitened circumstance, Davy?" he said. I was fresh from the stable yard and in my homespun must have looked somewhat different from the flash and shameless bridle cull that he remembered.

"I am in honest work," I said firmly, and meaning: therefore of no use to you.

"Yes, yes," he said dismissively, and plainly not believing me. "But you keep to your old haunts, no doubt? Our fair city's lower hostelries?" Then he added playfully: "Moorfields?"

I ignored that. "I do drink here and there," I agreed.

"And meet your old pals? Always glad to see a friend?"

I thought I saw what was coming.

He continued: "For instance, Jack Sheppard?"

"Oh no, sir, I never see Jack now."

The coach wheels trundled noisily beside me, grey with the dust of summer, shoving me closer to the wall. They slowed down almost to stopping. Mr Wild leaned suddenly a little from his window, and thrust his silver cane across my chest, barring my way. I looked at him.

"Fifty guineas, Davy, if you'll take me to where he is. Jump in beside me. Fifty guineas, Davy!"

"Mr Wild, I don't know where he is, I swear it."

He glared at me and grunted. Then he snapped: "You have done yourself no favours by this refusal." He tapped smartly upwards with his cane and the coach gathered speed and lurched forward.

I feared for Jack anew, it being plain that Mr Wild was out to get him. I was standing like a lummock, looking after his disappearing coach when in its wake a second coach appeared, this one more humble, the kind for hire on any street corner, the driver bearing down on me with a bawdy shout:

"Oy, gorgeous, shift your arse!"

His nearside leader missed me by an inch. He swerved at the last moment. I yelled abuse at him from the cobbles where I had landed. I heard him laugh as he careened away.

Harry Radley, damn him. Now I recalled he had said he was a coachman. Coachman, muttered I; not fit to drive a donkey cart. Then wiping down my dusty breeches I could not help but laugh, as I marvelled, full of admiration for the superb control he had in managing his horses.

Oh yes, he knew exactly what he was about. Son of a Bridewell bitch!

The news papers agreed it was a cunning piece of housebreaking. The house was broken into through the cellar. Three bolts and a padlock were breached. A second padlock and hasp were torn away. The shop above was entered. The housebreakers were within for long enough to choose at their leisure one hundred yards of wool-

271

len cloth, five yards of blue bays, a neat little wig, a beaver hat, two silver spoons, some handkerchiefs and a pen knife, the entire haul valued at fifty pounds.

And whose house was it? Mr Kneebone's. And Mr Kneebone went straight off to Mr Jonathan Wild to ask him to get his goods back for him and to catch the thief.

But Jack was not in town.

He had taken to the road with Blueskin Blake.

Chapter Thirty-Nine

I AWOKE to find Jack sitting on my bed. It was well after midnight. He had climbed in through my open window. That it was on the second storey and barely a foot square was of course no hindrance to the likes of him, and there he sat, like a leprechaun, small, winsome and grumbling.

"Feed me, Davy. Ain't yer got nothin' to eat here?"

It came as no surprise to me that Jack and Blueskin proved a dismal failure as Gentlemen of the Road. They flitted about Hampstead Heath. They got half a crown from a lady's maid alone and terrified in a small coach; they got three shillings from a drunken chandler; and a guinea from a stage coach. Then Jack quarrelled with his would-be partner.

" 'e's violent, Davy," Jack complained. " 'e would've done murder if I 'adn't stopped 'im. How'd 'e get like that? I s'pose it's keepin' company wiv villains."

I pulled on my breeches and we soft-footed downstairs, where we were eating cold beef slices in the kitchen when George found us. He came creeping round the door with a meat cleaver in his fist, and Jack pulled a pistol.

"No — it's all right," I said swiftly, in alarm. "George, this is my old friend Jack. Jack, this is dear George Page."

"Mr Page," said Jack, "I'm a wanted man with forty pound on my head and a known housebreaker, so you'll need to choose whether you want me to stay."

"Any friend of Davy's is welcome here," said George, and they shook hands and put down their weapons.

"Now I've eaten," Jack said cheerily, "I'll be on my way, sustained. I'm meetin' up wiv Blueskin to discuss our future plans."

"Not to Bess's?" I said hopefully.

"I couldn't find 'er. That's why I came 'ere."

He could not find Bess because, as we learned later, she had been arrested. Mr Wild arrested her. Roughly treated, she gave away the name of the place where Jack was likely to be found. Mr Wild's heavies went there, and the pistol that Jack drew on George misfired, and they took him off to Newgate and he came to trial.

Most of the folks that knew him were in the crowd at his trial. Jack Sheppard, of the parish of St Martin in the Fields. We saw Mr Kneebone, oh so holy. "I brought him up as my own. I was good to him. How could he return my generosity with deceit? How could he be so ungrateful?"

"It's true," says Jack. "I was ungrateful. I was drawn into it by ill company."

His brother Tom, who is sentenced to transportation.

And there is Mr Jonathan Wild, all sober and righteous, saying Mr Kneebone asked for his help to bring the accused to justice. But look who this is, speaking now, as the Evidence! It is one Will Field, who has been persuaded to impeach poor Jack, repenting of his own part in the crimes.

" 'e 'ad no part in them!" says Jack. " 'e lies! 'e w-wasn't w-wiv us!"

But Will Field swears he was, and it is his evidence that will convict the prisoner. Yes, he says, he went with Jack and Blueskin Blake and helped them break into the house. "We said it was impossible to break in, but Sheppard said that he could do it." Whoever peaches his accomplices gets off, and Will Field takes no risks here; besides, he is protected by Mr Wild. Jack is found guilty. He makes a plea for clemency.

"Can I 'ave transportation? Anywhere, as f-far away as you p-please, to the most extreme f-foot of 'is Majesty's dominions! I am young and ignorant. I didn't know what I was doin'."

The jury thinks he did. He is taken to the condemned hold to await the death warrant. The keeper says to him: "Make good use of your time." He means in prayer. "Thankyou, I will," says Jack.

So Bess and Poll and I got talking and we made some plans; and I went up from the Old Bailey to eat at Mother Clap's, and everyone was talking about the trial and how he ought to have had transportation, being young and not too clever.

"And he's only thin and little," Ma said. "It don't seem fair at all. I'd go in there and save him myself if I knew how!" Then eyeing me, she added: "And if anybody else knew how to save him they could bring him here and welcome, particularly if they came round the back way and did not draw attention to themselves."

"What they need," I said thoughtfully, "is a coach."

"You're not to steal anything, Davy, and get into trouble."

"No, Ma, I can hire it, all legal and proper. But I don't want a coachy who'll blab; I need a friend. George says he's never handled coach horses, so I'm going to have a try myself."

"My arse in a bandbox, you'll do no such thing! You'll ask Harry Radley. He has any number of coaches at his disposal, and unlike yourself he knows how to drive 'em."

"Oh no, I could not," I said at once. "Not go cap in hand to him. And I hardly know him, so why should he — ? Wounds, Ma, it is likely to be dangerous."

"Harry will take no persuading to live dangerously," Ma Clap promised me.

Harry Radley's coaching business was housed behind the Falcon, Fleet Street. He had two coaches, each with glazed windows, and six horses — three leaders, three wheelers. He was doing pretty well, always in work. He was mostly hired in the streets of London, but would do the country runs if necessary, charging more for them. I had no trouble finding him.

He was sitting on a mounting block in the stable yard, polishing a bridle. He was bare chested, his muscles lightly glistening with sweat, his black hair curling across his forehead as he leant forward. He looked up at me and wiped his brow. Blue eyes...

"Harry... I got to ask you a favour..."

I crouched down beside him. In a low voice I told him of my plans. I never heard such a stupid scheme, thought I, as the words came from my mouth. If I was him I'd clout me one and tell me to be off. I thought I'd have to beg and plead and work my balls off to convince him that we had a chance.

But no, it seemed, Harry Radley could not wait to put himself in danger on behalf of chaps he did not know, who came to him with a ridiculous notion that could get them all into the Whit.

"Of course, this all depends in the end on Jack," I finished lamely.

"And this Jack," said Harry. "What is he to you?"

I could not easily answer. I hesitated. "He is my oldest friend."

Harry nodded. "I see. And I meet you at the top of Old Bailey."

"Ah, Harry!" I marvelled. "Why? Why are you helping us? You never even met him."

Harry paused in his polishing. "Well, first because I will not willingly see any man hanged for housebreaking."

"And second?"

"Because you ask me."

It was thus that I found myself waiting beside a hired coach in the dusk of late August, gnawing my lip, and noticing that waiting in the London streets made me more apprehensive than ever I was in a hawthorn copse with Gry, and the rumble of a coach upon the road. Harry sat up top, holding the reins, speaking quietly to the horses, who were restive, surely sensing our own tenseness.

We were within spitting distance of Newgate. We could see its great black wall. When the two women approached, the smaller one walking stiffly and helped by the other, my heart went to my throat. The crazy plan had worked. I ran forward and helped Bess bundle Jack inside the coach. Harry urged the horses forward and we set off towards Ludgate.

"Wounds, what a sight you look, Jack!" I said, blunt in my relief. He was wearing some kind of nightgown and bonnet. From the folds of the nightgown his legs jutted stiffly, still complete with leg irons and chains.

"Give us the saw," he said.

"I haven't got a saw; you know I haven't. I thought you'd got one. Bess was supposed to take it in."

"I couldn't; they'd have found it," said Bess.

"You should've said; I'd have got one."

"We'll get one later. Just get clear of Newgate, will yer?" Jack said testily. "Who's the coachy?"

"A good pal of mine. Where d'you want to go?"

"Blackfriars, coachy!" Jack called with his head out of the window. Bess and I yanked him back inside, and we pushed on, down towards the river.

To Bess and Poll go all the credit for this astonishing escape. The condemned hold lies near the prison gate, where the turnkeys in the Lodge may keep an eye on those within. Here the guards lounge, drinking and dicing and swapping yarns, as 'Hangings I have known' and 'Women I have lain with'. Bess and Poll came in, well known now to the turnkeys, and made a great show of laughing noisily with Jack, through the partition. All this time he was making a gap to wriggle through, working away with a file. Bess thrust the nightgown and bonnet through the gap and Jack dressed up in them. A few yards further off they could hear the keepers recalling his wonderful escape from New Prison and reminding each other to keep an especial watch on him this time. Poll contrived to lose herself behind a post. Jack's fellow inmate shoved him through the gap, heels first, and he and Bess walked clear; Poll followed later. Did I not say that prison guards were stupid?

Jack's plan was to throw off the scent by taking to a boat and collecting some of his pickings from a lockup further up the river. There was only one waterman there at Blackfriars, a callow youth who viewed us with justifiable suspicion and most reluctantly accepted his fare of three passengers. Tense and edgy we waited at the river's edge for Poll; at last she arrived; her coach could not have been far behind our own. The three of them paid the waterman to take them upstream. Harry and I would wait at Blackfriars with the coach in case the river plan failed.

Poled by the most apprehensive waterman, who plainly suspected trouble, the boat set off into the darkness. Leaving the reins slack, Harry climbed down and we stood and watched it disappear from view.

I was full of misgivings. I turned to Harry. I said: "Whatever will become of him?"

The horses, jumpy as ourselves, tossed their heads, stamped and snorted. Harry suddenly reached for me and pulled me to him and kissed me hard. He shook me from him in a kind of exasperation, and climbed back into place, regaining control of the reins, soothing the horses with his voice.

Within a moment came the sound of muffled arguing and cursing and the vigorous splashing of the pole, and back towards us came the boat.

The wretched waterman had glimpsed the fetters on Jack's legs and would take no further part in it; his fear was like to have been their undoing, and they came back looking for the coach. The hapless waterman poled off at speed. Jack, in a foul temper for the time that had been wasted, threw himself into the coach.

"All the places I know will be full of Jonathan's heavies. Come on, Davy, you must know somewhere."

"Mother Clap's, Harry? She said she'd take him in."

"Who's Mother Clap?" said Jack.

"A dear good-hearted woman who will see you right."

"Excellent. To Mother Clap's then."

"But only Jack," I added.

"That's all right by us," said Bess. "I've had enough of muddlin' around. I could do with some sleep."

"I'll be in touch," Jack said; and once again the coach trundled forward, he and I together on the worn leather seat, Harry at the reins.

Jack and I entered Mother Clap's house through the yard beside the necessary house. A lanthorn above the door guided our steps, which in Jack's case were unsteady. It was Ma Clap herself that welcomed us and brought us in.

Suddenly the enormity of what we had done came over me.

"Ma! This is Jack, who has escaped from Newgate gaol!"

Proud and dewy as someone bringing home his bride I ushered Jack indoors. I fussed about him, gentle and protective. His flapping skirts were streaked with blood from where the fetters cut into his shins. We went into the kitchen where the fire embers glowed and the smell of cooking was delicious. Ma sent Billy Griffin her lodger to get hold of a saw, and she sat Jack down and said not a word about his odd attire; after all, such things were common hereabouts. Jack's good spirits instantly returned.

"This is real good of yer, ma'am; you're an angel."

"So I've been told," laughed Mother Clap. "But more often when I was younger, and in the privacy of the bedchamber."

Bill Griffin brought the saw and between us we sawed off the chains, and Ma Clap bathed Jack's bloody shins, and we ate a good beef soup with bread and buttered ale spiced up with cinnamon, while Jack recounted to her how he had escaped.

"I'm a new man now, thanks to you all," Jack said, stretching.

"Shall you stay the night?" said Mother Clap. "You're welcome."

"Thank you, ma'am, but I'm away to Spitalfields."

I frowned a query.

"To Bess," said Jack reasonably.

"But — " It was all I could do to hide my dismay. In my mind Bess had been so neatly written off. I thought I had him to myself.

"But Jonathan's men?" I protested.

"Bugger 'em." Jack stood up. "Truth to tell, I'd like a chance to stretch my legs. Sooner that, eh, than my neck!"

"I'll stay here, Ma," I said. "If that's all right."

She gave me an expansive hug. "You know it is."

As if the day had been an uneventful one Jack thanked us all and strolled off whistling into the night.

"Oh, Davy," said Ma Clap and put her arms about me. "Your face fell a mile."

"I know," I said glumly. "Ain't it stupid?"

"Listen, Davy dear, he ain't the one for you," said Mother Clap all sympathy. "He's sweet — but for a start all the world knows where he'd sooner take his pleasures. What about young Lucinda?

You look so good together. No?" She added vaguely: "Why didn't Harry come in with you and Jack?"

"He had to take his horses back and see to 'em."

"Of course."

"I can't get Jack out of my mind, Ma, and I know he'll go and do some foolery, he's that cocksure."

"Then let's not look for trouble, eh? You look tired out, dear. I shall bring a brandy posset to your bedside and I'll tuck you in and make believe you are my own young lad and not the terror of the road I've heard you are."

I laughed, but she insisted; and when I settled to sleep it occurred to me that no one had done as much for me before and I rather liked it.

With the imprint of her maternal kiss upon my brow I settled further into the feathers. But as I drifted off to sleep my thoughts were all of Jack. The jealousy I had felt on learning he would spend the night with Bess still stung and rankled. It was ridiculous how utterly I had counted upon his staying at Ma Clap's with me. I longed for us to be together and share a night alone, and sleep as we had done as boys, but with men's knowledge.

"It would be best," said George Page, "if you quit London, Master Sheppard. You are become as famous as His Majesty, though a damned sight better looking. And you are the talk of London. Everyone is looking out for you."

"Yeah," Jack agreed, not without pride. "I am become worth my weight in guineas."

He had come again by night to my lodgings and the three of us sat in the parlour with the shutters closed, and, elbows on the table, worked out what should be done.

"My sister Hannah lives in the country," George said. "She'd put you up. I'll write a letter. Stay there till the talk is of some other wonder. They farm some land. Northamptonshire."

"We could try it," Jack said doubtfully. "Will you come with me, Davy?"

"Of course I will."

"If I was to lend you a couple of butchers' smocks," said George, "you could pass for apprentices going for work in the country. After all, who knows your face outside London?"

You would have laughed to see us in our blue smocks setting off bearing west and trying to look nonchalant. We hired a horse for Jack and I rode Gry, and we rode at speed past Tyburn.

"Better to begin our journey here than end it!" Jack observed.

We took off towards the green fields and clear air of the countryside.

The place that we were aiming for was called Chipping Warden, but we never reached it. We got up to St Albans and we found Markyate and we passed the ancient church at Dunstable, but we blundered about on the edge of Whittlewood Forest, and Jack said that there was no point in what we were about.

"I hate the country," Jack said. "It's too green an' yeller. An' ain't it quiet, though? No street music, no yellin' an' shoutin'; all the women ugly, an' nothin' ter see but fields an' trees. Pretty scary. An' no one's heard of me! I could be anybody! Let's go back to London, eh?"

It had been with a light heart that I'd set out, Jack by my side and the open road ahead of us. I thought it was to be the fulfilment of a dream; but it was not to be. We rode pretty hard that first day, and slept in a barn, but Jack was so saddle sore I spent the first night rubbing his aching limbs. I was pretty sore myself, being sadly out of practice, but I had forgotten that as a rider Jack had no particiular talent. Not that I would deny the pleasure in the rubbing of his limbs and his pert round arse all softly furred with golden fuzz. Tomorrow night, I told myself... But our second night was very much spoiled by the barn where we slept being too near a farmhouse, and a barking hound chained in the yard having scented us; we left before daylight. The third night we risked recognition and slept at an inn, but because the inn was full an old chap was obliged to share the bed with us. When I prepared to make a fight of it, he said: "But why? The bed is big enough for three. Indeed, so many are arrived downstairs that we shall be fortunate to remain three!"

The following evening we arrived in London; and no sooner had we paused to take a drink than a man cried:"That's Jack Sheppard! I swear it — that's Jack Sheppard!"

Begins now a crazy game of cat and mouse. Further into London went we, still in our butchers' blue, sometimes with our horses, sometimes leaving them at an inn yard.

In Cooley's brandy shop in Bishopsgate a chap came in, turned about in meaningful fashion, plainly recognizing Jack; we fled.

"But we must eat," said Jack pained. So to the Cock and Pye in Drury Lane for Jack to dine on oysters and brandy, while I kept watch at the door. While he was there Jack had a haircut and a shave; then Jack took off while I was so served. The barber whispered to me: "Everyone has heard that Jack is back. The whole town is in terror!"

"Why?" I asked baffled.

"We heard he means to take a terrible revenge," the barber confided, pausing with his knife. "We heard that anyone who harmed him in the past or who spoke against him at his trial and anyone with property worth taking must quake in their beds this night. Mr Kneebone in particular is half dead with fear. He dreads Jack's terrible revenge."

"And so he should," said I. "You have heard right; it will be a terrible revenge."

Wounds, but it was good to eat a decent meal. I stuffed my face and took plenty of brandy with my meal. A great content came over me, a strength and merriment. Yes, it was good to be back in London.

In the doorway Jack beckoned me. I hurried away. We set off in the darkness towards Crane Court, where Jack's ma now lived, and Jack called in to cheer the hapless dame as best he might, while I kept watch outside. Further along Fleet Street we stopped before a well-lit window, where on black velvet lay displayed a glittering array of gold watches. Across the street the dainty spire of St Bride's church showed bone pale in the dark and smoky sky.

"Wounds! Gold watches! " Jack admired. Davy," then said he, "d'you want ter see me at work?"

"Yes! No!" I said, excited and appalled.

"Keep watch."

He fixed a nail piercer in the door post, and fastened the door shut by running a string through the knocker. No one could get out now.

"Pass me a stone! A big heavy one!"

"A stone? Damn me, I thought to see a grand master! You're going to break the window with a stone! The subtlety of it!"

Through the shattered window pane he stuck his hand and grabbed a fistful of the glittering gold within. We ran off.

"A constable!" I gasped.

We were pursued. We ran back towards Drury Lane. Past the Falcon, where Harry Radley lived and slumbered. We shook off our pursuer. As we ran pell mell up Wych Street I came slap up against a Newgate turnkey made suspicious by my breathlessness. He grabbed me by the arms and brought me up short. A coach came rumbling past.

"Now then, young man! Where d'you think you're going?"

"Sorry, sir! Her husband's after me!"

He laughed and let me go. Gasping I stood there till he had turned the corner and I looked around for Jack.

"Psst! Here!" He was on the other side of the street, grinning in a doorway.

"How'd you get there?"

"Rolled under the coach!"

"Jack, we got ter get out of this! Everyone knows yer!"

"All right. But not to the wilds of nowhere."

"Trust me," I said shining-eyed. "I know the best place for us. It's somewhere I know like the back of my hand, and so does Gry."

So we did what we should have done all along — retrieved our horses and took off up the Great North Road.

Chapter Forty

THE moon was up as we rode out of London. White amongst silver grey clouds it lit our way north. It was early September.

We were still riding as the dawn showed grey over trees and sward. The half light showed us the gibbet at Ring Cross. There was an occupant, creaking and swinging in his iron cage. I cast a glance at Jack. He grinned; and to whomsoever it was that hung there, our unknown brother, we blew a kiss and saluted him and we rode on.

As we came up Devil's Lane, which they say was named after Duval and has no business with the Devil, I thought briefly about the goal to which I thought my life was dedicated, the search for Duval's gold. What had happened to my resolution? Was I then to fail in that quest which had once seemed of such import? But what if Duval's gold was buried nearer London than Lord Staughton had believed? What if I were somehow to find it with Jack? What if this wild night ride was leading us towards it even now? I felt elated at the prospect.

We passed through the hilltop village of Highgate. Ahead of us lay Finchley Common, and our intention was to hide out in its wilderness. We slowed down to a gentle pace.

"There's a stone round here that Dick Whittington sat on," I remarked.

"Who?"

"Dick Whittington. Someone who quit London but came back. I often thought I must be like him. The number of times I've turned my back on London swearing never to return, but yet I do."

"I daresay 'e saw all them fields an' trees an' 'is 'eart sank just like mine does," Jack remarked.

"When I first came to London my pal the coachy said Finchley Common was the place where we'd see highwaymen."

"Did yer?"

"Yes; they were all dead."

"Dick Whittington," said Jack. "Not the one they say built Newgate?"

"That's the one."

"A pox on 'im," said Jack.

We had a good meal at the Three Tuns at the fork of the road, and the horses dined well. As we purposed to quit the road for the lesser travelled paths we crammed ourselves in anticipation — soup and bread, a pair of capons, a shoulder of mutton and some ham, all washed down with mulled ale, warm and sweet. We were well on the way to falling asleep, and so we took our leave, and as the day wore on were very much further into the safety of the common, where amongst its scrubby hedgerows, copses and furzey heaths, we proposed to lie low.

Some time in the afternoon we by great good fortune came across the remains of a cottage beside a little mere, a dwelling long since abandoned, dilapidated, but retaining enough of its former shape to provide us with a shelter. The thatch of its roof sagged, home to roosting birds, and brambles and nettles grew against its walls and twined their way through the window gaps.

We tethered the horses to the tree that hung down low over the tumbledown heap, and found within a fair amount of dry grass and straw, suggesting plainly that we were not the first to use this place as hideaway. We tumbled into it, and were discussing which of us should stay awake on watch as we fell asleep.

I awoke to darkness, stiff and chilled about the legs and back, but the front part of my body gloriously warm from the close proximity of Jack. I hugged him tighter to me, with a rustling of straw. A mouse ran along my thigh. Through a gap in the wall I could see the moon, a smudge of amber in the dark blue clouds. I could hear the wind in the branches of the tree that pressed upon the cottage roof. My lips were against Jack's hair. I kissed it.

We awoke to daylight, cramped, cold and stiff, and went outside. There was a slight mist which the sun was already dispersing, and the cobwebs gleamed amongst the brambles. We browsed the hedgerows, picking blackberries.

The sun's rays caught the surface of the mere in pinpoints of light, and we decided to bathe. We stripped, and broke the early morning silence by our yells and splashes — the water was pretty cold. Not deep though, about chest high at its deepest, and once the first shock over, we romped like boys and laughed like idiots, at nothing, until shivering and laughing still, we scrambled out on to the bank and ran about to shake ourselves dry.

The sun was warm now. We went back inside and dressed and lying side by side on the dried grass of our bed we dozed. We were very light of heart, and of head too, I suspect, being extremely hungry. We lay a while, talking a little, and the sunshaft inched its way across us and made us eager to go in search of food.

We saddled up and off we rode and reached by twisting paths a small inn on the outskirts of a village, where we and the horses put away a hearty meal. We lingered, much at our ease, drinking beer from leathern tankards which I swear had been old in the days of Queen Elizabeth, from their shape and taste.

At a table nearby sat a travelling puppeteer. He had the most miserable face that I had ever seen. He sat hunched and withdrawn, speaking to no one. From his fingers, on strings, hung two puppets with painted smiling faces, grimaces even. Every time his fingers twitched, these two puppets moved and shifted, in a curious stilted jig, grinning, gesturing; and the man above them gloomy as a wet day in November.

We quit that place when our drowsiness eased off. And then while daylight lasted we rode the horses hard for the enjoyment of it — Gry, I knew, was every whit as glad as I to gallop at speed across the heathland, his mane streaming in the wind, the dust of London shaken from his hooves, the weeks of inactivity forgotten. Jack's horse was not so happy, and one of the shoes came loose, and so we rejoined the road at a walk and made our way towards a smithy I remembered. I left Jack holding Gry, so that he would not be seen, and I dealt with the matter.

The forge was dark against the daylight, and I leaned against the door jamb, breathing in the pungent smells, watching the sparks upon the anvil as the smith hammered the shoe. What did they say — man is born to trouble, as the sparks fly upward? I wished I had not remembered those dismal lines, and was pleased to quit the smithy where they had occurred to me.

I rejoined Jack, and coming upon the outskirts of a village I found a small farmstead where I bought bread, cheese and beer. With these provisions we set off back to our cottage, for in all our wanderings we had not seen anywhere as useful to us for our night's lodging. The day had become cloudy, and a few light drops of rain flecked the wind.

We noticed a dark twist of smoke rising above a clump of trees, and then saw several gipsy horses grazing, sturdy long-maned beasts with a look of Gry; and beyond them a couple of covered wagons. There was a family about the one, with dark-haired children rooting in the hedge, and a man sitting in the doorway, making baskets, and a woman stirring the pot. Beside the other was an old man, sitting cross-legged on the ground on a mat of deerskin. He asked us in their tongue to sit down with them a while, so we dismounted and sat with them. They gave us a drink which they said was tea, but if it was, the leaves were hedgerow leaves and the brew dark green. The old man commented favourably on Gry. I asked him if he knew Nathan Grey. He laughed.

"Many of our people are called Nathan Grey."

I tried to describe him. He nodded and smiled, showing a patent wish to give me the information that I wanted.

"Ah," he grinned, gesturing expansively. "On the road."

He plainly had no idea where Nathan was; but somewhere between here and Scotland on the Great North Road, I guessed, Nathan was still travelling, still tuning his fiddle in the more disreputable inns, still sleeping under the stars.

I experienced a sharp pang of loss. For Nathan Grey or for the road? For my search for gold?

Jack fidgetted beside me. We thanked the gipsies and left them. When they said their goodbyes to us, they added to each of us: "*Warda tu coccorus* — take care of yourself."

"Maybe we should go north," I said to Jack as we rode away.

"I ain't goin' north. I'm goin' back to London as soon as ever I can."

"You've seen what it's like in London. Everybody recognizes you."

"Yeah," he grinned. "I'm famous, see."

"You'll be famous and dead if we go back."

"A short life and a merry, eh?"

"If you say so."

"It'd be more fun than drinkin' gnats' piss wiv gipsies."

"You should have thought about that before you flashed yourself about and got seen."

"I ain't goin' ter live like a frightened rabbit. What's the point of bein' famous if no one sees yer?"

It was dusk as we drew near the cottage.

Some short way off there lay a grassy meadow; here we tethered the horses, underneath some trees, and left them grazing.

Inside the tumbledown cottage we sat in the straw and made swift work of bread and cheese and beer. Jack said: "What d'you say we go an' find us some girls?"

I spluttered. "Are you mad? Tavern drabs are famous for betraying a cull to the turnkeys."

"You could keep watch for me. Then I'd do the same for you."

"Me? I don't want girls. What do I want with girls?"

"Don't be stupid; every chap does. What about Lucinda?"

"Eh?"

"Lucinda — the one you said was trouble for yer, an' you wouldn't go wiv Poll on account o' her."

"I thought you knew by now. Lucinda's a fellow. His name is Ralph."

"I didn't know, no, why should I? I fort she was a girl. You're very much the sort girls like — good lookin', tough. I fort you'd 'ave 'ad your pick of 'em."

"I never got the hang of it. I always thought a man was better. All my loves have been men, and I been lucky — all of 'em were pretty good."

After a while Jack said: "You've gone quiet. Are you thinkin' about 'em an' the good times you had?"

"No, I'm feeling bad about Lucinda. Oh, George Page'll tell him where I am, but he'll be pretty sore with me for riding off and not saying where I was going. And for being with you, I daresay."

"Me? What's that got to do wiv it?"

"He knows I care about you, always have done. He gets jealous."

"Yeah, Bess is the same. She'd claw the eyes out of Nan Cook and Moll Frisky if she knew all I got up to. I wish she was here now."

"I wouldn't mind seein' Ralph either. Just to explain."

We settled into the straw and put our arms about each other. A warm affection bound us. I thought that we had all the time in the world; and that same world seemed no bad place as I lay there with him with the rustling of the thatch and the creak and soughing of the leaning tree that crooked the little haven in its firm embrace.

"Tomorrow," I murmured, looking down at him and the moonlight on his golden hair, "we'll go up the Great North Road and I'll show you how to look for gold."

It was Gry's whinneying that awoke me. An odd sound, tinged

with alarm. Warning. I was on my feet like a shot, pulling my tangled clothes about me. Jack protested irritably as I trod on him. I looked through the window gap. It was day.

"Hell and damnation!"

"What?"

"They're here. They've found us."

Jack was behind me at the window. We could see a line of men moving across the heath, with pistols and muskets. Beyond them, other men on horses, and two small coaches coming slowly down the track.

Through my mind raced images of the people we had encountered — the innkeepers, the drinkers at the inn, the lugubrious puppeteer, the old woman selling bread and cheese, the smith, the gipsies — no, I did not think so — the nameless observers who had watched us quit London and set the turnkeys on the right road — our trail had been as clear, no doubt, as if we had strewn guineas.

"They're between us and the horses, dammit," I whispered through my teeth. "We're sitting ducks if we stay here. Best split up and each of us circle the field keeping close to the hedge and try and reach the horses. Take off up the Great North Road and meet at Newark. I'll see you there — good luck!"

"Good luck, Davy," Jack said. We hugged each other tightly. Then we crept out of the cottage, doubled over, and sneaked away in separate directions.

I plunged down a path bordered by two hedges and very much overgrown, with plenty of cover. Dozens of butterflies rose up around me like floating petals.

I must have gone all of a hundred yards when I walked straight into two of the turnkeys; they seemed to loom up out of the hedge, more approaching from behind, noisily now, wading through the undergrowth; I was surrounded.

"William Page! We arrest you in the King's name!" they all said at once, and with different pitch and speed, like a faulty choir, all eager to be the one that said it.

I was surprised to be arrested under that alias; but that was the least of my anxieties. Whether it were William Page or Davy Gadd, the fellow in question was in a damned unpleasant situation.

One of them held a pistol to my head and one fixed manacles about my wrists, and thus I found myself a prisoner of the Newgate turnkeys, trapped in a bramble patch, surrounded by butterflies.

Chapter Forty-One

I WAS taken to one of the waiting coaches, prodded forward with a pistol between my shoulder blades. I was ordered into the coach, and here I sat, with two of the turnkeys, and a pistol at my chest. I hoped that Jack had been more fortunate.

It seemed that he had. I heard snatches of the conversation taking place outside the coach.

"Jack Sheppard has got clean away!"

"Damn him! He was the one Mr Wild was after."

"He won't have got far. We'll have a hanging yet."

"Get this coach going. We'll get William Page to London and safely into Newgate — and then," he added poking his head inside the door, "it'll be transportation for you, boy. How d'you fancy a ride across the seas?"

"Did you get the horses?" one asked.

"We got the old nag. The gipsy horse took off. Wouldn't let anyone touch him."

The coach lurched forward and we trundled clumsily along the heath track to pick up the road. I looked hopefully around for some benighted highwayman desperate enough to attack a coach of turnkeys. There was none, and we continued our way southward at a reasonable speed.

Somewhere near Islington we stopped. We drew off the road. I could see the Red Lion further off, a wayside tavern; the turnkeys had paused here for refreshment. But there was something more going on, and several other riders were assembled there. I could see them milling about, hear the shouts, the jingling of bridles. A fast horse slithered to a standstill, stones flying up from the track.

"We have him! We got Jack Sheppard!"

I leaned forward in dismay, straining to hear.

"He first hid in a copse — we lost him there — but he was hiding in the stable of a farmhouse. We searched the straw — we saw his boots! He had the stuff on him from his last robbery, the watches from Martin's shop — he'd shoved them under his arms. We reckoned the occasion deserved a drink. He told us where there was a decent inn, and there we went, and had a fine and merry time. He's a good chap, ain't he? I was sorry that we had to bring him in."

"Not as sorry as he's going to be." I recognized the voice. It was Mr Jonathan Wild's and it was treacle-sweet with satisfaction.

Next thing I knew he was at the open coach door, looking in.

287

His piercing eyes surveyed me. I scowled back at him.

"Out!" he said to the remaining turnkey who sat opposite me.

"But sir — ?"

"Out. Give me the pistol. I'll look after William Page. Do you think I'm afraid of a butcher's lad?"

Jonathan Wild heaved himself into the coach and with a pistol in one hand and his silver cane in the other he regarded me intently. His perusal of me, handcuffed and dishevelled as I was, plainly gave him some enjoyment.

"Well," remarked he in a soft voice. "Mr Davy Gadd, you are come to a pretty pass."

I sat silent, vexed and sullen. There is very little pleasure to be found in being gloated over.

"Jack Sheppard is taken," said he.

I waited.

"I have come up from London to meet with my brave boys," he continued. "This is precisely the good news that I hoped to hear. Jack Sheppard caught at last. And...William Page." He smiled. He lifted his silver cane and poked me in the chest, with a kind of intimacy which I found repellent. "William Page," he said and chuckled. "Jack Sheppard's companion was believed to be William Page, a butcher's son. Now is that lucky for us, or is it not?"

"Mr Wild," I said irritably, "it seems to me to be neither here nor there, and of no relevance to yourself."

"There you are wrong," he said. "Everything to do with frolics upon the high road is of relevance to me. The stirring of every little blade of grass concerns me. How much more so then the capture of a wanted man and his accomplice! And my interest is lucky for you, Davy, in particular, because it could be the means of saving your life. And the life of your slippery friend."

"How?" I asked despairingly.

"William Page," said Mr Wild in that same low voice, and continuing to jab me in the belly with his silver staff in the pauses between his words, "is a condemned man. He has assisted a known criminal to escape the course of justice. He has assisted at a robbery. There is no way that William Page will escape transportation. But," he said, with a horrid prod that made me gasp, "Davy Gadd was elsewhere. I can vouch for that."

"Mr Wild, what do you mean?"

"Davy Gadd is one of my chaps. He was working for me. He was wherever I say he was. Listen here, Davy. I've always had my eye on you. I want you. You are wasted as a stable boy, a tapster —

even as an accomplice to Jack Sheppard. You should be out on the road. But working for me. If you agree, I'll undertake to get you out of this, and Sheppard also."

"You'd save Jack?" I said in disbelief.

"Of course I would," he assured me, with a further prod. "What use is Sheppard to me dead? I know he wants to be in London. He can take up with Burnside and Blake and start his own gang. The three of them would be unstoppable."

"But how can you achieve it?" said I in great gloom of spirit. "Both Jack and I are prisoners and the inn is full of Newgate turn-keys. And Newgate is where we shall sleep tonight."

"Bless you!" he laughed indulgently, as if I were a halfwit, endearing but stupid. "Have you learnt nothing about me? It is in my power to hang every thief in the metropolis. It is also in my power to save whomsoever I choose. If the evidence is not all it might be I will buy more. If new perjured evidence is insufficient I will buy judge and jury too. No man who works obediently for Jonathan need fear a ride to Tyburn."

"And you would save me and Jack? That's pretty decent of you, Mr Wild."

"I would! I swear upon my honour."

I winced. Was that a binding oath?

"Would you swear upon your own neck, sir, instead?"

"I swear it. That's a damn suspicious nature you have, Davy."

"I own it. But only a magician could get me and Jack clear of the mess we're in."

"Did they not tell you that I am such a magician? The Devil sits upon my shoulder. And now!" he said. "What about you, Davy? Will you agree to ply your trade for me, in return for your release and Jack's?"

"I will," I answered readily. "I'll work for you, Mr Wild."

I must admit that I did not think too deeply about what I was binding myself to. With the jaws of Newgate gaping before me the prospect of a closer involvement with Mr Wild suddenly appeared a curiously agreeable alternative.

Jonathan brought me at pistol point out of the coach. His habitual bodyguard were grouped about the inn door. I noticed Quilt Arnold; and Will Field was there also, his whole face a smirk. I was taken round the back of the inn and down into the cellar. There was a little room leading off the cellar, pitch dark and cold, with an earthen floor; and I was bundled inside and the door locked.

I was there for hours. During this captivity a thief in Mr Wild's employ was fetched and manacled and brought to London in the coach. He had no say in whether the game was to his liking. If he had refused, Mr Wild had evidence enough to send him to the gallows; he did not refuse. This cull — William Page, as everybody verified — was incarcerated in the Whit, was tried, and three months later was transported. Once you got to America you could be your own man. This unknown who would in England have gone to the gallows was now free to make a new life for himself. A sense of guilt obliges me to picture a good future for him. But now he fades from the story. William Page was nothing. It was Jack Sheppard they were after.

It was night when the door of my place of containment was unlocked. Will Field stood there with a lanthorn.

"Come on out," he said. "You're free."

"So get these cuffs off me."

"A moment."

"Why? What?"

"I have to be sure you know the way of it."

"Go on then."

"Mr Wild says you are to rob a coach this night in earnest of your good intent."

"My horse ran off. Am I to go on foot? You must be crazy."

"They've found you another horse."

"I can't work with any old nag."

"You don't have a choice."

"What if I rode off on it? You'd never catch me once I was on the road."

"No. But Jack Sheppard's on 'is way to Newgate, ain't he?"

"The deal was for us both," I frowned.

"And so it is. But Sheppard will be set free later. Mr Wild wants the praise and glory for bringin' 'im in. He'll be set free when Mr Wild is ready. Or not, if you turn difficult. I'd say you was over a barrel, Davy, except I know that's how you like to be." He sniggered. "So how about that coach?"

"And how am I to frighten the coachy?" I said scathingly. "Reasoned persuasion?"

Will Field tapped the pistol at his belt. "This is yours when you agree. And by the by, I am to go with yer, and see you do it."

"So you may peach me later, if the need arises," I said grimly. "That's how Mr Wild works, ain't it?"

"That's about it," said Will complacently. "You might as well accept you'll be in it now as deep as any of us, with all the risks and all the perks. Mr Wild won't have you peached if you behave; there's too many good years' work in you. So, do I unlock the cuffs and we get on with it?"

I held out my wrists. And thus it was, on a competent bay, with a borrowed pistol and a kerchief around my face, and Will Field lurking in the hedgerow, I held up a coach from Barnet and got twenty guineas from a fat-faced spluttering farmer, and two pocket books and a gold watch from his lean companion, and took off unscathed back towards the common. I shook off Will Field easily enough and I rode in darkness at a gentle pace, looking for Gry. I did not think he would have strayed far from where we parted, once the commotion had died down. I tried all the whistles that I knew, which mightily unsettled the horse I rode. As dawn came grey I found the gipsy encampment where Jack and I had drunk nettle tea, and even before I had drawn closer the old man came forth leading Gry.

With a whicker of pleasure Gry greeted me and I dismounted. Gry's muzzle pressed into my hand and I caressed his ears.

"We knew you would be back for him. We saw that he was one of ours. We kept him for you."

Now there might be those who would have thought the little group had other plans for Gry, to do with docking tails and dyeing hair and Bartholomew Fair; but I believed him and I thanked him heartily and gave him a guinea for his trouble. I took bread and soup with them, and the woman offered to tell my fortune.

"I'd sooner not know it," I replied. "But wish me well, if you would be so kind, and spare a thought for all those who have not their liberty."

When I arrived in London in the late afternoon I stabled Gry and the bay at the White Hart. I found that Jack's recapture was the talk of the town. Already ballad singers had composed fresh verses to the story of his previous escapes. I shuddered at the relish with which the details of his predicament were passed around. "Chained to the floor... padlocked... iron collars about his ankles... he'll not get out of there until he lies in Mother Tyburn's arms."

But I knew better, as I thought; for Mr Wild would have a plan and see to his release. He was just biding his time, waiting for the right moment. With this hope sustaining me I left Gry and walked to Aunty Mary's seeking Lucinda.

Not unnaturally, he was pretty sore at me; but his anger was of that kind that has been caused by great anxiety, and when he'd heard a swift account of my adventures he hardly knew whether to rage at me or comfort me.

"You see, I have been in considerable danger," I concluded, "and would have landed in the Whit but for Mr Wild's kindness. I can still feel the manacles upon me; the width of each one is pretty small and tight and damned uncomfortable and digs into your wrist."

"It was your own fault," railed Lucinda. "You could have stayed safe at the White Hart tending horses. You were lucky this time."

"I'm always lucky," I assured him. "And I'll be lucky again, you see if I'm not."

"Where do you mean to stay this time?"

"I best not go to George's. I must lose any connection with William Page for good."

"Sleep here," he urged me. "With me."

"You mean you'd have me back?"

"Lord knows why," he said darkly. "I suppose you didn't keep your hands off Jack?"

I did not answer, for the sudden recollection of Jack sleeping in my arms gave me such an ache about the heart that no words came. But Ralph was awaiting my reply.

"My heart was with you all the time I was away," I volunteered.

"Liar," he said predictably.

"*Almost* all the time."

No doubt of it, but there was a world of comfort to be found at Aunty Mary's. Everything was pretty — brocaded curtains, ornamented ceilings, fireplaces with mantle shelves held up by pillars, and mirrors above 'em, and much of veneered walnut and chairs with scallop-shell legs; and couch beds deep with cushions; and two jakes, one a two-seater, both always clean; and everywhere sponged over daily with camphor and wine against bugs and fleas. I couldn't help but notice these things, remembering the bed of hay and crumpled smocks that I had lain upon with Jack.

Ralph oversaw for me a warm bath in the kitchen tub, with coriander, a great restorative against the discomforts of the road.

Lucky, I thought, yes, that's what I was. I stood at the bedroom window for a moment, looking out onto the great shadowy gloom of London town. Distantly I heard the watchman calling "Twelve of the clock and all's well"; and St Giles' bells tolled agreement in the still air.

"What is it, Davy?" Ralph said from the bed.

"I can't bear to think of him, Ralph, with the cockroaches and chains."

"You said that Mr Wild has promised to arrange for his release."

"Yes, but when? How?"

"I would suppose that with his connections at the Old Bailey he'll work the trial so that Jack gets transportation. Or maybe pay the turnkeys to turn a blind eye."

"But till then?" I shuddered. "You've been past the Whit, same as I have. The frigging stench of it alone knocks you sideways."

"But Newgate does at least have a way out," said Ralph, "and Jack's got out of it before. I shouldn't worry overmuch."

Ralph, who did not like Jack, might possibly be forgiven for his dismissive remark. He continued: "It's you I fret for. You've bonded yourself to Mr Wild in return for a dubious promise. You did robbery, with Will Field as an accomplice. I gather that Will Field will turn evidence to anybody's bidding. It seems to me that Mr Wild has got you as securely as if you were in Newgate irons. Have you thought, Davy? However will you break free from his clutches?"

"Oh, I'll find a way," I shrugged. But I must confess I was uneasy.

St Giles' bell was quiet now, and in the silence that followed I seemed to hear a ghostly echo — the sound of St Sepulchre's deep toned bell, resonant, hollow, menacing, the bell that tolled the way to Tyburn.

Chapter Forty-Two

I TOOK a deal of care about my appearance when I presented myself at Mr Jonathan Wild's breakfast levée. Ralph helped me dress. Doeskin breeches, my white shirt and fine sewn waistcoat and lace cravat, tall well-polished boots, my beautiful well-cut coat with its embroidered buttons and side pleats, my elegant hat, and my silver pistols in my belt. How sure of myself had I been when I had refused his first invitation! If I was now to knuckle under I would go with a swagger.

Mr Wild's house in Old Bailey was a rich smart place betokening social success. It rose up from the cobbles, four storeys high, with neatly spaced windows and some kind of ornamental balustrade at the top.

You would have thought I was some long-lost dear relation, the way Mr Wild fell on me when I entered. The room was full of folk, and the impression convivial. Mr Wild, much at his ease, was wearing a dressing gown and slippers, and upon his shaven crown a red silk turban. My eyes strayed to that turban, low over the broad forehead and the bright darting eyes, and I wondered about the silver plates that joined together the gashes in the broken skull beneath.

"Mr Davy Gadd!" cried Jonathan. "How happy I am to see you here... at last. You're very welcome. How very handsome you are looking! Every inch the gentleman... of the road. Just what I would expect. May I offer you chocolate or sherry? Come and join the chaps."

The chaps! I knew some of 'em already. I'd seen Ned Burnworth and Kit Leonard at the Black Lion. Ned was the leader of a gang of a dozen roughs. He was lean and ugly with jagged teeth and always grinning; Kit was twice a murderer. There was Hell-and-Fury Sykes, Will Field of course, several foppish youths with painted faces, a couple of bookish fellows, maybe lawyers, and some raggedy street lads. Leaning against the door was Abraham Mendez, the little Portuguese Jew; and near at hand was Quilt Arnold, Mr Wild's favourite heavy. And this ill-assorted company were drinking chocolate out of pretty cups, and laughing, and watching one another, making deals and swapping information.

I half expected to see Blueskin Blake and looked around for his violet-skinned visage — which showed how out of touch I had become with the hierarchy of crime, for Will Field told me Blueskin was no longer under Mr Wild's protection.

"Ever since he took up with your pal Sheppard."

"But Jack had no time for him; they were not together long."

"It's no use. Mr Wild will nail 'im, just as 'e nailed Sheppard. They'll hang on the same day — you see if they don't."

"And what do you know about it? Friggin' nothin'."

"I know more'n you think. And where did you take off to after we had that coach? You'd better have the moveables on you, comin' here so flash and fancy. Your goose is cooked if you've already fenced 'em."

"Davy, my good friend!" Mr Wild was beside me. He was attended by two fawning servants who adjusted his turban and neatened his collar and filled his glass. The sherry was, I might add, of a very good quality and served in Venetian glasses on a silver tray.

"Mr Wild?"

"You have something for me."

"A curious admiration. But perhaps that's not enough for you, sir?"

He gave a crooked smile. His manservant held out the silver tray to me, empty of glass. I dropped the bag of guineas on to it, and the two pocket books.

"Good," said Mr Wild. "Pocket books I like. They lead to so many other deals. They are so often full of secrets."

"Much like yourself, sir."

"Yes indeed," he chortled good-humouredly.

"Mr Wild," I said urgently, "there was another part of our bargain."

Two small-time thieves jostled against us, showing lace handkerchiefs. Mr Wild gave them his full attention.

"Mr Wild," said I, "when may I expect to hear good news?"

"Yes, yes, by all means let's be subtle," Mr Wild said easily. "But don't pester me, Davy. All in good time. You'll hear your good news soon enough. And let's have more pocket books, eh? Of no value to anyone but the owner — you know the sort of thing. A diary — a fellow's business accounts — an indiscreet letter — a wad of folded bank drafts... will you do that for me? By tomorrow? There'll be no good news until I am sure of your good intentions. Every night, Davy. I want to hear that you've been busy every night. And take Will Field with you, eh? I'm just suspicious by nature and that's the way I am, and till I know your heart is in your work I like to know you did as you were told, eh? You did so well the other night, with a second-rate weapon. With two silver-butted jewels like those you should bring in a fortune, eh, a fortune!" Then he nudged me in the ribs. "Making any little visits to Moorfields these days?" he said, and cackling like a toothless old dame he turned and gave his attention elsewhere, leaving me scowling.

Most reluctantly I arranged to meet Will Field that evening. And though some folks could make a tale out of the exploits I undertook in his company, they are not deeds I am proud of and I recall them only with vexation. I was at my trade against my liking, with one I loathed and who loathed me. We were halfway through September then, and the darkening came early which made it easier for us. Seven nights we were abroad, waiting for coaches. I made sure that we never worked the same place twice, nor took a foolish risk, nor made any kind of name for ourselves, and all the while my heart was in my mouth for dread that Will Field might in some way let me down — which was to prove no idle suspicion. And we took pocket books enough to satisfy the voracious appetite of our employer, and a handsome array of jewellery. If he should decide it, he could have had me topped a dozen times over, for the work I did for him that week. It was uncomfortable knowledge.

I handed my pickings to Will Field, and how he disposed of them I cared not, but it was done in such a way that Mr Wild could say in all honesty that he had never touched the stolen goods, and that therefore he would never come under the Receiving Act, which dealt with felony.

Every morning when I presented myself at his house I said: "And now your part of the bargain, Mr Wild?" and every morning he said he was not yet satisfied; I must be patient; we must wait till the time was right. And I drank sherry with culls who thought nothing of putting a bullet into the chaps they robbed; and I would have despised myself utterly, except that I was doing it for Jack.

One morning I watched the painted fops being groomed for the work for which Mr Wild intended them. They were to be footmen in grand houses and must learn to be polite and dainty. Once in employment they were to rob the houses. There was a man playing the flute, and they must learn to dance to it; and there sat Mr Wild beaming approvingly, and slurping his chocolate from a silver spoon, the which he waved in time to the music.

All the talk was of Blueskin Blake.

"Twenty guineas to any one of you," said Mr Wild, "that brings him to justice, or to me."

One day Mr Wild took me aside and told me to accompany him to the upper floor of the house. Up the stairs we went and paused at a locked door, which he opened by the use of several keys. We entered an enclosed chamber with a sealed window. It smelt musty and unpleasant. Like a miser with his gold, Mr Wild showed me his treasures. He had them arranged on tables and stools and labelled in a Gothic hand — some scribe must have done this for him.

He went proudly from object to object, patting them, caressing them, explaining to me what they were — James Goodman's pistol — the bullet taken out of Timothy Dun's jaw when he was shot by Badger Riddlesdon — a piece of bloodstained cloth torn from Ben Child's shirt — a yard of the rope that hanged Sam Linn — a bird's nest taken from a corpse that hung too long on Shooter's Hill — a number of knives, some rusty with blood — some letters written from Newgate — a ring that someone swallowed in order to keep it, which passed out of their body in the natural course of events — a decomposing finger...

"This is a history of our time," said Jonathan, nodding, awed.

When we returned into the bedroom, from which his court was dispersing for the business of the day, he called forth one man from among them, a big tall man with a beard and a strong rough hand grasp.

"Here's a cull I want you to meet and shake his hand," said Jonathan in great good humour. "That's it, Davy, shake hands. A great pal of mine, a dear friend. D'you know who he is, Davy? It's a chap I hope you'll not have more close acquaintance with! It's Richard Arnett the hangman! The very chap who topped Sam Linn five years ago on the day I wed my sweet wife Mary. What a joyous day that was, eh? How we danced!"

I swear my hand burned for an hour afterwards.

I came away from Jonathan Wild's house angry and dismayed.

"Wounds, that man's unhinged," I told Ralph that night. "I cannot believe he passes amongst folk in civil fashion and is held in some regard. And yet he does. He says he is a just and honourable man, and they believe him.

I lay beside Ralph looking up into the darkness. A curious image came into my mind. I pictured Jonathan creeping by night to one of his safe houses; he had warehouses all over London — locks, as they were called. All alone, he entered, lit a candle, raised it, and then lit the wall brands, first one, then the next, until the whole place was alive with light and shadow. Revealed were great heaps of gold and silver, piles of guineas slithering like pebbles; rubies, opals, emeralds glittering and winking; and those plaguey pocket books edged with silver, strewn like fallen cards. Now I saw Mr Wild all crazed and cackling like a crone, running hither and yon amongst his treasure, tripping and kicking like a dancer at the fair, gyrating and putting his limbs out of joint and capering with his feet back to front, stooping and stretching and tossing the coins, rubbing his hands together in glee at how he had fooled the gullible — his trusting clients, the magistrates, the citizens, the thieves. And then he tossed his turban in the air and all the lights gleamed upon the silver plates that held his head together.

"He'll never free Jack," I said to Ralph. "I'll have to do it."

I said as much next day at Mother Clap's. As so often we would sit around her kitchen table, warmed at the hearth, the autumn winds a-blowing outside and the rain pittering at the window; wretched weather for the traveller on the heath. George Page was there, and Ralph and Gabriel.

"You're not to go into Newgate," Ralph said. "You'll be recognized as William Page."

"I won't; Mr Wild has taken care of all that."

"Mr Wild is not reliable." Ralph turned to Mother Clap. "Ma — tell him he's not to go into Newgate."

"Davy, I forbid it," Ma said. "If you are seen chatting to Jack Sheppard it might be too much for a turnkey if he recognizes you and he may think he'll get some glory by revealing who you are."

"I don't look like William Page now. He wore a butcher's smock; and I am pretty fancy. It's just a matter of slipping a file in and tucking it between the floorboards."

"Precisely," said Ralph. "So I'll go."

"You? Don't be stupid."

"You think I won't be able to go through with it?"

"I don't know, Ralph; it's pretty risky."

"We'll all go," said Mother Clap briskly. "Not you, Davy. But I'm quite ready to undertake the business."

"And so am I," said George.

"And I," said Gabriel. "It was never God's intention that a man should be caged like a beast." Gabriel of course was still pretty religious and carried his Bible about with him to read in quiet moments. It was a safeguard against too much fancying of Tommy Newton who teased him shamelessly at every opportunity; he pulled his breeches down in front of Gabriel once and waggled his bare bum to show him what he could not have.

I looked about me at their determined cheerful faces. "But why would you do this?" I marvelled. "Is it simple humankindness?"

"He's your friend, ain't he?"

It is a feature of this age that we love to gawp at marvels. Anyone could stroll into Newgate and be taken to see Jack. Visitors went in their droves. The turnkeys watched them to see if they were friends of Jack; these were searched. But the general populace, holding their handkerchiefs to their noses, filling an idle afternoon, might make their way up to his third-floor apartment and have a good look at the chains and padlocks and exchange merry banter with him.

Everyone who saw him commented upon what good spirits he was in, and how he jested and quipped with his jailors and the crowds. Some came away weeping; Mother Clap was one such; she was a tender-hearted female.

"When I think how he was here in this house," she told me, bustling about vigorously to disguise her distress. "So small and thin and sitting in that very chair. It's not right. It's just not right. What has he done? Stolen some watches and bits of cloth. Well!" she said proudly. "We left him one or two bits."

"I put a file in between the chimney bricks," said Ralph modestly. "But then I had to go out, as the stink of the place nearly made me vomit. I never smelt a stink like it. Gabriel gave him the Bible."

"There was a file in it," grinned Gabriel. "Amongst the Psalms."

Ma Clap laughed. "When I sat on the chair I tucked a chisel in between the rushes. It was all I could do not to let out a screech — there was already a small hammer, and so many nails tucked in there I feared for my posterior!"

"And is it true that he is keeping cheerful?"

"Oh yes! A man asked which was Sheppard, is this him? And Jack said: "Yes sir I am the shepherd and all the gaolers in this town are my flock, and I cannot stir into the country but they are all at my heels baaing after me!""

"He has every intention of escaping," Ralph said. "He makes no secret of it."

They caught Blueskin Blake. It was Mr Wild himself who got him, with Quilt Arnold and Abraham Mendez. The wretched Blueskin was hiding in a house in St Giles. He gave himself up and threw down his knife, by all accounts a gibbering wreck. He knew his goose was cooked and he would surely hang; and he was in mortal fear of being anatomized.

Mr Wild told us about it over his breakfast, licking his chocolate-covered lips. "Aye, Blueskin was ever a snivelling weakling. Easy. Easy to winkle out. So bold to begin with: *I'll kill the first man that comes in through this door!* Says Arnold: 'I am that first man, and Mr Wild is just behind me; throw down your knife or I'll chop your arm off!' 'Oh snivel, snivel,' goes Blueskin, 'they'll carve my body up and pull out all my guts and squint inside my belly and hang me up on a hook and measure all my limbs!' 'What of it,' Quilt says, 'you'll be dead, you will not feel a thing.' 'Oh snivel, snivel,' Blueskin goes again, 'they'll cut me into pieces...' 'No, no,' say I, all soft and sweet, 'they shall not, for I myself shall make sure you have a decent coffin and be buried with all proper ceremony, take my word.' So out he comes, all meek and mild, and he'll be tried within the fortnight. And hanged. And then," he sniggered, "just as he fears, they'll carve his body up and pull out all his guts; and serve him right, say I."

"How is he tolerated, Ralph?" I groaned. "He daily moves amongst the vilest cut-throats, all of whom he has the power to destroy, and most of 'em killers. Why has no one put an end to him?"

Then we heard two startling rumours — Mr Wild was murdered, and Jack was out of Newgate.

Unfortunately only one of these was true.

Chapter Forty-Three

THOUGH you may read the tale of Jack's escape in Mr Defoe's book, the subject is so marvellous and admirable I may not pass over it without some further explanation.

We are speaking of a small barred room on the third floor of the Whit, a room with a chimney, and Jack chained to the floor. On the night of the fifteenth of October with a nail which was hidden in his stocking he picked the lock of his handcuffs, with the nail in his teeth. He opened the padlock and released the chain about his ankles, though he still wore the iron collars and the chain attached. He went to the chimney and took it apart brick by brick, and with the iron bar within he battered his way into the room above. It was an empty room, pitch black and dusty. He picked the lock with a nail and came out into a passage. There was a locked door leading to the chapel. He smashed a hole through the brickwork and putting his arm through pulled the bolt back. The prison chapel had iron spikes between each partition, where the condemned were brought to pray. He broke off a spike and got through the gap. He picked another lock and came out through the door into a passage. On the other side of the door was the roof.

St Sepulchre's church bell chimed eight o'clock. He used the metal bar to wrench open the door. He came out on to the roof. He jumped and crawled from roof to roof. He could see below him the lights of Newgate Street. It was too far to jump. Tired and with a sinking heart he had to retrace his steps, room by room, stage by stage, back to the cell to get the blanket. Then back to the roof. Now he could climb down a little way. The attic window of a neighbouring house was open; he climbed inside. He crept down some stairs.

"Leanin' against a door post, breathin' hard," he said, "I heard this chap snorin' in 'is bed. I moved and the chains rattled. I thought: 'Damn!' 'What's that?' his wife said. 'Only a dog or a cat,' says her sleepy fellow; but I daren't go further. I was droppin wiv exhaustion so I crept back upstairs and found a bed and fell asleep. And when I woke I thought: 'You fool! Are you mad? Asleep in someone's garret!' So I waited, and I heard them at the front door and I saw they'd left it open, so I gathered up my chains and ran."

Now my first thought when I heard that Jack was free was that Mr Wild had kept his word and overseen the escape. But hot on the heels of the news of Jack's escape came news that Blueskin Blake had plunged a knife in Mr Wild's throat, therefore Mr Wild was in no condition to play the saviour.

What had happened was that Blueskin had been brought to the sessions at Old Bailey, and Jonathan had been strolling about with a glass of wine in his hand, and pretty smug.

"You'll promise me I won't be anatomized," whinged Blueskin.

"Now I can't promise that; how can I?" Mr Wild smirks. "Do you think that everyone does what I tell 'em? All I can promise you is that you are certainly a dead man, and will be tucked up very speedily."

Then Blueskin grabbed him by the neck in rage, and took a blunt knife to his throat and cut him, and had it not been for a muslin stock around his neck, Mr Wild would have been no more; but hey alas for muslin. They dragged Blueskin off him, screaming: "I 'ope you dies! I would have killed you! I would have cut off your head and thrown it into Sessions House Yard and made it bounce among the rabble. Damn my blunt knife! Damn my poor hand that could not do the deed..."

And Mr Wild was taken home and bandaged, and he was back among us for his breakfasts more grotesque than usual, with a bandage round his neck and round the side of his head. He must have seen my disappointment, for he grinned at me and looked at me askance: "Did I not tell you, Davy, that the Devil sits upon my shoulders?"

Like all of London I followed the rumours that buzzed abroad concerning Jack. I prayed he would have gone north — south — overseas — but I knew him better. He would be in London.

The mob now paid to see the empty cell, the pile of crumbled bricks, the smashed locks. Mr Bird whose attic Jack had slept in told his story again and again. 'It's just a dog or a cat,' I told my wife. 'Yes, this is the very bed. This hollow is the imprint of his sleeping form.'

The turnkey who had discovered Jack's absence was still in a state of shock and drinking copious amounts of gin for medicinal purposes.

It seemed no one could talk of any other subject.

"He's in Canterbury..."

"He was taken last night in Reading..."

"I saw him in an alehouse in Rupert Street..."

One evening at the end of October George Page came to Aunty Mary's, looking for me.

"Thank the Lord I found you, Davy," he said. "Best come back with me now to my place. You have a visitor."

"Is it — ?"

"Yes."

Jack was sitting in George's kitchen, eating cold boiled beef and bread. He looked pretty smart for one who had been ten days on the run. He was wearing a handsome black coat, a shirt with ruffles, a periwig, and, as he hastened to show me, a silver-hilted sword, a gold watch and a diamond ring.

"Who's your tailor?" I grinned; then I rushed at him and hugged him hard.

"Mr Rawlins," he sniggered. " 'e keeps a shop. 'e let me 'ave 'em for nothing; though the sword and watch and ring I got from a pawnbroker's. Well, I looked such a gipsy in my old clothes an' I wanted ter look nice for yer."

"I closed the shutters," George murmured. "We shall be quite safe here."

"Oh Jack! You should be miles away!" I groaned.

"What kind of a welcome is that, eh? Don't you want to hear about my travels?"

He'd walked to Tottenham village, hid in a cowhouse, persuaded a blacksmith to free him of his irons, lived as a beggar in Charing Cross, eaten at an alehouse in Rupert Street — ah, so that rumour had been true! — stopped and listened to a ballad singer warbling about his escape, stolen the suit...

"Davy, I want to write a letter to Ma and I want you to take it to her. Can I write a letter, George, here? If you'd be so kind..."

He wrote it, laboriously but impeccably:

"My dear loving mother, this with my duty to you, hoping these few lines will find you in good health as I am at this present writing. This is to let you know that in my attempt to make my escape from the castle of Newgate I have had the good fortune by the assistance of God to make it successful and to save my life; and I hope that by the grace of God I shall keep myself from any more of these heinous crimes which I have lately committed, and," he chuckled, " from the hands of my enemies. Dear mother, cast not yourself down but be of good heart for I hope to be as much comfort to you as ever I have been the occasion of your grief. You may let Mr Applebee the printer by Fleet Ditch know that I gave orders for you to receive, since I cannot come for it myself, the 8d a day which he agreed to allow me during my life for my Memorandums, which will be a good support to you. I would fain let you know where I am but dare not for fear of miscarriage. So no more at present, but I rest your loving dutiful misfortunate son, Jack Sheppard."

I admired it.

"I was always good at letters; Mr Kneebone taught me."

"What's this about Memorandums, Jack?"

"Mr Defoe is going to help me write my Memorandums. I've had such an interesting life, he says. 'e came an' saw me in the Whit. 'e said if I was to write my Memorandums he would like to be the one I told my story to, as he could write it well for me. I fort that seemed a good idea."

"And is it true that you are planning to give up your life of crime?"

"Oh, I don't know about that, Davy. How would I fill my time if not havin' adventures an' pickin' locks?"

"Did Mr Wild help you to escape?"

"I should say not!" Jack said indignantly. "What do you take me for? I could never work in conjunction with that gomph stick. My great escape was solely due to me, and the kind hand of the Almighty."

"And what will you do now? Will you stay?" I was torn — I wished that he would do so, but with daylight would come recognition and danger. I need not have troubled.

"Nah, I'm off. You know who's waitin' for me?"

"Who? Bess?"

"Nah; she's still in gaol. And anyway, she turned out no good, didn't she? Told on me. Nah — I'm with Kate Cook and Cathy Keys. Both of 'em! Ain't I the lucky one, eh? Both!"

He slipped away.

"What can you tell him?" George said in exasperation. "He's askin' for it. Anyone with any sense would go across the seas. I don't think he's right in the head."

"George, I'll sleep here for a night or two if that's all right. In case he comes back."

"I wish you would. I missed you."

Mulling over what Jack had said about his great escape I asked Mr Wild outright whether he himself had had a hand in it.

"Ad's Heart, it was my own clever plan," he beamed, as if the answer was quite plain for all to see. "You know the turnkeys are in my pocket. Why do you think they kept so long away from

Sheppard's cell and gave him time enough to get clear? It was all down to me. I always keep my word."

"Then Mr Wild, since Jack is free and I have worked hard for you while he was in captivity, I would say our bargain was now at an end, would not you?"

His little bright eyes narrowed. "It sounds to me as if you may have misunderstood the terms of our agreement, Davy. I do not recall a time limit set upon our friendship. I was under the impression that you were become closely bound to me; and so you are, Davy, so you are, *now*. I'm afraid you have committed crimes, Davy, hanging offences; and you need the protection that only I can give. Think about it, Davy, think what it would be like for you if my care for you should be withdrawn. The answer must be pretty clear, I think, even to one such as yourself, Davy, who is none too clever."

Everything he said was true; I had dug myself a pit and readily jumped into it. But even so...

"How long must I be bound to you?" I said in some desperation.

"For as long as you are useful to me," Mr Wild said. "And you have grown lazy latterly, haven't you? Perhaps you should set about to prove your worth to me and remind me why I took you under my wing. I have not heard of any pickings brought in by yourself these past few days."

And I went away scowling, cursing Blueskin Blake's blunt knife.

A couple of nights later Jack came back. He climbed up the low roof round the back and up through the upper window.

"Davy! Hey, Davy."

I sat up in bed. He took off his coat and shoes and climbed in beside me. His hair was damp. He smelt of beer. He snuggled up against me. "It was good in that old cottage, eh, on Finchley?" he said.

"Pretty good."

"Girls are all very well, but a chap needs a good pal. You was always my best pal, Davy."

"Thank you; I hope I am."

"Ma says you brought the letter."

"Yes. You've seen her?"

"I sent Kate to bring her where I was hidin' out. I'm real sorry about Ma. Two bad sons. An' she fort I was a little angel. Still does, I reckon. Says I should get out of London. Cried. It made me real upset."

"She's right; you should get out of London."

"And so I will. Hey, Davy," he began to laugh. "Guess what I just did."

"What?"

"Me an' the girls had a good meal at the Ram, then took a hackney coach — guess where we drove!"

"Where?"

"Right past Newgate! Straight underneath the arch of the gateway! We were this close to the doorway! We could've leaned out an' spat on the guards!"

"Wounds! What is the matter with you?"

"We were laughin' fit to burst!"

"Jack, you've got to get out of London."

"Will you come with me?"

"All right."

"We can go back on the Great North Road. You were goin' ter show me how to look for gold."

"That's right, I was."

"Then let's go now." I could see the glint of his excited eyes.

"No, wait, I can't go tonight."

"Why not?"

"I'd have to let Ralph know, and Ma Clap. I can't go off without saying goodbye and explaining, not after all they've done."

"Well, when?"

"Tomorrow night, after I've seen Ralph and the others."

"Why d'you 'ave ter see them?"

"They've been real good to me. And to you — Ralph brought a nail in for you. It might have been the very nail you used to pick the lock of the handcuffs."

"Tomorrow night then. Shall I come here?"

"Yes. But till then stay indoors; stay in your room all day. Wait till dark before you meet me. But Jack," I sensed him moving, "don't go yet; stay with me, it's early; it's not midnight."

"I got Moll Frisky waitin' for me at the Rose and Crown."

"Oh well," I snapped, "best not keep her waiting."

"But tomorrow night," said Jack, "we'll go up the Great North Road and look for gold. Claude Duval's gold, eh?"

"Come here, Jack," I said, grabbing for him. "Don't go."

He lay back and let me kiss him.

"I love you, Jack, you know it, don't you?"

"I love you too an' all, Davy. Odd, ain't it, but I do."

"Stay."

"I best not. But you'll see me again. You'll see me tomorrow."

Reluctantly I let him go. I went with him to the back window; he wriggled through, and slithered to the yard.

There was a full moon, eerily bright in a cold sky, and scudding silver clouds beneath. I padded back to bed, shivering. It could not have been for very long that I lay there, half asleep. An hour perhaps. And then came such a roar and rumpus up and down the street. Running footsteps, a piercing whistle, a woman's scream. Nothing odd in that. But the noise continued. Horses neighing, the clatter of a coach's wheels, the woman screaming, people shouting; and then loudest of all, Jack's voice crying: "Help me! Murder! I am in the hands of bloodhounds!"

George and I both, heaving on our clothes, went thudding down to the front door, in time to see the back of a coach swaying from side to side, careering at speed around the corner of the street in the direction of Newgate. We stood there stupidly, in our bare feet, half dressed and half awake.

"What can we do?" George said to me. There was exasperation in his tone. "Is it a surprise to you? I've never met such a buffoon. I'm sorry, Davy, I know he is a friend of yours and he was very likeable. You know what? I think he just likes being famous. It goes to his head. He just likes people to be standing in line to marvel at him. It was just too quiet for him away from all the cheering."

It transpired that after leaving me Jack went with Moll Frisky on a boozing spree and everyone who saw him recognized him. They sent for a constable. The people drinking in Mrs Campbell's dramshop and the Rose and Crown came out to witness the arrest. This is what happens when you're famous and Pass into Legend.

George said: "Sitting in Newgate with his chains on and the people crowding round him — you never saw him, Davy — he was like a prince holding court. On the run, what is he? Just another thief of the streets."

Doubtful of my allegiance Jonathan Wild asked me to rob a coach the following night.

"I need reassurance, Davy," he croaked, still in his bandage. "I need your loyalties at this difficult time. Oh, and take Will Field along with you."

"You don't need that safeguard, Mr Wild. You know you've got me safe as if I was chained hand and foot."

"Ah well," he said waggishly, "and that's no safety these days! Believe me, I am desolate that Sheppard is back in gaol. I can't help it, can I, if the fool gets caught?"

"But that's no problem to you, is it, Mr Wild? You can fix him up with a second escape. That was the bargain — I work for you, you free Jack. And like you say, you always keep your word."

Jonathan Wild gave me that laugh that was not a laugh but a noise that came out of his nose. He patted my sleeve.

"Pocket books, Davy; try for pocket books."

It was not a good night for that kind of venture. The moon was too bright. It was asking for trouble to go out with the moon so soon after the full. But I went; and Will Field with me. We went quite a way out of London up the north road, and in time we caught a glimpse of what appeared to be a gentleman's coach some way off; we lay in wait accordingly. I rode forth and brought the coach to a standstill.

"Out! Come on now, out!" I heard my voice; it sounded edgy, jumpy, lacking in authority, not the way I was accustomed to sound. I was tense and sweating and in no way at ease. Because of this, Gry was pretty fidgetty and all. But I had no particular difficulty. The coachman had a blunderbuss but he could not get at it, and at my direction out came three young gentlemen and, to my astonishment, three wicker baskets, each containing a cockerel, which they set on the ground with great care. It was clear that they were on their way to a private cock fight. They grumbled and muttered as they parted with their rings and watches but I believe that if I had chosen to take the birds instead of their gold they would have put up more resistance.

I turned and rode off down the road and had gone but a hundred yards or so when Will Field cut across in front of me and caused me to rein sharply, and for a moment we were illumined against the moon. From behind us a couple of shots rang out; they must have had some weapons somewhere inside the coach — what astonishing ill luck! Gry turned swiftly, thereby saving my life; but a bullet grazed my arm, and Will Field, acting very oddly, I thought, contrived to block my path, preventing a quick getaway, shoving me in the chest as he turned his horse and fled. Thoroughly unsettled, Gry reared up in the confusion, and I came tumbling off and found myself on my back in the bracken looking stupidly up at a moon that was swinging to and fro like a windblown lanthorn. It had all only taken a moment.

Gry came and stood over me; I could feel his warm breath on my face. The coachman must have believed I had the wit and strength to get into the saddle, for he began to take pot shots at him, and fearful for Gry's safety I gave him a signal to lose himself and quickly.

The gentlemen from the coach now came running up in great good spirits at their unexpected luck, and I had the pistols taken from my belt and myself turned over and my hands behind me bound at the wrists, before the world had yet righted itself from its peculiar motions. Jamie Goodman's mask came off, and they peered closely at me.

"Do you know who he is?"

"No."

"Is he famous?"

"I don't believe so."

Damn me, I thought in gathering alarm, I shall be now.

"Well, sirrah," said one. "It's up before the magistrate for you! You're going to be very sorry for this night's work!"

And then another one said: "But there's a magistrate amongst us at the cock fight!"

"So there is! What luck!" And it was decided there was nothing for it but that I must be taken in the coach and handed over to him there and then.

They got me to my feet and I was bundled in amongst them and the cockerel baskets, with many shouts of "Careful as you go — that bird's worth more than this chap can make in a year!" "Mind my Hercules; he has a delicate nature!" and "Here, Duval, you'll have to have Demon's basket on your knees and mind you sit still and keep him steady; there's a fortune hanging on him."

The three then settled themselves around me and ordered the coachy forward, and we trundled off.

Now that I had recovered my senses I was pretty scared. I had been nabbed fair and square in the act of robbery upon the highway. These gents would get a forty pound reward — maybe a hundred — and my possessions, and Gry if they could catch him, and I would be joining Jack in Newgate, with transportation if the judge was kind, it being the first time that I was accused. But Will Field could peach me and bring our other offences to light if Mr Wild had decided that my time was up; and it did seem pretty certain Will had either on his own account or directed by Mr Wild, set out to get me taken.

My captors were all young, about my own age or younger, gentlemen's sons of small brain and much wealth. They were like boys with a trophy, sniggering and boasting and repeating their intention to see me safely into the clutches of the magistrate. I felt pretty sour to see them all reclaim their rings and watches from my pockets, and handle my pistols with some admiration ("Italian..."

"Silver!") and arrange to dice for who should have 'em. They were plainly proud of themselves for their night's work and intending to dine off the story of their bravery for weeks. I daresay I would increase in size, malevolence and villainy as the tale progressed.

James Goodman's velvet mask was passed around; each tried it on, and leered and chuckled; and between us all the wicker cages bounced and their occupants flapped and squawked and worked with beak and claw to free themselves.

I considered myself a fool to find myself in the hands of such, I who had so latterly given Jack advice on keeping out of trouble. Moreover, I had not supposed the stinging of a bullet graze to be so damned uncomfortable, enhanced by the fact that the owner of the coach kept heaving me back and forth by that same arm, protesting piteously: "But he's bleeding on to my plush!"

A few miles further down the road the coach turned off down a narrow byway, and pulled up. In something of a tangle the three young gentlemen, myself and the cockerels extricated ourselves from the coach.

The bright moonlight and several lanthorns showed that we were outside some kind of ruined building with a small tower, grey and shadowy, half hidden by trees. Another coach was waiting, a couple of gentlemen were looking at their watches in impatience, and some other wretched cockerels clucked in their baskets, with no doubt the irons already fixed on to their claws.

The three who had brought me here now seized hold of me and dragged me forward, making a deal of noise about it, showing off the pistols, explaining what had happened and why they were late; and if I had been Duval himself I am sure I could not complain of the enthusiasm of my reception. At length a voice said:

"Hand me the lanthorn; let me have a look at him."

The magistrate came forward, and two of the bold young gentlemen took hold of my arms and stood me before him. He raised the lanthorn high and looked me in the face. I eyed him warily, bleeding and dishevelled. In his hands rested my fate. It was a damned unpleasant thought.

He studied me at some length. Then he said: "It looks as if I'll have to cry off the game tonight. Much as it breaks my heart. Tambourlaine was in great form and would have mangled your paltry chickens to ribbons. But I had best get this villain under lock and key at my house. Oh, and hand me his pistols; I shall need them as evidence."

Groans of disappointment, murmurs of assent, promises of

further fights, threats of further mangling all followed, and cries of "See you at Tyburn!" to myself. I found myself propelled towards the second coach, to wreck somebody else's plush.

"Forward!" said the owner of the coach.

We were alone now, the magistrate and I, and the coach was taking us towards his home, where I would learn what was to become of me.

The magistrate began to chuckle. He was fat, and his belly heaved beneath his satin waistcoat as he rollicked.

"Now, Davy, what's all this about? How did you get in this pickle, and what will you give me to get you out of it?"

The magistrate was my old companion Tubs, my pal from Bishopsgate school, the benefactor of my youth and childhood, and if his manner was any indication of his state of mind, one who had long since forgiven me for the lies I told him about my thundering exploits with the women of the Rose.

It looked pretty much as if I was to land upon my feet this time.

Like I say, lucky.

Chapter Forty-Four

"YOU recognized me then!" I marvelled.

"No, I didn't," Tubs replied. "I recognized the silver pistols. After all, they're mine."

"They are not; they were given to me by your grandfather."

"I am sure he did not intend them to be used against poor benighted travellers going about their business."

"Poor benighted — ? You were about to cause innocent creatures to murder one another for your own amusement. And it was not me that fired the shot."

"Cocks adore to fight," said Tubs blandly. "Are you badly hurt?" he added concerned and setting about to cut my bonds. "I shall attend to it when we reach Ashfield."

"That's very kind, Tubs. I don't believe I am much hurt but there's a deal of blood."

"And how came you, Davy, to be on the road and fallen to such straits?"

"Straits? It was always my ambition, if you remember, to follow in Claude Duval's footsteps; there is no shame in it."

In the time it took for the coach to reach Ashfield we had

swapped accounts of our respective lives, a version, in my case, heavily censored, and for all I know in Tubs's case also. Tubs had become very much the country gentleman, with the virtues and vices of his kind, and in the years since I had last beheld him he had married and engendered sons, two small creatures Jeremy and George, each fat as he. His wife the lady Augusta was a big affable lass whom he called Gussie, and her interests being similar to his, it would appear that they lived a life of conjugal harmony, in which food and gambling played a large part and bookishness none at all.

As we drew in to the curved drive that I remembered I said urgently: "You do mean to save me then, Tubs?"

"Of course I do," he said heartily. "You were the nearest thing I had to a brother, for all that we did sometimes quarrel."

"And how will you explain your behaviour to your friends?"

"You overcame me by devious means and fled. I see no problem here. Did no one tell you that magistrates are corrupt?"

I ignored that. "Then may we go and find my horse?"

"In the morning," said Tubs placidly.

"Tubs, is my dear horse Willow still with you?"

"Yes and gentle as ever. Jeremy rides him. But please be free to renew your acquaintance with the fellow."

At Ashfield manor I was treated with great warmth and kindness. I had a hot bath in the bedroom, and Gussie herself attended to my arm and bathed and bound it. The sleeves of my shirt and coat were soaked in cold water to remove the bloodstains, and dried before the fire. I borrowed Tubs's enormous dressing gown and I slept out the remainder of the night and much of the next day in the bed I had used as a lad, the very room that I had left nine years ago to begin my life upon the road.

I went down with Tubs to the stables where I made a glad reunion with Willow who I swear remembered me, and nuzzled my neck with great affection. I saddled him and rode off to look for Gry. I was pretty careful, as you may imagine, watching out for the chaps I had encountered last night, but I did not see them, and returning to the place where I had stopped the coach, by dint of gipsy whistling I brought Gry to me. I saw him some way off but he refused to come up close. I had never seen him act so coy, and was at a loss to understand his reticence, till it occurred to me that he was simply jealous. This astonished and amused me, and only when I dismounted and came forward to him would he approach and permit me to mount him. We led Willow home to Ashfield, Gry frequently turning his head in a manner I could not but believe complacent.

For all Tubs's assurances to the contrary I considered my portly friend to be in danger while I stayed with him, and so quit Ashfield the next day; but not before a serious talk with him about our mutual friend from boyhood.

"I was not sure whether it was indeed the same Jack Sheppard that we knew," admitted Tubs. "Remember I have had nothing to do with him since we were six years old. I knew our Jack was little and wiry and could climb like a monkey. But that he was the great Jack Sheppard, who has twice escaped from Newgate... And do you truly believe that we could save him?"

"I believe we must," I said, "for it is becoming plain to me that Mr Wild has no intention of so doing."

"Have you any plan in mind?"

"None at all," I replied despondently. "It is gone beyond a matter of leaving files and nails in the cell. He is manacled beyond all human aid, and weighed down with three hundred pounds' weight of iron. It had occurred to me that his friends might work to save him when he's in the open air, on the way to the gallows. It's a long road from Newgate to Tyburn."

"I wonder..." Tubs then said. "I wonder whether we might try the truth of a scientific notion I have heard propounded. It is this: a friend of mine has assured me that a hanged body may be resuscitated, even when it seems to all intents and purposes to be lifeless."

"I have heard the same. There is a chap who lived to tell the tale; they call him Half-Hanged Smith. His neck was purple, and he saw wild visions, but he was cut down in good time, and lived and breathed."

"Then why not so with Jack?"

"I would sooner try a rescue from the cart. This other idea smacks of too close a dicing with death."

"Were you never a gambling man, Davy?"

"I never was."

"I have some friends that I might interest in the rescue," Tubs said thoughtfully. "They would take a wager on his chances."

"Why would they care about what happens to a housebreaker?"

"They would care nothing. They would do it for the sport."

"This was not how I pictured saving Jack," I demurred.

"Believe me, this is not a time to question motive," Tubs said. "I may very well be able to persuade my friends to hire a coach and get the body clear and rush it to a surgeon, for a wager, Davy, just to see if it may be done. After the hanging, a coach waits, does it not, for the body to be taken away to the dissecting table? Our coach will wait, but we shall take the body to a different surgeon — one who will save." Tubs's eyes gleamed. "It will be the most marvellous prank! And if we succeed, it will be in the nature of an experiment beneficial to mankind. Men of science will be grateful to us."

I winced. "Jack also, perhaps."

"Jack also," Tubs conceded.

"Well then," said I, "if all else fails..."

I returned to London and Lucinda with my arm in a sling and my pistols in my belt. But Jamie Goodman's mask I never saw again, and maybe those young gentlemen deserved a trophy to remind them of their triumph. I told Lucinda what had happened and enjoyed his care of me. I went to Mr Wild's morning levée and made out that my arm was in worse case than it was, and he said he would not send me out on any venture till I was recovered. But truth to tell, his mind was on other matters. He plainly had no intention of freeing Jack, and I surmised that now for him there was but one burning issue — would he get Jack Sheppard hanged and add that final feather to his turban — or would some rogue foil his triumph?

Tubs — and I should call him Lord Endymion Vale, for whether it were done for love or sport, his part became now of the noblest — moved to his town house, with a motley crew of sporting gentlemen. I met him privily every day at the Barley Mow, Long Acre, for him to reveal the flowering of his plans. They had procured a surgeon eager to perform the resuscitation. All that we had to do was to get hold of the body with all speed and rush it to the waiting coach.

I dared not attend Jack's trial for fear concerning my own part in the events which had led up to it, but Ralph went to the Court of the King's Bench that November day, and he told me what Jack said concerning the affair.

The judge said to Jack that if he would give any information leading to the arrest of an accomplice he might be treated with leniency. At this moment, did I but know it, my life hung in the balance. All the court waited, in case Jack might take up this offer in so public a place.

"Who helped you, Jack?" the judge said. "Now's the time to tell. Who was your helper?"

And Jack said: "No one. Only God Almighty." And everybody gasped at such a boldness, and the judge reproved him for his profanity.

"I suppose it was deemed an unbelievable arrogance to boast that God protected him against the officers of the law," said Ralph.

"Ah, Ralph," I said. "That boast of his was the gesture of a kind good friend." And I found my eyes were full of tears and I believed that I was one that never cried.

They hanged poor Blueskin Blake that month. No intrigue and plot for that poor cull. Will Field peached him at his trial. You wanted a chap to peach his friend — you asked Will Field, and he would do it, pat.

I went to pay my respects to Blueskin at St Andrew's burying ground, along with just about all the thieves and cutpurses in London, and, as far as I could tell, the anatomizing surgeon never got his knife to him after all, for he certainly went down into the ground, and the rain poured down along of him, and there we stood, wet and drenched, to see him on his way.

Jack meanwhile with all the glamour of a condemned man was praised and lauded and visited by everyone who was anyone. Lords and earls trod the cockroach path to his cell, the beautiful women of the day, with handkerchiefs to their noses, came and wept over him, and the drabs and wenches who had known him pretty well came in; and I went, with Lucinda.

We reckoned if we went as a wedded couple we would draw less attention to ourselves, and in Ralph's bedroom at Aunty Mary's we dressed ourselves for the part. Ralph in his female attire was, as I have remarked and been amazed at, utterly convincing, and I wore a sombre black coat and breeches and a powdered light-coloured periwig, my own chestnut mop well hidden, and we powdered out my eyebrows and I daresay I might well have passed for older than I was.

On the day that we went to Newgate, which was the afternoon before the execution date, we could hardly move for the crowds, and the stink was pretty foul. It made my guts heave simply to enter the place, but I knew in my heart it was not the stench that caused it but base fear. The spectre of this place had haunted my fancy for so many years that to know myself inside its walls unmanned me quite; whereas Ralph, who had been once before, was positively brazen in his nonchalance, and not a little superiority tinged his concern as he observed my ashen visage and dry lips as we shuffled forward.

I was astonished at the laxity of the terms of the imprisonment, for after having paid our four shillings to the turnkeys at the door, we might wander at will into the condemned cell, whose door was open to let the sightseers in and out. Granted there was no way Jack could move, since he was fettered enough to keep an entire army out of combat; but the peculiar gaiety and bawdiness about it all was disturbing and amazing.

Jack, seated in a chair, was half suffocated by the embraces of all manner of women, who came forth sighing and crowing: "I kissed Jack Sheppard!" and by gentlemen eager to shake his manacled hands.

Beside Jack on a stool sat an elderly chap, lean and dark with a pointed chin; he was engaging in converse with Jack and plainly vexed at all the interruptions.

When it was our turn to be let in, both Lucinda and I embraced Jack with a great spreading of Lucinda's long-fringed shawl, under which I contrived to fix a sheathed knife behind the buttons of his waistcoat. It was customary to take off the iron manacles of the condemned man as he set off for Tyburn and replace them with bonds of cord. Jack would understand what I meant.

"You lean forwards as the cart approaches Little Turnstile," I breathed. "Cut the rope. Jump into the crowd. I'll block the alley after you." Jack looked so dazed, I added urgently: "You know where Little Turnstile is? The seventh alley after the George Inn."

"I know it, Davy, ta," said Jack.

"If that fails, don't lose heart. Trust me."

"Hurry along there!" called the chap behind us. "Others are waiting."

"Have yer met Mr Defoe?" Jack said, directing his glance towards the old chap on the stool. "He's writin' my Memorandums, ain't yer, Mr Defoe? Tell Davy wotcher said I was — tell Davy wotcher fink I am!"

"A Supernatural," obliged Mr Defoe.

"Yeah, what was it? — a Creature something more than man! And the other bit, Mr Defoe, about the Bars and the Bosom."

"'Bars are not made that can either keep him out or keep him in. He has fled from the very bosom of death'. And," added Mr Defoe, "might I say that he has endured his dismal ordeal throughout with the temper of a philosopher."

"I say, move on!" cried our impatient neighbour.

"Goodbye, dear Jack," I said and kissed his cheek.

"Goodbye, Davy," answered he; and Ralph and I wove our way into the crowds, and pushed a hurried pathway to the door.

I was at the Barley Mow that night with Tubs and his cronies. Our converse was muttered and macabre.

"The soldier will pass the inert body to Southwell here. He

will pass it to you, Davy. You pass it to Macy. He passes it to Wilmot who gives it to Palmer who gives it to me at the coach..."

I spent the night at Ma Clap's just nearby, though understandably I did not sleep, but sat up in the kitchen with Lucinda, watchers of the night. Ma brought us food and drink and told us we should eat and keep our strength up. Bill Griffin said the crowds began to gather along Holborn long before dawn. He said there were already hot-potato sellers on the street, and braziers of roast chestnuts, and people gathered round them to keep warm.

We could hear the gloomy bell of St Sepulchre's. We knew the moment when the bellman went along the underground passage from the church to Newgate to ring the handbell and declaim the horrid verse that warned the condemned man to consider his soul.

As soon as it was light I went out.

"Good luck, my dear," said Ma and hugged me.

I stepped out into the wet sludge of Field Lane. The sky was a dull watery grey, the air was chill. All was activity outside St Sepulchre's church — soldiers with pikes and any number of dignitaries in gold-braided coats on restless horses. I saw Under City Marshall Charles Hitchin, bulky as ever, very prominent. There was the cart with the coffin laid across it, and the prison chaplain with his Bible, a breed of men universally despised, for under cover of comforting the condemned they tried to get salacious details of his life, to sell after the event. The crowd was pretty dense; and when Jack was brought out they went wild, and cheered and yelled; you could hardly hear the bellman's voice as he called out to us to pray for the poor sinner; but we heard his bell all right — a horrid high-pitched clangy thing.

Jack in the elegant black suit he'd filched looked abominably cheerful. I wondered whether George was right about his being 'not right in the head'. This was a man that was on his way to Tyburn. He was grinning and calling out to folk he recognized, and swapping banter with anyone that cared to crack a joke. Trust me, I had said. Was his cheerfulness a result of his belief in my ability to procure a release? Did he know something other? Or was he merely in his element, the hero of the crowd, taking pleasure in the moment?

"They have not taken the manacles off," I said dismayed.

"They fear he will escape, even now," said one beside me. "They found a knife on him, inside his waistcoat."

My heart sank. So no chance of the Turnstile Alley plan. Everything depended upon Tubs and his gang of gentlemen, waiting by the gallows.

Nonetheless, in case of miracle, I ran on ahead along Holborn to wait at Little Turnstile. The procession was long in coming — it must pause when girls climbed up into the cart to kiss him, for Jack to drink mulled sack at a hostelry and to send the mob into a frenzy of hilarity by calling out the time-honoured response: "Tell the landlord I'll pay for it on the way back!"

But nothing happened at Little Turnstile. The procession continued on its way, and I ran on ahead to Tyburn, past the open fields of Marylebone and the wall of Hyde Park.

The people who had paid for seats were coming into their places, helping each other up the steps of the great tiered blocks that encircled the Triple Tree, unpacking wine and cold chicken, spreading their feast out across their knees. Sellers of wine and biscuits moved obsequiously amongst them.

All space was now filling up. A mob of hundreds, all of whom seemed to have a yapping dog with them, and hordes of brats, all bawling. The hot-potato men, the beer sellers now shouted their wares, the doxies plied their trade, the pickpockets got to work; there were a dozen fights. A man was selling dead rabbits dangling from a pole.

There was Tubs's coach, some way off, and his pals about it, drinking wine from bottles. Tubs was sitting on the roof. He waved to me. I saw the pigeon go flapping up into the air, released to show the procession was approaching. The soldiers forced us back, and made a ring about the gallows.

I watched it all. I saw him hanged. It seemed a lifetime before the soldier cut him down. Now Southwell seized the inert body, looked around for me; I was there. I took it from him, ran with it in my arms, warm and living, but unconscious.

"To me!" yelled Macy. I passed Jack to him. He turned and passed him further back, along a line of men that stretched towards the coach.

"Stop!" the man beside me roared. "They mean to take the body to Surgeons' Hall!"

Jonathan Wild! He raised his silver cane aloft like some weird wizard with his wand, and the crowd heard and saw him. Suddenly all was mayhem.

"They're stealing the body for dissection! They're taking our Jack to be cut to pieces!"

The mob went wild. They grabbed at Jack, to save him, as they thought, with every second endangering our plan, and seeping Jack's faint life away.

"No!" I shouted. "Let them be! They're saving him!"

"But they're too late," said Jonathan Wild, close to me, and quiet, and looked me in the eyes.

It was as if a little circle held us in a still point within the surge and clamour of the crowd.

"You shouldn't have done that," I gasped.

"I'm pleased to see your arm is healed," said Jonathan and smiled. "To lift a man above your head — even a man as light as Sheppard — that takes a muscle or two."

"You shouldn't have done that, Mr Wild," I repeated and went for his throat. I dug my thumbs into his neck, all thickly bandaged as it was. I heard him gulp, and his eyes bulged. But Sykes and Arnold rose up like pillars one each side of him and dragged me off and slung me to the ground, and worse would have followed had the heaving crowd not closed about us. I had to save myself from being trampled underfoot. I was buffeted this way and that. Driftwood on the tide I struggled to find a way to Tubs, to Jack, to the coach, trying to see what was happening, seeing at last that it was all over, that last chance, that wager for sport so gallantly undertaken by Tubs's cronies.

The mob rushed the coach, like a great wave on a broken ship, tore it apart and smashed it up, and now were hurling the seats to and fro, and the wheels and the lamps and the doors; and the terrified horses were running hither and yon, and Tubs nowhere to be seen, nor Jack neither, and the whole brave impractical design in ruins.

The scene had now become a riot, with the soldiers taking charge. I stumbled clear and made my way back towards the city. The streets were full of people running. I heard windows smashed, and everywhere screaming, shouting.

I went by back ways towards Covent Garden, running, and I found myself in Knave's Acre, suddenly quiet and alone, and I leaned against a wall and hit my head against a timbered upright till the pain brought me up sharp, and I fell forward on to my hands and knees, choking and retching, like a shipwrecked man washed up on the sand. I heaved myself up, cursing myself at my uselessness. I was shaking like a leaf. I went into a boozing ken, a one-roomed place, smoky and dark, and drank my way through a dose of gin. I could see in my mind's eye with horrible clarity Jack dangling in the noose, all in his fancy black suit, and I reckoned gin would blur the image, but damn me, how many cracked cups of the vile liquor would it take? — I still could see him there.

I limped my way to St Martin's Lane and so by indirect means to the backyard of the Barley Mow, where I guessed Tubs would make for, all the way accompanied by the distant clamour of a restless mob loose in the streets, rampaging, looting, drinking, starting fires. I had never heard or seen the like.

The Barley Mow was strangely silent. The shutters were all drawn. It was dark as a tomb. The first person I saw was Tubs, with a bloodstained bandage round his head and a candle in his hand.

"Davy! Come in quickly! How did you get past the soldiers?"

"What soldiers?"

"In Long Acre. They're closing off the streets... arresting people."

"I was lucky."

"Davy... come and see."

He led me up the narrow stairs to a bedchamber and pulled aside a curtain. On a bed lay Jack, very pale and small and dead.

"I wanted to leave a candle burning. But I thought the place would burn down. The town's gone crazy."

"What a frigging shambles."

"As you say."

"There is no chance, I suppose...?" — the remark of an idiot.

"I know you've been drinking heavily, but even you must see..."

I sat down on the bed beside Jack, my knees giving out. Tubs arranged himself carefully on the other side.

"Your forehead, Tubs? Are you all right?"

"I was one of those defending the coach," Tubs said ruefully.

"The others?"

"All downstairs; a little worse for wear, but planning their next wager."

"I'll see Jonathan Wild dead, I swear it. You are my witness."

"My own ambition is merely to get back to Ashfield in one piece, once we have buried Jack."

"And how shall that be done?" We each lay back upon the bed, one on either side of Jack.

Tubs surprised me. "It is all arranged. Mr Applebee the printer has procured a coach. He's the chap who's printing Mr Defoe's pamphlet. I paid for the coffin, which should be on its way. There'll have to be an armed guard."

"Where?"

"St Martin's in the Fields, that new church they're building; it was his parish."

"Who'd have thought it, Tubs, eh, when we all lay in one bed

319

in Bishopsgate?"

"Who indeed?" said Tubs. We were silent then, and the three of us lay as if we were asleep, and Jack the more peacefully, for Tubs and I were much weighed down with thought.

"I'll go and fetch his ma," I said at last.

We gave Jack a hero's burial, a king's. It took place that night, by torchlight. Soldiers escorted the coach which bore the coffin. The crowds lined the streets, but they were silent. We put him to rest.

I was dispirited beyond belief. Time was, to ease my pain and grief I would have saddled Gry and taken off up the Great North Road.

Instead, I went to Mother Clap's.

Part VI
The Search continued

Chapter Forty-Five

HABITUATED as I was to a lifetime of that mental solitude which finds it difficult to share grief or joy but handles both conditions with a shrug, I was perplexed to find how much I needed to be among friendly faces in the days that followed the loss of Jack.

Mother Clap turned out to be more of a parent to me than I had any right to expect, for what was I to her but some stray that Lucinda had brought in? But her warmth was given out regardless.

I had been pretty low when Jamie Goodman died; but this was a hundred times worse. Then I had fled from London, to the road and to the Crown and as humdrum a life as I could fix for myself. But flight had not proved the answer, and I had been drawn back to London like that gold-seeker Whittington, and much good had it done me.

I went to ground at Ma Clap's, where she looked after me with kindness, leaving me to sleep, or drink my own way to oblivion in a room beneath the eaves, while outside December hung upon us, dark and leaden, passing overhead like a great crow's wing, whose touch sent shivers into every limb.

I was not so far gone that I did not know Lucinda came to see me and sat by my bed, or that George was looking after Gry; but I knew this from far off, as if I was at the back of a cave and these events were going on in daylight.

Some time towards the end of January I came out of that cave. It was good to be sitting in the kitchen by the fire. I felt ashamed at having traded on Ma Clap's goodwill and at the weakness I had shown; but she didn't see it thus. She said grief was not weakness, and weakness was human, and she would always look after her own dear mollies and I was one and very dear to her. I winced.

"What have I said?" she asked.

"I don't like the name."

"What name?"

"Mollies. It seems an odd name for the likes of coal heavers and butchers — and highwaymen."

"Well then, dear, I'll not use it. What shall I say — my own dear boys? Whatever you like to call yourself you are most dear to me."

"And you to me, Ma. You've been so good an' all."

She got me talking about Jack, and I was glad to tell her all the good things I remembered. It made me snivel a bit, but oddly that seemed to ease the stiffness at the heart; and Ma was no stranger to witnessing emotion, glad or sorrowful.

"You see, it was my fault he died," I blurted out.

"How so?"

"I tried to organize a grand escape. It failed so spectacularly. I should have seen it coming and had plans ready."

"How many of you were there, planning that escape? Don't tell me their names; just count them on your fingers."

"About a dozen, as I guess, all in all."

"And what's so marvellous about yourself, Davy Gadd, that you should bear the blame out of a dozen! Circumstance was against you. It was all as a result of that minx called Bad Luck; that's all."

I thought about it. "I suppose I take the blame because I told Jack to trust me. When something goes so disastrously wrong you look for reasons. The reason isn't hard to find. It was Jonathan Wild. He was always after Jack. At first I thought he meant to save him and use him to work for him. But Jack would never do something so demeaning — I should have thought about it more. Wounds, how can such a villain live! I know how Blueskin felt. I'd like to have a chance like that, only my knife would be sharp."

"Davy, promise me you won't be so stupid."

"He's never without Mendez and Arnold, and he wears a tin shield under his shirt." I shrugged. "They say he has the marks of seventeen gashes on his body. I wouldn't be the only one to try to rid the world of such a villain. Believe me, Ma, I've thought about it."

"Davy, could he not be taken by the law?"

I said bitterly: "What law will get Jonathan Wild, who owns the law and makes it work for him?"

I went out in my working clothes into the wintry streets and trudged my way to the White Hart, and there found Gry. He received me coolly and standoffishly, and rightly so, for I had been neglectful of his needs. I had to work hard to regain his favour. I was surprised to find him nonetheless in excellent condition, and impressed that George had left him so.

I saddled him and out we set, gently at first, then swiftly, riding towards Islington; but the road being poor, we did not go far, and we returned, but nonetheless the better for the trip. I was stiff as a board and very much out of practice. The next day we went further and found a bit of heathland and had a good gallop till our manes streamed out behind us and our eyes grew bright and our misty breath was white on the cold air. We came back into the city at a steady pace, hungry. I was rubbing Gry down in his stall when behind me came a meaningful cough. It proved to be the indication of no lingering consumptive, but of Will Field, who was leaning jauntily against a post, observing me.

I finished with Gry and patted him, and turned to face Will Field. I watched him latch the stable door and kick an empty barrel against it. He set the barrel upright, temporarily blocking the way in or out. We were alone and private.

A tingling of the loins suggested to me that my vital spark was not entirely lost. This cockroach who had once beaten me half senseless, who had tried to get me nabbed on the high road, this creature of Jonathan Wild's, still caused a crude attraction, as inexplicable as it was pleasurable. Lean as a stoat, with lizard eyes, this predatory reptile was urging me to take hold of life again.

"I knew you'd sooner or later come for your horse," said Will Field. "Mr Wild wants to see you."

"Oh, does he? Why?"

"You ain't been attending his breakfasts and gettin' your orders."

"I was indisposed."

"That bullet? That healed up long ago. We saw you lift Jack Sheppard above your head."

His mention of Jack which I had feared would unman me, had the opposite effect. A glorious anger surged through my body. I ran at Will and clamped myself upon him, and then close against his body rammed my fists into his ribs, and we went down in a writhing tangle of limbs, rolling over and over in the muddy straw, till we fetched up against a feeding trough, and I sat astride him and laid into him with all my rage and strength. I freely confess it was one of the happiest moments of my life.

At last exhausted I hung over him, breathing hard, leaning on his wrists, my thighs taut each side of him, my balls moving on his belly. He was pretty bloody. He croaked: "Stop! Enough!"

When I could speak I said: "Will Field — you've peached everybody else. Why can't you peach Jonathan Wild?"

"Oh Christ, I dursn't!" he said thickly.

"Oh, do it, Will! It'd be a service to humanity."

"I dursn't. He'd kill me."

"You must know all manner of things about him. Tell the High Constable. Go to the magistrates — they'd let you off..."

"They wouldn't an' you know it. I'd be straight for the steps an' the string, same as you."

We panted there together, bonded by Jonathan Wild and our years of mutual sparring. Beneath me his body writhed. My cock hardened. He could not have been unaware of it. I suddenly found that I did not care. I leaned forward, till my hair fell across my face. I worked my thighs. I freed my cock and rubbed it up and down his belly — the pleasure was excruciating. I laughed out loud.

"You slut," Will Field said almost conversationally. "You whore. You bum-firking molly." But he did not struggle; he let me get on with it, and I came with a great shout, with my head back and my throat arched, and my grip on him as flaccid as a daisy chain. At which point he shoved me off himself and crawled to his feet, wiping his face with his fist, with plenty of oaths. He edged towards the door. I was on my hands and knees, my spine weak as string.

"Do you hear me?" he said. "Do you know what you are? You're a damned molly. You're like Mr Hitchin."

"Yes," I grinned and looked at him. "I suppose I am."

"You'd best be at Mr Wild's tomorrow," Will Field said. "Or you'll be sorry."

Then he shifted the barrel and unlatched the door and was gone.

There was a dismal ring of truth in his threat. I could not afford to play about with Mr Wild's displeasure. My personal hatred of him was irrelevant to this unassailable fact. In the morning I went round to his house in Old Bailey, as smart as I could make myself, which, dammit, was pretty good, with my tall boots and tight breeches and a clean white shirt and ornate waistcoat, and my coat of dusky blue. I smelt like a lord, with a good deal of Hungary water about my person. No pistols; I was always searched on entering. I walked in with all appearance of nonchalance.

The upper room was as always full of folk, mostly of a disreputable nature, and very few of whom had bothered with Hungary water. The room was warm and stuffy, body heat and a bright fire contributing to this effect. Will Field I saw, his eyes black, his lips swollen up, his cheeks bruised, in despite of which he managed to convey to me a brooding scowl. A servant gave me a glass of sherry, which was agreeably warming; Mr Wild gave me a nasty smile, which was not.

"Ho!" he said. "Mr Davy Gadd honouring us with his presence at last. How very good it is to see you."

"Your servant, sir," said I with a flourish.

"And so you are, sir, and so you are," said he, "and in a fair way of forgetting it."

"I daresay you intend reminding me," said I.

"We shall talk, you and I," said Mr Wild, "but not here, not amongst this riff raff. I want you to attend me afterwards — let's say in my chamber of trophies, eh? Wait for me there. I shall soon have finished with this genial rabble. Take another glass of sherry. Or would you sooner take chocolate? It's very good."

I knocked back the sherry in a throatful. I left the heated chamber and made my way up the twisting stair to the horrid little room where Mr Wild kept his gory pickings. I opened the door; it was unlocked. This room was cold. It was as vile as I remembered. I paced about, unable to shut out from the corners of my vision the bloodstained cloths, the manacles and padlocks and the coils of rope, all neatly labelled, all with their own sorry tale to tell. I stopped short.

There was a new display, upon a little table. I half guessed what it would be, even as I read the script.

"Jack Sheppard's manacles... the padlock first unlocked by Jack Sheppard on his great escape... a brick from the chimney up which Jack Sheppard climbed... a portion of the noose..."

My guts heaved. With my boot toe I kicked the wretched table across the room. I was standing amongst the wreckage, feeling — and no doubt looking — like a trapped dog as Jonathan Wild entered.

In he came, and stood, contemplatively, tapping his silver cane against his leg. To right and left of him Quilt Arnold and Abraham Mendez took up their positions, immobile, expressionless, like door posts.

Mr Wild's eyes surveyed the desecration of his shrine with no visible emotion whatsoever. This studied unconcern when I knew that he was experiencing something very different caused me more apprehension than if he had exploded into fury there and then. Unarmed and outnumbered I was pretty scared and I could not but suppose that my adversary surmised as much.

Jonathan Wild grimaced. "Those stairs!" he said. "Killers."

I looked blankly at him.

"Gout," he explained. "I get it in my toes. The right great toe particularly. No joke, Davy, gout. I pray that you'll be spared it."

"Amen," I said cautiously.

"Now," he said. "I have some cole for you."

"You have?" This was not the line I was expecting.

"The last but one ride you did for me, before your various disappearances. You brought me some pocket books and I owe you for it. Are you so wealthy now that you have forgotten?"

"I do remember."

"So," he said, and smiled. "You thought that you would save Jack Sheppard, eh?"

So now we came to it. I found my fists were clenched.

"I have no wish to speak of that," I said, "but since you have done so, sir, it did cross my mind that you have an odd way of keeping your word."

"You have to tell the odd lie in my business, Davy," he returned. "The end and the means, you understand. I had to have Jack Sheppard. I could not let him remain at large. He made me a laughing stock, with his darting round London, drinking in every tavern from here to Wapping. I thought you understood that."

"I do now."

"It was a clever plan," he said, taking a step closer to me. I stood my ground. "I too had heard about the chance of pulling back a half-hanged man from the jaws of death. I wondered if some rogue might try it. And there you were, Davy, all ready to foil my greatest triumph. It could not be allowed. You see that, don't you?" His eyes glazed over. He was talking partly to himself. "You see," he said, "I am invincible. No one can better me. I am the Law. I am at the centre of it all. You understand that, Davy. Don't you?"

I caught Quilt Arnold's eye. He nodded.

"Yes sir," I said uncomfortably.

"I've worked so hard for my success," Wild continued, much like a guilty child explaining a misdemeanour. "Don't suppose it has been easy. I was nothing — a poor buckle-maker from the Midland shires. No one understands the grind of it, the whittling away, the slow building up... and on all sides misunderstood. Some people, Davy, do not like me!"

"No sir," I said, uneasy and appalled.

"Years of my life," continued Jonathan in that awful dreamy voice. "Years to grow successful. It was cruel of you to try and take it from me."

"I ain't takin' it from you, Mr Wild." I was growing pretty

326

jittery. I just wanted to be out of there. "You said you had some cole for me," I prompted hopefully.

Wild blinked and stared me in the face. Then he moved to one side and stepped over to a table, mercifully clear of trophies. In some relief I followed him and stood and watched him count out a little pile of coins.

"Here you are, Davy. These are rightfully yours."

I put my hand down on the coins. Quick as a flash he banged his silver staff down on my hand. I yelled; the pain was fearsome. I stuffed my fist into my mouth, cupping my other hand around it. I backed away. I had believed him crazed and drifting. He was here all right now.

"You went for me at Tyburn!" he said accusingly. "I your master and you went for me! You took yourself off without my say so. I have not finished with you yet. When you can hold a pistol once again I'll have my moneysworth from you, you damned molly. You'll be out on that road day in, day out and you'll do it, or I'll have you hung up by your twatling strings. Till then you had best go seek employment with your fellow buggeranto Mr Hitchin and take your arse to Moorfields. Do you hear me?"

"Yes sir!" I said, backed against the door. Mendez and Arnold now bundled me through it and shoved me towards the stairs; but not before I caught a last glimpse of Jonathan Wild, down upon his knees, gathering up the scattered relics of Jack's imprisonment, and crooning over them, cradling them to his chest.

I grabbed hold of the banisters to get my balance; I thudded down the stairs at a great pace and so out into the street.

It was bitterly cold outside, but even the foul-smelling smoky air of Old Bailey seemed fresh compared with the place whence I had come. I walked I know not where, striding hither and yon to walk away my anger; I was also in no little pain, which added to my hatred of the villain who had caused it. Having assessed that I could move my fingers I perceived that my disability was not of a permanent nature; but my hand, the right, was swollen and discoloured and burned like the devil and of no use to me if I was obliged to defend myself against attack.

When my passion eased a little I found I had walked to Long Lane and I went into the Goat and took a cup of gin. The inn parlour was dark and musty. I sat on a bench with my back against the wall, knocked back the blue ruin, and fetched a long sigh, thinking of my recent confrontation.

I thought that Mr Wild had seemed odd in his manner, which

in no way consoled me as to my own case, but what stayed with me was his accusation 'you damned molly'. So Will Field had told him, had he? So now he had that hold over me as well, a pillory offence if he could prove it. And that jibe about Moorfields, where men paid for their pleasure on the Sodomites' Walk... your fellow buggeranto Mr Hitchin... Mr Hitchin, Under City Marshall.

Under City Marshall... surely this must count for something... surely it must mean that Mr Hitchin had some power...

A woman sidled up to me, a short fat repulsive drab nearer forty than thirty, and she nudged my arm and put her face against my shoulder.

"What a handsome gentleman it is," she wheezed. "It's not every day we see the likes of you in here, sir. You know, sir," she continued, "my life has not been easy. Men have been unkind. I was old before my time. And it's my misfortune that I prefer handsome men. But they would never look at me. I had to take what I could get..."

I blinked. This was Grizel Peabody. This was the dame whose messenger I became when they sent me out from school to make myself useful, she who would not cross Moorfields because it was a filthy place. I remembered her particular grumbles and her great capacity to laugh at what to most would seem misfortune.

Thanks to her I had met that day some of the most celebrated names of our time — Isaac Rag, Badger Riddlesdon... I would have met Obadiah Lemon if he had not been in the debtors' prison. Inside those walls that day, unknown to me, was Mr Jonathan Wild himself, a nobody, a man scraping acquaintants among his fellow riff-raff, a man about to begin his career of deception and crime. Like a great net, the city of London encircled us all, binding us in, small fry and large, emeshed in its coils, now jostled together, now separated, now pushed up against each other, rolling round in its tangled confines.

"I had to take what I could get," said Grizel Peabody.

"Life ain't easy," I agreed.

How doleful I had been upon that day! Too young and too poor to ride off up the Great North Road, and aching in the heart because they'd taken Jack away from school, what had I done? I'd looked into the window of the Blue Boar, Barbican, and through the dark whorled glass I had seen the kindly ugly face of Mr Hitchin, a man for whom, upon reflection, I found I could not help but feel a curious if misguided affection. He had beckoned me inside and given me advice, a beef pie and a kiss, and told me he would have me in the end.

I began to laugh, seeing the way my thoughts were tending.

Grizel Peabody, surprised, joined in, with great hiccoughing guffaws. "That's the way," she said. "Find something to laugh at — that's the way. Why, only last week I saw a slate come tumbling off a roof and hit a fellow on the head, and when he looked up to see what had hit him he put his foot in a great hole in the ground and tumbled in. I never laughed so much in all my life to see him disappear."

The day was yet young, or not too far from middle age. It was not improbable that Mr Charles Hitchin even now was sitting in the Blue Boar by a warm fire eating beef pie and perusing lists of missing property where words like 'gold' and 'stolen' and 'pocket books' and 'reward' were like to figure largely.

I left Grizel Peabody the price of a decent meal and said farewell; then I set off in the direction of Barbican.

Chapter Forty-Six

IN some respects it might be said that little had changed in the intervening years. The Blue Boar, Barbican, still had dark whorled-glass windows. The inn sign yet creaked lopsidedly. Mr Charles Hitchin was seated at a table in the window bay in his braided coat, his three-cornered hat upon the seat beside him.

Mr Charles Hitchin had changed a little. He was grown bulkier with the years. He would be now about fifty years of age. His waistcoat bulged, the dainty buttons barely containing the heaving breathing of the mass beneath. His face had become rounder, his eyes more sunken in their flaccid bags, his chins piled one atop the other above his cloth cravat. He wore a light tie wig. It had slipped a little to one side.

I too had changed. Where before the high-backed settle had seemed very large and tall, now it did not, and I filled my place there with a man's completeness.

"Good day to thee, Mr Davy Gadd," said Mr Hitchin. "I would ask thee to sit down, but thee has already done so. Sure of thee welcome, eh?"

"We are old friends, Mr Hitchin, are we not? So you told Mistress Clap when you visited her house in your capacity of Under City Marshall, keeper of the Law."

"It is true that I am a person of some importance," said Mr

Hitchin comfortably. "I should offer thee wine. Shall thee partake?"

I took a glass and any number of the biscuits on the plate he offered; I was ravenously hungry.

"Ah, thee's hurt thee hand," he said and touched it. An angry weal a good two inches wide was now raised from wrist to knuckle.

"I walked into somebody's silver staff."

"So," said Mr Hitchin, "thee has fallen out with the buckle maker?"

"Mr Hitchin," I leaned forward urgently. "You said yourself you are a person of some importance. You surely do possess powers far more than common. There can be no love lost between you and Jonathan Wild. You know his hypocrisy and double dealing — how he persuades the world that he is a thief catcher working for the general good to rid the streets of crime, and all along he is the power behind that crime."

"Zounds now! Be careful in thee accusations, Davy!"

"Let's not waste time in games of that kind, Mr Hitchin. I know it and you know it. What I need to hear is whether you can put a stop to it. You must have friends in high places. And you understand the working of the Law. Is there not a law that deals with such as Mr Wild?"

"Jonathan is a very clever man."

"He used to be, in setting up his empire. But I believe he is not what he was. I believe that he could be led to make mistakes. I think he has become a little crazed."

"I understand thee," Mr Hitchin said. "He has had too much power for too long. He believes himself a cut above the rest. And I have remarked some oddities in his manner. Since he must be protected all the time from enemies, he must retire a little from the world; but maybe also in his head. And thee is right — laws there are. But sometimes justice needs a little nudge."

"Mr Hitchin! You are the man to do it!"

"But Davy," Mr Hitchin said, "who is the man to nudge me?"

I suppose that foolishly I had hoped it would not come to this. But I had known it would, and must confess to no surprise.

"What would it take, Mr Hitchin, for you to set the wheels in motion?"

"Which wheels in particular, Davy?"

"Any course of action which would lead to Mr Wild's arrest and trial... and hanging."

"Does thee so hate the man?"

"He had the power to save Jack Sheppard. He could have got

him transportation at his trial. Then later at the Triple Tree he could have stood back and let Jack's friends attempt a rash rescue. And he has me in thrall," I finished in despair.

"Fortunate he," said Mr Hitchin drily. "Another biscuit?"

"Mr Hitchin," I said. "Will you work to bring down Jonathan Wild? I know you mislike him; everyone knows it. You would be following your natural inclinations."

"Aye... my natural inclinations..." He was looking at me in a manner that needed no interpreting. I looked down at the biscuits.

"If I was to do as thee wish," said Mr Hitchin, "and work against whom thee hate... at thee request — at thee particular request — then thee would be in my debt and thee would owe me... one favour for another."

"It could be seen so, yes."

"It would be so. It would most certainly be so."

"Yes, I suppose that it would," I reluctantly agreed.

"I saw thee at the molly house, in most becoming rags. In the rents of thee breeches a little of thee flesh was to be seen. I found it teasing and pleasing."

I waited, toying with the biscuits. He suddenly slapped my fingers. "Davy! Other folk may want to eat the biscuits thee is mauling with thee dirty fingers!"

I began to laugh at the incongruity of our position. "What, are you my tutor?" I enquired.

He also smiled. "There is that I could teach thee," he admitted.

"If it includes honesty," said I. "I mean the keeping of a bargain."

"I will keep any bargain," he said with a lewd leer.

"But can you promise me his arrest? Nothing less will do."

"I believe I can. Ah, Zounds, I know I can. But this is a corrupt age, Davy. Nothing is done for nothing. What will thee do for me in return?"

"What," I coughed, "had you in mind?"

"Thee company tonight." For a stupid moment I wondered whether company was all he wanted. But I had not misread my man. He added bluntly: "Zounds, what does thee think? I want to fuck thee."

"And if you do so, and are unable to arrest him?"

"Then I shall have good memories, and thee must learn the uses of philosophy."

I smiled in spite of myself.

"What does thee say then, sweetheart?" Mr Hitchin wheedled.

"Have we a bargain?"

"One night," I said.

"At Mistress Clap's?"

"No, not there. Somewhere else."

"A reputation to preserve, eh? Very well. Do thee know Mr Wright's molly house in Beech Lane?"

"No."

"Next door to the Queen's Head. An old house, with a great brass knocker shaped like a laughing fox."

"Is it a place like Mother Clap's?"

"Mostly. But Mr Wright, unlike the lovely Mistress Clap, makes use of the facilities. One of which, by the way, is Tommy Newton, whose presence is a great enticer. Whereas the lovely lady rules her house with maternal graces, Mr Wright is not so particular. Money changes hands a deal more often there. At Ma Clap's there is more sweet affection."

"I've met Tommy Newton. He was the prize for a masquerade we had. Someone said he was the neighbourhood whore."

"Tommy picks and chooses; and as I was once one of those choices I have to admit that Tom shows some discrimination. But let's not talk of whores and sluts. Thee and me are old friends. So, go thee to Mr Wright's house at dusk; tell him to make ready Mr Hitchin's chamber and wait there for me. Oh and sweetheart," added he, "without thee clothes. I hate to waste time undoing buttons."

Mr Hitchin gathered up his hat and papers and shuffled from his seat. After he had gone I moved to a shadowed alcove and ordered a substantial meal and ate my way through several courses as the afternoon wore on. I have to admit that I was not entirely comfortable about the proposition I had undertaken, particularly as we had just dismissed Tom Newton with a shrug for being a whore. At that moment I did not consider myself so very different from him. However, barter is acceptable coinage in this wicked age of ours, and a chap's body is his own to do with as he wishes. I could no longer tolerate my servitude to Mr Wild, nor indeed any further close proximity to his person. If the law did not bring him down I knew that I would end up shooting him myself; and I had no wish to spend my life on the run evading a charge of murder, or to tackle the steps and the string even for so worthy a cause.

I found, however, that whereas I was able to justify my proposed course of action adequately to myself, I had no particular desire to bump into anyone I knew who might ask me where I was going; therefore I spent the afternoon where I was, and dozed undisturbed, till dusk.

The month being January, the darkening came early, and the lanthorns above the doors were lit when I left the tavern. It was raining, pretty cold and bleak, the rain like golden needles in the lamplight, and the mucky wet streets glimmering where the puddles caught the light.

Mr Wright's molly house was easy to find. The door was open, with a lamp glowing above it, and a couple of chaps were going in, their arms about each other, hands on each other's bums. After they had gone inside, someone looked out of the doorway, up and down the street, and was about to shut the door when he saw me and waited. "Coming in?" he said.

Although the last time I had seen him he had been naked and I had therefore paid more attention to his body than his face, I recognized Tommy Newton. He was in his late twenties. He had dark hair, thick and short, a small forehead, a well-shaped nose and a small mean mouth. There was a hard line to his lips; his eyes also were hard, his brows dark. He had big hands but he was slight across the chest, and wiry. He wore tight breeches and a shirt unbuttoned to the waist. I knew he had a firm round arse and a good-sized cock, and he was standing very provocatively, draped around the door jamb, one hand on his hip, crotch thrust forward, and his head jerked enquiringly to one side.

"Mm," he said and looked me up and down. "Tasty."

"You too," I said.

"Want to bugger me?" he said.

"I'm with Mr Hitchin," I hedged, basely wondering whether there was time before my patron arrived, to take advantage of the offer.

"I charge two guineas," added Tommy, which made up my mind for me.

"I'd best go in and wait for him."

"I'll show you the way." He unwound himself from the door. "Thomas!" he called, peering in through a door on the left. He turned to me. "Mr Wright and I have the same name. And the same tastes! Thomas!" he called again into what seemed to be a crowded room and was proved to be so by the throaty guffaws that greeted his revelation: "Here's one of Mr Hitchin's bum boys come to use the room — get Toby to take the tub up." He smirked. "Mr Hitchin likes his poppets clean to start with, however they may finish up. Follow me."

The stairs were dark and twisty and led to a narrow passage

with uneven floorboards and a low ceiling, latched doors leading off. We went into a room at the back. Tommy lit a great branched candelabra which stood on a table. It showed a biggish room containing a big old four-poster bed and some cumbersome chairs. The window curtains were drawn. There was a little smoky fire in the chimney place.

"You'll be pretty cosy in here," said Tommy. He eyed me speculatively. "Have you done much of it?"

"Of what?"

"Buggery of course — wotcher fink?"

I looked around the room.

"You don't like me teasin' yer, do yer?" he said, sidling up to me.

"What are you still here for? Haven't you got no cocks to suck or something?"

"Ooh! Peevish!" he said with an affected mince. "All right, I'm going." He stood in the doorway. He offered a parting shot before leaving. "Sleep well. But you won't sleep much tonight if I know Mr Hitchin. And I do."

I kicked the fire into life. In came Toby, a heavily built manservant carrying a bath tub, and then to and fro with buckets of hot water. He said nothing, which was a relief to me, as Tommy Newton had been right about the teasing. When he had finished and left I took off my clothes and had a bath before the fire and padded over to the bed. The sheets were cold. I could hear a buzz of conversation from the room below, with a sudden shriek of mirth and longer bouts of hearty laughter. I sat there, knees drawn up to my chin and wondered what kind of a pickle I had got myself into.

I did not have long to wait. In came a great draught of cold air and Mr Hitchin, who stood and opened wide his arms. "Well now, Davy! Come and kiss me!"

I got out of bed and went to him and put myself against his person, and his arms enclosed me in a great bear hug, pressing me so tightly that the buttons of his waistcoat imprinted my skin. His mouth clamped on to mine, his tongue went in so deep I all but swallowed it and there we remained till he had had his fill. "Help me off with my coat," he said.

"Now stand thee by the fire," he said, and he sat down at the table by the candelabra with all appearance of ease, and by his observations about the loveliness of the fireglow upon the human skin, the amber tints upon the flesh, the play of light and shadow, I perceived that Mr Hitchin must be something of an artist, an appreciator of life's varied forms. He lifted up a hand bell and rang it vigorously, and in came Toby once again, bearing a tray of steaming food, and Tommy Newton bearing wine, a bottle in both fists, and winking like someone with a pretty bad twitch.

"Thank you," Mr Hitchin said tranquilly. "And now I think we have all we need and we don't expect to be disturbed."

"Just as you say, Mr Hitchin," Tommy said obligingly as they withdrew. "I wish you both a happy night."

Although I thought it somewhat odd to sit with nothing but a blanket round my shoulders in the company of Mr Hitchin in his winter garments, it was certainly a decent meal and plenty of it — a dish of beef swimming in red wine, and a lemon syllabub with white wine and browned cream. We talked most conversationally of London Life and Roads I have Known, and what makes a good horse, and which were the best coffee houses — this latter a monologue, I having nothing to contribute. The room was well supplied, in that it had its own close-stool in a little closet, so no one need tramp outside into the chilly air; a person could live pretty comfortably here. Mr Hitchin rang the bell, and Toby came to take away the tray. Beneath us in the room downstairs a fiddler set up and tuned, and there was dancing down there, which went on merrily most of the night.

"Sit thee on my knee," said Mr Hitchin, and I did so, with my arm about his neck, and he handled me till I was hard, and kissed me and got me to unlace his breeches and sit astride him, and he told me not to stint myself but to go on and emit upon his belly, which I did; and all the while he held me round the arse, cupping my cheeks, his fingers digging in my flesh. Then he told me to go down upon my knees between his thighs. He pressed my face against the wetness of his belly. I could sense him holding back, prolonging his enjoyment.

"Quick, over the bed," he said; and I got up and did as he bid, and he stood behind me and entered me and took his pleasure on me, coming with such sounds as left me in no doubt of his satisfaction. As for myself it had been some time since I had participated in the Pleasant Deed and must admit I gasped a bit at first; but, a little to my surprise, enjoyment rapidly supervened. We then washed ourselves and lay upon the bed.

Mr Hitchin, however, had no intention of wasting the night in sleep. He did not take off his clothes, except for his buckled shoes, but lay there in his shirt, waistcoat and breeches, with his hand between my thighs, and we passed the night thus, dozing, while he waited for the renewal of his strength. Nature being as it is, and he a man whom portliness had rendered less active than a leaner man of his age, once more was all he could achieve, but with such honest relish in what he was about as left me in no doubt of his appreciation of me, and my own pleasure in his treatment of me was lively also.

Afterwards he fell asleep, and snored so loud that if it had not been for the fiddlers' tunes downstairs I am sure the whole house would have heard him; and I lay in his noisy embrace and reflected on life's devious courses.

In the morning Mr Hitchin became brisk and businesslike. He rang for Toby to bring fresh water and take away the old. We washed, we dressed, and we had breakfast.

"Well then, Davy," Mr Hitchin said, stirring his tea. "Thee did not pass too terrible a night, I think?"

I mumbled something.

"Not as bad as thee feared, perhaps?"

"No sir," I admitted.

"The business being not without some small enjoyment for theeself?"

I agreed that such had been the case.

"Myself," said Mr Hitchin stretching, "am well content. Thee are a good fuck, Davy."

"I am pleased to hear it, Mr Hitchin." It was true that I had striven to fulfil my part of the bargain with wholeheartedness, but now I wondered modestly whether Mr Hitchin would consider twice an adequate amount in exchange for the arrest of Jonathan Wild.

"Mr Hitchin," I said urgently. "You won't forget? You'll see to the matter which we spoke of?"

"I'll do my best," said Mr Hitchin. "It won't be easy, mind. I'll have to work to change the minds of all the magistrates. Hard-hearted men. It'll take all my guile and cunning."

"I do appreciate it, Mr Hitchin. It's real good of you."

He beamed and nodded. He certainly seemed content enough. I helped him tie his cravat and fix his sword. He gave me a parting kiss and a pat on the bum and went on his way whistling.

I was unable to quit that place without a further encounter with Tommy Newton, who had certainly been lurking in the passageway and greeted me with a fleer.

"Not too sore, dear? He's a very devil, isn't he? And not a young man. I hope I'm that spry when I'm fifty!"

"The pox'll get you first," I answered waspishly.

Two weeks later they arrested Jonathan Wild. Five days after that he was in Newgate. I was pretty smug about my own part in his downfall, and though naturally I told no one about it, privately I claimed all the credit. I thought of Mr Hitchin with the greatest affection. What an honourable gentleman! What an easy and delightful bargain we had made — what a pleasure it had been to do his bidding!

I bumped into Tubs in Holborn. I recognized his coach, and waved to him. He gave orders for his coach to pull up, and called me in beside him, saying he would take me to the Rose to celebrate with the very best claret.

"We'll drink the night away," he promised. "You and I have some droll memories of the Rose, have we not, and a mutual friend at last avenged. Some merriment, I think, is called for, and no expense spared!"

"Who'd have thought it?" I sighed rapturously, settling into the plush. "Jonathan Wild arrested! Jonathan Wild in Newgate! Who'd have thought it!"

"Who?" laughed Tubs. "Well, I would, for one. We've been after Mr Wild for weeks now. I was talking about it to Sir John Fryer only yesterday. The magistrates have been drawing up a list of charges since before Christmastide. It was only a matter of time... Davy? You look surprised. Did you think it was a sudden matter?"

"What — all the magistrates agreed?" I said blankly.

"Of course! The greatest villain of our time? What else would they do?"

"They needed no persuading? No one particular person worked hard to convince them that this was the right and proper thing to do? Mr Hitchin, for example?"

"Lord, no — there was no need. They could hardly wait to draw up the charges! Davy? Why? Is anything the matter?"

I began to laugh.

"No. Just take me to the Rose."

Chapter Forty-Seven

THE news of Mr Jonathan Wild's arrest was brought to me at Mother Clap's by Harry Radley, who had better reason than most to know about it, because his was the coach that took the prisoner to the magistrates.

We were sitting around Ma Clap's kitchen table — there was herself, and Billy Griffin and Thomas Phillips who both lodged at the house. We were eating potato soup, and Ma was ladling it out from a great steaming pot. She loved to play the mother to her lads, and we were pretty happy that she should. When she heard the disturbance at the door she hurried out, returning with a very merry countenance.

"Someone to see you, Davy," Ma Clap said.

Harry's hair was soaking wet and plastered to his head. Rain-drops dribbled down his face. They say the bearer of good tidings becomes beautiful. Something about feet upon the mountaintops. I could not see Harry's feet, but his face was the loveliest thing I had ever seen.

He dried his hands before the fire.

"I was driving along Rose Street," he said, "empty and for hire. There was a crowd gathered. I had to pull up as I could not get past. Then this chap says to me: hey, coachy, wait there — we'll be need-ing you in just a moment. I could see he was someone of a certain importance. It turns out he was the High Constable of Holborn. Then they brought out Jonathan Wild, and all the people jeered and clamoured, and Mr Wild protested. He said: 'I wonder, good peo-ple, what it is you would see? I am a poor honest man who have done all I could to serve the people who have had the misfortune to lose their goods by the villainy of thieves. Why do you insult me? I never injured any of you. Look at me, lame in body and afflicted in mind...' And then he did something with his hip, Davy, so his leg went out of joint, and walked oddly as if he were a cripple. But then when he got into the coach he put it back; I could not help but marvel at it. I heard the crack it made as it went back in place."

"It is one of his tricks," I murmured, stunned as I tried to take in the sense of Harry's account. I still could not believe it.

"Arrested, Harry? Truly arrested?"

"True as I stand here," said Harry steaming in the warmth. "And believing him a villain, black in heart and mind, I was sur-prised to see the way he went to pieces. 'Please don't use me ill,' he whimpered. 'It is not fair.' And I thought to myself 'Aha! There'll be a deal of folk made happy by this day's work! And one of them'll be Davy Gadd.' Eh, Davy?"

"Ah, Harry, if your news be true I'll kiss your feet!" I cried, still cherishing the Biblical notion of those feet upon the mountain-tops, that brought good news.

Harry looked thoughtfully at his muddy boots and then at me, as if he thought it would be no bad idea; but Ma began to pace about between us, swishing her skirts and shaking her head.

"I call that a pretty sad business," she said.

"What? Why so?" said Harry.

"That a chap is taken to the magistrates and all that may be said of him is good riddance! He must be hated and despised by everyone who knows him. Who will have a good word to say for such a monster? What will happen to him?"

"He'll get off," I said morosely. "He has the magistrates in his pocket. Or so he has always said."

"So we must not celebrate yet, then?" said Harry with a disconsolate expression and another glance down at his boots.

"Stay and have some soup," said Ma.

"No, I've left my coach with a boy holding the horses; best be off."

The next three months proved to be a very odd time indeed. From April onward there was incessant rain and gales, and everyone dolefully promised a disastrous harvest. People were wary and ill at ease. No one knew who was going to peach their neighbour and bring him down in the wake of Jonathan. I met Will Field once, at the Cat and Fiddle. He was pretty glum.

"I went to the magistrates," he said. "I offered to peach Mr Wild, like you suggested. I reckoned that was damned generous of me. I could have told 'em a good deal. Know what they said? I'd peached so many in my time I wasn't no use as an Evidence!"

I laughed, but hollowly. We were all apprehensive. Dozens of chaps were arrested. Rumour had it that Mr Wild was going to name all his associates in return for his release. No one slept easy. But Will Field and I did not peach one another, which we well could have done. The world as we knew it, vile and corrupt, yet with its own curious rules and logic, was disintegrating; maybe we were bound somehow in brotherhood. But anyway, Will Field was in the business pretty deep, and there were plenty of others after his guts. Quilt Arnold was arrested. Will Field peached Mendez; Mendez peached Will Field. Will Field came to trial, but got off. Mendez went to prison. Everybody seemed to think that now that Mr Wild was taken, Mr Hitchin would be next to go.

Jonathan Wild was charged with many crimes, among them buying stolen goods; keeping company with villains, highwaymen, pickpockets, housebreakers and thieves; and seeming to bring thieves to justice but only peaching those that would not work for him; and procuring false evidences to swear persons into facts they were not guilty of.

In his prison he took mercury ointment, but it failed to have the desired effect and did not kill him, only caused his teeth to fall out. Everything he did was grotesque.

I found that I could think of nothing else. I was drawn to Newgate walls. I kept pacing to and fro in the rain beside the grim place, looking up at the barred windows, undeterred by the vile stench that hung upon the air. It seemed to be composed of all that was contained therein, but finely distilled, ready to be bottled and sold as an example of all that symbolized this wicked age — body sweat, sir-reverence, rotted meat, beer, the sickly sweet fevers of the plague, rancid breath in a confined space, strong perfume to disguise the other; fear, corruption, lust...

And now, having sent so many there ahead of him, Jonathan was there. In my fancy he grew monstrous, more than human. Toothless, with a skull like a cracked egg, a quill pen in his talons, ready to betray all those whom he considered enemies, writing letters to the corrupt and powerful, promising information, lies, anything, in return for freedom, life. I perceived him growing larger, like some creature of myth, spreading like a jelly, oozing from beneath a door, till the door burst open, the very walls cracking under the pressure. Could mere brick and stone contain him? I caught myself leaning a shoulder to the stonework, testing its strength, making sure no man could push his way out; and I laughed and half began to suspect my reason.

One day I saw Constable Willis coming out of the Lodge. I made myself known to him.

"Have you perhaps been visiting Jonathan Wild, sir?"

"I have seen Mr Wild, yes, though that was not the purpose of my visit. I am pleased to see you looking better than you did when I last spoke with you. Are you in honest employment now, I hope?"

"Oh yes," I lied. "Working with horses. And how did you find Mr Wild, sir? A strange business, is it not? His seeming to be such an honest man..."

"As to that, it is not for me to say," said Constable Willis gravely. "The jury will decide that when he comes to trial. But his case is a sorry one, I will say that. He has no religion to console him in his hour of need. He seems to have no conception of Almighty God. He knows nothing of Heaven or of Divine Mercy. His ignorance upon these matters is incredible, and may partly be the cause of his being where he is today."

"Let us hope he remains there, if he is bad as people say."

"Charity, Davy," Constable Willis reproved. I recalled that I had heard that Constable Willis belonged to the Society for the Reformation of Manners — a Holy! He continued in crusading vein: "A man that knows not the Lord is to be pitied. I did attempt to rectify this sad omission. I spoke to him about Our Lord. He did not seem to understand the seriousness of his position, but quipped and jested. 'Come, man,' said I, 'if things fall ill with you, you are like to be hanged.' 'What is hanging,' said he, 'but a dance without music?'"

"I see it as something other," I said.

"As do I. I have witnessed any number, but each case is as awesome as the last, and leaves a man bad dreams."

"*Will* he be hanged?" said I.

"Let justice take its course," was all the hope that Constable Willis could promise me.

Meanwhile the case against Jonathan Wild was prepared, and the rain poured down and the blossom gusted from the trees and speckled the gutters and the horse dung with petals of white and rose.

Jonathan Wild was brought to trial in May at the Old Bailey. He was found guilty and sentenced to death. He took laudanum in his cell, but once again he failed to carry himself off; and he was taken to Tyburn slumped in the coffin cart in a doped condition, with the crowd in the streets throwing bottles and stones. I saw him hanged; and Mr Hitchin rode in the procession.

But I learned an odd lesson — pain is a strong emotion, triumph a weak one. After Jack's death I suffered greatly, but after Wild's there was no corresponding elation; only an emptiness where the hatred for Jonathan had been, and before that, the love for Jack.

One night a few days after the hanging, Lucinda and I went to Ma Clap's to catch up on the gossip. Billy Griffin, Ma Clap's lodger, came rolling home, singing at the top of his voice. And for why? Because he had buggered Tommy Newton and it had been a joy beyond his wildest dreams. Everyone congratulated him, but all that I could feel was envy, envy, envy, to find cause for singing over so simple a matter. It struck me pretty forcibly that I had had enough of being the plaything of the great emotions — love and hatred left your heart in tatters, possessed you, weakened your judgement. London wore you down, made you jittery and nervous.

I was scowling amongst so many that were merry. I said aloud and sourly to the one that stood beside me:

"I don't think the answer lies in fucking Tommy Newton."

It was Harry Radley. He said — but so angrily that I was startled: "Perhaps you should try fucking someone else." And then he strode away with never a backward glance.

Now what cause had I given him for such a display? People were so difficult, with their unfathomable motives and reactions and I had had enough of them. A good horse was worth 'em all.

I found my mind was filling once again with images of the road, the road that always served as panacea for my pains, the road amongst whose wildernesses and open spaces I would clear my head and find my strength and solace.

Next day I retrieved faithful Gry and headed north.

That summer Will Field's luck ran out. When Abraham Mendez came out of prison he took his revenge and peached Will Field and got him on a charge of receiving. Will was sent to Newgate. His sentence was for one year; and when I thought about his lean hard body and his lizard eyes I thought it was a waste and a shame.

Again that summer Gabriel Lawrence fought with his religious principles and lost. He buggered Tommy Newton at Mr Wright's molly house. Peter Bavidge was beside himself with fury. What was it about Tommy Newton? He was everybody's heart's desire! Whoever had him raved about it afterwards. Gabriel had desired him constantly for months, one hand on his Bible, the other elsewhere. And now he had achieved his satisfaction.

Will Field, Tommy Newton... reason and morality have no place in the tortuous meanderings of lust.

Something of the same was on my mind when I returned to London in November.

Chapter Forty-Eight

"AND are you back for good?" said Harry Radley. "You and your old gipsy nag?"

"I daresay," I replied.

"The road too rough for you in November?" he said, curling his lip.

We glowered inimically at one another. He was whittling the dry mud off the wheels of his coach, kneeling on a wad of sacking in the stable yard of the Falcon Inn. I was leaning against the doorpost watching him, and Gry beside me, while the autumn wind shifted the loose straw idly over the flagstones.

Harry paused in his work, eyeing me from brows so nearly

drawn together as to almost make a frown.

"A fine-weather traveller?" he continued, needling me.

"I've been on the road in all weathers," I shrugged. "I don't fear no storms."

"That's as maybe," he said, standing up. He was taller than me, and pretty broad, his neck thick and his arms powerful. His blue eyes pierced my self-command.

"From what I've seen of you," he said, "you take to the road as some take laudanum."

"Maybe I do, but what's it to you, Harry Radley?" I said stung.

"More than I want, damn you," answered Harry. Then he reached and threw a cloth at me; I caught it. "Suppose you make yourself useful polishing my door, instead of leaning there like a curtain?"

I led Gry carefully into the stable yard.

"I'll see to this old crock," he said and took the bridle.

I laughed scornfully. "Gry won't let you touch him."

"We'll see about that," he said.

I gawped as Gry went placidly with Harry into the stable, where Harry's own horses waited in their stalls. I followed him in.

"He treats you like a friend," I said.

"I am a friend," he said.

"You handle him as if you know him."

"And so I do," shrugged Harry. "Who do you think looked after him when you were sick at Mother Clap's in those weeks after Sheppard died?"

"Well, I thought George did," I said blankly.

"George? What does he know about a decent beast like this? All he knows is that plodder that pulls his meat cart."

"You saw to Gry while I was at Ma Clap's..." I marvelled.

"I'm good with horses," Harry laughed.

"Yes. I remember how well Gry was looking; I was impressed."

"We didn't tell you, since you'd asked George to do it. You have a damn good horse there, wiser than most men I know; and certainly wiser than you."

"Yes, I know. Thankyou, Harry; it was real good of you."

"Didn't I tell you to polish my coach?"

There was a deal of metal on Harry's small town coach. Studs edged the roof and base, each window was framed, and on the doors an embossed design. It was a pretty smart coach.

"You have struck luckier than you know," I called. "I am a skilful hand at polishing coach doors. My dad was a chair man. He had the best chair in London. We used to polish that chair like it was holy."

"Let's see you do it then, or I shall believe you an idle braggart."

Now Harry leaned against the door post watching me.

"I thought you were seeing to Gry," I said.

"Gry will wait."

I began to polish.

"You won't need that handsome coat," said Harry.

I took it off and handed it to him.

"Nor the embroidered waistcoat," he continued.

I gave the waistcoat to him. I polished his coach. After a while, warm and dishevelled, I said: "Harry? What's the point in my polishing the studs and shafts on your coach? The first time you take it out, the streets being what they are, this coach will be mud-spattered and all my efforts for nothing."

"The point of it is the pleasure I now take in seeing you do it, in your shirt, and your tight breeches."

I turned back to my polishing, more thoughtful than before.

"Davy," Harry said. "I'm short of a chap to see to the horses."

"Are you?"

"I always am. They never stay long. You can't get a dependable lad."

"I'm not a dependable lad."

"I know that. But you know about horses. You can bring that mangy old nag of yours along and stable him here. There's a stable loft above where you can bed down. Or if we find that we get on together you might move in with me. I have a room here at the inn. But that's as may be. If you'd like to work with me I would be glad of your help. What do you say?"

"I say yes. For a while."

"For a while? Why? What's more important to you?"

"Some business on the Great North Road."

I stepped back and admired my handiwork. Those brass studs gleamed.

"That holy chair of yours," said Harry. "What was it like?"

"What, my dad's chair?" I laughed. "A damn sight prettier than this old rattler. It was like a throne. There were naked nymphs all over it, and leaves and flowers and fringes, and birds and creatures; and ivy leaves and roses... I haven't thought of it in years. The crazy fellow loved it like it was a woman. Or an altar. If I didn't polish it right, he clouted me."

"Now you are putting ideas into my head," said Harry.

I grinned. "Now why would you want to do that, clout me?"

"Thwarted desire, I guess," said Harry ruefully. "Do you remember our first meeting? Under the stairs at Mother Clap's?"

"Of course I do. How could I not?"

"It must have occurred to you I would have liked to know you better," Harry said. "But every time I have been close to you since then, you were in love with someone else. Or if you weren't in love you were prowling about after Jonathan Wild. You had no time for anything but that."

"Well," I said lightly, "I am not in love with anybody this time."

Harry grunted sourly. "For all I know you have some little sweetheart up in York or Lincoln waiting for you."

"I haven't, no, truly I haven't," I laughed.

"What is it then? You said you had some business on the road."

"It isn't what you think. It's something else."

Then Harry frowned. "Did you come directly here? I mean, am I your first port of call?"

"Yes."

"Not Lucinda?"

"No."

"Mother Clap?"

"No."

"Well, damn me, what kind of host am I? Get you inside and get you a meal. I'll join you when I've finished with Gry."

I was munching my way through a roast chicken when Harry came into the inn parlour and sat down at my table.

"You know that holy chair of yours," he said. "The one with the bare doxies and the birds and roses on it — I know where it is."

"Never!" I laughed. "How do you know?"

"I've seen it. I'll tell you how it came about. The chap that used to own it died. But he hadn't the same name as you. Mind, it was something short. It was Bate."

"That's right. He was the back end of the chair."

"When he died this other chap had it, and this was the chap I knew, and he only had it a short while when a gentleman bought it, one he was carrying, who took a fancy to it."

"A gentleman bought that chair? Whatever for?"

"It took his fancy. I'll show you where it is. I'll take you there now if you like. In the coach you have so beautifully polished."

I laughed. "All right. Where is it?"

"Just up Gray's Inn Lane. You can ride up beside me if you

like."

I helped Harry harness up the horses — Boxer, Star, Rowan and Colly. We drove out into the miry streets, and so up Gray's Inn Lane. Soon we were out amongst the fields that flanked the road to Hampstead and Highgate. A short distance from the town and we came to a high stone wall that plainly surrounded parkland and gardens. Harry drew rein and the four horses came to a standstill. He jumped down to give me a leg up to look over the wall, and went back to the horses. I sat astride the wall.

There in the grass below, between two stone statues, stood that same sedan chair that I had tended as a lad, with all its nymphs and foliage, the chair in which I found my old Dad dead. A rich man's folly, now it stood, in a carpet of yellow leaves, wound about with ivy leaves, whose curly tendrils twined inside the windows and out again, while about it tumbled in the wind the russet leaves of autumn.

I dropped back to earth, and regained my seat beside my coachy.

"My father died in that chair," I remarked. "I found him stiff and staring. That chair was his pride and joy."

"In the summer," Harry said, "it's covered with flowers."

We drove back to London. As we came slowly into the town a man asked if we were for hire. We took him down to the Strand, and so were paid for our indulgent trip. As we came towards the Falcon Harry said: "So, are you working for me, then?" He gave a crooked smile. "For a while."

"I said I would."

"Then help me with the horses."

We worked together, and I began to get to know the four, and the two still in their stalls. It was agreeable, companionable. When we finished Harry said: "Now clean the mud from the coach, so it begins tomorrow afresh."

I raised my eyebrows. "And what will you be doing?"

"I'll be in the Falcon, ordering us a meal. You know how coachies are — they strut about and think that they are lords of the road. Join me by the hearth when you are finished."

As dusk fell we were each side of the fireplace, our boots steaming gently in the warmth, and a fat tabby cat dozing between us. Harry leaned forward.

"So what is special about the road? What did you do this summer when you quit the town?"

"I looked for gold."

"Did you find any?"

"Yes. I always do; that's the pleasure of it. Buckles, pins, rings — the north road is a treasure house if you want baubles from the earth. I have a pendant made of leather and glass." I took it from my inner pocket. I let it dangle from my forefinger, so that the firelight caught it. It hung and glimmered there. The cat looked up and watched it sway. "It belonged to a treasure hunter, Jerry Dowlan, who taught me how to look for gold. Over metal it will quiver as if it had life in it. Then it swings violently round in a circle. That usually means gold. Sometimes it makes the wrist ache. It's an odd business. I don't understand it. When I work it, it takes me over — I forget time and place."

"And friends," said Harry.

"I told Lucinda I was going; I told Ma; and I'm laden down with gifts for 'em now I'm back."

"Did you not think you'd be missed?"

"No," I shrugged. I carefully replaced the pendulum.

"Anything can happen on the road," Harry said. "Folk fear the worst."

"I can look after myself all right. I don't like being bound."

"You would sooner look for gold."

"A particular gold. Claude Duval's gold."

"And what is that?"

"A thousand guineas, Harry, somewhere on the north road between Tollentone and Alconbury. I've been looking for it all my life." It sounded a curiously pointless thing to have been doing as I looked into Harry's bleak unsympathetic gaze. "I'm not the only one," I added defensively. "Clever men — lords — have devoted their time to this same search. And come away as disappointed."

"Then why do it?" Harry asked, eminently reasonable.

I remembered Lord Staughton, when he once explained the same to me. "It's a hope, a dream, a kind of joining with Duval, becoming one with him. It gives meaning to each day, because of the search, and you discover things, as you search."

"Is that so?" said Harry, plainly unimpressed.

"Pox on it," I said irritably. "Why should I bother to give you account of that you do not please to understand?"

"Why?" said Harry. "Because I want to take you to my bed and would have more of you than use of your pretty arse."

My throat tightened. "But what more?" I asked cautiously.

"Your friendship," Harry answered bluntly, "and that means some amount of trust and confidence, the which, I think, you do not readily give."

"That is not easy to explain without whingeing," I said uncomfortably. "Simply there has been from my boyhood some indifference from whom I would have preferred stronger emotion, and where I have felt affection, there has been loss."

"It is already a year since Jack Sheppard died," said Harry roughly. "Long enough, I would have thought, in this uncertain world, to pass in vain regret."

"It wasn't only Jack," I said defensively. "But yes, you are right, particularly now that Jonathan Wild has also gone." I grinned. "I heard they dug up his body, you know, and took out all the innards for dissection, and left only the hide and guts, all strewn like offal on the streets, scarcely recognizable as human!"

"For Christ's sake, Davy," Harry interrupted, "take that look of unholy joy off your face or I will clout you here and now."

"Ah, Harry, you don't know how much I hated him!"

"I do. I've watched you eaten up with hatred even as with love. All that time I have been somewhat near at hand, waiting for the strong possessings to be gone, and only a workaday honest affection to put in their place."

"I'm touched by your kindness," I began.

"Are you, dammit?" Harry said angrily, and stood up, brushing himself down smartly as if shaking off something unwanted. "I feel like honest company; shall we go to Mother Clap's?"

"By all means," I said; and we went there, slushing through the mud ruts, each preoccupied in thought.

There, amongst the lights and music, it was very merry. Ma welcomed me with open arms and dabbed her neck liberally with the Hungary water I had brought her. Lucinda squealed in wild delight and hustled me away to tell me his secret:

"I have a new Friend in High Places, Davy! As wonderful as Lord S- !" He looked around, as if the room were full of spies. "We will call him Lord M- . He is a personnage of very great import, high in the Government. A married man. His wife does not understand him. I am his solace."

I hugged him close. "Dear Ralph — dear Lucinda! I'm so glad for you."

"And you, Davy? Have you found someone?"

"I believe I have," I said and looked around for Harry. I saw him. He was dancing ostentatiously with Orange Deb. He was cuddling him and nibbling his ear.

"I'm so happy for you," said Lucinda and hugged me in return. then he looked again more quizzically. "Harry? You are sure you

348

did mean Harry?" Then he passed on the latest gossip to me.

Gabriel Lawrence and Peter Bavidge had fallen out quite startlingly over Tommy Newton. Nobody seemed quite clear what exactly had occurred — something to do with Peter wanting Tommy and Tommy choosing Gabriel, but saucily and provocatively, and Peter taking offence, and Gabriel and Tommy laughing at him, and carrying on in front of him till he could take no more and strode away and vowed he would be revenged. Oh, and there were two new faces here tonight — how would I like to meet them? I stole another glance at Harry — he was kissing Billy Griffin — and I said I would. Their names were Sam and Joe.

Lucinda led me into the dance. It was a round where you danced with anybody; but I did not get a chance to talk to our new acquaintance, merely touched palms as we went round. They were both exceedingly pretty, with fair hair — Sam had a cherubic look, blue-eyed and boyish; Joe was older, with an ear ring, and his lips painted, showing white even teeth, and the tip of his tongue between. Peter Bavidge had brought Sam. His split from Gabriel was now complete. Sam was his new spouse. He was to be called Miss Strawberry Sue.

I met Tommy Newton in the dance also.

"And how is Mr Hitchin, your especial friend?" he enquired with a sweet smile; but the music drowned my answer.

Then we watched Orange Deb misbehaving with Joe. He was all over him, kissing and cuddling — Wounds! — practically devouring him. And he sat him down in a chair and danced about in front of him. Joe was grinning but he looked embarrassed. Maybe Deb was overdoing the welcome for a chap's first visit. But Deb had only just begun, and now had pulled his breeches down and shown his bending bum, and now tried to sit bare-arsed in Joe's lap. Joe did not seem to know what was required of him. We who were watching laughed and laughed. Then Peter Bavidge suddenly strode forward and dragged Deb away.

"You fool!" he hissed. "Put on your clothes — you don't know what you're doing!"

"Where is your old husband Susan Sweetlips?" said Lucinda. "Deb, are you no longer married? You were such a lovely couple in the marrying room; I was quite overcome with jealousy!"

I found that I was standing beside Gabriel. I thought that he looked troubled.

"Ah, Gabriel," I said. "Cheer up. You were such a bonny singer when you first brought me to London, sitting in your cart."

"Aye," he remembered, smiling. "How did it go? Yes, yes, the maid of Islington, that fair conniving hussy!" And then he grew despondent once again. "Ah, Davy, life would be an easy passage if the Lord did not give us that wayward member!"

"Then how would we piss?" said I.

"Perhaps it might be converted into a kind of perspiration," Gabriel said lugubriously, "and evaporate from us, like autumn mist."

I put my arms around him and kissed him on the lips to make him merry. Then Peter Bavidge and his new spouse Sam along with Joe and Orange Deb set off to go on to a molly house in Drury Lane, at which Deb hoped to try again with Joe; and Deb called Gabriel to go along with them. I believe he did, though I did not see him go, as I was otherwise engaged.

A brawny arm came round my neck and pulled me away from Gabriel. Wounds! — I had not believed that Harry was so strong. I had always thought I had been pretty much able to take care of myself, but not so in this instance; Harry could shift me with one arm. His knee came up in the small of my back and propelled me forward. I saw a circle of beaming faces — Ralph, George, Ma, and Tommy Newton — watching us in blatant delight.

"I'm not leaving here tonight," Harry told them, "without fucking him. Upstairs," he ordered me and I put up no resistance.

There was a little room on the second floor at the front of the house, no more than a box room, with a low bed and little else. Harry kicked the door open, threw me in and bolted the door behind us. For the second time that day, as he had for the polishing of the coach, he told me to take off my coat, my waistcoat. "And the rest," he now added, and I heard in the darkness the sound of his own undressing.

Naked I reached for him to kiss him.

"Later," he said brusquely. "I've waited years for this." He slung me down upon the bed. His body covered mine, pressing my face into the pillow. I shivered at the intensity of his need for me, and gave myself up to our pleasure.

Down in the street below, with a timing that was humorous in its aptness, the bellman croaked that all was well.

Chapter Forty-Nine

"IF we find that we get on together," Harry had said, "you could move in with me."

It turned out that we got on pretty well.

The candle burning on the old dark coffer in Harry's room at the Falcon showed low beams, a leaded window-pane gleaming with rain, and a big bed.

"You can put your things there," he offered generously, opening a drawer in a chest. "Have you possessions?" he wondered dubiously.

"I have some clothes at Aunty Mary's and my two silver pistols, and a tidy sum in a locked box under a floorboard."

"Ah," said Harry. "So the tales were true. Are you still in your old trade?"

"Not while I work for you. Why? Does it trouble you?"

"Davy Gadd!" he laughed. "Think about it! A chap in my kind of work has no time for a chap in yours!"

I laughed with him.

"I've spent most of my life ordering coachies to stand and deliver and now I'm moving in with one."

"It's lucky you never lurked in wait for me and my coach and tried that line on me, my lad," said Harry. "I would not have stood meekly by."

"There's no answering a pair of pistols, Harry. You'd have stood."

"Promise me, Davy — you'll not take up the old trade. A law-abiding life now you're with me."

"Don't ask me to make promises, Harry; it's not in my nature."

"No. You'd sooner take to the road than pledge yourself to anything."

"I never found anything I liked enough to pledge myself to it."

"Well, I daresay that hard work with coach and horses is not like to succeed where all else has failed," said Harry sourly.

"I daresay not," I agreed blithely, "unless I liked the coachy."

Harry grunted tolerantly. He had cause enough to suppose that I did.

"Davy," Harry said and put his arm about me. "It is my greatest wish to see you well content." And he gave me a kiss of such tenderness that I believed my bones were like to melt.

I wondered how Gry would take to the close proximity of six other horses. For that first month or so I was fully taken up with making sure that all was well with him and his new companions. Gry would have been about fourteen years old then; he had been my trusty friend for eleven years. But placid and dependable by nature he showed no sign of discontent in the stable which now became his dwelling.

The darkest time of the winter passed in work by day and love-making and sleep by night. We went sometimes to Mother Clap's, sometimes to one of the other houses — Parsloe's in Drury Lane, for one. I had not realized how many molly houses there were and I only knew a few of them — secret havens of companionship and merriment, with music and dancing and talk. It seemed to me that all was set for a pretty agreeable existence. Though neither Harry nor I spoke of love, it was plain to us both that we found pleasure in each other's company and worked harmoniously together.

And then an odd thing happened. I was kneeling by the coach wheel, greasing the axle, when a metal cane prodded me between the shoulder blades. I jumped as if I had been burned. I thought that it was Jonathan Wild; I thought it was his silver staff. I jumped to my feet in an instant and turned to face him.

Of course it was not Wild. But the first shock was succeeded by a second. The man who stood there, dressed in black, with start-lingly white hair, and a silver-knobbed cane in his hand, was Dr Sylvanus, my mother's Holy husband.

"Young man," he said. "I need to hire your coach for this after-noon." And then as the light of recognition dawned: "Lord save us! It is my stepson Davy!"

Rather stiltedly we shook hands.

"Yes, I work here now," I said, a little unnecessarily. "I help Harry Radley the coachman. But are you here on a visit, sir? And is my mother with you?"

"No, she is at home with Susan and her studies. Under my tuition Selina is acquiring literary skills. I flatter myself that I have helped her to develop her mind."

"Will you take a meal with me here at the Falcon?" I offered, feeling some obligation to be host to this country visitor. To my surprise he accepted. We sat in the inn parlour and talked at first about Buckden and the old Crown and such inconsequential matter as chickens, the cost of a good horse and of leather-bound books. By and by we came down to the reason for his visit.

"There are to be several meetings of the Society for the Reformation of Manners. As you know, I have always considered it my especial crusade to try to rid the world of the threat posed by the sodomite. You would be surprised, Davy, to learn how virulently they flourish in this city. But their time is at hand."

"Why, sir? What are you going to do?"

"We have many plans. My own particular interest is to bring down those who have attained positions of power. A man with power has the power to corrupt."

"I understand that the powerful also have the power to keep themselves secret. Will you not find it difficult to track them down?"

"They are not all secret," said Dr Sylvanus. "Some we know about."

"Oh? Who?"

"Well, even you must know that the Under City Marshall is a sodomite."

"No! Do you mean — no, you cannot mean Mr Hitchin?"

"Have you never seen him in the company of boys?"

"No, sir, never. Always on his own. Besides, I believe he has a wife."

"Now, Davy, don't be simple. They take a wife to fool the crowd. Are you sure that you have never heard anything of a pathick nature about Mr Hitchin? No gossip, no rumour? Nothing?"

"No sir. All I have heard tell is that he works hard to bring the wicked to justice and is kind to the poor."

Harry drove Dr Sylvanus to his meeting. I trudged round to the haunts of Mr Hitchin and finally tracked him down in the King's Head, Ivy Lane, in the company of boys. Street urchins, ragged rapscallions of about ten years old, with knowing eyes, three of 'em, all munching on oat biscuits, and Mr Hitchin placidly patting their heads, and drinking red wine from a tall glass.

"My dear pal Davy!" he beamed. "How pleasant to renew thee acquaintance! And looking very fit and well and comely, if I may say so, even in thee sturdy working clothes. Boys, offer Davy a biscuit."

"Thank you, I have eaten," I said, as three pairs of hands came down protectively over the plate.

"How happily I recall the circumstances of our last meeting, Davy," Mr Hitchin continued. "Do not thee?"

"Very happily, Mr Hitchin," I said drily. "Indeed, I have not yet seen you to thank you for your part in the downfall of Jonathan Wild. I heard that you had a deal of difficulty in persuading the magistrates to proceed against him. I thank you most heartily for your trouble."

"Justice, Davy, that's all it was," said Mr Hitchin tranquilly. "And I was her right hand. Sit down, Davy. Boys, make a place for Davy. He is one of us."

I lodged myself upon the end of the bench.

"I am afraid that so firm an upholder of the Law as yourself, Mr Hitchin, must inevitably bring yourself to the attention of the vulgar, not always with beneficial effects," I said.

"Thee mean that I have enemies. I know that."

I lowered my voice. "Some of them are growing stronger."

"What is it thee know, Davy?"

"The Society for the Reformation of Manners..."

"Zounds, Davy, I am a member of the same!" he said dismissively.

"Then take care, sir, for some who seem to be your friends have taken against you and would like to make an example of you."

"Do thee mean in the field of bribery, corruption, thief taking, teaching these lads to pick pockets, receiving what they bring me, or sodomy?" enquired Mr Hitchin.

I blanched a little. "Sodomy," I whispered.

He chuckled. "That was a happy night we shared, was it not, sweetheart? Is there anyone else thee'd like me to bring down — another Jonathan Wild? — for a repetition of the pleasure that I took upon thee?"

"Mr Hitchin!" I urged. "I am here to warn you. Please take care!"

"Davy," Mr Hitchin said. "I have been a molly all my life, though I have not always put that name to what I do. I am not going to change my ways for anybody, least of all for the Society for the Reformation of Manners. Even as the Last Trump sounds I shall be reaching for a handsome chap's bare arse. And now do have a biscuit, Davy, while there are some left."

So I sat there, with Mr Hitchin's other boys, and we all finished off the biscuits.

But I was uneasy as I came away; and for good reason, as it turned out. The very next year Mr Hitchin was indeed accused of sodomy, following an incident at the Talbot Inn. He was sentenced to the pillory and prison. In the stoop he was treated with brutality amazing even in our age, from the which he never did recover, and having served out his prison term he died some six months after.

Harry was a little subdued when he came back from taking Dr Sylvanus to the meeting of the Society for the Reformation of Manners.

"I never heard the like of it," he said. "They were in some side room off St Anne's church. They had a rabble-rousing speaker. I could hear snatches of his bellowing even as I waited outside the walls. I heard the like of 'Word of God — the gates of Jerusalem — sodomital dogs — pollution of this fair city...', and in between, such hurrahing and halloing and such stamping of their Holy shoes, and at last the singing of a hymn, some loud thing; and before I knew it out they trooped. I half expected monsters with jaws dripping blood, but no, these were the most humdrum of creatures — you'd say tailors, grocers, clerks and their wives, anybody's fathers, sons, mothers. I half thought that I had better take off before they set upon me and tore me limb from limb, being one of the damned crew they mean to rid the city of; but they greeted me most pleasantly and said it looked as if it might rain and asked if I were for hire. I took your Dr Sylvanus and three of his pals back to their lodgings, and they paid their fare most politely, and wished me good night."

"But are they to be feared?" I frowned. "What can they do?"

"I'd like to see them try to do anything," said Harry. "I'd soon send them nearer to the gates of Jerusalem. They leave a sour taste in the mouth. We'll to Parsloe's, shall we, and dance away vexation?"

It was a small place, Parsloe's, being but two adjoining rooms next door to the Blackbird, Drury Lane. Three fiddlers played, standing on chairs, and sometimes in excitement tumbled off. There was always a great press, the rooms being small, and folk danced up against each other, taking pleasure in the brushing against one another's bodies. I danced sometimes with Harry, sometimes with anyone at all, and there was certainly some lewd embracing and the singing of songs of a disreputable nature. So, what with dancing and singing and drinking, we were well away, and when there came a thunderous knocking on the door it was several minutes before anyone was aware of it. But it continued, and at last the fiddling petered out, the dancers rollicked to a halt, the singing drained away, and someone let in the icy winds of winter and three constables.

"Now sirs!" cried the first of these. "You must all come with us!"

There were cries of: "What for?" "No chance!" and "It's too cold!"

Harry stepped forward. "Now, sir, I perceive you are a constable," says he, "and we are folk that like to sing and dance. Wherein lies the harm? And why do you ask us to accompany you and where would you have us go?"

"You are to come to the watch house," said the constable.

"And why should we do that?"

"I order it," said the bold fellow. "We believe that you are what they term 'molly culls'. And for that, because it is a sin and vile and against the Law, you are to come with us and answer the charge against you."

I stood side by side with Harry.

"We refuse," I said. "We are well content exactly where we are, and shall not go with you."

"What makes you think you can withstand us," said the constable, "who stand for the King's Law?"

"Because," said I, "you are three and we are many!"

Everyone gave a great cheer and suddenly the room erupted — men seized tables and chairs as if they would turn them into weapons, and drummed with their fists and feet, and gathered round the constables who, in spite of the sturdy poles they carried, began to step back towards the door.

"We order you — " one shouted, but his voice was drowned in a chorus of noise. There were some thirty of us, and nothing for us to fear from these poor fellows. We wrested their poles from them and pushed them out of the door with them, and whacked their retreating limbs; and two of our number did a morris dance with those same poles in celebration. We locked the door upon the constables. We heard them in the street, thumping on the door, shouting: "You'll not be so merry in Newgate!" and then they went away.

The fiddlers struck up anew and we returned to our dancing. Jem Parsloe watched at the window for half an hour or so, but the constables did not come back, nor sent for others of their kind.

In the small hours of the morning Harry and I walked back to the Falcon. It was an unquiet night. There were shouts further off, and the ringing of a bell near at hand — a summoning sound — the noise of running feet and pursuit. We thought nothing of it; London was often so. We were a little drunk, a little unsteady on our feet. Our hearts were happy. We floated still upon the elation of having seen off the constables, a merry crew of mollies, all as one, none of us questioning our course of action, but all joining in, making a force to be reckoned with. None had come back against us. We had scared them off.

Harry and I climbed the dark stair to our chamber. We bolted the door. We flung our arms around each other, not needing words, the shared emotion binding us, making us joyful. We tumbled on to the bed, kissing, laughing, tugging off our clothes. At last we lay still, breathing hard, recovering stability, in each other's arms.

"I reckon we do well together, you and me," said Harry.

"I reckon we do."

"What do you say to letting other folk in on the secret?"

"How'd you mean?"

"I'd like to take you into the marrying room at Ma Clap's."

I laughed. "Would you? What, a celebration?"

"Yes, a celebration. Of how good we are together, and of how we drove the constables away."

"I think that's a damn good idea."

"You agree? Ah, Davy..." Harry seemed quite taken aback, and touched. He began to kiss me, and for a while we lay and hugged.

"I thought you'd say it would make you feel bound," said Harry.

I grinned. "I think I might enjoy being bound up with you, Harry."

"I think you might," he agreed, "if I have anything to do with it."

I began to kiss his face, his neck, his shoulders. The dormant strength in his powerful body excited me; my handling of him stirred a like response. He gripped a handful of my hair and pushed me downwards. "I seem to remember," he said, "you once promised something about kissing my feet."

His feet, his legs, his balls — my lips and tongue went happily about his body. At last when passion could no longer be contained we lay in each other's arms and brought ourselves to our satisfaction; and I slept against him in a peaceful sleep, his strong arms cradling me.

Next morning as we dressed, Harry said: "Are you still game to face the marrying room, or was that part of my dreaming?"

"I'll do it gladly. You know, I once told Lucinda I wouldn't fancy it, with folks gawping and the door open and the jokes and all. But I must have changed or something. With you I'd rather like it. I'd like everyone to see how big and beautiful you are without your clothes, and let them envy me."

"No — it's me they would be envying. Come on now, Davy, they all fancy you. They always have done. I can see 'em now — Gabriel fighting his demons of lust, Lucinda wishing he had stayed with you instead of chasing the nobility, George calling you his darling. And Ma Clap beaming and smiling and throwing paper flowers and ribbons, and we two lapping it up like cats with cream."

"Yeah. Ma'll be so pleased. She'll think it was all down to her.

We'll go round there straightaway, shall we, and tell Ma to make arrangements for a marrying next Sunday night?"

"If there's to be a marrying," said Harry, "we had best get each other a ring."

"I might have one already," I began. "A fine gold one, once belonging to a gentleman."

"None of your stolen trinkets! I don't want to be nabbed walking about with it. You'll buy me one, honest, in a jeweller's shop."

So in the sleet and wind of a February morning we called into a jeweller's shop and solemnly tried on rings, but each kept the other's, to put on in the marrying room when we would have our celebration on the Sunday night. We then continued on our way to Field Lane to make arrangements.

We reached Ma Clap's door and were about to knock when we noticed that the door was ajar and shifting on its hinges. Surprised, we pushed it open and went in.

A scene of devastation met our eyes. Chairs lay overturned. The curtains hung loose, flapping in the draught. A fiddle lay smashed, incongruously, next to a discarded shoe; broken glass was strewn across the floor, with fallen candlesticks and one red wig and a pair of white stockings. A similar confusion met us in the kitchen, and as we went upstairs and looked into the rooms, we saw sheets heaved back and pillows and mattresses burst open, with the feathers gusting up suddenly, like snowflakes. With gathering unease we went downstairs and back into the street.

We went then to the Bunch o' Grapes next door, where Ma had always got her liquor. This too was pretty quiet, but in no way strangely so, as Ma Clap's was. Mr Blaine the innkeeper was cleaning tables.

"Whatever has become of Mother Clap? Where's Mr Eccleston? What's happened?"

"And well may you ask," said Mr Blaine. "The constables came here last night. Dozens of 'em. Some of them must have got inside the building and opened up the doors — though how nobody saw them is beyond me. All the streets were blocked, and the back yard. Then suddenly they all went rushing in, they rounded everybody up, and took 'em off to Newgate."

"Ma Clap and all?"

"Everybody."

Chapter Fifty

"**P**SST! Davy Gadd!" I turned from polishing the windows of the coach to see Tommy Newton looking as uneasy as a fox that's strayed too far from cover.

"I need to speak to you, but," and he looked behind him to the street, "nobody must see me."

I opened the coach door and jerked a thumb towards the interior. He scuttled inside. I joined him. There we sat, he pressed against the leather, in the shadows.

It was a month or so since the constables had raided Ma Clap's molly house. In that time Harry and I had learnt that other molly houses had been raided on the same night. Parsloe's, where Harry and I had been, was one of them, but because we had put up resistance the raid had come to nothing. If we had meekly gone along with the constables we would now be in Newgate. As it was, we had spent a very quiet month, living in apprehension. Jem Parsloe had closed down his molly house. All kinds of rumours were about.

When I went round to Aunty Mary's I found Ralph there, very white and shaken.

"Weren't you at Ma Clap's?" I asked him.

"Yes I was! And taken off to Newgate. I nearly died of fright. But I was set free immediately. Lord M- heard about it and he got me out. But just for the moment he daren't visit me. Oh Davy! What a dreadful business!"

It was so indeed. It was like a wave of shock that lifted and fell, all over London. The Society for the Reformation of Manners had made its move. The molly houses were in disarray, some raided and broken up, others gone to ground. There were to be trials, punishment...

Now here I sat, knee to knee with Tommy Newton and he was plainly in a state of fright.

"I've come to warn you, Davy. Where d'you think I've been these past three weeks?"

"Where?"

"Locked up. But Constable Willis let me out."

"What? Charity?"

"My arse in a bandbox! Charity? No chance. He wants examples. And I gave 'em."

"What do you mean, examples?"

"Well, like they can't hang everybody, can they, not hundreds, so they'll go for one or two, as an example, to keep people scared. Like when you throw meat to the dogs that chase you, one joint is enough."

"Wounds, whatever have you done?"

"I didn't tell no lies. Just gave some names of who had fucked me. Only one or two. All the others'll go free. I had to think of my own skin."

"Who did you name? Lord save us, Tommy, you had hundreds to choose from! Constable Willis knew what he was doing when he nobbled you."

He didn't answer. He said: "Now listen, Davy, and this is why I'm here. Don't go to any of the houses. Just don't put a foot out of line while this is goin' on. And then it'll all die down."

"All what's going on? Do you mean there's more?"

"You know Ned Courtenay?"

I thought. "Yes. He broke some windows once at another molly house. A black-haired chap, thin as a pole. Constable Willis took him away. The chap I was with said he was a nobody."

"Well, he's leapt to fame now," Tommy sneered. "He gave 'em examples, same as me."

"Why are you warning me, me particularly?"

"No, don't fret, nothing to fear. Why? Because you brought Mr Hitchin to Wright's place, and I knew you were like me. And when I saw you stripped I thought you were pretty tasty. Good bum, I thought. Like I say, any time you want to bugger me, the offer stands."

I was half speechless. "With all this going on — ?"

"Yeah," he grinned. "But we don't stop fancyin' folk, even though they're takin' us to prison for it, do we?"

"Listen, Tom, I'd fuck you any time you like if it'd keep you away from the constables. You're free now — you don't have to play their games. Tell 'em you forgot who had you. Tell 'em you were lying. Tell 'em to stuff their protection."

"I daren't, Davy. They know me. I'll be for it if I back out now. I'm a marked man on all sides. You won't see me again after the trials. I'm gettin' out as soon as ever I can." He put a hand on my knee and squeezed it hard. "I'm sorry, Davy... I'm sorry..." And then he wriggled from the coach, and he was gone.

Little by little, those mollies against whom nothing could be proven were set free. George Page slunk back to his butcher's shop, telling his customers he had been called away unexpectedly to visit his sister in the country. Peter Bavidge disappeared. Some found long lost relations in other parts of the country. Some, like me and Harry, lived very soberly. Some went overseas.

But there remained Tommy Newton's examples. They were Gabriel Lawrence, Billy Griffin and Thomas Wright, at whose molly house Tommy had provided services, and who, it seemed, had availed himself of the same.

I recalled how last May Billy Griffin had rolled home to Ma Clap's singing, because he had got his way at last with Tommy Newton. I recalled how Gabriel had pursued Tom Newton as if he were possessed, tormented the while by his fear of the Lord, how he had achieved his heart's desire and how he was mortified with guilt when he had done so. Just as he had said, Tom Newton would need to tell no lies, and the dogs would get their meat.

The procedings of the trials at the Old Bailey Sessions House became common knowledge on the streets and in the boozing kens; broadsheets and gossip passed the news around and gave the details to the eager greedy. You would see them in little groups, reading, passing it all on, whistling and catcalling, delighted with each revelation.

"He said many times he wanted to take me to his bed; he said I was a very pretty fellow..."

"They call each other dearie and little darling. They call each other by the names of women..."

"They go into a marrying room and kiss each other on a bed..."

Gabriel brought any number of witnesses to speak in his defence. I knew one of them — it was Henry Yoxam the cowkeeper from Islington, where Gabriel got his milk. As in a dream I saw again that barn where as a lad I hid, and saw Gabriel and Peter Bavidge below. *A young good-looking fellow naked is the best sight in the world.* And he had hid me in the manger when the pursuers came after that handsome highwayman, and brought me to London in his milk cart, and gave me a bed for the night when Tubs had left me stranded. And now he was on trial for his life — and for what? For going with a willing whore, which men did every day and came home to their wives.

I heard that Gabriel comported himself with dignity. They said he prayed and spent time in the prison chapel, quiet. Nonetheless it did him no favours. He was condemned to death.

It was the same for Billy Griffin. He said he did not know that Ma Clap's house was a molly house. He said he was so poor he must live where he could. Not surprisingly, no one believed him.

And then we had a shock.

"Sam and Joe are constables! Sam Stevens is a Holy!"

At last it dawned on us the extent to which this operation had been planned. They must have been after the molly houses for months. They must have chosen their prettiest constables. There had been Sam and Joe, and a chap we had not met, one Davison, who went to Wright's place on the same errand. How thoroughly we had been fooled! I remembered well Joe's torn breeches, his painted mouth... Sam's blue eyes and angel face. And each was a reforming constable. Now Sam was giving evidence against Bill Griffin. And Billy was to die for it.

Joe Sellers testified against Thomas Wright. I winced to hear of the details of our gatherings trumpeted to the world. "They fiddle and they dance — they sit in one another's laps — they practice indecencies, talk bawdy. They have a room with a bed in it. They call it the marrying room. They go into it and leave the door open. They call each other Sweetlips, Gloriana, Orange Deb..." And we had welcomed him and made him one of us. With a sick feeling I remembered Orange Deb and his bare-arsed dance in front of Joe. Peter Bavidge had warned him to stop. Was Deb to suffer for so foolish an indiscretion? For larking and teasing?

"Harry," I said, lying in his arms. "Whatever will become of it?"

He held me close and could give no particular comfort. All he could say was that he loved me. But what good was that?

I received another visitor in the yard of the Falcon. It was Dr Sylvanus. His face was all smiles. Plainly his sweetest dreams were coming true. He handed me a letter; I took it.

"This was sent to the old Crown," he said. "It is addressed to you. Your mother sent it down to me, knowing that I was in touch with you. It is well sealed," he added, a little regretfully, I thought.

I put the letter down upon the coach seat.

"Now Davy!" he cried. "And how are you this fine day?"

His smug complacent handsome face was close to mine. I stepped back and I drove a punch into it, hard. It knocked him to the ground. The look of astonishment on his face was the funniest sight I had seen for months. It almost made me laugh.

"Get up," I said. "Get out of here. And don't come back. And don't you set the constables on me. I've got pals who know who you are and where to find you. They'll be after you with knives."

"You're mad!" he choked, spitting blood. "You're crazed. Spawn of your father! Villain of vile degree! I knew you always hated me

362

for marrying your mother."

He was right, but that wasn't why I hit him. But I must have frightened him. He never came back, and he never sent the constables.

The letter took me by surprise. It was sent to me from Edinburgh and was written by Lord Staughton, the handsomest man I had ever known, my Jacobite lord, who had searched for Duval's gold with me and taught me the pleasures of male love; then dropped me from his life.

"I am living now in Edinburgh, but I intend to take ship for France in the autumn. I've often thought about you, Davy, and recalled our time together. Why not join me? Do you still travel the Great North Road? You will find me at the end of it. Does that make me the hidden treasure you were seeking? Is Duval's gold no gold at all, but merely the attainment of the heart's desire? I wait for you in hope."

I must admit that some sweet memories and some bitter were stirred up by this letter. But at that moment it seemed to belong to another world. And just at present, one of startling irrelevance.

On a day in May, Gabriel, Billy and Thomas Wright were taken by the same road Jack had taken, Jonathan Wild had taken, past St Sepulchre's, along Holborn, towards Tyburn; and there hanged.

"I think," said Harry, "we will take a leaf out of your book and take ourselves towards the north road. I have no desire to be in London."

We took the coach and drove as far as Highgate, past the windy flowering hawthorn blossoms and the waysides white with keck. We were quiet and kept to our own thoughts. We came back in the evening, and by then the deed was done, and Gabriel's body was slit open at the Surgeons' Hall and the lungs whereby he sang so heartily were offered up to the furtherance of scientific knowledge.

As we lay in each other's arms that night I said: "They hang folk for all kinds of reasons. But Gabriel is hanged for fucking Tommy Newton who wanted him to do it."

Orange Deb was next to come to judgement. But he was lucky. For his having wanted to fuck Joe Sellers, for his having kissed him with his tongue and desired him and said as much, for his having shown his arse and offered to sit on his lap, he must stand in the pillory and pay a fine and go to prison for one year. He was an exuberant fool, was Deb, and in this day and age it seems that is the price of folly. Harry and I went to the stoop in Bloomsbury Square and watched to make sure he was not killed by the crowd. I would have shot to maim whoever tried as much; but they were a more refined mob in Bloomsbury, and merely yelled abuse till they grew hoarse.

That left Ma Clap and Mr Eccleston. Mr Eccleston had the foresight to die in prison, he being elderly, and so robbed the town of further spectacle; but Ma was made of sterner stuff and survived to face a trial with the accusation of keeping a disorderly house. Needless to say, she was found guilty. For making a home for us in which folk sang and danced and played, providing a private place where men might love each other freely, she was sentenced to the pillory and two years in prison. Her fine we paid for her, but the other she must endure.

The collapse of the pleasant world that I had grown to love was something I might grow accustomed to — the loss of friends, the venomous spite of the Holies, the concentrated attack upon a matter that concerned only its own participants. But to see that dear dame who had been more mother to me than my own fainting in the stoop on that oppressive summer day all in the name of Law and Justice, with the jibes of the crowd, and the peace officers waiting to take her away to prison, where I did not lay much odds on her survival, tipped the balance for me.

Harry was right — I would always run from what I could not face. I took Gry from the stable while Harry was out with the coach. My horse and I set out for the path we knew so well.

St John's Street, the Hollow Way, the road north.

Chapter Fifty-One

I SCARCE knew which villages I passed through. The ground was hard and easy; Gry and I knew one another so well we moved as one. The air was clean and clear. The city smoke was far behind us. It was late summer time. Leafy trees passed by us — furzy heaths —field already under plough. The wind played in my hair. My head was empty of thought. Such actions as I undertook were done as in a dream. I slept in barns. I saw the stars through open doorways. I heard the owls hunt, and the rustling of mice and rats. I bathed my face in a brook by starlight. I ate at wayside inns. I rode away my pain; I tasted tears.

I found myself at Alconbury.

It is indeed a place that requires pause, both of the mind and body. The hill tired Gry, and I dismounted and walked along beside him, stretching, rubbing my behind, aware now of the ache of limb, a plain old-fashioned tiredness.

Ahead of us the gibbet that is a landmark for the surrounding countryside. Swinging in his irons some poor cull that made one mistake too many. In the silence you could hear the squeak and creak of the metal as the wind took it. I saluted him. Then I climbed clear of the road, and sat upon the yellowy grass, Gry standing close by, eyeing me with that wise gaze, as if to say: And what are you about now?

On all sides fields and woods stretched away from me, sloping gently down. The wind lifted my hair, a warm wind beneath a heavy sultry sky of dappled cloud. Here I sat, part looking, part reflecting.

What indeed was I about?

I was in physical terms well on my way northward. I could soon make Stamford, and by easy stages York. Swift Nicks had done that in one fell swoop, they reckoned. And after that, Edinburgh.

My hand went to my inner pocket. Lord Staughton's letter rustled as I touched it. What if I were to join with him? What if I rode all the way, straight to his arms, to sleep with him in Edinburgh, and know again his skilful and exquisite lovemaking? What a prize awaiting me for that ride! He had been so beautiful... I lay back in the grass, my arms behind my head, looking up at the sky, remembering Lord Staughton. His black hair, his white skin, his melodious voice, the pleasure that he showed me... I had been so young then; I had thought I knew so much — I had known nothing. But his lovemaking had been superb — my cock hardened thinking about it. Gry made a restless sound; I clapped my hand to my pistol and sat up.

Nothing. A crow had perched upon our speechless companion's cage.

And on the way to Edinburgh... all those untapped miles where maybe gold lay hidden. I had Jerry Dowlan's pendulum with me, all its powers intact. The mystery unsolved, the riches still for the taking. And riches of a different kind — the potential for the unexpected meeting. Nathan Grey — where was he now? Somewhere on the road, always on the road... the man who brought my unskilled body to life with his rough passion. The man who gave me Gry, my well-beloved friend, always dependable, true of heart and faithful. What a treasure he had been to me!

But for how long now? How would such a life as I was contemplating prove in company with a younger horse? I could not picture it. It must be Gry.

All we had to do was set our faces north.

I stood up, I paced about. I looked up at our grim companion. I spoke to him, asked his advice. I told him something of my situation. He heard me calmly, never interrupting. All around us stretched the distant fields, the woodlands, the copses, under any bush of which Duval's gold might lie hidden. It was time to follow my dreams at last, to turn my youthful hopes into reality.

I hugged Gry's neck, burying my face in his long mane. I led him slowly down the hill. I mounted and I turned his head and we set off —

In the direction of London, dammit.

What business had I to pursue the elusive phantoms of my imaginings? What was Lord Staughton to me now but a beautiful faithless nobleman who would leave me when it suited him, what Nathan Grey but a good memory, a man to whom I would be forever grateful?

And what of Harry? What must he be thinking? How could I explain my flight and keep his good regard? I must get back and make it up to him and show him that I loved him. That I loved him... Whyever had it taken me so long to know it?

No sooner had I struggled with this flash of inspiration than came others pushing at its heels: Lucinda, he would need a friend if Lord M- let him down, my pal George Page, Jem Parsloe. And what if the Holies should set out to bring down Mr Hitchin — we could not allow it. And we might work some way of helping Ma Clap and Orange Deb... Wounds, I knew better than most that you could get out of a prison if you had friends and skills. And there was Jack's ma to provide for. And Will Field would be once again at large. My place was there amongst it all; I was needed; I could be of use.

As I went south I laughed and wondered whatever was I towards? A hostile city where I would have to tread carefully, where if I escaped hanging as a highwayman I risked hanging as a molly. What kind of fool had I turned out to be? I had not even heard the bells of London telling me to turn again. I wondered once again about that poxy cull Whittington who turned back to London only to put his money into building the Whit. I was pretty sure that I could make better use of my return than he did.

As I urged Gry forward I reached into my inner pocket and took out Jerry Dowlan's pendulum. I kissed it, and I flung it with all my might over the hedge; I never saw where it came to earth. Probably smack on an old earth-encrusted box buried fifty years ago by a French highwayman, I grinned; but I never stopped to look.

I rode south. As I drew nearer to London I rode faster. Somewhere on Finchley Common I rode past a coach that was travelling north. I recognised Boxer and Star from far off. I pulled Gry round, and we chased after them.

I cast a glance round about me, making sure that no passer-by would misinterpret what I was about to do. But there were no travellers nearby. We were alone upon the road.

I overtook the coach. We slithered to a halt ahead of it. I drew my pistol. I called: "Stand and deliver!"

Harry slowed the horses to a walk and drew rein. He glowered at me.

"What the hell are you playing at?"

"Harry! I love you! I'm coming back!"

"What makes you think I want you?"

"*Do* you want me?"

"Damn you, wasn't I coming to fetch you back?"

"How far would you have got in that old barrel?"

"Far enough to find you and take you by the scruff of the neck and shake you senseless."

"And I deserve it."

Harry gave me a look that turned my bones to water. "Put away that fancy silver pistol or someone will arrest you for frightening a poor coachy."

With a skill that had to be seen to be believed Harry turned the coach and horses. I tucked the pistol in my belt, and Gry and I fell into a slow accompaniment to his vehicle.

"Have you still got my ring?" said Harry.

"Have you still got mine?"

We reached across, exchanging rings. We put them on.

"Jem Parsloe has opened his doors again," said Harry. "If you agree I thought we might go there when we get back. It's time we had a dance."

"Gladly. And I daresay he'll not be the only one to start up again, given time."

"I'm sure of it. It's an odd notion, to think that by going out and dancing in a crowd you're saying something — even taking a step some might consider brave. Or foolhardy. But we have to do it, else we might as well be dead and underground. What made you come back, Davy?"

"That sort of thing."

"Anything else?"

"You, maybe."

"Me, *maybe?*"

"You, most of all."

"And are you sure this time?"

"Harry, no one can ever be sure of anything in this uncertain world."

"I didn't ask for a lesson in philosophy. I asked you are you sure this time?"

"I am."

Harry eyed me quizzically. "And Duval's gold?"

"Let some other fool go find it."

— THE END —